IN TH...
TUDOR C...

Outlaw
IN THE
TUDOR COURT
ANNE
HERRIES

April 2014

Libertine
IN THE
TUDOR COURT
JULIET
LANDON

May 2014

Notorious
IN THE
TUDOR COURT
AMANDA
McCABE

June 2014

Maiden
IN THE
TUDOR COURT
JUNE
FRANCIS

July 2014

Outlaw
IN THE
TUDOR COURT

ANNE
HERRIES

MILLS & BOON

Published in Great Britain 2014
by Mills & Boon, an imprint of Harlequin (UK) Limited,
Eton House, 18-24 Paradise Road, Richmond, Surrey, TW9 1SR

OUTLAW IN THE TUDOR COURT © 2014 Harlequin Books S.A.

Ransom Bride © 2005 Anne Herries
The Pirate's Willing Captive © 2010 Anne Herries

ISBN: 978 0 263 24618 6

052-0414

Harlequin (UK) Limited's policy is to use papers that are natural, renewable and recyclable products and made from wood grown in sustainable forests. The logging and manufacturing processes conform to the legal environmental regulations of the country of origin.

Printed and bound by
CPI Group (UK) Ltd, Croydon, CR0 4YY

Anne Herries lives in Cambridgeshire, where she is fond of watching wildlife and spoils the birds and squirrels that are frequent visitors to her garden. Anne loves to write about the beauty of nature and sometimes puts a little into her books, although they are mostly about love and romance. She writes for her own enjoyment and to give pleasure to her readers. She is a winner of the Romantic Novelists' Association Romance Prize.

Ransom Bride

ANNE HERRIES

Chapter One

Kathryn stood at the top of the cliff, looking down at the sea as it swirled about the rocks far below her. The wind tore at her hair, catching at her cloak, buffeting her from all sides as she stared out to the far horizon, her thoughts returning as always when she came here to that day in her childhood—the day when the bravery of her companion had saved her life. Never would she forget how they had gone down to the cove in direct disobedience to their fathers' commands; how their curiosity about the strange ship in the bay had brought disaster.

Kathryn's cheeks were wet as she wiped the tears with the back of her hand. There was no point in weeping. Dickon had gone from her, from his family, taken by the Corsairs who had come ashore to find water and food. It seemed that some of the villagers had been trading with these evil men who plagued the seas of the Mediterranean and occasionally ventured as far as the coasts of England and Cornwall. How often she had regretted that she had not been more mindful of her duty, for it was she who had prompted her companion to go down and investigate the strange ship.

Shivering, Kathryn recalled the way the fierce pirates had suddenly swooped on them as they walked innocently towards where the pirates were plying their trade with the rogue villager. That man had long disappeared from the village, for when Kathryn escaped from the clutches of the men who had tried to seize her, he must have known she would tell her story. But her beloved Dickon had not escaped. He had pushed her behind him, telling her to run for help while he had bravely fought against the men who attacked them. At the top of the cliff, she had stopped, turning to see that they were carrying Dickon on board the boat that had brought them ashore, and that he appeared to be unconscious.

Kathryn had run as fast as she could to her father's house, spilling out her tale of abduction and treachery, but when the party of men had arrived at the beach it was to find it empty, with no sign of the brave lad who had fought against impossible odds. He was but fifteen when they took him, but Kathryn knew he would have been sold as a slave, perhaps to work in the kitchens of some eastern potentate. Or perhaps, because he was tall and strong for his age, he had been chained to an oar in one of the raiders' galleys.

She had wept bitter tears, for she had loved Dickon. He was her friend and her soulmate and, though their families lived some leagues distant from one another, they had known each other well. Kathryn believed that it was the intention of both fathers that they should marry one day, when she was nineteen. She was almost nineteen now and soon her father would make arrangements for her to marry someone else. But in her heart she belonged to Richard Mountfitchet—her own Dickon.

'Dickon…' Kathryn whispered, her words whipped

away by the wind, drowned by the cries of seabirds and the crashing of the waves against the rocky Cornish coastline. 'Forgive me. I never thought it would happen. I did not know that such evil men existed until that day. I miss you. I still love you. I shall always love you.'

It was ten years to the day, Kathryn thought, and every year she came here at the same time hoping to see Dickon, praying that he might return to her and his family. Yet she knew it was impossible. How could he return? Their fathers had sent men to search the slave markets in Algiers. They had contacted friends in Cyprus, Venice and Constantinople, the city that the Turks now called Istanbul, but which was still known in the Christian world by its old name. Always, there was unrest between the Turks and the Christians; wars, quarrels, and differences of religion and culture made it difficult to conduct a search within the Ottoman Empire. For Sultan Selim II was constantly seeking to push out the boundaries of his empire and had boasted that one day he would stand victorious in Rome itself. However, there were a few men who could help and one of them was Suleiman Bakhar.

Suleiman had an English wife. He was a clever, educated man and travelled tirelessly, trading, trying to reach out to the world beyond the Ottoman Empire, and hoping to bring about peace, though there was such hatred, such a history of conflict between their peoples that it seemed the breach could not be bridged.

Kathryn knew that Suleiman Bakhar was in England at this time. He had promised to make inquiries on behalf of Lord Mountfitchet, but as far as she knew he had discovered nothing that could help them. Sir John Rowlands and Lord Mountfitchet had gone to London to speak with him, for they had other business of which Kathryn knew nothing, and it would suit them to meet with Suleiman at the same time. But they were expected to return today, and Kathryn felt a flicker of hope as she turned her steps towards the beautiful old manor house that was her home. It had once been fortified against attack from the sea, but, in these more peaceful times of Queen Elizabeth's reign, it had become simply a family home rather than a fortress, with many improvements to make it more comfortable.

As she reached her home, she saw that a cumbersome travelling coach had pulled up in the courtyard and she began to run, her heart racing. Perhaps this time there would be news of Dickon…

Lorenzo Santorini stood on the steps of his palace. It was built at the edges of the Grand Canal, the huge lagoon that wound through the city and beneath the many bridges of Venice. The city had established trading arrangements with the Muslim world that had helped it to become one of the most powerful seagoing nations on earth a hundred years earlier. It was from here that the great Marco Polo had set out on his voyage of expedition that had taken him as far as the court of Kublai Khan, opening up the known world far beyond what it had been previously. However, the Turkish invasions and the unrest of recent years had led to gradual erosion of the Republic's supremacy.

The Venetian galleys were, however, still thought to be some of the best craft available and remained a force to be reckoned with; the merchants of Venice were rich and influential—and Lorenzo Santorini was one of the most powerful amongst them. His galleys were famed for their speed, fighting abilities and the discipline of his men, none of whom were slaves.

He frowned as he saw the galley making its way towards

the small jetty where he stood waiting. It was one of the fleet that he owned which guarded his merchant ships, and it was late returning from what should have been a routine trip to Cyprus to buy wine. As it drew closer, he could see that it had taken part in some fighting—which could only mean that it had been attacked by a Turkish or Corsair galley.

'Welcome back, Michael,' Lorenzo said as the captain mounted the steps towards him. He extended his hand, helping him jump up to the steps of the palace. 'I thought there must have been some trouble—was it Rachid again?'

'Is it not always Rachid?' Michael dei Ignacio replied with a grimace. 'He hates us and will harry our vessels whenever he gets the chance. Fortunately, I had left Cyprus in company with three other galleys and the ship that carried your wine. We lost one of our fighting galleys, but the merchant ship is safe. It is but an hour behind me, accompanied by two galleys. We came ahead because we have several injured men on board.'

'They must be tended by the physicians,' Lorenzo said with a frown, 'and all shall be compensated for the hurt they have suffered.' In Lorenzo's galleys the men were paid for their work, not chained to their oars the way the wretched prisoners were in the galleys of those men most feared in these waters. The Corsairs, or Barbary pirates, as some were wont to call them, roamed the seas from the Mediterranean and Adriatic to the Barbary Coast and the Atlantic. They were fearsome men who were a law unto themselves, owing no allegiance to anyone, though some paid tribute to the Ottoman Empire.

'It shall be attended to,' Michael promised. Lorenzo was a good master to work for, and a mystery to most, for few knew anything of his history. Michael himself knew that Lorenzo was the adopted son of the man whose name he bore; of much of what had gone before he was as ignorant as the next man.

'I know I can leave their welfare in your hands,' Lorenzo said. His eyes were the colour of violets, a dark blue and as unreadable as his thoughts. His hair, the colour of sun-ripened corn bleached white at the tips, was worn longer than the fashion of the time; thick and strong, it curled in his neck. 'I leave for Rome in the morning. I have been summoned to a meeting concerning these pirates.' His lip curled in scorn, for he included the Turks, who had caused the merchants of Venice so much trouble these past fifty years or so and now had the audacity to demand Cyprus of the Doge, something that would be fiercely resisted by the Venetians. 'As you know, there is talk of gathering a force to curb Selim's power, otherwise he will sweep further into Europe. The Emperor is concerned and he hopes to bring in Spain as well as other allies to break the power of the Turks.'

Michael nodded, for he knew that his friend was considered an important man by certain men of influence in the Holy Roman Empire. Lorenzo owned twenty fighting galleys besides his fleet of four merchant ships, and he would certainly be asked to join any force that attempted to sweep the menace of the Turkish invaders from the seas. There was a widely held belief that, could they but break the power of the Ottoman Empire, many of the Corsairs would lose much of their own power.

'They need to be curbed,' Michael agreed. 'In the meantime, we have captured one of Rachid's oarsmen. We sank one of his galleys and this man was brought out of the water, still chained to the wooden spar that prevented him from drowning. We shall see what information we can persuade him to give us about his master's stronghold—'

'I will not have him tortured,' Lorenzo said. 'No matter that he is a Turk and an enemy, he shall be treated as a man. If he is willing to help us, we shall offer him employment in our ranks. If he refuses to co-operate, we will see if he can be ransomed to his family.'

Lorenzo rubbed at one of the wide leather bands he habitually wore on his wrists, his eyes as dark as the deepest waters of the Mediterranean and as impenetrable.

'I do not believe he is of Turkish origin,' Michael said. 'He will not answer when spoken to, though he understands the language of his masters, also some French and, I think, English.'

Lorenzo looked at him in silence for a moment. 'This man is not to be ill treated,' he said. 'You will leave his questioning to me when I return, if you please, my friend. And now you must rest, enjoy the benefits of home and family for a few days. You have earned them. When I return from Rome we shall meet again.'

'As you command,' Michael said, watching as his friend signalled to a small gondola that was waiting to ferry him out to his personal galley, which was further out in the lagoon. He was curious as to why his commander had suddenly decided that he wanted to interrogate the prisoner himself, but he would obey his orders. The reason Michael, born of good family, had chosen to sail with Lorenzo Santorini was because he respected him; he was a fair man, not cruel—though he would not suffer disobedience lightly.

Lorenzo was thoughtful as he boarded the galley, which was the flagship of his fleet, the fastest and newest of the vessels he owned, with the benefit of three sails, to be used when the wind was fair, thus giving the oarsmen a chance to rest. Such galleys were still much faster and easier to manoeuvre than the top-heavy galleons the Spanish favoured. Even the smaller, lighter craft of the English merchant adventurers, who had begun to be a considerable force in these seas, would find it difficult to keep pace with this galley. Turkish galleys seldom attacked his ships—they knew that he was a man to be reckoned with.

His real quarrel, however, was with Rachid the Feared One, a man of such cruelty that his name was well earned. The pitiful creatures that served at the oar in his fleet were wretched indeed, few surviving more than three years of beatings and torture.

Lorenzo's eyes darkened as he remembered one such object of pity, a man who had survived by chance. He would never rest until Rachid was brought to justice, either at the end of a rope or by the sword. He had vowed it at the deathbed of the man who had adopted him, and one day he would keep his promise.

He regretted that he had lost one of his galleys in this struggle, for men must have died, though their comrades would have saved all they could. Rachid had also lost men and galleys, but for him life was cheap. He would replenish his oarsmen from the slave markets of Algiers or simply send a raiding party to one of the islands of the Aegean to capture men, women and children. The men would serve in his galleys, the women and children would be sold as house slaves—a trade that revolted all good Christian men and women.

It would be interesting to hear what plans were afoot in Rome, for he would welcome any fight that lead to the demise of such men. Rachid paid tribute to the Sultan of the Ottoman Empire and was free to pillage and murder as he would in these waters. If the power of the Turks could be curbed, it would make his enemy that much more vulnerable.

But even if he had to enter his very stronghold to do it, one day he would find and kill the man he hated.

'It is so good to see you, sir.' Kathryn kissed the cheek of their visitor. Lord Mountfitchet was almost as dear to her as her own father, and she looked forward to his visits. They had been rare enough since Dickon was stolen all those years ago. 'Did you see the man of whom Father told me—Suleiman Bakhar?'

'Yes, we spoke with him at length,' Lord Mountfitchet told her with a sigh. 'But there is no news. He has made inquiries for us, for, as you must know, his influence is far reaching in that part of the world. However, he has not given up hope—though he says that it would be rare for a man to survive that long in the galleys. It depends what happened to Richard when he was taken. If he was sold as a house slave…he could be anywhere.'

'We must pray that he was,' Kathryn's father said, shaking his head over the sad business. 'Otherwise…' He looked sorrowful. For his own part he believed that Richard Mountfitchet must be long dead, but his friend had refused to give up his search and he did not blame him. If it had been his own son or—God forbid—Kathryn, he might have felt the same.

'I do not believe that Dickon is dead,' Kathryn said. 'I am sure that I would have felt it in here.' She pressed her clenched hands to her breast as if in prayer. 'You *must* go on searching for him, sir.'

'Yes, Kathryn.' Lord Mountfitchet smiled at her. She was lovely with her dark red hair and green eyes, a sweetness about her mouth that was testament to her tender nature, but more than that she had helped him to retain the hope of his son being restored to him one day. 'That is why

I have come to stay with you for a while. It is in my mind to visit Venice and Cyprus. As you know, I have recently begun to import wine from Cyprus and Italy to this country. I began to take an interest in the region when I started my search for Richard, and I am thinking that I might decide to live out there in the future.'

'You would leave England?' Kathryn stared at him in surprise; she had heard nothing of this before now. 'But what of your estate?'

'The house and land could be left to my agents to administer. It might be that I shall want to return one day, but there is little for me here now. In Elizabeth's England, Catholics like myself and your father are not given an equal chance. I mean no disrespect to the Queen, for I know she must take the advice of her ministers—and they live in fear of a Catholic plot against her. I have taken no part in such plots nor would I, for she is our rightful Queen, but there is nothing to keep me here. If our poor Dickon lives, he must be somewhere in that region of the world— perhaps Algiers, or Constantinople.'

'We shall miss you,' Kathryn said and her throat caught with tears at the thought that she might never see him again. 'How shall we know if there is news of Dickon?'

'I should write to you, of course,' he said and smiled at her. 'But if I live there I shall need a good friend in this country to keep an eye on my affairs. I have asked Sir John if he would join me in this venture of importing wines, and he has been good enough to agree.'

Kathryn looked at her father, who confirmed his satisfaction with the arrangement. 'Then at least we shall hear from you sometimes.'

Lord Mountfitchet nodded, looking at her thoughtfully. 'Your father is too busy to accompany me on this voyage of exploration, Kathryn, but I would like him to have first-hand knowledge of what I intend to do there. He has suggested to me that you might accompany my party. My sister, Lady Mary Rivers, was widowed a few months past and has agreed to make the journey with me, for she has nothing to keep her here either and we shall be company for each other in our dotage.'

'You are not yet in your dotage, sir!'

'No, you are right—but it comes to us all in time, Kathryn. Mary and I get on well enough, and I have no wish to marry again. She thinks me a fool to search for Dickon, but keeps a still tongue on the subject. She will be your chaperon on the journey, and I believe we shall find a suitable guardian to accompany you on the return journey—unless you meet someone that you would wish to marry.'

'Oh…' Kathryn looked at her father, a faint colour in her cheeks.

'I had it in mind to look about for a suitable husband for you, daughter,' her father said, and paused. 'But Lord Mount-fitchet is right. There is little opportunity for Catholics in this country these days. If you should chance to meet someone suitable who you liked while on your travels, I should be pleased. I know that Mary and Charles would take care of you and make sure that any suitor was worthy of you before advising me. Indeed, I shall probably make the journey to fetch you home myself. If I were not so busy at the moment, I would come with you. Your brother Philip will be home from Oxford next year and, if I cannot come myself, he will be happy to take my place, for he longs to travel.'

'Yes, I know.' Kathryn gave him a look of affection, for she was fond of her brother. 'Would you truly not mind if I went with Lord Mountfitchet and Lady Mary?'

'I should miss you, Kathryn,' her father said, his eyes warm with affection. 'Had your mother lived I might have been able to introduce you to a gentleman you could like before this. I have been too busy to see to it, and, besides, I think you need a woman to help you make such a decision. When Lady Mary told me she was to accompany Charles I thought it an opportunity for you to see a little of the world. I fear you must have been too often lonely since your dear mother left us.'

Kathryn smiled, but it was true enough. She had her good friends, neighbours and the elderly nurse who had been almost as a mother to her, but she had missed the time she had spent with her mother, talking and working at her sewing. It was nine years since the fever had taken her, just a year or so after Dickon was abducted.

'Where do you intend to go first, sir?' she asked, turning her clear green eyes on Lord Mountfitchet.

'We should return to London and my sister,' he replied. 'Then we should travel to Dover, and from thence to Venice. I have made contact with a merchant there, a rich, powerful man from whom I have been buying fine wines these past three years. It is he who has encouraged me to expand my business. I shall consult with him before I make my final choice, though I believe Cyprus will suit me rather than Italy itself. I have it in my mind to establish a vineyard there.'

'May I think about this for a little and give you my answer in the morning?'

'Yes, of course. I know it is a grave decision—it would mean that you would be away from your home for many months.'

'I believe I know my answer, but I would think about it,' Kathryn said and smiled at him. 'If you will excuse me now, sir, I shall leave you both, for I have things to attend to.'

'Until the morning, my dear.' Lord Mountfitchet bowed to her as she walked away.

'She is a good girl,' Sir John Rowlands said as the door closed behind her and sighed regretfully. 'Her feelings for Dickon went deep and she has never forgotten him. I think they made some childish pact between them, but she has not told me the details. Until she accepts that all hope of Dickon is gone, I believe she will resist the idea of marriage with another.'

'It would be a shame if she were to waste her life,' Lord Mountfitchet said. 'Much as I hope that we shall find some news of him in Venice, I would not have Kathryn grieve for my son for ever. She is young and beautiful of face as well as nature, and she deserves some happiness.'

'Do you think this merchant of whom you spoke may have news?'

'I pray it may be so. Suleiman Bakhar knows him well. He told me that Lorenzo Santorini has helped several slaves who have managed to escape from their masters. He sometimes buys them in the slave markets of Algiers or takes prisoners from the pirate galleys he sinks, and he will ransom a Corsair captain for galley slaves. I think he exchanged ten slaves for one such man just a few months back. He gives them the chance to work for him, and sometimes he will return them to their families. He might ask for a ransom for his trouble, but for myself I would gladly pay it.'

'He sounds a man to be reckoned with?'

'Indeed, he is. Suleiman admires him—they have a mutual respect, I believe, though Santorini hath no love for Corsairs or the Turks. Indeed, I have heard that he hates them.'

'Yet Suleiman Bakhar calls him friend.'

'Suleiman is a man of enlightenment, as you know. He has only one wife, Eleanor, though his religion allows him to have several, and he adores her. They travel together and though she adopts Muslim dress when in his country, she wears English garb in ours. Suleiman says that if anyone can find Dickon, it is Santorini.'

Sir John nodded. 'And that is the true reason you want Kathryn to accompany you, isn't it? You believe that Dickon will need both you and her if he is found.'

'What will he be like if he has survived?' Lord Mountfitchet said, his face grey with grief. The abduction of his son had haunted him these many years, giving him no peace. 'He is bound to have suffered terribly. He will need nursing and care if we are to teach him how to live again.'

'Yes, I fear you are right,' Sir John agreed. 'Perhaps Kathryn is the only one who might help him. They were so close as children.'

'I have not told her my thoughts on this matter,' Charles Mountfitchet said. 'It would make her feel that she ought to accompany us—but I would have her come only if she wishes it.'

'Yes, it must be as she wishes,' Sir John said. 'I would not have it otherwise. Yet if she should want to marry…'

'I shall write to you at once,' his friend promised. 'But Mary will have a care to her. We shall not allow some ruthless fortune hunter to snare her.'

'Her fortune is adequate, but not huge,' Sir John said. 'I have my son to think of and, as you said, Catholics are not given the chance to rise these days. Philip will not be given a post at court as I was when Mary was Queen.'

'That is why you do well to join me in my venture,'

Lord Mountfitchet said. 'We may trade where we will, for the world is bigger than this country of ours.'

'Yes, I believe you are right,' Sir John said, 'though for myself I would be loath to leave it as you intend.'

'Perhaps I might have thought as you if…' Lord Mountfitchet sighed and shook his head. 'It does no good to repine. If Santorini can give me no hope, then I may accept that I shall never see my son again.'

Kathryn looked at herself in her small hand mirror. It had come all the way from Venice and had once belonged to her mother. She touched the smooth silver handle with her fingertips. The merchants of Venice were known for the quality of their wares, and it was from that city that the beautiful glass posset set, which her mother had treasured, had come.

It would be a great adventure to go with Lady Mary and Lord Mountfitchet. She had never expected to leave the shores of her homeland, for her father was not a great traveller. Yet she had read the histories in his library, those rare and valuable books and bound manuscripts that she was privileged to share, and her mind was open to new things. And of course Venice was renowned as a centre of publishing, particularly of the poets and of great histories. She thought that she would like to see new countries, new places—and there was always the possibility that they might discover something concerning Dickon's whereabouts.

Her hair was hanging loose about her shoulders, a dark, shining red mass of waves that gleamed with fire when it caught the candlelight. She got up and went over to the window, gazing out into the darkness. She could see very little for there were no stars to light the sky that night. Her father had spoken of her finding someone she might wish to marry—but how could she ever do that when her heart belonged to Dickon? She had given him her promise as a girl and he had taken his knife and cut her initial into the back of his wrist. She had cried out in alarm, for it had bled a lot, and had given him a lace kerchief to bind it.

'Does it hurt very much?' she had asked and he had laughed, his eyes bold and daring.

'It is nothing, for I know that this blood binds you to me for ever.'

She had kissed the wound then, tasting his blood, and had known that she would always love him. She would resist any attempts to marry her to a man she did not love. She would behave modestly when travelling and listen to Lady Mary's advice, but she would not let them marry her to a man she did not respect or feel some affection for. Perhaps one day she would feel inside her that Dickon was dead. If that happened, she might consider marriage. If not…

Her thoughts seemed to come up against a blank wall, for she did not know what she would do if Dickon never returned to her. There was no alternative to marriage for a woman of her class, unless she wished to retire to a convent. Women married or became nuns, unless their male relatives had a use for them. Perhaps Philip would accept her as a dependent in his household if she grew old and past the age of being a wife.

It was a sad prospect, but what else was there for her? Laying down her mirror, Kathryn went to her bed, which was a heavy box base with four posts and a carved tester overhead. A handsome thing, it was piled high with soft mattresses filled with goose feathers, for the slats were wooden and hard. Slipping beneath the luxury of silken quilts, she wondered what life was like on board ship.

Yet she would put up with any discomfort if, at the end of the journey, she could find the man she loved.

The momentum was gathering, Lorenzo thought as he left the meeting to which he had been summoned. There had been talk of forming an alliance to fight a campaign against the Turks for a long time, but now, at last, it looked as though it might actually happen later that year. Pope Pius V had formed the Holy League with Spain and Venice, and it was hoped that others would bring their ships to help fight the menace that had haunted the Mediterranean seas and the Messina Strait for so long. Many had thought the talking would simply go on and on, and negotiations would probably continue for a while. However, after these latest threats against Cyprus and Rome itself, it seemed that His Holiness was determined to strike against the enemy that had for so long threatened the nations of Christendom.

Leaving the palace, Lorenzo was thoughtful as he walked, his mind dwelling not on the conference that he had attended, but on a letter that had reached him shortly before he left Venice. It was from an Englishman with whom he had done business in the past, telling him that he was coming to Venice and asking if he could help to trace a youth who had been abducted from the shores of his homeland over ten years previously.

Lorenzo frowned, for it was a thankless task. He knew as well as any man how unlikely it was that the youth had survived.

He would, of course, do what he could to help Lord Mountfitchet, for although they had never met he had heard good things of the gentleman. His father, Antonio Santorini, had visited England some years previously and had spoken of meeting Lord Mountfitchet, saying that he was both honest and decent. Therefore, Lorenzo would help him, but to trace a man who had been taken by Corsairs so long ago...

Lorenzo's instincts remained alert even while his mind wrestled with his problems, and he was aware that he was being followed. So when the attack was made, he was ready for it, drawing his sword as he turned to meet the three ruffians who rushed upon him out of the darkness.

'Come, my friends,' he invited with a cold smile that only served to intensify the ice of his eyes. 'Would you have my purse? Come, take it if you can...'

One of the three, bolder than the others, took him at his word. They clashed swords, contesting the fight fiercely, but the rogue was no match for a master swordsman and called for help from his comrades. The other two came at Lorenzo warily, for they had seen that he was no easy mark. Outnumbered three to one, he held his own for some minutes, slashing to left and right as each one attacked in turn, whirling out of reach, retreating, then advancing as he fought with the skill and ferocity his years as master of a war galley had brought him. Even so, the odds were against him and it might have gone ill with him in the end had not a newcomer joined in the fray, bringing his own skill and courage to Lorenzo's assistance.

Lorenzo's sword found its mark, disabling one of the three. Finding that the odds were now even and that they were being driven back, the other two rogues broke and ran, whilst the wounded fellow leaned against a wall, clutching his arm, blood oozing through his fingers.

Lorenzo had sheathed his sword when the others ran, but the stranger who had come to his aid still held his, regarding the would-be assassin speculatively.

'Shall we kill him?' he asked of Lorenzo. ''Tis what the dog deserves—or do you wish to question him?'

'His purpose was to rob me,' Lorenzo answered with a careless shrug. 'Let him go to join his companions—unless he would prefer a quick death?' His hand moved to his sword hilt suggestively.

The man gave a squeak of fear, suddenly finding the strength to run in the wake of his comrades. A harsh laugh escaped the stranger, who turned to Lorenzo.

'You are merciful, sir. I think he would have killed you if he could.'

'I do not doubt it.' Lorenzo smiled. 'I thank you for your help, sir. I am—'

'I know you, Signor Santorini,' the stranger said before he could continue. 'I am Pablo Dominicus and you were pointed out to me at the conference we both attended. I followed you because I wish to speak with you.'

'Then good fortune followed me this night,' Lorenzo said. 'Shall we find an inn where we can sit and talk, if you have some business you would discuss?'

'My business is twofold,' Pablo Dominicus said. 'I am on the one hand an emissary from His Holiness the Pope—and on the other I am a man seeking revenge. I believe we have a common enemy.'

'Indeed?' Lorenzo's eyes narrowed. It seemed the stranger was a Spaniard. He had no great love of the Spanish, for the Inquisition was a fearful thing, practised by many in the name of Catholicism, but stronger and more powerful in Spain than most countries. And it was known that Spain resented Venice for its independence, and considered that some of its inhabitants would benefit from the attention of the Inquisition. There were men who served in Lorenzo's galleys who had known what it was to suffer torture and beatings at the hands of the fanatics who ruled the religious order. Yet there was only polite inquiry in Lorenzo's voice as he said, 'Pray tell me more, *señor*. I would know how I may serve you?'

'Let us find somewhere we can be private, Signor Santorini. I have a request from His Holiness, for your name is well known to him—and another of my own.'

'There is an inn I know in the next street,' Lorenzo said. 'If your business is secret we can take a private chamber and be sure that we are not overheard.'

Lorenzo drank sparingly of the rich red wine Dominicus had ordered, listening to the request being made of him. In the darkness of the streets he had been unable to see the face of Don Pablo clearly, but now he saw that he was a man in his middle years. Heavily built, he wore a small, dark pointed beard, his hair short and thinning at the temples. And there was a faint unease in his manner that Lorenzo found interesting.

'His Holiness requests that you pledge your support to our cause,' Don Pablo said. 'Your galleys are some of the finest and your men are strong and brave, and, I am told, loyal to you. If you join us in the League, others will surely follow.'

'It was my intention to make my offer once I had consulted with my captains,' Lorenzo said, his eyes thoughtful as he studied the other man. Why was it that he did not quite believe him as honest as he appeared? 'I shall join your cause for it is also mine, but the men who serve me are free to choose. I believe most will follow me, for they have cause to hate the Turks and their allies.' Some hated the Spanish just as much, but he would not say that. 'Now, perhaps you would care to tell me the true reason you chose to follow me this evening?'

Don Pablo smiled. 'They told me you were clever. I shall not insult your intelligence by holding to the claim that I am here on the Pope's behalf, for that might have been left to others, though I know His Holiness intends to approach you. I followed you because I believe you have good cause to hate Rachid—he they call the Feared One. I have heard it said that you hate him and would see him dead if it were possible.'

Lorenzo was silent for a moment, then, 'What has Rachid done to you?'

'Three months ago his galleys attacked and captured one of my merchant ships,' Don Pablo said and his fist clenched on the table. It was clear that he was suffering some deep emotion. 'That cost me a great deal of money— and one of the men he killed was my son-in-law.'

'I am sorry for your loss, sir.'

'My daughter and grandchildren are living in Cyprus,' Don Pablo went on and his hand shook as if he were in the grip of some strong emotion. 'Immacula wants to return to Spain with her children. I would send ships to fetch her myself—but I have suffered other losses of late. Those accursed English privateers, as they call themselves, have been harrying my ships as they return from the New World…'

'You are asking me to bring your daughter to you?' Lorenzo's brows arched as he studied the other's face.

'I am willing to pay for your time, of course.' Don Pablo's eyes dropped before Lorenzo's intense gaze.

'My galleys are meant for war. They are not suitable for a woman and children. I think you must look elsewhere for your escort, Señor Dominicus.'

'You mistake me, *signor*. Immacula will naturally travel in our own ship. I but ask for an escort to see her safely to Spain.'

'You want my galleys to escort your ship?' Lorenzo nodded, his gaze narrowing as he studied the Spaniard. Something was not right about this. His instincts were telling him to be wary, and they were seldom wrong. 'My men work for me. They are not for hire to others.'

'Surely they would do as you bid them?' Don Pablo's eyes were dark with suppressed anger and something more—was it fear? Lorenzo could not decide, but sensed that there was more to this than he had been told. 'I believed you commanded. Do not tell me that those who serve you dictate what you do, for I should not believe it!'

Lorenzo's mouth curved in a strange, cold smile that sent a shiver down the spine of his companion. 'Forgive me if I speak plainly, Don Pablo. Some of my men have suffered at the hands of the Spanish Inquisition. They would spit in your face rather than fight for you.'

Don Pablo's face suffused with anger, his neck a dark red colour. He started to his feet as if he would strike out in anger. 'You refuse me? I had heard that you were a man of business. Surely my gold is as good as the next man's?'

'For myself I would take your money,' Lorenzo said, his face a stone mask that revealed nothing of his thoughts, 'but I cannot expect my men to fight for a Spaniard.' He stood up and inclined his head. 'I am sorry, but I believe you may find others willing to assist you.'

'You may name your own price.' Don Pablo flung the words after him, seeming desperate. 'I beg you to help me, *signor*.'

'My answer remains the same, Don Pablo.' Lorenzo turned to look at him, his eyes cold and resolute. He was certain now that his instincts had been right; this was not a simple matter of business. 'When you decide to tell me the truth, I may reconsider, sir—but until then, farewell.'

A look of fear mixed with horror came to the Spaniard's eyes and for a moment he seemed as if he would speak, but he shook his head and in another moment Lorenzo closed the door behind him.

His instincts had served him well as always. He believed that the attack on him had been planned, not random, a ploy to make him grateful to Dominicus—to make him accept the commission that was offered in a sense of friendship and trust. Lorenzo had learned in a hard school that few men were to be trusted.

There was more behind this than met the eye, and it smelled wrong. If his enemies had set a trap, it would need to be baited more cleverly than this.

Chapter Two

So this was Venice! Kathryn looked about her eagerly as their ship weighed anchor in the great lagoon. They were too far out to see the shoreline clearly, but the grand palaces of the rich merchant princes lay shimmering in the sunshine, the waters of the lagoon lapping over the steps at which brightly coloured gondolas were moored.

'What do you think of Venice, my dear?' Lady Mary asked as she came to stand beside the girl. 'Is it what you expected?'

'It is beautiful. I did not know what to expect. I have seen a pastel of the Grand Canal and its palaces, ma'am, but reality far exceeds the artist's imagination. Those palaces seem almost to be floating.'

Lady Mary laughed. She was a stout, good-tempered lady, who had been pretty in her youth, and her smile was warm with affection, for she had grown fond of Kathryn on their journey. They had been together some months and it was now the spring of 1570. In England it would still be very cool, but here it was much warmer as the sun turned the water to a sparkling blue.

'Yes, it has a magical appeal, does it not? My late husband was an enthusiastic traveller in his youth. He told me of his visit to Venice. We must visit St Mark's Square and gaze upon the Doge's palace while your uncle is at his business, Kathryn.'

It had been decided that she should look upon her kind friends as Aunt Mary and Uncle Charles.

'We may not be blood related,' Charles Mountfitchet had told her at the beginning of their journey, as they set out to London to meet his sister. 'But we shall be together *en famille* for some months and must be comfortable with one another.'

Kathryn had been very willing to accept him as an honorary uncle, for she had long felt close to him. They had comforted each other throughout the years since Dickon's abduction and she was fonder of him than anyone other than her father.

'Oh, I want to see everything,' she said now. Her eyes had a glow of excitement that had been missing for a long time. The journey had suited her for she had not been seasick, as Lady Mary had for the first few days of their voyage. 'And you will feel so much better to be on land again, Aunt.'

'Indeed, I shall. I might wish to go no further,' Lady Mary said with some feeling. 'I fear that this is but a temporary respite, for my brother wishes to settle in Cyprus and so we must put to sea once more.'

'He plans to grow his own wine,' Kathryn said. 'But who knows? His plans may change.'

'You are thinking of Richard, of course.' Lady Mary frowned. 'I know that both you and my brother hope for a miracle, my dear, but I fear you will be sadly disappointed.'

'But it does happen,' Kathryn said. 'Suleiman Bakhar

told my uncle that sometimes slaves may be either rescued or bought from their masters. If Dickon was sold as a house slave, it is possible that we might be able to find him and purchase his bond.'

'My brother has tried to find his son,' Lady Mary said, sighing deeply. She did not believe their search would come to anything and feared that they merely brought more pain on themselves. 'For years he petitioned men of influence to help him in his search, to no avail. I believe that Richard is dead. I am sorry, but I think that some trace of him would have come to light before this if he were alive.'

'I know what you say is sensible,' Kathryn said, her eyes bright with the fervour of her belief. 'But I feel that he lives. Here inside me.' She pressed her hands to her breast. 'I cannot explain it, for it must sound foolish, but if Dickon had died—a part of me would have died too.'

Lady Mary shook her head, but said no more on the subject. In her own opinion Kathryn was living on false hope. Even if her nephew had somehow survived, he would not be the same. Any man who had endured years of slavery must have changed; he might be hard and bitter or broken in spirit. Either way, Kathryn was doomed to grief. It might be better if no trace of Richard was ever found, for surely in time she would learn to love someone else.

The girl had blossomed under her care. While in London they had visited the silk merchants, buying materials to make into gowns suitable for a warmer climate. Lady Mary had been pleased to take the girl about, introducing her to her friends, giving her a taste of what life could be, and the change in Kathryn had pleased her. She smiled more and her laughter was warm, infectious, though there was a stubborn streak beneath her pretty manners. Yet she had thrown off the air of sadness that had haunted her lovely face and was revealed as a charming, intelligent girl.

Lady Mary had great hopes of finding a suitable husband for her charge before the time came for Kathryn to return home.

'I believe this is the gondola come to take us ashore,' Kathryn said as she turned to her companion. 'We are to be taken to the house Uncle Charles has hired for our use, but he is to meet that friend of his immediately. Signor Santorini, I believe he called him.'

'He hopes for news, I dare say.' Lady Mary smothered a sigh. 'Well, at least it will give us time to settle in. Men are always in the way at such times.'

Kathryn smiled, but made no answer. Given a free choice she would have wished to go with her uncle to the meeting, but she had not been asked. She would be of much more help to Lady Mary—but she would be impatient for news.

'I trust your journey was a good one, sir?' Lorenzo rose to meet his visitor. He had chosen to receive him in one of the smaller salons to the right of the grand entrance hall, for it was more welcoming and more conducive to privacy. 'I am pleased to meet you at last, Lord Mountfitchet.'

His words were spoken frankly, his eyes going over the older man and finding that he was drawn to him in a way that was not often the case with strangers. He saw suffering in the other's face, the greying at his temples and in his beard; it was a face grown old before its time. It was the face of a man who had known terrible grief. For some reason Lorenzo was saddened by his grief, though the man was a stranger to him.

'Come, sir, will you not take a glass of wine with me? Pray be seated.' He indicated the principal chair, which was of a kind not common in England, the seat well padded, and the low back comfortable and shaped to accommodate a man's bulk. 'I dare say you are weary from your journey?'

'Indeed, a glass of wine would be welcome, Signor Santorini,' Charles Mountfitchet said as he took his seat. 'My sister and niece wanted me to accompany them to our lodgings and rest for a day or so, but I was impatient to meet you.'

'Unfortunately, I have no definite news of your son,' Lorenzo said. 'However, there is a man I would have you meet, sir. He was rescued from a Corsair galley two months ago, but has been too ill to question. We believe that he may be English, though as yet he has hardly spoken a word.'

'What does he look like?' Charles asked barely able to contain his excitement. 'What colour are his hair and eyes?'

'What colour hair did your son have? Were there any distinguishing features?'

Charles thought for a moment. 'It distresses me to say it, but I can no longer see Richard's face. His hair was fair—darker than yours, but of a similar texture. His eyes were blue...' He frowned. 'I might be describing a thousand men. I fear I have given you but poor help, sir. But loath as I am to admit it, I spent little time with my son when he was young. He was there and I took my good fortune for granted. It was only when I lost him that I understood what he had meant to me.' His voice broke with emotion.

'Yes, it is often so, I believe,' Lorenzo said. He was not certain why he felt affected by Lord Mountfitchet's story, for he was not a sentimental man. 'We all take what we have for granted. My father died some months ago and I miss him sorely. I was away much of the time and afterwards regretted that I did not show more gratitude towards him.'

'I was sorry to learn of Antonio's death. We met only twice when he visited England, but we were drawn to each other.' Charles hesitated, then said, 'I did not realise at the time that he had a son.'

'I was adopted some years ago,' Lorenzo said, revealing more than was his wont. 'My father was a good and generous man. I owe him much. He was not a wealthy man, so it was given to me to improve our fortunes and I was happy that I was able to see him end his days in comfort.'

'He was fortunate to have you. I have tried to preserve my estate for Richard, but it would have been a relief to me to have him with me. I fear I grow old and the days seem lonely.' His eyes were clouded with grief, the years of futile searching carved deep into his face.

'The man I would have you meet has blue eyes,' Lorenzo said with a frown. 'As for his hair—it has turned grey from the suffering he endured at the hands of his captors. I must warn you that this man has terrible scars on his arms, back and legs.'

'The poor devil,' Charles said and his hands shook as he sipped his wine. He took a deep breath, trying to control the images in his mind—images that had haunted his dreams for years of his son being beaten and tortured. 'This wine is excellent.' He made an effort to banish his nightmares. 'A new one, I think? You have not sent me this before?'

'It came from a vineyard in Cyprus,' Lorenzo told him.

'I have been trying it before adding it to the shipment.' He refilled his guest's cup. 'I shall speak to the man I mentioned myself, ask him if he will see you.' He saw the surprise in the other's eyes. 'He is not my prisoner. He was saved from the wreck of a galley and we have nursed him through his illness. Now that he is well, he will be given a choice. He may work for me as a free man or return to his homeland. If he asks me for help to find his family, I shall give it.'

'Do you ask a ransom for him?'

'If his family can afford to pay. I am a man of business, sir.'

'And if he has no family?'

'Then he is free to go where he will—or stay with me.' Lorenzo's eyes held a glint of ice. He lifted his head defiantly. 'He has his life returned to him. What more would you have of me?'

'Nothing you have not given,' Charles replied. 'For myself, I would be glad to pay for the return of my son.'

'I wish that I might give you more hope,' Lorenzo said. 'But let us speak of other things. You have an idea of settling on Cyprus, I believe?'

'I have thoughts of my own vineyard.'

'Then I may be of more help to you there,' Lorenzo said. 'Come to dinner tomorrow evening. Bring your sister and niece to dine. I may have more news for you by then.'

'Thank you. I shall look forward to it.'

Charles was thoughtful as he took his leave. He believed Lorenzo Santorini an honest man. His manner was somewhat reserved and at times his eyes were cold. He was clearly unsentimental about his business, a man of purpose. Some might think him harsh to take ransom money for men he rescued from slavery, but Charles found no fault in his seeking some profit from what he did. There were others who would simply have left the galley slave to die or even have sent him back to the markets to be sold again.

No doubt it was Santorini's keen intelligence and lack of sentiment that had made him wealthy. Yes, perhaps he was a little harsh in matters of business, but who knew what had caused him to be that way? He sensed some mystery in the man's past, but it was not his affair. Santorini would deal fairly with him and he could ask for no more.

His thoughts turned to the man he had been told of—a man who might be English with blue eyes. Could he possibly be Richard? Charles felt a flicker of hope. Yet it was ridiculous to allow himself to hope. There must be many blue-eyed Englishmen who had been lost at sea and taken as galley slaves, and not only by the Corsairs. Some served in Spanish galleys and there was little to choose between their masters, for they were beaten and tortured, made to work until they collapsed at the oar and were tossed into the sea to die. The Spanish hated the heretic English and it was often said that they were crueller than the Corsairs to those they took in battle.

Charles closed his eyes, trying to shut out the pictures that crowded into his mind. God forgive him, he could almost wish his son dead rather than know that he had suffered such a terrible fate.

'But that is wicked!' Kathryn exclaimed as Charles spoke of the ransom he would pay if the man he had been told of should by some extreme chance be his son. 'Why, this Lorenzo Santorini is little better than those evil men whose business is to trade in slaves.'

'No, Kathryn,' he said. 'You do not understand, my dear. I would be willing to pay any sum for Richard's return and should be grateful to the man who found him for me.'

'But a decent man would not ask for money, Uncle Charles.' She was outraged, her eyes scornful of this man she had yet to meet.

'Hush, Kathryn,' he chided. 'We must not judge him. He does much good, I think, and if he makes a profit by it…' Charles shrugged his shoulders. 'I found him honest. He is a man I can do business with. You may feel it wrong to take money for restoring a man to his family, but others would have let the poor fellow die.'

'Please, Charles,' Lady Mary said with a little shudder, 'I wish you would not say such things. You will give Kathryn nightmares.'

'No, dear Aunt Mary,' Kathryn said and smiled at her. 'My nightmares have become a thing of the past since we began our journey. I do not know why, but my heart has become much lighter.' It was as if she felt that she was going to meet Dickon, that she would find him at her journey's end. In her dreams he seemed very close and he was no longer in pain or distress. She seemed to see him smiling at her, opening his arms to enfold her and kiss her.

'Well, I am happy for it,' Charles said with a smile. 'But it would be too much to expect to find Richard so swiftly. It may be months or years—or perhaps never—but Signor Santorini has promised to do what he can. I pray you, Kathryn, do nothing to antagonise him this evening.'

'Of course I shall not, Uncle Charles,' Kathryn said. 'If you believe he can help us, then I shall do nothing to make him change his mind. I may think him unprincipled and wrong, but I shall not say it.'

He smiled at her, nodding his satisfaction with her promise. It was time for them to leave, and the gondola was waiting at the steps outside their house to take them to Lorenzo Santorini's palace.

Kathryn's eyes widened as she saw it, for it was surely one of the most important and attractive of the many beautiful buildings built by the Grand Lagoon. This Signor Santorini must be very wealthy; if that were so, he did not need to ask for money from the families of the poor wretches he rescued from cruel masters.

Her antagonism was growing towards the man she had never met, her feelings of outrage at the obvious trappings of his great wealth building a picture in her mind so that, when the tall, golden-haired man came towards them, she did not at first imagine that he was Lorenzo Santorini. She had seldom seen a more attractive man, Kathryn thought, and as she looked into his deep blue eyes her breath caught and she felt very strange. She had only ever known one person with eyes that colour and so strong was the emotion that gripped her then that she almost fainted. Indeed, she swayed and put out her hand to steady herself, finding her arm gripped by a firm hand.

'Are you ill, Madonna?'

His voice was so deep and husky; yet she heard only the echoes of the sea against a rocky shore on a windswept night, her mind whirling in confusion. For a moment she was there again, looking down as the Corsairs carried her beloved Dickon away with them, her feeling of terror so strong that she almost fainted.

'Kathryn? Is something wrong, my dear?'

Lady Mary's voice brought her back from the edge of the precipice and her head cleared. She looked at the man, who still held her arm in a vicelike grip, her eyes suddenly dark with revulsion as she dismissed the foolish notion that had come to her. How could she have thought even for one moment that this man was her beloved Dickon? His face was deeply tanned, with sculptured cheekbones and lines about his eyes. Richard Mountfitchet would be no more than five and twenty; this man must be some years older, of course, the set of his mouth harsh and unforgiving, so different from the easy smile that she had been wont to see on Dickon's lips.

Why, from what she had heard of him, he was little better than the evil men who had abducted her dearest friend!

She moved her arm and his grip relaxed, releasing her as her head went up proudly, daring him to touch her again. 'I am all right, Aunt Mary,' she said, smiling at the woman who was clearly concerned for her. 'It was just a moment of faintness. Perhaps the change from the bright sunlight to darkness?'

It was a weak excuse, of course, for it was not truly dark in the palace, which was a place of colour and sunshine from the many windows high above that gave the grand hall a churchlike feel.

'It has been very warm today,' Lorenzo said, his eyes narrowing as he sensed her hostility. What ailed her—and why had she looked at him so oddly for a moment? 'And I believe it may be cool in here. Please come through to my private chambers, ladies. I believe you may be more comfortable there.'

Lorenzo led the way to another, smaller chamber, which was lavishly appointed with beautiful tiled walls and floors, the colours rich and vibrant. It was furnished with the most exquisite things that Kathryn had ever seen, some of them with a distinctly Byzantine look to them. For surely those silken couches belonged more properly in the harem of an eastern potentate?

'I have never seen such a lovely room,' Lady Mary declared, echoing the thoughts Kathryn would not for pride's sake utter. 'Where did you find all these lovely things, Signor Santorini?'

'Some of them were given me in gratitude for saving the life of a precious son,' Lorenzo told her. His eyes were on Kathryn as he spoke, a mocking gleam deep in their mysterious depths. 'It was in Granada and the boy was a Moor, the son of a merchant prince—a man whose wealth would make me seem a pauper by comparison.'

'How interesting,' Lady Mary said. 'Pray do tell us more, sir.'

'It was nothing,' Lorenzo told her with a fleeting smile, his eyes becoming colder than deep water ice as he saw that Kathryn's mouth had curled in scorn. 'I happened to be in the right place at the right time—and the grateful father showered me with gifts of all kinds, some of which you see here.'

'You must also be a very wealthy man,' Kathryn said and her tone made it sound like the worst of insults. 'Might it not have been nobler to refuse the gifts and be satisfied with the pleasure of saving a life?' Her eyes flashed with green fire, challenging him so clearly that the air seemed to crackle between them.

'No, no, Kathryn,' Charles reminded her uneasily. He was afraid she would antagonise the Venetian, and Santorini was his best hope of ever finding his son. Indeed, since they had met, he had been filled with new hope. 'You must not say such things, my dear. It is not for you to judge these matters.'

'Kathryn's fault lies in her ignorance,' Lorenzo said

easily and she saw that there was an amused curl to his mouth. His eyes glinted with ice and she felt her heart catch, for something about him drew her despite herself. 'To have refused the gifts from such a man after rendering him a significant service would have been to offer him a deadly insult. Had I been unwise enough to do so, he would have thought that I believed he owed me more and would simply have increased the size of his gift—even to beggaring himself, if I demanded it. But of course, your niece could not know anything of the customs, or indeed the pride, that prevails amongst such people.'

He was looking at her as if she were a foolish child!

Kathryn felt as if she were in the hands of her old nurse, being scolded for some childish misdemeanour. He was humiliating her, stripping her to the status of an ignorant girl, making her feel foolish—and she hated him for it. If she had not remembered her promise to Lord Mountfitchet at that moment, she might have given him an honest opinion of his morals, telling him what she thought of his habit of asking a ransom from his victims.

'I bow to your superior judgement, sir,' she said, her nails turned inwards to the palms of her hands as she fought her instinct to rage at him. Dickon's father was relying on his help. It was through him that they might learn something that would lead them to find Dickon. She must remember that, no matter how great her disgust of this man and his trade. 'Forgive me, I did not know…'

The apology was the hardest she had ever had to make and she tasted its bitterness; she was determined to say nothing more that evening, for it would kill her to be civil to him! She could not know that the look in her eyes and the tilt of her head betrayed her, nor that he found her defiance amusing.

'No, do not apologise, sweet Madonna,' he murmured and the mockery in his voice stung her like the lash of a whip. 'We should be churlish indeed not to forgive such beauty a small mistake of judgement.'

Kathryn inclined her head. Oh, he was so sure of himself, so secure in his position of power and wealth! She would like to wipe that mocking expression from his face and were she alone with him she would do it! But no, she must not let him drive her to further indiscretion. She would behave as befitted an English gentlewoman.

'I bow to your generosity, sir.' The look she gave him was so haughty that it would have slain any other man, but he merely smiled and turned his attention to Lord Mountfitchet.

Wine was served and there was a choice of a sweeter wine for the ladies, but Kathryn stubbornly chose the same as he and her uncle drank and nearly gagged on the dryness of it. She took one sip and set the glass down, her irritation mounting as she saw that he had noted her distaste. When they were directed outside to a small courtyard garden, where a table had been set for them, she noticed that he made a small signal to his servant, and when she looked for her wineglass her wine had been changed.

Oh, was there no ending to this torture? Kathryn asked the servant who served her from the many delicious varieties of fish, meat and rice dishes to bring her some water, refusing to be tempted by the wine, which Lady Mary had declared was delicious.

The food was wonderful too. Used to the more heavily spiced dishes her father's cooks served at home and sickened by the awful food on board ship, she could not resist trying the delicious prawns and unusual fruits and vegetables that were served to her. After each main course a cold ice sherbet was served, which cleared the palate, and the sweet courses included a delicious sticky jelly that she simply could not resist.

'I see you approve of one of the gifts my friend from Granada sends me from time to time,' Lorenzo said, smiling at her. 'You see, as his son grows to a man, his gratitude increases and he will not allow me to forget that he considers me as another son.'

Kathryn had been reaching for another piece of the sticky sweet and her hand froze in mid-air, then withdrew, her eyes darting a glare at him that would have made most men retreat in confusion. His answer was to smile so wolfishly that it sent a chill through her, the flash of white teeth sudden and menacing, as if he would devour her.

'Please continue to enjoy them, Madonna,' he told her. 'It will please my friend mightily to know that his generosity is not wasted. He fears that I do not appreciate it, but now I can tell him quite truthfully that it brought me favour in your eyes.'

'I am glad that your friend will be pleased,' Kathryn said and defiantly took the piece of lemon-flavoured sweetmeat that she desired, biting into it with such venom that she saw his eyes flicker with laughter. He enjoyed taunting her! She could see it in his face, but there was nothing she could do, for she was at his mercy. Please God, let this meal be over soon and then, perhaps, she need not ever see him again.

'I was thinking,' Charles said, seemingly unaware of the duel going on between Kathryn and their host. 'I have cudgelled my brains to think of a distinguishing mark that might help you find Richard, sir—but I cannot recall a thing.'

'Oh, but—' Kathryn began and then stopped as all eyes turned on her. She shook her head. 'I cannot be sure that it would still be there.'

'If you know of something, you should tell us, Kathryn,' Charles said. 'I believe you knew Richard better than anyone.'

'Pray do give me any information you can,' Lorenzo said and reached for his wineglass. As he did so she caught sight of a leather wristband chased with silver symbols. The wristbands were so at odds with the richness of his dress that she was mesmerised for a moment and he saw her interest. 'You are admiring my bracelets, Kathryn?' He pulled back his sleeves so that she could see that he wore the curious bands on each wrist. 'The symbols may not be familiar to you, for they are in Arabic. One stands for life, the other for death.' There was something in his eyes that made her shiver inwardly, an expression so different to any other that she had seen in him that her stomach clenched with fear. 'It is to remind me, lest I should forget, that one is the close companion of the other.'

'Surely…' The words died on her lips, for now she felt a sense of desolation in him and it touched her, reaching down inside her so that she shared his grief, his pain, and it almost sent her reeling into darkness. 'They are remarkable, sir,' she said, fighting to pull herself back from that deep pit. 'But you asked about a distinguishing mark. There was one that Uncle Charles would not know about.' She paused, for the memory was so strong in her mind then that it made her ache with the grief of her loss. 'Dickon was my closest companion, my dearest friend. One day he told me that he would always love only me, even though I was but nine years to his fifteen. I said that when he grew up he would forget me, and he drew his knife. He cut my initial into his arm, just above his wrist.' She saw Lorenzo's eyes darken, his gaze intensifying on her face. 'It bled a great deal and I was frightened. I gave him my kerchief to bind his wrist, but it was deep and the bleeding would not stop. My nurse bound it for him when we went home and scolded me for allowing him to hurt himself. When it began to heal, there was a livid mark in the shape of a K.'

'You have never told me this, Kathryn,' Charles said and frowned. 'It might help in the search—if it still remains.'

'It might have been obliterated by other marks,' Lorenzo said and he looked thoughtful, serious now, all mockery gone. 'I do not wish to distress the ladies, Lord Mountfitchet, but you must realise that the manacles galley slaves wear leave deep scars. Even if the scar that Richard inflicted on himself remained, it might not be easy to see after so many years of being chained to an oar.'

'If he was a galley slave,' Kathryn said. 'He was but fifteen, sir. Might he not have been sold as a house slave?' She had prayed so often that it might be so, otherwise there was little hope that Dickon would have survived.

'It is possible—but if he was strong for his age he would more likely have been put to the oars. The rate of death amongst such unfortunates is high and anyone with the strength to pull an oar might be used if the Corsairs had lost some of their oarsmen.'

'Yet that makes it all the more likely that the mark may still be there,' Kathryn said. 'For if he lives, it is unlikely that he was in the galleys.'

'You speak truly, for I doubt that any man could survive ten years in the galleys,' Lorenzo told her and the expression in his eyes sent a shiver down her spine. 'We must hope that for at least some part of the time your cousin was more fortunate.'

Kathryn looked at him, seeing an odd expression in his eyes. What was he thinking now?

'Would your friend in Granada help us to find Dickon?' she asked.

'Yes, that is possible,' Lorenzo said. 'I will write to him and ask if he will make inquiries, though after so long…' His words drifted away and he lifted his shoulders in a gesture that made her want to defy him all the more.

'You think it is impossible, don't you?' Kathryn saw the answer in his face. 'But I don't believe that Dickon is dead. I am certain he lives. I feel it in here.' She put her hands to her breast, her face wearing an expression of such expectation, such hope, that he was moved. 'As we journeyed here my feeling grew stronger. I believe that he is alive and may be closer than we think.'

'All things are possible,' Lorenzo said, for he found that he did not wish to dim the light in those beautiful eyes by telling her she was wrong. 'My friend would tell you that it is the will of Allah, but I believe it is the will of man. If Dickon was strong enough, if he wanted to live badly enough, he would find a way to survive. And perhaps he might have been fortunate. Not all slaves are ill treated, Kathryn. Some masters are better than others.'

'You speak as if you have some experience of these things, sir?'

Lorenzo smiled oddly. 'Perhaps…'

Kathryn would have pressed for an answer, but he turned to Lord Mountfitchet and began to talk of Cyprus and the land most suitable for wine growing. Kathryn sat and listened, her first disgust of him waning a little as she realised that he was a man of knowledge and influence.

She could not condone what he did in the matter of the ransoms he demanded from the families of those he rescued, and yet she began to understand that it could be but a small part of his business and not the source of his vast wealth.

She could not like him, she decided, for he was too arrogant, too certain of his position, and he could not understand how she felt—how Lord Mountfitchet felt—about the loss of Dickon. But perhaps Uncle Charles was right and he would deal honestly with them.

Besides, what right had she to judge him when she did not know him?

Lorenzo turned his gaze on her again for a moment, and she felt that strange sensation that had almost made her faint when they first met. Why was it that she felt as if they had met before?

'This is so beautiful,' Kathryn exclaimed as they wandered about the square that was the centre of Venice. 'Is it true that the Church of Saint Mark was built to house his body when it was brought from Alexandria?'

'That is what I have been told,' Lorenzo answered her though she had addressed her question to her aunt. 'The building you see near by is the Palazzo Ducale—and over there is the Cathedral, which was first begun in the ninth century and rebuilt after a fire in the eleventh. Notice the architecture, which bears a distinctly Byzantine influence.'

'It is very fine,' Kathryn replied. 'I had thought the people of Byzantium were barbarians, but it seems that they knew how to build.'

'They knew many things,' Lorenzo replied with a smile. 'It was a great empire that demands our respect.'

'You seem to know so much,' she said, a little overcome by all the things he had told them as they explored the beautiful city of Venice and its waterways. 'What, pray tell me, are those buildings over there?'

'That is the Procuratie Vecchie, and used by the procurators or magistrates, from amongst whom the Doge is chosen, and is built, as you see, in the Italian style, as are many of the palaces themselves. And those columns were erected in the twelfth century. That one bears the winged lion of St Mark and the other portrays St Theodore on a crocodile.' He looked at Kathryn, a faint smile on his lips. 'Would you wish to visit the Bridge of Sighs—or would you prefer return to my home and take some refreshment?'

'Tell me, why is it called the Bridge of Sighs?'

'I imagine Signor Santorini has had enough of your questions for one day,' Lady Mary said. 'It was kind of him to accompany us, but perhaps like me he is ready to return home for some refreshment.'

'Oh, forgive me,' Kathryn said, for she was not in the least tired and might have carried on exploring for another hour or more. 'Yes, we shall go home—at least, we shall return to your home, *signor.*'

'It is also yours for the duration of your stay,' Lorenzo said. On discovering the previous evening that the lodgings they had taken were less than they had hoped for, he had sent his servants to remove their baggage, insisting that they stay with him until they left for Cyprus. It was also his suggestion that he accompany Lady Mary and Kathryn on their tour of the city, for Lord Mountfitchet had other business and, despite Kathryn's protests, he did not think it suitable that they should go alone. 'And as to the matter of why the bridge has that name, it is because the palace connects to the prison and the bridge is the route by which prisoners are taken to the judgement hall.'

'Ah, I see,' Kathryn said and smiled. 'I had thought it might have had a more romantic story attached to it.'

'Perhaps a lover who had cast himself into the water after having his heart broken?' Lorenzo laughed huskily. 'I can see that you are a follower of the poets, Madonna.

You have come to the right country, for this is a land of beauty and romance. You have only to look at our fine sculptures and paintings.'

She blushed, looking away from the mockery in his eyes, for her heart was behaving very oddly. 'I have noticed some very fine paintings in your home, sir.'

'Tell me, which ones do you admire?'

'I noticed one that had wonderful colours…' Kathryn wrinkled her brow. 'It was in the great hall and I saw that the colours seemed to glow like jewels when the sunlight touched them. Most of the paintings I have been used to admiring were tempera, but I believe that one was done in oils, was it not?'

'Indeed, you are right,' he said. 'The artist was a man called Giovanni Bellini and my father bought the painting some years ago. I have others that I have bought that you might like to see one day.'

'Yes, I believe I should, if you have the time to spare, sir. I know you must be a very busy man and— Have a care, sir!' Kathryn gave a little cry as she saw someone suddenly lunge at his back with what looked like a curved and deadly knife.

Lorenzo whirled round even as she spoke, catching the would-be assassin's wrist as he raised his arm to strike. There was a sharp tussle and she heard something that sounded like a bone cracking, and then, before she knew what was happening, three men rushed up and overpowered the assassin, dragging him away with them.

'Forgive us, Madonna,' Lorenzo said and his face had become the customary hard mask that she found so disturbing, all trace of softness and laughter gone. 'I believe your safety was not in doubt, but it should not have happened. My men were instructed to keep a look out for anything that might cause an unpleasant incident.'

'What a terrible thing,' Lady Mary said, looking distressed. 'I trust you are not hurt, sir?'

'I thank you for your concern,' he said, but his eyes were on Kathryn, an odd expression in their depths. 'Perhaps now you will understand why it would not be safe for you to wander at will in this city.'

'But why did he attack you?' Kathryn had been startled by the incident, but he had dealt with it so swiftly that she was not frightened, though Lady Mary looked shaken. 'Do you have enemies, sir?'

Lorenzo frowned. 'I believe that any man in my position must have his share of enemies, but I did not know until today that I had one prepared to attack me here in Venice.'

'Do you know who the man was?'

'A hired assassin,' Lorenzo dismissed the man with a twist of his lips. 'I dare say I know who paid him.'

'Someone who hates you?'

'He has cause enough,' Lorenzo said. 'He belongs to that fraternity you despise so much, Kathryn—a Corsair by trade and inclination. He is called the Feared One, for his cruelty exceeds that practised by most of his brethren. Even they fear and hate him, but they do not dare to betray him.'

'Why does he hate you enough to pay someone to kill you?'

'Because I have made it my life's work to destroy as many of his galleys as I can.' Lorenzo's eyes were colder than she had ever seen them. Gazing into them, she was caught up in an emotion so strong that it robbed her of breath. 'I have nineteen galleys at the moment—we recently lost one in a battle with Rachid—but I have ordered six more. Soon my fleet will be large enough to

meet him wherever and whenever he takes to the seas—
and then I shall destroy him, little by little.'

Kathryn gazed into his eyes, feeling herself drawn into
a vortex that had her spinning down and down, drowning
in the bottomless depths of his eyes. 'Then I must tell you
that I owe you an apology,' she said when she could
breathe again. 'I believed that you were as guilty as those
men who enslave others because you asked for a ransom
for those you rescued, but if you have dedicated your life
and your fortune to destroying such an evil man, then—'

'Pray do not continue,' Lorenzo said and she saw that his
eyes had lost their haunted look and were filled with
laughter. 'You run the risk of flattering me, Madonna. Say
only that you approve of what I do and I'll not ask for more.'

'You are mocking me,' she said and could not quite
hide her pique.

'Indeed, it is very unkind in me,' he said, 'but do not
grudge me the pleasure that teasing you has brought into
a life that has hitherto known very little, Madonna.'

Once again she was aware of powerful emotions
swirling beneath the mask he showed to the world and was
silent for the moment. They had been walking as they
talked, a little ahead of Lady Mary and two men who now
shadowed them more closely than before, and had now
reached one of the canals where Lorenzo's gondola was
waiting to convey them to his palace.

'You are not what you seem,' she said. 'Will you tell
me the reason you hate Rachid so much? For there must
be other pirates almost as feared, and yet it is he whom
you wish to destroy.'

'That is something I have told to very few,' Lorenzo
replied. 'One day perhaps I may tell you, Kathryn. But for
the moment I think I shall keep my secret.'

Chapter Three

Here within the courtyard garden, where brightly coloured flowers spilled over from warm terracotta pots, their perfume wafting on the soft night air, Kathryn could almost believe that she was in the knot garden of her home. It was odd, but there was something English about this garden, though many of the flowers were Mediterranean. The roses were fully bloomed and scented, very similar to some that her mother had grown at home.

She thought of her father, wondering if he was missing her. But Philip might be home from college now and so he would have company, though she was sure enough of his love to know that he would think of her. She missed her family and yet she was moving in a new world that she found interesting and colourful.

Her thoughts turned to the incident in St Mark's Square earlier that day. Had Lorenzo not acted so swiftly it might have ended very differently. It was true that she had called a warning to him, but she did not flatter herself that she had saved his life; he had acted instinctively, as if he had heard or perhaps sensed the assassin's approach. What kind of a man was he that he needed to be so alert to danger?

He had begun to haunt her thoughts, for she had dreamt of him the previous night. He had been in danger and she had tried to reach him, but a strong wind had been blowing, carrying her further and further away. She had woken from her dream with tears on her face, though she did not understand why she wept.

Kathryn's feelings were mixed—she did not know how she felt about Lorenzo Santorini. He was such a strange mixture, at one moment as cold as ice, his features rock hard, his mouth an unforgiving line. Yet when his eyes were bright with laughter…it was then that she had this strange feeling of having known him for ever.

What had he meant when he said he would keep his secret for the moment? That he was a man of mystery she did not doubt, but—

Her thoughts were interrupted by the sound of voices. Charles Mountfitchet and Lorenzo were talking together. They spoke in English as always, for Lorenzo's grasp of the English language was much better than their grasp of Italian. He, of course, spoke several languages.

'It may be that it would be better for you to buy land in Italy,' Lorenzo was saying. 'With this threat of invasion from the Turks…'

'Do you really believe that they will try to invade the island?'

'I cannot say, sir. I merely sought to warn you of the possibility.'

'I doubt there is much danger for the moment,' Charles said, for he had set his heart upon buying land in Cyprus, an island rich in sugar, fruit and fertile wine-growing soil. 'I visited the man you told me of—poor fellow.'

'Would he speak to you?' Lorenzo was saying.

'He asked if I had come to buy him,' Charles said, sounding distressed. 'When I told him that I was trying to find my son he wept, but would not answer me. I could not tell him that he would not be sold to another master, for it was not in my power, despite what you have told me, sir.'

'From what you saw of him, was there anything that reminded you of your son?'

The two men had come into the courtyard now, clearly unaware that Kathryn was there, standing just behind a tall flowering bush.

'It is impossible to tell,' Charles said with a heavy sigh. 'He could be Richard, but I do not recognise him.'

Kathryn moved towards them and saw the startled expression in both their faces. 'Will you let me see him?' she asked. 'I would know Dickon if I saw him, I am sure of it.'

'The scar you told us of…' Charles shook his head sadly. 'It would not help you to look for that, Kathryn. His wrists are so badly scarred and callused by the wearing of manacles and chains for all that time that any previous scar would have been obliterated.'

'Oh, the poor man—' Kathryn began but was interrupted.

'It would not be fitting for you to see him,' Lorenzo said. 'It caused your uncle much grief and a woman would find it too upsetting.'

'Have you such a low opinion of our sex, sir?' Kathryn's head was up, her eyes flashing with pride. Why must he always imagine that she was foolish? 'Do you think I have not seen suffering before? My dear mother was ill some months before she died of a wasting sickness, and I have seen beggars with sores that were infected with maggots in the marketplace at home. If I saw this man, I might know if he is Dickon.'

'Kathryn knew my son better than anyone,' Charles said, looking at her uncertainly. 'She is a woman of some spirit, Signor Santorini. I think—with your permission—I should like her to see him. After all, what harm can it do for her to speak with him if someone is near by?'

Lorenzo's eyes flickered with what might have been anger, but it was controlled, not allowed to flare into life. 'Very well, I shall arrange it for tomorrow. But I warn you, Kathryn, he has suffered things that you cannot begin to contemplate. I fear your tender heart may sway your good sense.'

'I shall know if he is Dickon,' Kathryn said stubbornly, though in her heart she was not sure that she would truly know. For that one moment when her senses had betrayed her, she had thought that Lorenzo himself might be her lost love, though that was impossible, of course. There was no possibility that Dickon and this cold, arrogant Venetian could be the same man. He had clearly been born to privilege and wealth and could never have suffered as this poor slave he would deny the chance of a new life.

'Very well, you may see him tomorrow. I shall have him brought here for you.' He inclined his head curtly, clearly not pleased to be overruled in this matter. 'I fear I have an appointment this evening. In my absence, I beg you to make yourselves free of my home. My servants will serve you supper and care for your needs. Do not hesitate to ask for whatever you want.'

'You are generous,' Charles said. 'I myself have a business meeting this evening, but Mary and Kathryn will be company for each other.'

'Yes, of course we shall,' Kathryn said and smiled at

him. She did not look at Lorenzo, annoyed with him because he had tried to deny her the chance to identify Dickon. 'We have many little tasks that need our attention.'

'Then I shall wish you a pleasant evening.' Lorenzo inclined his head, turned and left them together.

Charles looked at her for a moment in silence, then said, 'It was a harrowing experience, my dear. Signor Santorini is probably right in thinking that it will upset you.'

'I do not expect otherwise,' Kathryn said. 'Who could remain unaffected by suffering such as he describes? But it was for this that I came with you, Uncle. I can only trust my instincts. If I do not feel it is Dickon, I shall tell you.' She looked thoughtful. 'You said that he hardly spoke to you—do you think he might tell me more?'

'Perhaps he does not remember,' Charles said. 'Signor Santorini believes that he has been a slave for many years, perhaps not always in the galleys. He might have been a house slave for a while and sent to the galleys for some misdemeanour. It is the way of things. Youths make amusing slaves for some men, but when they grow older and stronger they become too dangerous to keep in the house. I shall not tell you of the things these youths are forced to endure, for it is not fitting, but it may be that a man would prefer to forget rather than remember such abuses.'

Kathryn's eyes were wet with tears, for she could guess what he would not say. She brushed her cheek with the back of her hand. 'How can men be so cruel to one another?'

'I do not know, Kathryn,' Charles said with a deep sigh.

'How can anyone survive such terrible things?' Kathryn asked. 'It seems impossible. Yet this man has done so and deserves our kindness, if no more.'

'Yes, you are right,' Charles said, looking thoughtful. 'I must leave you now, Kathryn. Go into your aunt, my dear, and do not dwell on this too much. I think it unlikely the poor wretch I saw today is my son, but I should value your opinion.'

Kathryn kissed his cheek, doing as he bid her.

She spent the evening with Lady Mary, working on her sewing, for they had purchased many materials before they left England and had not had time to complete their wardrobes. One or other of the servants they had brought with them did much of the plain sewing, but they liked to finish the garments with embroidery and ribbons themselves.

Kathryn was not tired when she retired for the night. She felt a restless energy that would not let her sleep, and sat by the open window looking out over the courtyard. The sky was dark, but there were many stars, besides a crescent moon, and she found it fascinating to look at them, for it was possible to see far more here than at home where there was so often clouds to obscure them.

She became aware of someone in the sunken courtyard. A man just standing there alone, staring at the little fountain that played into a lily pool. He was so still that he might have been one of the beautiful statues that adorned his house and garden, and yet she knew him.

What was he thinking? Was he too unable to sleep? He was such a difficult man to understand, and sometimes she wanted to fly at him in a rage, though at others…she liked him. Yes, despite herself she had begun to like him.

Sighing, Kathryn turned from the window as the man moved towards the house. It was time she was in bed, even if she did not sleep, for Aunt Mary wished to go exploring again in the morning. They were to be taken in a gondola through the waterways so that they might see more of the city.

Lorenzo unbuckled his sword, dropping it on to one of the silken couches that he preferred about him, something he had learned to appreciate at the house of Ali Khayr. A wry smile touched his mouth, for his friend had tried hard to convert him to Islam, though as yet he resisted.

'You are more at home here with us than in the Christian world,' Ali Khayr had said to him once as they debated religion and culture. 'And no one hates the Inquisition more than you, Lorenzo—and yet you resist the true faith.'

'Perhaps there is good reason,' Lorenzo said and smiled as the other raised his brow. 'I do not believe in a god— neither yours, nor the Christian variety.'

'And yet it was by the will of Allah that you came to me and my son was saved,' Ali Khayr said. 'Why do you not accept the teachings of the Prophet? It might help to heal your soul and bring you happiness.'

'I think I am beyond redemption from your god or the god the Inquisition uses as an excuse for torture and murder.'

'Hush, Lorenzo,' Ali Khayr told him. 'What a man may do in the name of religion may not be called murder, though it would not be our way. We use our slaves more kindly, and those that convert to Islam may rise to positions of importance and a life of ease.'

'You may choose that way,' Lorenzo said, a glint in his eyes, 'but others of your people are less tolerant.'

'You speak of pirates and thugs,' Ali Khayr said with a dismissive wave of his hand. 'There are men of all races in that fraternity, Lorenzo: Christians as well as Muslims.

They say that Rachid, your enemy, was from the Western world, though I do not know if it be true.'

'It is true,' Lorenzo said. 'He wears the clothes of Islam and he speaks the language like a native, but a clever man may learn many languages. I have seen him close to, though he did not look at me, for I was beneath him—a beast of labour, no more.'

'You have good cause to hate him,' Ali Khayr said. 'And I do not condemn you for what you do—but I would bring ease to your soul, Lorenzo. If you put your faith in Allah, you might die a warrior's death safe in the knowledge that you would be born again in Paradise.'

'And what is Paradise?' Lorenzo smiled at him. 'You would have it a place of beautiful women, and wine such as you have never tasted? My business is fine wines and if I cared for it I could have a beautiful houri when I chose.'

Ali had laughed at his realism. 'You are stubborn, my friend, but I shall win you in the end.'

Now, alone in his private chamber, Lorenzo smiled grimly as he removed the leather bracelets from his wrists, rubbing at the scars that sometimes irritated him beyond bearing—the badges of his endurance and his slavery. The three years he had served as a slave in Rachid's personal galley had almost ended his life. Had he been taken sick at sea he would no doubt have been thrown overboard, for there was no mercy for slaves who could not work aboard Rachid's galley. His good fortune had been that they were near the shores of Granada and he had been taken ashore when the men went to buy fruit and water from traders on the waterfront. He had been left where he fell on the beach, left to die because he was no longer strong enough to work.

It was luck, and only luck, that had brought the Venetian galley to that same shore later that day. He had no memory of how it happened, but he had been taken aboard the personal galley of Antonio Santorini and brought back to life by the devotion of that good man—a man who had also suffered pain and torture, but at the hands of the Inquisition.

Lorenzo recalled the time shortly after he was brought to his father's house. He had been broken in body, though not in spirit, and it was the gentleness, the kindness of a good man who had brought him back to life. Antonio had taken him in, treating him first as an honoured guest and then as a son, adopting him so that he had a name and a family. For Lorenzo did not know his own name. He had no memory of his life before the years he had spent as a galley slave.

This was the secret he so jealously guarded. No one but his father had known of his loss of a past life, and only Michael amongst his friends knew that he had served in Rachid's galley, though some might guess. There was a look about him, a hardness that came from endurance. For, once he had regained his strength and health, Lorenzo had worked tirelessly to be the best swordsman, the best galley master, the best judge of fine wines. No softness was allowed into his life. On his galleys he lived as his men lived, worked and trained as hard as they did, and he treated them with decency, though never with softness. He was known as a hard man, ruthless in business, but fair. He had repaid Antonio Santorini for his kindness, taking the Venetian's small fortune and increasing it a thousand-fold.

'God was kind to me when he sent me you,' Antonio had told him on his deathbed. 'I know that you have cause to hate Rachid and all his kind, my son—as I have cause to hate the Inquisition. I was tortured for what they said was blasphemy, though it was merely the debate of learned men who questioned the Bible in some aspects. They would have us all follow their word in blind obedience, my son. Yet the God I believe in is a gentle god and forgives us our sins. I pray that you will let Him into your heart one day, Lorenzo, for only then may you find happiness.'

It was strange, Lorenzo thought, as he prepared for bed, that two good men would convert him to their faith, though they believed in different gods. A wry smile touched his mouth as he buckled on his bracelets again. He wore them to guard his secret, for knowledge was power and he knew that some would use it against him.

As he lay on his couch, he thought for a moment of Kathryn. He had deliberately shut her out of his mind, for she was too dangerous. When he was with her he forgot to be on his guard, he forgot that he had sworn to dedicate his life to destroying evil.

To feel warmth and affection for a woman would weaken him, nibble away at his resolve so that he became soft, forgot his hatred, the hatred that fed his determination to destroy Rachid. He could not love. He had felt something approaching it for Antonio—but a man might feel that kind of affection for another man and remain a man. To love a woman… He could not afford to let her beneath his guard, though at times she tempted him sorely. Had she been a tavern wench he would have bedded her and no doubt forgotten her, but a woman like that was for marrying.

He smiled as he remembered the way her eyes flashed with temper when she was aroused. She gave the appearance of being modest and obedient until something made her betray her true self. The man she loved—her cousin, it seemed—would have been fortunate had pirates not taken him that day.

It was a sad story, but one that Lorenzo had heard often enough through the years. He thought of the poor creature she had insisted on seeing. If he was indeed the man they sought, she would probably devote the rest of her life to him—and that would be a shame.

Lorenzo glared at the ceiling as he lay sleepless, Kathryn invading his thoughts now though he had tried to keep her out. It would be a waste of all that beauty and spirit if she considered it her duty to care for a man who might never be a husband to her.

Kathryn had chosen to receive the former galley slave in the courtyard of Lorenzo's home. She thought that it might be easier for him than the splendid rooms of the palace, where he might be afraid of what was happening to him. Here in the garden, she could sit on one of the benches and wait in the warmth of the sunshine until he was brought to her.

'You do not mind if I join you?'

Looking up, she saw Lorenzo and frowned. 'I had hoped I might be allowed to see him alone, sir. He may be frightened of you and refuse to speak to me.'

'I have not harmed him, nor would I.'

'Yet he may fear you.' Kathryn hesitated. 'Your expression is sometimes harsh, sir. If I were a slave, I would fear you.'

'Do you fear me, Kathryn?'

'No, for I have no reason,' she replied with a smile. 'I find you…difficult, for you seem to be not always the same. At times—' She broke off, for she heard voices and then three men came into the courtyard. One of them was clearly the former galley slave—he was thin almost to the point of emaciation and his hair was grey, straggling about his face. His clothes hung on his body, though they were not rags, and some attempt had been made to keep him clean, his beard neatly trimmed.

Kathryn's throat closed and she could hardly keep from crying out in distress as she saw him, for pity stirred her and her eyes stung. She got up and moved towards him, a smile upon her lips.

'Will you not come and sit by me, sir?' she invited. 'I would like to hear your story if you will tell it to me.'

His eyes were deep blue, though not quite the colour of Lorenzo's—or Dickon's. Kathryn felt the disappointment keenly. A man might change in many respects, but his eyes would surely not change their colour?

For a moment the man seemed confused, as if he feared to believe his eyes, and then he shuffled forward, sitting on the bench she indicated. He stared at her, seeming bewildered, not truly afraid, but wary.

Kathryn sat beside him. She saw that Lorenzo made a dismissive movement of his hand, causing his men to withdraw to a distance, though he still stood closer than she would have liked.

'There is no need to be afraid,' she said to the former slave. 'No one will hurt you. I promise you that, sir. I only wish to hear your story.'

'I am not afraid,' he replied. He spoke English, but hesitantly as though the words came hard to him. Yet that was not surprising, for he must have become accustomed to another language, the language of his cruel masters.

'What is your name?'

'I do not know,' he said. 'I am called dog. I am less than a dog.'

Kathryn swallowed hard, for the tears were close. 'Do you have no memory of what you were before…?'

'I am an infidel dog,' he repeated. 'I do not think, therefore I am not a man.'

'That is so wrong, so cruel,' Kathryn cried and saw him flinch as she put out a hand to touch him. 'No, no, I would not hurt you.'

'Am I yours now?' he asked. 'Have you bought me?'

'You are not to be sold.' Kathryn turned to Lorenzo with a look of appeal in her eyes. 'Tell him that he is not a slave…please?'

Lorenzo hesitated, then inclined his head. 'If you recover your strength, you might work for me, but you are not a slave. If you wish to leave here, you are free to go when you wish.'

'Where would I go?' The man's blue eyes were so bewildered that Kathryn spoke without thinking.

'You may come to Cyprus with my uncle and me,' she said impulsively. 'Not as our slave, but as one of our people. When you are well, you may perhaps work in the gardens or some such thing, but you will be paid for what you do.'

'You would take me with you?'

'Yes,' Kathryn promised recklessly. 'You shall be my friend and help me when you can.' Her heart caught as she saw tears trickle from the corner of his eyes and she had to wipe away her own tears. She was shocked as the man fell to his knees before her and kissed the toes of her shoes that were peeping from beneath her gown. 'No, no, you must not do that. You are not a slave. I shall take care of you.'

'Get up,' Lorenzo commanded, his voice harsh. 'You are a man, not a dog. Since you understand English you shall be called William. You will return to the house where you have been cared for until Mistress Rowlands leaves for Cyprus with her uncle and aunt.' He signalled to his men, who came to help the newly named William to his feet.

Kathryn watched as the former galley slave shuffled off, helped by Lorenzo's men. She turned to look at him, her eyes bright with anger.

'Why were you so harsh to him?'

'He needed to be told, for you had unmanned him with your kindness. He is not used to that, Kathryn. You must give him time to become accustomed to his new life.'

She felt hurt by his accusation. 'He needs kindness, not harsh words.'

'I have dealt with many such victims. You do not know what you do, Kathryn. If you treat him too kindly he will become as your lapdog, a pet to beg at your feet for scraps. No man should feel that way. It is better that he hates, for hatred makes a man strong.'

Kathryn's eyes widened as she looked at him. 'Is that how you became so strong?' she asked. 'Do you hate so much that you cannot feel kindness, Lorenzo?'

It was the first time she had used his given name and she did not know what had prompted her to do it, and yet she felt that somehow she was closer to him, closer to knowing him than she had ever been.

'I learned from a master,' he said. 'What will you do if your uncle refuses to have the man as one of his people?'

Kathryn dropped her eyes, for she did not know. Lord Mountfitchet had come to find his son and she knew that William was not Dickon, felt it instinctively inside her. She had wanted it to be so, but it was not—and yet her heart was filled with pity for the former slave.

'I do not think he will refuse me,' she said. 'Lord Mountfitchet has always been kind and generous to me—especially since we lost Dickon.'

'You called him Lord Mountfitchet then—is he not your uncle?'

'We are not blood relations,' Kathryn said. 'My father and Uncle Charles are lifelong friends and I would have married Richard Mountfitchet if…' She shook her head sadly. 'This man is not the one I loved. I would have known it—besides, his eyes are too pale a blue. Dickon had eyes like…' She looked up and found herself gazing into eyes so blue that they took her breath. 'He had your eyes, Lorenzo. If I did not know it was impossible, I would say that you were more likely to be Richard Mountfitchet than that poor creature.'

'I am not the man you seek!' Lorenzo's tone was harsh, even angry.

'I know that. Forgive me,' she apologised. 'How could you be a poor galley slave? You have too much pride, too much arrogance.'

To her surprise, Lorenzo threw back his head and laughed. She had not expected him to be amused and was at a loss for words.

'Nay, Madonna, do not look so bewildered. Should I be angry when you pay me a compliment?'

'It was not meant as one,' she came back swiftly.

'Perhaps not, but I take it as one,' he said. 'You think me a Venetian prince, perhaps, born to the life I lead?'

'Is that not the case?' she asked and for a moment as she looked deep into his eyes her heart raced. Something in his eyes made her think that he would take her in his arms and kiss her, and her heart leapt with sudden excitement. Her breath caught, her eyes opening wider as she looked up into his face.

'It might be—and then again it might not,' Lorenzo told her, a smile of mockery in his eyes now. His laughter had been genuine, but this was meant to put her in her place. 'You will not gain my secret so easily, Kathryn.'

'Why should I wish to know it?' she asked and turned on her heel, walking into the house, her back stiff with a mixture of anger and pride.

'Why indeed?' he called after her, and then, in a softer tone that she could not hear, 'Better that you should not know the devil you would rouse, sweet Kathryn. Better for you…and for me.'

Kathryn did not look back, but she was shivering with some strange emotion that she did not understand. When he had looked at her a moment or so earlier she had felt that she was drowning in the ocean of those blue eyes, and she had wanted him to kiss her.

'You will take him with us, won't you, sir?' Kathryn asked when her uncle came in from his business later that day. 'I know that I should have asked you before I gave my promise, but he looked so…desperate.'

'It was in my mind to ask Santorini what he wanted as a ransom,' Charles told her with a smile. 'I am not sorry that you do not think he is Dickon, for to see my son like that…' He drew a deep breath, a look of sadness in his eyes. 'The search for Dickon will go on, but I have room enough in my household for this poor wretch. He may never be able to do much for his keep, but I dare say we shall find him something to keep him out of mischief.'

'Oh, thank you, dearest Uncle,' Kathryn said and hugged him. She did not know whether to laugh or cry, but her smile won through. 'Lorenzo thought you might refuse to take him and then I should not have known what to do.'

'You might have taken him as your own servant,' her uncle said. 'Your father has provided money for anything you might need. This man may be your servant if you choose. If he knows how to write, he may be of some use as a scribe. We shall have to see how he goes on as he recovers his strength.'

'He speaks English and understands it, though he is hesitant,' Kathryn said. 'But he will learn once he is living with us.'

'I am certain that he will,' Charles said. 'And I am proud of your tender heart, my dear. I wish that we might find Dickon safe and well, but I would not have you live your life in expectation of it. If you should find yourself able to love another, I would rejoice in your happiness.'

'You are so good to me,' Kathryn said with a smile that lit up her whole face. 'But as yet I have not met anyone I would wish to marry.'

There was someone who could make her heart beat faster, but he could also rouse her to anger and despair and he was not at all the kind of man she would wish to marry. Nor, indeed, did she flatter herself that he would ever think of her as a woman he might take as a wife.

'My business here should be done within another week,' Charles told her. 'I advise you to make the most of your stay here, Kathryn, for I imagine the life on Cyprus will be very different. I do not believe you will find merchants there of the kind that are here, and we shall be reliant on ships that call at the island for much of our provisions, though I believe we may be self-sufficient for the food we eat and such things. However, any luxuries you need should be bought before we go.'

'Lady Mary has already suggested another shopping expedition,' she said. 'Perhaps you could send some of your servants with us, sir. I do not like to ask Signor Santorini for his escort again.'

'Yes, of course, my dear. I shall arrange it myself and there is no need for Santorini to know. He has been a considerate host and we should not take up more of his time.'

Kathryn tossed and turned restlessly. Her dream had been pleasant at the start for she had been walking in a beautiful garden and she had been happy. Someone was with her—a man. The man was Lorenzo Santorini, but not as she knew him. This man laughed and teased her, looking at her with eyes of love. He had taken her into his arms and kissed her, telling her that she was everything to him.

And then, just as she was about to answer him, a great tide of water had come rolling towards them, sweeping her up and carrying her away from him. She woke suddenly, shivering and frightened.

Why was she having these dreams? It was not as if she even liked Signor Santorini, and yet…when she was torn from his arms she had felt as if her heart was breaking.

Kathryn shook her head, clearing it of the troubling images that had caused her so much distress. She was being very foolish. She was confusing Dickon with the proud Venetian in her dreams, for it was her dearest friend who had been torn away from her. She must put all this nonsense from her mind and get ready for the shopping expedition later that day.

'Well, my dear, I think we have spent our time and our money profitably,' Lady Mary said as they turned their steps towards the gondola that was to take them back to the Santorini Palace. 'When our stores are delivered to Charles's ship we shall be ready to leave. I do not think we shall go short of anything we require for the next six months, and before then we may order what we need.'

'I am glad to have so many beautiful embroidery silks and such fine cloth—I dare say we shall find the life a little quiet after our time in Venice, Aunt Mary. At home I had my father's library whenever I needed something to fill my time, but Uncle Charles was unable to bring everything he might have wished for and I believe many of his books were left behind.'

'I shall mention it to him this evening at supper,' Lady Mary promised. 'It may well be that he has already thought to order books for himself and might do the same for us.'

They had reached the steps leading down to the lagoon where their gondola was waiting. Kathryn was a little ahead of Lady Mary and the two servants who had accompanied them. She ran down the steps, accepting the hand of a man who came forward to help her. As she stepped on board, she glanced back at the steps, expecting to see Lady Mary follow, but to her surprise she saw that she was being restrained by one man, while the servants were engaged in a battle with several burly rogues armed with cudgels.

'It is a trap, Kathryn,' Lady Mary cried. 'Come back!'

Kathryn gave a cry of alarm, trying to jump back to the steps, but it was too late. Already the gondolier was pushing off from the steps and someone grabbed her from behind, clasping her in a strong hold as she struggled to get free. She watched as the shore receded, seeing that her aunt seemed to have been released and was standing on the steps staring after her. She sensed Lady Mary's distress, realising too late that it was not her friend who had been in danger, but herself. Lady Mary and the servants, who had now joined her on the steps, had been diverted for long enough for the abduction to be carried out.

'Stop struggling, girl, and you will not be harmed,' a voice said and all at once she felt herself released. Turning, she saw a man of middle years. Heavily built, he had a small pointed beard in the Spanish fashion, his hair cut short and thinning at the temples.

'I beg your pardon for this inconvenience,' he said, speaking in English, but in an odd accent that told her he was unused to the language. 'Please believe me when I say that I mean you no harm. You are simply the means to an end, Mistress Rowlands.'

'Who are you?' Kathryn demanded. Her heart was racing, for she could not help but be afraid despite the words that were meant to calm her. 'And why have you abducted me?'

'My name is Don Pablo Dominicus,' he said. 'And you are my guest. I mean you no harm, mistress. Providing you are sensible and do not try anything foolish, you will be made comfortable aboard my ship.'

'Your ship?' Kathryn stared at him in horror. 'Where are you taking me?' It was like something out of one of her nightmares! She was being taken from her friends, just as in her dream.

'To my home in the hills of Granada,' he replied. 'It is a temporary arrangement, Mistress Rowlands. You are to be held until you can restore my younger daughter Maria to me.'

'But I do not understand,' Kathryn said. 'How can I help your daughter? I do not know her.'

'Maria is being held by a man called Rachid,' Don Pablo said, a look of anger in his eyes. 'His price for her release was that I should deliver his enemy to him—dead or alive. He would prefer to have him alive, for I believe he has a score to settle with Lorenzo Santorini.' He smiled cruelly as Kathryn gave a little gasp. 'Yes, I see that you begin to understand. I asked Signor Santorini for his help, but he would not give it, therefore I have taken you. We shall see what he is prepared to offer in exchange for you.'

Kathryn's head went up proudly. 'Why should he offer anything? Signor Santorini is merely a business acquaintance of my uncle. My father might be prepared to ransom me, but Signor Santorini will not be interested in your proposition. You have made a mistake if you believe that he will give into your blackmail on my behalf.'

'Then I shall offer you to Rachid in exchange for my daughter,' Don Pablo said. 'If Santorini will not come for you himself, you may be my only chance of regaining my daughter.'

A thrill of horror went through her. He could not mean it!

'Surely you would not…that man is a pirate of the worst kind…'

'I see that you have heard of him, from Santorini, I dare say.' An unpleasant smile curved Don Pablo's mouth. 'No, Mistress Rowlands, I do not believe that I have made a mistake. I think that Santorini will come for you and when he does…'

'You mean to trap him! It is his life for mine, is that not what you are saying?' Kathryn felt icy shivers all over her body. It was worse than any of her nightmares. This man was desperate for the return of his daughter. He would stop at nothing to get her back—and that meant he would kill Lorenzo if he could. No, she could not bear it if he were to sacrifice his life for hers. Lifting her head, her eyes glittering with angry pride, she said, 'You are a fool if you think he will come. I mean nothing to

Lorenzo—nothing at all.' Yet, she was beginning to realise, it seemed that he meant something to her.

'How could she have been so foolish as to go without the proper escort?' Lorenzo's anger was fearful to see and Lady Mary felt quite faint. 'God only knows where she is now or who has taken her!'

'But we had our servants to protect us…'

'Little good they did you,' Lorenzo growled. 'Surely the attack on me in St Mark's Square was enough to warn you that it was dangerous for ladies to go out without sufficient protection?'

'I thought the attack was against you personally…' Lady Mary swallowed hard as she saw the flash of fire in his eyes. 'Forgive me. My brother believed that two servants should be enough.'

'No,' Lorenzo said, 'do not apologise, ma'am. This is my fault, as you so rightly say. I acknowledge it freely. Kathryn has been taken because my enemy believes she is important to me—this was done against me.'

'Against you?' Lady Mary fanned herself, for the heat and the shock of what had happened that day had overset her and she was feeling quite unwell. 'Then…what will they do with her?'

'I am not sure,' Lorenzo said. 'It depends who has taken her. She might be used as a hostage—in that case we shall receive a ransom demand for her, but…' If she had been abducted by his enemy she might pay with her life.

Lady Mary gave a cry of distress as she saw the look in his eyes. 'Mercy on us! You do not think that they will kill her?'

'If she should fall into the hands of Rachid, he would do so without a flicker of remorse,' Lorenzo said. 'However,

I believe there may be more to this than meets the eye.' He frowned, taking a turn about the salon. 'For the moment there is little I can do but make some inquiries. I beg you to be patient, Lady Mary. Be assured that I shall do all I can to return Kathryn to you safely.'

'I can do no other than trust you,' Lady Mary replied. 'She is very dear to us, sir. It would break her father's heart if she were lost—and I believe my brother would be deeply distressed. It almost killed him to lose Richard. I do not think he could bear the responsibility of losing Kathryn too. And her father would be devastated.' She gave a little sob. 'This is terrible—terrible…'

'The responsibility for this is mine and mine alone,' Lorenzo said and something in his eyes shocked Lady Mary, for she suddenly understood something that she had not guessed before. 'I promise you that I shall do all in my power to find her. If she lives, she shall be restored to you, no matter what it costs.'

Lorenzo left her, for he had much to do. He was not a man to wait for news. He would make searches, discover what he could before his enemy could demand whatever it was he intended.

His mind was working furiously. This was the third unpleasant incident to occur since his trip to Rome—was it possible they were connected? He had suspected Don Pablo of some treachery, and it was unlikely that Rachid would have had the necessary contacts in Venice to make that attack on him in St Mark's Square.

It was more likely to be the Spaniard—but why? Why should Dominicus hate him that much? He could not think that they had met before that night in Rome. Was it only that he had refused to help him escort his daughter from Cyprus? Surely not.

He had been used to danger and hardship and could bear with them—but Kathryn had never faced the kind of danger that threatened her now. Lorenzo was consumed with a terrible anger, and fear—fear that he might not be able to help her.

Chapter Four

Kathryn made no attempt to escape as she was taken on board the Spanish galleon. She had considered jumping into the lagoon, but she could not swim and the weight of her clothes would soon drag her under. As yet she was not desperate enough to take her own life. Lorenzo would not walk into the trap that Don Pablo had set for him—why should he? But perhaps a ransom could be paid? Don Pablo had told her that in the last resort he would try to exchange her for his daughter Maria, and perhaps Rachid would accept a ransom for her.

It was very frightening, but she comforted herself as best she could. Perhaps Rachid would not be interested in exchanging the other girl for her and then Don Pablo might release her.

Once on board the ship, Kathryn was treated well. She was shown to a cabin, which clearly belonged either to Don Pablo himself or another important member of his crew. It was furnished with a heavily carved, ornate wooden box bed, on which was a mattress of feathers covered by a silken quilt and several pillows. There was also a table, chair and two sea chests. Looking about her, she noted the iron sconces that held lanthorns secured to the wooden panelling, and when she glanced inside one of the chests she discovered a quantity of women's clothing, also silver items and ivory combs that she might need for her toilette. There was, however, nothing that she might use as a weapon to defend herself. It seemed that this abduction had been planned with some care.

The door to her cabin had been locked once she was inside and when she looked out of the small square window, she saw that the cabin was situated at the stern of the ship, and she realised that they were leaving the waters of the Grand Lagoon far behind. They were heading out to the open sea, on their way to Spain as her captor had promised.

She whirled around as the cabin door opened, half-expecting to see Don Pablo, but it was merely a sailor come to bring her food and wine.

'Where is your captain?' she asked. 'Has a ransom demand been sent to my uncle?'

The sailor shook his head, saying something in Spanish that she took to mean he did not understand her. It was useless to ask questions—he probably would not have dared to tell her had he known what she was asking.

Kathryn sat down at the table where the tray awaited her. She looked at the bread, meat and fruit provided warily, wondering if it might be drugged or even poisoned. The sailor watched her for a moment, then picked up the wine cup and took a sip as if to show her it was harmless. Afterwards, he wiped the cup with his fingers and gave it back to her.

Kathryn took the cup. She realised that she was actually feeling hungry for she had not eaten since early that morning and it was now late in the afternoon. It would do no good to starve herself, she decided, and ate one of the rich black grapes, the juice running down over her chin. The fruit was crisp and delicious and she reached for a peach as the sailor nodded his satisfaction and left her to her meal.

Kathryn ate most of the fruit and some of the bread. Her fear had begun to abate. It seemed that she was to be treated as a guest as Don Pablo had promised, and, since there was no possibility of her escaping while on board this ship, she must accept the situation and wait as patiently as she could.

Please come for me. The words were in her mind. She knew that she was hoping Lorenzo would find some way to rescue her, but why should he? He had no reason to care what happened to her. Besides, she did not want him to risk his life for hers.

Lorenzo took the letter his servant offered, breaking the wax seal at once. He read the brief message it contained, cursing aloud as it confirmed his fears. Ever since Kathryn's abduction he had suspected something of the sort.

'You have news of Kathryn?' asked Charles, his face drawn with concern. 'Do they ask for a ransom?'

'Yes, but not the kind that you can supply, my friend.' Lorenzo handed him the letter, but he stared at it blankly and gave it back. 'Forgive me. You do not read Spanish. It is from a man called Don Pablo Dominicus. He is holding Kathryn hostage. He promises she is unharmed, and will be exchanged for his daughter Maria.'

'What does this mean? Do you have the girl of whom he writes?'

'No—but Rachid does.' Lorenzo frowned as he saw that Lord Mountfitchet was puzzled. 'Some weeks ago Don Pablo came to me with an offer I refused. He asked me to escort his elder daughter Immacula from Cyprus to Spain, but I believe he wanted me to commit myself to him so that I was at a certain place at a certain time.'

Charles stared at him in silence, then, understanding, finished, 'So that Rachid would know where to find you?'

'It has a certain logic. One thing that Rachid can never know is where I am at any given time or how many galleys will be with me. If I had agreed to commit three of my galleys and accompany the lady myself as he asked...' Lorenzo shrugged. 'At the time I was not sure. My instincts told me that Domincus was lying, hiding something, but I did not know why. Now I understand. Rachid has his younger daughter Maria and demands a ransom from him.'

'He was prepared to trap you for Rachid so that he might regain his daughter?'

'A fair exchange in his mind.' Lorenzo's face was set in stone. 'Would not any man be prepared for such a bargain?'

'Are you suggesting...?' Charles stared at him in horror. 'Good grief, sir! No, I cannot ask such a thing of you. Surely we can arrange a ransom for Kathryn? I know that most men have their price.'

'Rachid's price is my life,' Lorenzo said. 'It seems he would do anything to have me at his mercy. Only if I can return Don Pablo's daughter to him will he release Kathryn to you.'

'But that is hardly possible,' Charles objected. 'Even if you were willing to make such a sacrifice, how could you trust a man such as you have described to me? You do not know that the Spanish girl is still alive. Besides, what is to stop Rachid murdering you and retaining the girl?'

'Nothing at all,' Lorenzo agreed, a hard glint in his eyes. 'That is why I shall not walk tamely into his trap. At least I know that Don Pablo has taken Kathryn to his home not far from Granada. I have a friend living near there who may be able to help me.'

'So you will try to rescue her?' Charles looked at him with respect. 'You will be at risk, sir. Should you be discovered or captured…'

'I have survived Rachid's loving attentions once,' Lorenzo said with a wry smile. 'I am prepared to risk it again for Kathryn's good—but I prefer to believe that it will not be necessary. I may yet bring her out safely. If I fail…' He shrugged his shoulders.

'I shall pray that you do not, for Kathryn's sake and your own.'

'Perhaps your god will listen,' Lorenzo said, his eyes glinting with some deep emotion that he tried to suppress. 'For myself I have little faith in prayer, but for Kathryn's sake I shall hope that your prayers are answered.'

Inwardly, he shuddered as he imagined her fate if he should fail. She was beautiful and would fetch a huge price in the slave markets of Algiers.

'And what would you have me do?'

'Go on to Cyprus as you planned. Find your vineyard and begin a new life. If I succeed, I shall bring Kathryn to you.' Lorenzo smiled oddly. 'If not, you must send her father my apologies.'

Charles nodded, guessing that the other's manner was deliberately reserved, hiding the swirling passion, the anger inside him. 'It shall be as you say—and may God protect and keep you, sir.'

Lorenzo inclined his head, his eyes dark with an emotion he could not hide, try as he might. 'May your god go with you, sir. Please excuse me, there are things I must do.'

Charles watched as Lorenzo strode from the room. He must put his trust in this man, for there was no other way. It was strange, but he felt a bond between them, an understanding that went beyond words. Perhaps only such a man as this could save Kathryn, a man who knew far more about the suffering of those who served in the Corsair galleys than he would ever tell.

Kathryn looked at the house to which she had been brought. Nestling on a plateau in the mountains overlooking the city, it was a substantial building of grey stone with small windows, most of which had iron grilles. Once within its walls she would truly be a prisoner. She shivered as Don Pablo came himself to help her down from the horse she was riding.

'Welcome to my home,' he said, smiling at her as he took her arm, steering her through the heavy iron gate, which enclosed the house and gardens and swung to behind them with an ominous clink. 'Think of yourself as my guest, *señorita*. You are at liberty to walk in the gardens and my home is yours for the duration of your stay.'

'You are gracious, Don Pablo.'

She held her anger inside. It would do no good to rage at him, for he would only keep her closer. She knew that she was a prisoner, for all his conciliatory words—he would not have allowed her the privilege unless he was sure she could not escape. The walls that enclosed his garden were too high for her to climb. Besides, she had no doubt that she would be watched whenever she was allowed to walk there, but at least it would be better than being kept a prisoner in her room the whole time.

Her good behaviour thus far had been accepted at face value by the Spaniard, who thought her suitably cowed by her situation. Indeed, she was helpless, because his hacienda was almost a fortress. For the moment she could do nothing, but she would remain watchful, waiting for her chance. One of these times her captors might grow careless and then...she would take her chance to escape if she could.

Kathryn would rather die in the attempt to escape than be sold to Rachid, for she knew what her fate would be, and it turned her stomach sour. Better to die than live as a harem slave.

Lorenzo stood in the prow of his galley looking out to sea. They were a day behind the galleon, but his men were pulling at attack speed for long periods. They would not catch the Spanish ship before it reached harbour, but they would not be far behind. With luck they could reach Granada long before they were expected and take Don Pablo off guard.

Lorenzo had not confided his plans to Lord Mount-fitchet—they involved serious risk of injury to Kathryn. It was possible that she might be harmed in the attack on the Spaniard, but there was no real alternative. To give himself up in return for Kathryn's safety was no guarantee that she would be freed. His only true chance of getting her back was to storm the hacienda, hoping for the element of surprise. And the alternative was unthinkable. Better for her that she should die in the attempt to free her than be sold to Rachid.

Don Pablo would think himself safe for a few days, but in believing that he would have mistaken his enemy. Lorenzo's instincts had warned him of the reason for Kathryn's abduction. He had begun to make his plans from the moment he had learned she had been snatched.

Lorenzo motioned for the speed to be taken down. The men could only keep up the fast stroke for a certain length of time, but all his men would take their turn at the oar, including Lorenzo himself. He would not demand anything of others that he was not prepared to do himself.

These men were his most loyal, the strongest and the best. Every man aboard this galley was prepared to die if need be.

Kathryn had noticed that the main gates were kept locked at all times, opened only when a body of men went in or out. However, there was a small side gate that the servants used. She had seen an old man with a donkey bringing fruit and vegetables early in the morning. He had left the gate open for several minutes while he carried the produce into the house. From the window of her bedchamber she had watched carefully to see if it was locked after he left, but no one had come for some minutes afterwards.

If the old man came at the same time every day it was possible that she might be able to slip out of the side gate during the period that he was in the kitchens.

Kathryn did not know what she would do if she succeeded in escaping from her prison. She was alone in a foreign country and penniless. It might be that she would make her situation worse, for thus far Don Pablo had kept to his word to treat her as his guest. If she escaped and was mistaken for a woman of loose morals, which she might well be if she approached a stranger for help, her virtue might be in as much danger as her life.

Yet what was the alternative? If she did nothing, she might find herself being exchanged for Don Pablo's daughter. Kathryn thought that almost anything would be better than to become Rachid's slave. Lorenzo had spared her the details of the Corsair's cruelty, but she was not so innocent that she could not guess what her destiny might be once she was in his hands.

Even if Lorenzo were fool enough to come for her, to offer his life for hers, it was unlikely that she would be returned to her family. She would be sold to the highest bidder!

Lorenzo cursed the delay, for more than two days had passed since they landed on the shores of Spain. It had taken that long to contact his friend Ali Khayr and to buy horses for the small party of men he had chosen to accompany him inland. He would have preferred to attack at once, but Ali had counselled against it.

'I know the man of whom you speak,' he had told Lorenzo. 'If he has taken the girl hostage, she will not be harmed. Yet if you attack his hacienda with no plan you may fail. It is well defended and you would be seen before you could get near. Anything could happen to her then. She might be spirited away while you were kept busy at the gates. You would do better to take her by stealth.'

'Your words are wise as always,' Lorenzo said, controlling his impatience as best he could. 'But it would be dangerous—unless I could discover where Kathryn is being kept.'

'If you will wait in patience for a while, my friend, it may be that I can help you. My servants may go where you may not. Stay your hand for the moment, Lorenzo.'

Against his inclination, Lorenzo had waited, chafing at the bit at the enforced idleness. Some of his men were able to mingle with the townspeople and discover what they could about Don Pablo and his hacienda, but it seemed true that it was almost impregnable to a frontal attack.

Now, at last, Ali Khayr had news for him.

'There is a side gate,' Ali began. 'The main gate is kept locked and heavily guarded. There are armed men patrolling the garden all the time, though the girl you seek is allowed to spend some time there. Sometimes the men grow careless and forget their duty.'

'Do you think we could gain entrance through the side gate?'

'One man could do so,' Ali told him. 'There are two paths to it. One passes the main gate and would be impossible to negotiate without being seen. The other is difficult terrain, which is why it is undefended. If the girl you seek were near the gate at the right time it would be a simple thing, if she were brave enough, to bring her down to where you and your men were waiting.'

'I should be the one to go in and fetch her!'

'With your eyes? A blue-eyed Arab is very rare,' Ali said with a smile to ease his words. 'No, my friend, I think not. You would never get past the gate. However, every morning at a certain time an old man delivers fruit and vegetables. He is an Arab and they know him; they scarcely look at him.'

'Then who…?' Lorenzo cast his mind over his men. 'It must be someone who is willing to risk his life. Surely if I stained my face and kept my head down I might pass for a Moor?'

'Your eyes remain as blue. You need not concern yourself about who shall enter the hacienda,' Ali told him. 'Just be there ready at the foot of the descent. You may need to repel an attack—if they realise she has gone, they will try to take her back.'

'How will this man know where to find her?'

'I have not lived peacefully in Granada all these years under Spanish rule without knowing their ways. When

Bobadil was driven weeping from the Alhambra most of my people left for other shores, but some of us stayed. We live quietly, peacefully, and we watch our backs. Even when Galera was under siege my people and I were left in peace, because we make no trouble for our Spanish masters. The Spanish hardly see us, for we do nothing to make them notice we are still here. We are nothing, of no importance, mere shadows in the night. Some of our people work for them and they take our service for granted. Money is a great persuader. Someone will make sure that the girl is near the gate and the guards are not. If Allah wills it, she will be with you tomorrow at the appointed time.'

'I shall owe you much if you can arrange this, Ali.'

'It will be repayment for the debt I owe you,' Ali Khayr said. 'Had you not acted so swiftly the day my son was attacked in the marketplace by a mad dog, he would have died. You put your life at risk, for to be bitten by such dogs is to die of the foaming disease. Without my son I should have had no reason to live. Therefore my life is yours.'

'It was instinctive,' Lorenzo said. 'And you have repaid the debt.'

'Gold alone cannot repay such a debt. But if I give you back this woman the debt is ended. We may meet then as friends.'

'We are friends now,' Lorenzo said. 'And I shall be for ever in your debt.'

Ali smiled and opened his hands. 'Allah will provide, my friend. Only if he wills it shall our plan succeed.'

Kathryn was unable to sleep. She had risen with the dawn, washing and dressing in the clothes provided for her use, which were Spanish and heavier than she was accustomed to wearing. She stood by the window, looking out at the garden, which was rich with lush greenery and exotic flowers. Soon now the old man would come with the fruit and vegetables and it was in her mind to go down to the garden and take her chance of escape.

'*Señorita…*'

Kathryn looked round as she heard the woman's voice. She had seen the old woman before when walking in the garden and believed she worked in the kitchens. Her skin was a dark olive tone and Kathryn thought that she might be of Moorish descent. Once the Moors had ruled the province of Granada until they were defeated and driven out by the Spanish king, but, though many had sought a life elsewhere, some had remained.

'What is it?' Kathryn asked, but the woman placed a finger to her lips, shaking her head. The Morisco woman put her hand on Kathryn's arm, seeming to want her to go with her and saying something that she could not understand.

Kathryn hesitated, but the woman pulled urgently at her, speaking rapidly, repeating the same instruction over and over. There was no point in resisting, for if she did Don Pablo would send his men to fetch her. She nodded to show that she would go with her, but when she attempted to speak to her the woman put her finger to her lips again and smiled.

Suddenly, Kathryn was alert. Something was happening. She had the strangest feeling that this woman was attempting to help her and that Don Pablo knew nothing of it. When the old woman led her down to the door that led out to the back of the garden and pointed to the far end, she knew that she must mean the gate. She smiled and gave Kathryn a little push, then waved her hands as if she were shooing a goose.

Kathryn smiled, but when she would have spoken the old woman shook her head and disappeared into the house. Feeling nervous and yet excited, Kathryn walked in the direction she had been shown, and as she did so the gate opened and an old man came in with his donkey. She hesitated, but he beckoned to her urgently and she ran the last few steps towards him.

'Go quickly,' he said, pulling her through the gate. 'Down that path. See where it curves to the right and follow. The way is steep and hard, but you will find what you seek there.'

Kathryn's heart was racing—he had spoken to her in English, though from his looks he was a Moor. She whispered her thanks and heard the gate shut behind him as she began to walk down the steep path he had indicated. It was not the road by which they had come and, as she paused to look back, she realised that only a couple of small windows at the back of the house looked out this way. Once she was past the place where the rock jutted at an angle, it would be impossible to see from the house. Perhaps the path was too narrow and steep to be thought a likely approach for any surprise attack. Indeed, it was not easy for Kathryn to negotiate the path, for some of the rock was loose and twice a shower of debris went hurtling from beneath her feet, tumbling down the side of the rocky crag. Her progress was slow and her heavy skirts made it difficult for her to keep her balance. Had she had a choice she would never have ventured down such a path as this, but she steeled her nerves, knowing that it was her only chance. The old man had promised she would find what she needed at the bottom, and therefore someone must be waiting there for her.

When she reached the place where the rock jutted out at

Ransom Bride

an angle, she paused—the path was so narrow that she did not know if she dared to pass the protrusion. If she fell, she would surely go plunging down the side of the mountain to her death. As she took a deep breath she heard a slithering sound as some loose shingle went sliding down into the valley and then a muffled curse, and then, as she held her breath, a man came round the path and beckoned to her.

'Come, Kathryn,' he commanded. 'Take my hand and I shall help you.'

'Lorenzo…' she breathed, her heart leaping. She moved towards him, and somehow she was not surprised that he should be there. Ever since the woman had taken her to the garden she had believed that only one person could have arranged to have her freed.

He frowned as she came towards him, his eyes going over her with disapproval. 'What is the matter?'

'Take off those wide skirts,' he told her. 'You will never be able to negotiate this path in that gown, Kathryn.'

Kathryn did not hesitate. Untying the strings that held her overskirt, she let it fall to the ground. At once she felt so much easier in the petticoat that fitted to her body more closely than the cumbersome panniers she had donned that morning. She went to him with new confidence, taking the hand he offered. His fingers closed about it tightly and he smiled at her in a way that set her spirit soaring.

'You are a good, brave girl,' he told her. 'Trust me, for this next bit is difficult, but I shall not let you fall.'

'Thank you.' She nodded at him bravely, trusting him, confident that he would not let her slip.

He smiled but said nothing, and, looking down, Kathryn saw that the brownish-grey rock jutted out to an alarming degree over what was a sheer fall. The path around it was no more than a ledge and could never have been intended as a path at all. It looked as if at some time a part of the rock had fallen away, leaving this overhanging ledge dangling precariously. It was hardly surprising that the Don had not considered it necessary to guard this side of his mountain home, for a party of men could not pass this way, and the only other approach was past the main gate.

She could never have done it alone! Her heart was in her mouth as she took a tentative step on to the narrow ledge, and only the firm grip of Lorenzo's hand on her arm kept her steady. They had their backs to the rock, which pressed into Kathryn's flesh, scraping her as she pushed back against it, edging one tiny step at a time, moving sideways, inch by inch, not daring to look down. Only the firm pressure of Lorenzo's hand kept her from falling as her eyes closed against the dizziness that seemed to take her mind and for a moment she felt that she could not go on.

'Not much further,' Lorenzo said. 'We are almost there, Kathryn.'

She could not answer—she was too terrified. She breathed slowly, deeply, hanging on to her nerve by the merest of threads, and then, all at once, she found that her feet were on more solid ground and she was suddenly swept into a crushing embrace. Lorenzo held her so fiercely that she almost swooned from the surging emotion that possessed her body and mind. She held on to him, her breath coming in great sobbing gasps as she clung to his strong body and felt the relief wash over her. She wanted to weep, but the feel of his body warmed her, giving her courage.

'You are safe now, Madonna,' Lorenzo said. 'Come, my brave one. My men and the horses are waiting. We have no time to waste—once they know you are missing they will come after us.'

As she looked up at him, he bent his head, his lips brushing hers in the lightest of kisses, so light that she hardly felt it, yet it was enough to set her heart fluttering wildly.

Kathryn blinked as he let her go. She longed to be back in his arms, for she had felt so warm and safe there, but he was already hurrying her down further to where a small party of men and horses were waiting. From there the way was a gentle slope, widening out into the valley, and in the distance the grandeur of the sleeping city lay shimmering in the first rays of the morning sun.

'Once we reach the galleys we are safe,' he told her. 'We shall talk then, Kathryn. But first we have some hard riding ahead.'

She nodded at him, recovering her breath now as he lifted her on to the back of one of the horses and then mounted his own. There was a sense of urgency about him that made Kathryn realise they were not yet safe and she did not need to be told to urge her horse first to a canter, and then, as they left the steep roads behind, to a gallop.

The pursuit did not begin until they had almost reached the shore. One of Lorenzo's men gave a shout and pointed to a party of horsemen outlined against the sky. The alarm must have been given soon after Kathryn's disappearance, for the Don's men were not that far behind them. Lorenzo's party were urged to make a final effort, and then they were within sight of the cove.

The horses were abandoned to one of the party, who rode off with them in another direction as Lorenzo, Kathryn and half a dozen men began the scramble down to the sandy beach where the boat was ready to take them out to the galley moored in the bay. From above them they could hear shouting and, as she paused to look up, she saw that some of Don Pablo's men were preparing to fire at them with their deadly mosquettes, a superior weapon of Spanish invention.

Lorenzo pushed her into the boat and climbed in himself, though two of his men had fired their match-locks at the Spaniards above; however, they were useless at such a distance and did nothing to deter the pursuers from beginning to scramble down the rocky incline to the beach below.

Now they were all in the boat and pushing off from the shore. Don Pablo's men had reached the beach and were racing to the water's edge, some of them wading out to take aim at the rowers. One found his mark and an oarsman fell wounded. Lorenzo took his place while Kathryn bent over him, distressed to see that he was bleeding from a shoulder wound.

She tore strips from her petticoat, making a wedge and then binding him as best she could, her attention given to her task as the shots of the men on the beach began to fall short of their target. By the time she had finished her work they had reached the galley and many hands reached out to take both her and the wounded man aboard. She heard Lorenzo giving orders and then a cannon boomed out and she looked towards the shore, seeing that the men there had fled back to the cliffs and were scrambling up them.

'Kathryn.' Lorenzo came to her as she stood shivering and at a loss to know what to do. Around her the men were preparing to put some distance between them and the shores of Spain. She alone could do nothing and she suddenly felt lost and terribly alone. 'Come, you must go to my cabin and rest. This has been a harrowing experience for you. Forgive me, but there was no other way.'

'There is nothing to forgive,' she said in a trembling tone. 'I must thank you for my life.'

'I did very little. The friend I told you of—Ali Khayr— it was he who risked his life to come to you at the hacienda. I pray that he was not taken, for it will go ill with him. He lives in Granada only because his neighbours tolerate him. He says that money buys him freedom, but it was a great risk he took for our sakes.'

'Then I shall pray for his safety,' Kathryn said. She raised her head to look at Lorenzo, seeing the customary hard line of his mouth, his eyes giving no hint of his feelings. 'I have had time to think of and to regret my own folly. Had I not ignored your advice, this would not have happened. I hope that you will forgive me for causing you so much trouble?'

A faint smile curved his lips. 'Would that I could believe it will be the last time, Madonna.'

'What do you mean?' Her eyes sparked with indignation.

Lorenzo merely shook his head. 'Forgive me, I have work to do. I must stay on deck in case we are followed and attacked. I do not think it, for Don Pablo does not have galleys swift enough to match ours. However, I must be here to direct the men. Michael will take you below.' He nodded to a man standing nearby, who smiled at her as he approached.

'I hope you will permit me to say how pleased I am to see you safe, Mistress Rowlands. Please, follow me and I will show you where you can rest.'

Kathryn thanked him. When she glanced back she saw that Lorenzo was bending over the man who had been wounded while rowing them back to the galley. She felt a little hurt—clearly she was less important to him than his men. He had saved her and for that she must be grateful but, for a few moments on that mountainside, he had seemed so different. When he held her in his arms, when he had kissed her so softly, she had believed that he truly cared for her, that she was more than an errant girl he had rescued, perhaps for a price.

But she would be foolish to imagine that she was anything more than another captive he had rescued, no more than a galley slave he might snatch from a watery grave. She wondered how much her uncle had promised to pay him for her safe return, and the thought made her heart ache.

She could not but be grateful to him for what he had done, but she did wish that he had done it because he cared for her and not for money.

Following Michael into the cabin, she saw that it was sparsely furnished, unlike the cabin in Don Pablo's galleon. There was a plain wooden cot with a straw mattress and one thin blanket, a sea chest and a table with maps spread upon it, but nothing else. Clearly the master of this galley lived much as his men did with no concessions to comfort. His home might be the height of luxury, but here there was no softness of any kind.

'Forgive us, Mistress Rowlands,' Michael apologised. 'There was no time to make provision for your comfort. We did not dare delay for we could not be sure what Don Pablo intended. Had he decided to sell you to Rachid in exchange for his daughter, we might have been too late. Taking you from the Spanish merchant was an easier task, for Rachid's fortress is guarded day and night. No one who is taken there comes out alive unless Rachid wishes it.'

Kathryn shivered as she realised how great had been the

danger of her being lost for ever in some harem. 'Do not apologise,' she said. 'I am grateful for all that you and the others have done, sir. If this is how Lorenzo lives on board ship, then it is good enough for me.'

'Captain Santorini claims no privileges that are not given to the rest of us,' Michael said. 'But I know he would not have chosen that you should travel in this way.'

'Please, no more apologies,' Kathryn told him, lifting her head proudly. 'I shall be perfectly comfortable here. I dare say it is more than I should have been given had I been sold to Rachid.'

'You may thank God for it that you were not,' Michael said and made the sign of the cross over his breast. 'Please rest as best you can and food will be brought to you once we are underway.'

Kathryn nodded. After he had gone she went to look out of the tiny porthole at the sea, which seemed wide and empty, then returned to sit on the edge of the bed. Now that she was alone she was beginning to feel the effects of her desperate escape and to realise how close to death she had been on that mountainside. She closed her eyes, shutting out the memory. It was over. She was here on Lorenzo's galley and safe.

Tears stung her eyes but she would not release them. There was no sense in giving way to her emotions now. She was safe because Lorenzo had risked his life and others to rescue her. He must be angry with her for causing him so much trouble. As yet, he had not chided her for her foolishness, but no doubt that was to come.

Kathryn lay down for a while. She was tired and hungry, and, waking after a fretful sleep that had not re-freshed her, she discovered that Michael seemed to have forgotten his promise to bring her food. She got to her feet and pushed a strand of hair back from her face, feeling dirty and crumpled, and also a little cold in her torn petticoat. When Michael returned she would ask him if there was anything she could wear instead of the clothes that had been given her in Don Pablo's home.

She had just decided that she would go up on deck when she heard a loud boom and the galley shook from stern to prow. Startled, she rushed to the porthole and looked out. It seemed that two galleys were attacking them, and from the flag they were flying, looked as if they might be Corsairs. The pennant had a white background and bore the sign of the crescent and the letter R in a blood-red colour. Something about the bold statement of the Corsair's flag made her shiver.

It must be some of Rachid's men! Kathryn felt chilled as she looked out and saw that the shot Lorenzo's galley had fired had gone home. One of the galleys had been holed and was clearly in some difficulty. The other galley had fired at them and as their vessel rocked, she knew that they had taken a hit, but then several of Lorenzo's guns roared at once and the second galley, which was very close, was holed. It went down so fast that she could hardly believe her eyes. One moment it was there, firing at them, and she could see fierce-looking men on deck preparing to board and fight. And now it had gone—but there were some men in the water.

The second galley was retreating, leaving their comrades in the water. She could see them screaming, calling out to the men who had deserted them, but as Lorenzo's guns roared once more she knew that the second Corsair galley dared not stop to pick them up. Surely they would not leave the men to die?

Kathryn went to the door of her cabin, opening it and going to stand on the little deck that was directly above the rows of oarsmen. For a moment she thought that Lorenzo's crew were going to ignore the men in the water, for they were cheering as they saw that they had routed their enemy. But then she saw that some of the men were at the rails as if to snatch those they could from a watery grave.

'You should go below, Mistress Rowlands,' Michael said, coming to her. 'It is not fitting for you to be here—and like that.'

She glanced down at herself, realising that she must look as if she were in her nightgown. 'May I not help with the wounded?'

'We have our own surgeon to do that,' he told her. 'Please go below.'

'But those men in the water…'

'We shall do what we can. Please go!'

Kathryn retreated, feeling angry and disturbed. She could hear shouting on deck and men moving about, also the movement of oars that told her they were going on. Looking out of the porthole, she saw that there were several bodies floating in the water, but could not tell whether any of them were still alive. She felt the sting of tears, because she knew that those left behind would surely die.

How could Lorenzo abandon them? She had thought he had more compassion. Yet she was foolish to believe in a softer side. For a moment she had glimpsed another man on that mountainside, but in truth he was ruthless. A hard, cold man who saved only those he believed would bring him a profit.

Kathryn felt chilled. She had believed herself to be falling in love with him—but how could she love such a man?

Chapter Five

'Forgive us,' Michael said when he brought food and wine to her later. 'We were attacked by two of Rachid's galleys, as no doubt you saw, and there was no time for anyone to eat.'

'Those men in the water…' Kathryn said. She felt sick to her stomach, revolted by the sight of food. 'Why did you not stop to pick them up?'

'We rescued a few, most of them galley slaves,' Michael said, but she noticed that he would not look at her as he set down the tray of food. 'Do not concern yourself for the others. Most were already dead and, besides, they were not worth your pity, mistress.'

'Is not any man worthy of help?' she asked, a catch in her voice. 'In God's eyes even a sparrow is worthy of notice.'

'Thank you, Michael,' Lorenzo said, his voice harsh. 'You will leave us now if you please.'

Kathryn turned her accusing gaze on Lorenzo as he stood aside for his captain to leave the cabin. 'There were so many,' she said, a choke in her voice. 'Surely they were not all dead?'

Lorenzo's face showed no emotion as he answered her. 'They were Rachid's men—ruthless pirates. They take no prisoners. Can you imagine what would have happened if they had been the victors? Save your tears for those that deserve it.'

'But they were beaten…' Her words died as she saw that he was angry. He was arrogant and ruthless. He would not listen to her. She was merely a foolish girl who had caused him enough trouble.

'Has it not occurred to you that there might have been more of his galleys waiting for us? If we had spent too much time trying to rescue men, most of whom were already dead—or likely to be hung for their crimes if we had rescued them—we might have been attacked again. I do not think that Lord Mountfitchet would have been pleased if you had escaped from Don Pablo to fall into the hands of Corsairs, Kathryn.'

'Are you saying that it was for my sake that you did not stop?'

'Does that grieve your tender heart, Kathryn? Do not take my guilt upon your shoulders, Madonna. I saw no profit in saving men I would have to either hang or kill another day if I set them free.'

'Is everything a matter of profit?' Kathryn said angrily. 'Tell me, how much did Lord Mountfitchet pay you to rescue me?' She saw him flinch and regretted the words as soon as she had said them, but her pride would not allow her to take them back. Raising her head proudly, she looked into his eyes. 'Perhaps you should know that I am an heiress and my true worth is what my father will give to have me back.'

'I shall bear that in mind,' Lorenzo said, his eyes glinting. 'Perhaps I shall not take your uncle's ransom after all, Madonna. It might be that you would fetch a higher price elsewhere.' He moved towards her, towering above her so that she felt shivers run down her spine. For a moment she thought he meant to take her into his arms, and his expression frightened her, but then he shook his head and stepped back. 'You are a troublesome girl and I have better things to do! Be careful or I may find it easier to be rid of you.'

Kathryn stared as he turned and walked from the cabin. He could not mean that! Surely he was merely punishing her for what she had said to him? He could not seriously mean to sell her to the highest bidder?

No, of course he didn't. He would hand her back to Lord Mountfitchet and take the agreed price—wouldn't he? And yet what did she really know of this man? He guarded his feelings so well that anything might be going on inside his head.

Kathryn sat on the edge of the bed, hugging herself as she tried to come to terms with her feelings. For a moment as she gazed into his eyes she had wanted him to kiss her. How foolish she was! He was a hard, cruel, dangerous man and the sooner she was with Charles and Lady Mary the better.

Lorenzo stood staring out to sea. It was a dark night with only a few stars to guide them, but within hours they would enter the Grand Lagoon. He had decided to return to Venice before setting out to Cyprus. His galley had received some serious damage and was not fit to fight again without repairs. It would be sensible to send Kathryn with another of his ships. She might travel on one of his merchant galleys with an escort of fighting ships to protect her. She had found a way to get beneath his guard, and it would be madness to keep her near him—and yet he was reluctant to let her go.

What was it about this woman that had got through to that secret part of him he had kept so well hidden these past years? He had known other beautiful women, sophisticated lovers, who had given him the pleasure of their company and their bodies, but none of them had touched him. There was something about Kathryn that tugged at his heartstrings, making him feel things that he did not wish to feel.

For so long he had kept all his emotions under rigid control, feeding only on his hatred of the man who had enslaved him. Lorenzo had no memory of being captured. His first memory was of being chained to an oar and the lash of a whip on his shoulders to make him pull harder. He could remember the pain of the cuts on his back, which had been tended by another, older slave during the hours of darkness, and the constant chafing of the manacles on his wrists. The memory made the rough skin beneath his wristbands itch, but he resisted the urge to take them off. To ease them he needed a salve that he kept in his cabin, and he would not expose his one weakness to the eyes of the woman who already had too much power over his emotions.

'Kathryn…' he said the words without realising he was speaking. 'Kathy…sweet little Kathy…'

For a moment there was a roaring in his ears and his mind whirled as the stars disappeared and there was only blackness, deep, deep blackness, and then terrible pain. He made a moaning sound as for one moment he saw something—a girl's face and blood…

'Did you speak, sir?'

Lorenzo's mind cleared as his captain approached him.

He frowned, for he was not quite sure what had happened to him. It was as if a curtain had lifted in his mind, revealing some incident from the past, which had never happened before. The time prior to his enslavement had been a complete blank, but just for a moment he had seemed to remember.

'No, I merely cleared my throat,' he said, banishing the images that would sap his strength. He must banish her from his mind! He could not allow himself the luxury of caring for a woman like that. 'We were fortunate today, Michael. Somehow Rachid must have known that we were unaccompanied. It was a mistake. When you deal with wolves you should hunt as they do, in a pack.'

'There was no time to waste if you were to rescue her,' Michael said and frowned. 'I fear she does not understand the law of the sea, Lorenzo. It seems cruel to her to leave men in the sea, but she cannot know what they are capable of or that we were in no position to rescue them.'

'Women and war do not mix,' Lorenzo said; he had re-covered his usual calm. A little smile touched his mouth, though it did not reach the icy blue of his eyes. 'Do not allow her to make you feel guilt, my friend. The men we killed today served a cruel master because they wished it and we should feel no pity for them. They would have killed us and used her for their pleasure.'

'Some did not serve willingly.'

Lorenzo saw the doubts in the other's face. 'We pulled three alive from the water,' he said. 'The others had no chance, chained to their oars—they went down with the galley. We did not make them slaves, Michael. If we are to rid the seas of such men as Rachid, there will be innocent men who must die. We too may die for our beliefs. Only if we accept this can we carry on our chosen path.'

'Of course.' Michael smiled wryly. He should not have allowed himself to weaken because of the accusation in a woman's eyes. 'She is very beautiful, Lorenzo, and I am a fool. Forgive me.'

Lorenzo smiled. 'If we let them, women may make fools of us all, my friend.'

Kathryn saw the deep blue waters of the lagoon and felt a sense of relief to know that she would soon be back with Aunt Mary and Uncle Charles. They had been forced to delay their departure for Cyprus and would no doubt be impatient to leave. They could be no more impatient than she, for then she would not have to see Lorenzo Santorini again.

A part of her knew that she was being both ungrateful and wrong-headed in her judgement of him, but she could not help her feelings of irritation. He was such an arrogant man, so sure of himself. So many men must have died when that galley sunk so quickly, and he had saved only a few of them. How would he feel if he were one of those poor creatures chained to an oar and doomed to die unless someone rescued them? He could know nothing of their suffering or their pain.

She remembered his harshness towards the man he had named William. Was there no softness in him, no compassion? For a moment as he held her on the mountainside she had felt such…warmth, love…desire.

Kathryn's cheeks flamed as she admitted to herself the mixture of emotions that had swirled through her in those brief moments in his arms. No, it was imagination, she could not have felt anything like that! It would be impossible to love such a cold man. What she had felt had merely been relief.

She turned as the door to her cabin was opened and saw

Lorenzo standing there, watching her with those deep blue eyes that stirred such feeling in her.

'My gondola will take you to my home,' he told her. 'Please feel free to do as you please within the house and garden—but do not leave it without my escort.'

'I shall be only too pleased to be with my aunt again, sir.'

'Lady Mary and Lord Mountfitchet have gone ahead of us to Cyprus,' he told her. 'My galley needs urgent repairs and so I returned to Venice for that purpose.'

'But…' Kathryn stared at him in dismay. 'How am I to… It is not fitting that I stay in your house without Aunt Mary, sir.'

His eyes mocked her. 'You have lately been a prisoner of Don Pablo, Kathryn. Your reputation must have suffered. If, however, you worry for your virtue, you should know that you are quite safe from me. I have no interest in foolish children.'

Her cheeks burned as she saw the mocking light in his eyes. 'I did not mean—but my reputation…' She faltered as she realised that in truth she could no longer claim to have one. She had been Don Pablo's captive, living on board his ship and in his house for several days. Anything might have happened to her during that time, and some might believe it had. 'I dare say it is too late to worry what others may think of me…'

Lorenzo's laughter was low and husky. 'Let them think what they will, Kathryn,' he said. 'The man who weds you will know your innocence is untouched and the others are as nothing.'

'Yes, you are right, sir.' She lifted her head proudly, though she was sorely troubled. Reputation was everything to an unmarried girl and hers had been tarnished through no fault of her own.

'We took three galley slaves from the wreck,' Lorenzo said. 'None of them have blue eyes, but when they are well enough they will be questioned for any information concerning Richard Mountfitchet that they may have.'

'I always called him Dickon,' Kathryn said, her eyes sad and slightly dreamy. 'And he called me Kathy…his sweet Kathy. We were but children, but we loved each other well.'

Lorenzo's gaze narrowed intently. A little nerve was flicking at his temple as he said, 'If you think of any other information that may be relevant, you may tell me. It should take no more than a week to repair my galley and then I shall escort you to your uncle. I believe he took William with him as you asked.'

'Thank you…' She looked into his eyes despite her determination to keep her distance, and her heart caught. Oh, no! She was being foolish. She could not be attracted to this man. It was impossible—wrong! Her heart belonged to Dickon and she would never marry someone who could do the things this man had done. 'I shall be glad to be with my friends again.'

'Yes, of course,' he said. 'Now, if you please, the gondola is waiting.'

Kathryn paced the floor of her chamber, feeling restless. They had been in Venice for two days now and she had hardly seen Lorenzo at all. Her meals were served to her wherever she wished, but she ate them in solitary state, which only made her feel more alone than ever. It seemed that in being rescued from Don Pablo she had merely exchanged one prison for another.

She was so tired of being in the house! She decided to go down to the courtyard and walk in the garden, but as she went down the stairs and into the main hall, she heard voices and saw that Lorenzo had that moment come in with Michael dei Ignacio. They both turned to look at her. Michael smiled warmly as he saw her, but Lorenzo's eyes were as cool as ever.

'I was about to go into the garden,' she said, feeling it necessary to explain. 'It is warmer today and the house seems too confining.'

'You must be tired of being shut in the house,' Michael told her. 'I fear we have been too busy to entertain you, mistress. However, this evening there is a masque being held in the open air—perhaps you would care to attend? I shall be going and I dare say Lorenzo may be persuaded to spend a little time with us. And I shall take several of our men to protect you, though I think it unlikely that Don Pablo will try another such trick.'

'I should like to go with you, sir.' Kathryn looked at Lorenzo. 'Have I your permission to go?'

His mouth seemed hard and censorious as he said, 'You are not my prisoner, Kathryn. I am sure that Michael will take good care of you, though I have business that will prevent me from attending. You will need clothes for the masque, which is said to be very entertaining, I believe. I shall instruct my servants to bring you gowns and masks that you may like to wear for the occasion.'

'Thank you.' She sensed his disapproval, which was almost anger that she had agreed so willingly. 'I shall look forward to it, Signor Ignacio.'

'I shall be here at the hour of seven to collect you,' he said and bowed to her. 'And now, if you will excuse me, I have some business I must attend.'

Kathryn turned away as he left, but Lorenzo followed

her into the courtyard. She waited, wondering what more he had to say to her.

'I shall do nothing foolish,' she told him before he could speak.

'Michael will make sure that you are well protected. Besides, I do not think that Don Pablo will try another abduction. I have sent him a message and I believe you are safe from him in future, Kathryn.'

'What kind of a message?'

'It is not necessary for you to know that,' he replied, a wintry expression in his eyes. 'I wanted to tell you that we shall be ready to leave for Cyprus the day after tomorrow.'

'Oh.' Kathryn did not know why her spirits had suddenly fallen so low. 'Thank you, sir. I shall be pleased to be with my friends again.'

'Once there you will have the freedom that has been denied you here.'

'Yes…' She felt her throat closing and was suddenly emotional though she did not know why. 'Lorenzo…' She swayed towards him, wanting him to take her in his arms, to hold her as he had for that brief moment on the mountainside. She saw something in his eyes, a glow deep down that made her tremble with anticipation, with a strange longing that she could not name. For a brief moment she thought she saw that longing reflected in his eyes and believed that he was struggling with some fierce emotion, but then he moved back and it was as if a barrier had sprung up between them.

'Excuse me, I have business,' he said in a curt tone that brought her swiftly back to reality. 'You should rest, for you will find our Venetian festivals somewhat riotous.'

He inclined his head, turned on his heel and left her. Kathryn's cheeks flamed. Had she given herself away?

Had he seen that longing in her eyes? Oh, what a fool she was! She did not like what he was or what he did—so how could she feel such tempestuous emotions when he looked at her?

Kathryn chose a gown of white silk trimmed with black ribbons. Her mask was a pretty thing of white, silver and black that fitted over the top half of her face and fastened with ribbons. Her cloak was fashioned of fine soft velvet that felt so comforting to wear, for, though the sun had been warm during the day, the night air was much cooler.

She was waiting downstairs in one of the salons when Michael came to collect her. He wore a harlequin costume in the colours of black and white, which complemented her gown perfectly, and looked the picture of a courtier. He was a handsome man, his dark hair and eyes enough to set the hearts of most ladies fluttering. Kathryn wondered why she could not feel something more for him, for he was much kinder and more courteous than his commander.

'We make a pretty pair, sir,' she said and curtsied to him.

'You are beautiful, Mistress Rowlands,' he told her. 'I am but a simple sea captain, but you are a lady and far beyond me.'

Kathryn did not know how to answer him, for she was surprised by his words, which seemed to hint at something much deeper and stronger than mere friendship. She smiled and gave him her hand, blushing as he held it to his lips before leading her out to the front of the palace and down the steps to the waiting gondola.

'I thought that you might like to see the sights before we join the revellers in St Mark's Square,' he said. 'For this evening is a celebration.'

Kathryn allowed him to hand her into the gondola. Their oarsman took them through the narrow waterways of the city, which was lit with many tiny lanterns and torches, and bedecked with ribbons, flowers and flags.

When they reached the square it was already crowded. Music was playing and people were dancing, everyone dressed in beautiful clothes and carrying or wearing masks. Some were very exotic, resembling the heads of animals or mythical beasts, others were sad or comic, though most were very simple, like hers.

She danced with Michael three times, and then stood to one side to watch the others dancing while he fetched her a cool drink mixed with fruits that tasted sweet. She sipped it and then set the glass down, just as someone caught her arm and she was suddenly whirled back into the throng of dancers. Her heart raced for a moment as she thought it might be an attempt at abduction, and then, as she looked up at the masked man, she knew him.

'Are you enjoying yourself, Madonna?'

'Yes, very much,' she said. 'I thought you were too busy to come with us?'

'My business was finished sooner than I thought,' Lorenzo said and smiled. His mask, like hers, was plain and fitted over the top half of his face, but he was dressed all in black, though the sash at his waist was of silver. 'I thought I would discover for myself what happens on this night of mystery and feasting.'

'Why mystery?'

'Do you not know the legend of the Seventh Moon?'

Kathryn shook her head, her eyes wide with curiosity. 'What is the Seventh Moon?'

'It is said that if a virgin looks at the full moon in a bowl of water for seven nights without fail, on the last night she will see the face of her lover—and by morning she will no longer be a virgin.' There was a wicked, teasing note in his voice that made her want to laugh. 'Have you looked to see the face of your lover, Madonna? And whose is the face you see, I wonder?'

'Oh!' Kathryn felt her cheeks grow warm. She looked away hastily for she did not know how to interpret his teasing. 'But why is the feast held on this night?'

'That I cannot tell you,' he said and she knew that he was laughing at her. 'Perhaps to celebrate the beginning of the legend—who knows?'

'I think you invented your story, sir,' Kathryn said and her heart beat faster as she heard his laughter.

'Did I, Kathryn?' he asked. 'Now, why should I do that?'

She shook her head. Her heart was beating so fast that she felt a little faint, as if she were swept away with some emotion that thrilled and yet terrified her. He seemed so different from the cold, hard man she had become accustomed to thinking him, reminding her of someone she had known long ago. Dickon had told her stories, making them up on the spur of the moment to tease her and make her laugh.

The music had ended for the moment and people were moving away to find food and refreshment. Kathryn stood looking up at him, caught by some strange sensation that gripped her, sweeping her back through the years so that she seemed to be a child again.

'Who are you?' she asked, her eyes seeming to be locked with his.

'I do not know who I am, Kathryn,' he said, and then, as her breath caught in her throat, he bent his head and kissed her on the lips very softly. 'Since you came I do not know anything…'

'Lorenzo.' Her mouth seemed to tingle from his kiss though it had been sweet and gentle, and her heart was racing wildly. 'What do you mean?'

'Who knows what words mean?' he asked, an odd smile touching his mouth. 'Did I not tell you this was a night of mystery? Michael is looking for you. I shall take you back to him, Kathryn.'

She wanted to stay with him, to be back in his arms, but she knew that the moment had passed as he took her arm, steering her back to where Michael awaited her. Then, before she could say or do anything, he turned and disappeared through the throngs of people crowding the square.

'I have never known Lorenzo to attend the masque before,' Michael said, watching him go. 'Nor have I known him to dance.'

'Not ever—with anyone?' Kathryn's heart jerked as he shook his head. How strange that was! 'He said that his business had finished early.'

'Even so…' Michael looked thoughtful. 'Will you eat something, Mistress Rowlands?'

'I am not very hungry,' Kathryn confessed. 'Would you mind very much if I asked you to take me home?'

'No, of course not,' he said and smiled at her. 'I am here to serve you.'

'You were very kind to bring me this evening. I have enjoyed myself.'

'Lorenzo asked me to bring you. He said that you had been confined to the house too long. I asked him why he did not bring you himself, and he said that you would be safer with me. I did not understand him.' Michael frowned. 'I would give my life for Lorenzo Santorini, but…' He paused, then rushed on. 'I do not think he is a man who would make a woman such as you happy, Kathryn. There are things in his past that he can never forget.'

'What do you mean?' She looked at him, her eyes wide, feeling coldness at the nape of her neck. 'What kind of things?'

'Forgive me, I may not tell you. I have perhaps said too much. It is not my business to interfere—but I have a deep regard for you, Kathryn. Forgive me if I use your name without permission.' She shook her head. 'You are as brave and generous as you are beautiful. I do not know what Lorenzo intends towards you, but I would not have you hurt.'

'Thank you for your concern, sir. But I do not think he intends anything towards me—other than to deliver me safely to Lord Mountfitchet and collect the ransom.'

'What ransom?' Michael stared at her. 'If you imagine that he snatched you from that Spaniard for a ransom, you are much mistaken. You do not understand him, Kathryn. Yes, sometimes he takes money for restoring a man to his family. Most are only too eager to pay it and he puts that money to good use. For every man that can be restored to his family there are a hundred that cannot; some can never work and without help would simply starve.'

Kathryn felt very strange, her throat tight with emotion. 'Are you telling me that the money…?' Her voice caught on a sob as she realised how badly she had misjudged Lorenzo. 'He helps the men he rescues if they are not strong enough to work?'

'Did you imagine that he cast them out to fend for themselves? Better that they should die quickly than starve, Kathryn. Lorenzo is rich, but he cares little for money for its own sake. His purpose in life is to destroy those evil men who prey on others, enslaving them and using them like beasts. That is why I warned you not to love him, for there is such pain in him…' He shook his head as her eyes begged the question. 'No, I may not tell you more. I have already said too much and I beg that you will not speak of this to Lorenzo. He would be angry. He makes no apology for what he does to any man—or woman.'

'I shall never tell him what you have said this night,' Kathryn said. 'But I do thank you for telling me. I did not understand.'

She had had no idea what lay behind that mask of coldness, the apparent ruthlessness of his business, the way he saved or took life seemingly at will. Even now she could not think of the men left behind in the water without shuddering, but she could begin to understand.

Lorenzo removed the leather wristbands, rubbing at the ridge of dark purplish-red flesh beneath. The badge of his slavery, a constant reminder that would never let him forget those years of pain and humiliation or the hatred that had festered inside him. At Antonio Santorini's deathbed, he had sworn that he would not rest until he had brought Rachid down and freed all those he held prisoner. That purpose had driven him from this day until now, and he could not let anything change that—not even the enticing lips of a woman who filled his senses as no other ever had.

She had felt so good as he'd held her in his arms during their dance that the temptation to kiss her had been overwhelming. She filled his mind even now, making him burn with desire such as he had never known. Only the strength of his will was keeping him from going to her now and making her his own. He wanted to feel her soft skin as she lay beside him, to touch her, kiss her, know her fully. To make love to her, to love her, have her always…

No! That way lay madness! He could not lie with Kathryn without letting down his guard. He could not seduce her without offering her his home and his name—but what was his name?

A shiver went through him as he recalled the moment she had looked into his eyes and asked him who he was, and his answer had surprised even himself. He was Lorenzo Santorini, a man dedicated to destroying his enemy. Of course he knew who he was! To let himself dwell on the past—on things that could never be proved—would be to invite confusion.

He rubbed at his left wrist. It was always this one that irritated the most. The flesh was swollen now for he did not use the healing salve as often as he should. Getting out of bed, he took the pot of lotion that had been given him by Ali Khayr, rubbing it into the ridges of tortured flesh. He frowned as he traced the thin line, which extended from beneath the welt of scarred skin. It looked darker than the other scars, older and in some way different. He had not really noticed it until lately. His finger traced it absently, sliding down over the welt of disfigured flesh, making the sign of a letter.

Kathryn! She was too often in his mind. If he allowed her to take over she would destroy him. He had begun to imagine things, impossible dreams that were not for a man such as he—and there were the images that came to him now. Flashes of memory, perhaps? He could not be sure. For so many years he had remembered nothing, had wanted to remember nothing beyond the moment he had seen the face of his enemy and known that he lived only to kill him.

Rachid was not of Arab descent, nor was he a Turk. His skin was sunburned and his eyes were grey, but he was from the Western world—something that had made Lorenzo despise him more. How could he, a man raised to Christian values, use and torture other men so cruelly? He was evil, a disciple of Satan—and Lorenzo could not rest until he was dead.

Nothing must deflect him from his purpose. He must not allow himself to be softened by a woman's smile—nor must he let those disturbing flashes of memory rob him of his identity. It did not matter who he had been. He was Lorenzo Santorini. A man with no mercy for his enemy.

The sooner he could return Kathryn to her friends the better. If he were sensible, he would send her with Michael as her escort, finish it now. The longer she stayed with him the more enmeshed in her web he might become.

Kathryn looked around the cabin to which she had been shown. It was much more luxuriously appointed than the one she had used on board Lorenzo's war galley. This was the largest and finest of his merchant ships. It was carrying a cargo of goods to the island, which would be sold to the merchants there in return for another cargo of fine wines and citrus fruits. These fruits were much valued by those who spent their lives at sea, for they were believed to help prevent the dreaded disease that some called scurvy.

She turned as she heard someone behind her, and, looking towards the door, saw that Lorenzo stood there. His eyes were thoughtful as they looked at her, almost brooding. She felt herself tremble inside and knew a longing to be in his arms as she had been on the night of the Seventh Moon.

'I hope you will be comfortable here, Kathryn. My own

cabin was not fitting for you, but we have made more provision this time.'

'I was happy enough to live as you do,' she said. 'Do you travel with me on this ship, sir?' Her heart was fluttering as she waited for his response, for though she feared what he did to her with those devastating eyes, she also longed for it.

'No, on my personal galley,' Lorenzo replied. 'You will be safe enough for we shall escort you to Cyprus. I have some business there with Lord Mountfitchet.'

'Yes, of course,' she said, though she sensed that he was not telling her the whole truth. 'It is good of you to go to so much trouble for my sake.'

'But I do not want to lose my ransom,' he said, an odd smile on his lips. 'Surely you must know that, Kathryn?'

'You shame me, sir,' she said, blushing. 'I was wrong to say such things to you.'

'Were you?' His eyes narrowed, intent on her face. 'I am not ashamed of what I do.'

'Why should you be?' She flushed deeper as he looked at her more closely, clearly wondering why she had changed her mind, and knew that she must be careful or she would betray Michael's confidence. 'Any man is worthy of his hire. If you do someone a service, they should expect to pay for it.'

Lorenzo inclined his head. 'I have questioned the men we took from Rachid's galley. No one knows anything of a youth taken from Cornwall all those years ago. It was not likely that they would. I believe that you will never find the man you seek, Kathryn. And if you did…he would not be the same man.'

'I know…' She sighed. 'I have begun to think that it may be best if Dickon is never found. Sometimes I hope that he died long ago. I had heard stories of men being put to the galleys as slaves, but I did not understand what it meant until now. It must be the most soul-destroying thing that a man can suffer, to be forced to work so hard and to know that he is a slave…'

'Dickon is dead,' Lorenzo said, his eyes violet dark. 'The youth you once loved would not have survived without becoming someone very different, believe me.'

'Yes, I know,' she said and her voice caught with tears. 'I know that his father will go on searching for him, but I shall try to remember him as a friend that died.'

'It would be a waste if you were to spend your life waiting for a man who will never come back to you,' Lorenzo told her. 'You should marry, Kathryn. I dare say you would not look at Michael Ignacio, though I know he cares for you. And I can vouch for him as a man of good family and honest values. You could do much worse than to marry a man such as he, for I dare say he would give up the sea for your sake.'

'If I felt that way for him, I should be pleased to wed him,' she replied, her eyes stinging with the tears she held back. He was doing his best to persuade her to think of Michael as a husband. Why should he do that? It could only mean that he was telling her not to think of him. She looked at him proudly, coldly. 'Perhaps I may marry one day—when I return to England. But I am not sure that I could be happy with any other man than Dickon. It may be that I shall never marry.'

Lorenzo nodded and frowned, silent for a moment, then he said, 'When do you plan to return home?'

'I do not know,' Kathryn said. 'I shall stay with Lady Mary and Lord Mountfitchet for some months and then…' She could not go on, for her heart felt as if it were breaking, and she wanted to say that she would stay for ever if only he cared for her. His eyes seemed dark with some hidden emotion as he looked at her, but he said nothing that could give her encouragement, nothing to indicate that she meant anything to him. She must put her foolish notions from her head. She could not love a man such as Lorenzo Santorini.

But of course she didn't! He had called her a foolish child enough times, and she knew that he must despise her for the trouble she had caused him.

'I believe there will be a campaign in a few months,' Lorenzo told her, changing the subject abruptly. 'His Holiness the Pope has gathered a great alliance to try and wipe the scourge of the Turkish invaders from our seas, and, with the demise of their power, much of the piracy that takes place under their flag. I have pledged my support, but if you waited until the following spring I should be happy to escort you to your home.'

'Thank you, sir,' Kathryn said. She lifted her head proudly, blinking back her tears. 'I think my father or brother may come to fetch me—but if I should need your help, I shall ask for it.'

'As you wish,' he said and smiled. 'We shall meet again on Cyprus. Excuse me, I have work to do.'

Kathryn felt the tears she could no longer restrain trickle down her face as he walked from the cabin. He was so withdrawn, so distant. How could she have been so foolish as to fall in love with him?

No, no, of course she wasn't in love with him. It was just that he had saved her from a terrible fate, and she was grateful to him. Yes, that was it. She was grateful to him, and she liked him. It was reasonable to like him for she owed him a great deal. But she did not love him. She must remember who and what he was, a cold, harsh man who lived by the sword.

No, she could never love such a man.

Chapter Six

Why had the ship stopped moving? Kathryn went to the porthole and looked out, her heart beating wildly as she wondered if they were being attacked. She was relieved as she saw that they had halted so that Lorenzo could come aboard. It was a tricky manoeuvre, but she saw him swing himself over the rigging with an ease she could only admire. He had an air of authority, seeming so strong and sure, a natural ability to lead that was apparent in the way his men greeted him. For a moment she was lost in admiration, her pulses racing.

Kathryn sat down to wait, her heart beating faster than normal. Several minutes passed before he knocked at her cabin door and then entered. She was shocked by the gravity of his expression. Her knees felt like jelly and she was trembling from head to foot. What had made him look like that?

'Kathryn…' She thought that she had never heard him speak with such emotion, except perhaps for one moment on that Spanish mountainside. 'I fear I have received bad news. The Turks have invaded Cyprus. It is believed that Nicosia has fallen.'

'Invaded?' Kathryn looked at him in dismay. 'But Lady Mary, Lord Mountfitchet—what will happen to them?' She had risen as he entered, but now sat down on the edge of the bed, overcome by her concern.

'We must hope that they have somehow escaped,' Lorenzo said. 'Or that a ransom may be paid for their safe return. Sometimes that is the case, especially for those who might not be worthwhile as slaves.'

'Because they are not young and beautiful—or strong enough to work in the galleys?' Kathryn's throat tightened and she felt the sting of tears as she thought of the people she loved become prisoners of the Turks. 'This is so terrible. How could such a thing have happened? I thought Cyprus belonged to Venice?'

'As it does,' Lorenzo said, looking angry. 'We refused their demands to surrender the island to them, but it seems that the invasion has gone ahead. This means the Pope must marshal the forces of the Holy League. I must go to Rome, Kathryn, and you must come with me. You will wait there for me until I know how things stand.'

Kathryn was silent. Had she been with Lady Mary and Lord Mountfitchet, she would have been on Cyprus when the invasion happened. She might even now be dead or a captive of the Turks, perhaps destined for a harem. She felt shocked by the news, unable to come to terms with the loss of her friends.

'I have been nothing but trouble to you,' she said, on the verge of tears. 'I must accept your offer, sir, for I do not know what else to do.'

'There is nothing you can do,' he told her, his words and manner seeming harsh to her. 'It seems that fate has delivered you into my care, and we must both make the best of it. Now I must ask you to transfer to my galley, for this ship will return to Venice. I must muster my war captains and a ship like this is little use for the task that awaits us now.'

'Would it not be better if I were to return with this ship?'

'No, I think not. I cannot afford to send an escort with it and in these uncertain times anything might happen. Besides, I shall not be returning to Venice for some months. I shall leave you with a friend in Rome. You will be safer there until I can decide what best to do with you.'

Kathryn was too subdued to answer him. The possible loss of two people who had been dear to her was heartbreaking and she could not fight Lorenzo this time. Without him she would have been even more vulnerable, for she had little money of her own and could not return to England without help. She was, in fact, completely dependent on him, even for the clothes she wore and the food she ate. It was a humiliating feeling and she hardly knew how to face him.

'Come, Kathryn,' Lorenzo demanded. 'Do not despair. Lord Mountfitchet was warned that invasion was a possibility. It may be that he changed his mind at the last minute.'

She knew that he was trying to comfort her, but her heart was heavy. Despite Lorenzo's words, she doubted that Lord Mountfitchet would have changed his plans without good cause. All she could hope was that he and Lady Mary had somehow escaped with their lives.

Kathryn looked around the room she had been given at the home of Lorenzo's friend. The Contessa Rosa dei Corleone had welcomed him with a smile and the warmth of old acquaintance. Kathryn was not certain that she was so pleased to have a stranger as her guest, though she had accepted her graciously.

'Of course Mistress Rowlands may stay with me, Lorenzo,' she said, her dark eyes sparkling as she looked at him. 'You know that I would do anything you asked of me.'

Why, she was flirting with him! Kathryn realised it and felt a spurt of disgust. The Contessa was years older than him!

'You are generous, Contessa,' Lorenzo said, an amused glint in his eyes. 'I shall return as soon as possible. In the meantime, I shall make some provision for Kathryn. Should I not return from the coming encounter, there will be sufficient money to see her safely back to England.'

'As you wish, my friend.'

The dark eyes were speculative as the Contessa looked at Kathryn.

'My servant will take you to your room. I am sure you must wish to tidy yourself after so long at sea.'

Kathryn sent Lorenzo a look of appeal. Now that he was about to leave her, she felt as if she were being abandoned. She wanted to cling to him, to beg him not to leave her, but knew that she must not let him see how she felt.

'I shall see you again before we leave,' he said, smiling at her reassuringly. 'There are preparations to be made and I have much to do. It may be three or four days before the rest of my fleet can join me, and another two before we put to sea.'

Kathryn nodded. She fought her tears. Her heart felt as if it were being ripped in two, but she must not weep.

'You must not think of me. You have your duty—but I would have news of my uncle and aunt…'

'I shall not abandon you,' he said and smiled. For a moment her heart lifted as she saw something in his eyes— a look that she had seen only once before. 'Go with the Contessa's woman now. She will take you to your chamber. You should rest for a while.'

Kathryn had obeyed him. There was so much she wished to say and could not. Now, alone in this room, the guest of a woman she instinctively knew disliked her, Kathryn admitted to herself that she was in love with Lorenzo Santorini. She did not know how it could have happened, for she had been determined to dislike him. Now she knew that she would find it unbearable if she were never to see him again. If he should be killed… She could not think about it. It was too painful.

'The Contessa asks that you will come down to her salon as soon as you are ready.'

Kathryn turned, her heart sinking as she looked into the hostile eyes of the Contessa's servant. She was not welcome here in this house—but what could she do? Lorenzo had brought her here and there was nowhere else for her. Her abduction had taught her how vulnerable she was. She was dependent on Lorenzo's generosity, at least until there was some news of her friends.

She followed the servant down to the grand salon where the Contessa was waiting for her, and her heart sank as she saw the expression in the older woman's eyes. She had pretended to be welcoming while Lorenzo was here, but there was no mistaking her hostility now.

'So,' the Contessa said. 'I must make you welcome since Lorenzo asks it of me. In return I demand that you behave with proper modesty while in my house, Mistress Rowlands. I would not have you disgrace me before my friends.'

'In what way do you fear I shall disgrace you?' Kathryn lifted her head, eyes flashing with pride. She felt humiliated and was angry. What was this woman implying?

'You have been travelling alone with Lorenzo Santorini. You stayed with him at the Santorini Palace in Venice. What do you imagine people will think of you if they discover your shame?'

'I have done nothing to be ashamed of—and I had my maid with me at the palace, and on the journey from Venice to Rome.' Kathryn did not tell her of the time she had spent alone on Lorenzo's galley after her abduction, for it could only make her situation worse. 'This awkwardness is not of my making.'

'A servant is not a chaperon. You have forfeited your reputation, girl,' the Contessa said harshly, her mouth twisting with spite. 'What you choose to do is your own affair, but do not shame me by speaking of it in public, if you please.'

Kathryn's cheeks flamed. Her anger at being spoken to so unfairly banished the tears that had been hovering. Had there been any other alternative she would have left this woman's house at once, but there was no way out for her. She must endure the Contessa's spite, at least until Lorenzo was ready to escort her to her home.

'I shall behave as befits an English gentlewoman,' she said with dignity. She lifted her head high, refusing to be cowed by the woman's hostility. 'I cannot change your opinion of me, Contessa. For both our sakes, I hope that Lorenzo will remove me from your house very soon.'

'Very well. This has been distasteful to me, Mistress Rowlands. This evening I attend a private supper at a friend's house. Tomorrow evening there is a grand reception, which you will attend with me. I hope you have suitable clothes?' Her tone suggested that she thought it unlikely, stinging Kathryn on the raw.

'My trunks are on the ship. Once they are delivered, I believe I shall not disgrace you.'

'See that you do not.' The Contessa waved her hand. 'You may go. I shall tell you when I require your presence. If you wish, you may use the gardens and the salons at the back of the house.'

Kathryn left the room, her back very straight. She was humiliated and upset, but anger made her keep her spirits up. How could Lorenzo have brought her to the house of such a woman?

Kathryn dressed in a gown of dark green silk the following evening. She wore a small ruff of gauze that was stiffened with wire and stood up at the back of her neck. Her hair was swept up on her head and covered by a green velvet hood trimmed with silver and brilliants. It was the most matronly of her gowns and chosen to make her look as ordinary and respectable as possible.

The Contessa looked her over as she went down to join her in the salon. 'Yes, that is well enough,' she said, her mouth sour with disapproval, for even in this plain apparel Kathryn was beautiful, young and desirable. 'Do not forget what I have told you.'

'I shall not forget.'

Kathryn would have preferred not to accompany the Contessa to the reception that evening, but she had little choice. She must do as she was told while she lived under this woman's roof.

The reception was being held in a large villa built in the hills overlooking the city. Kathryn joined the other guests, smiling but saying very little as she was introduced to the Contessa's friends as the ward of a dear friend. She was in public a very different woman, smiling and calling Kathryn a sweet child, which made Kathryn want to run away and hide.

However, she stood obediently at the Contessa's side, speaking only when addressed and wishing that the evening might be over. She liked none of these people and remembered how kind Aunt Mary's friends had been to her in

London, something that made her heart ache as she wondered if her friend was still alive. Would she ever see her kind friends again? Would she ever be able to return to her home?

Seeing that the Contessa appeared to have forgotten her, Kathryn moved towards the marble arches that opened out into the huge gardens, needing suddenly to be alone. She felt lost and alone and so unhappy that she was having to fight very hard to hold back her tears. She went out into the cool of the night air, looking at the stars. Somehow she must find a way to bear this time of unhappiness.

'Why are you out here?' Lorenzo's voice close behind her made her jump for she had not been aware of him. 'The Contessa was anxious about you.'

Kathryn turned to look at him. Was he angry with her too? She felt a tear slip down her cheek and turned aside, not wanting him to see. She walked away, wanting to escape deeper into the gardens.

He came after her, catching her arm, swinging her round to face him. 'What is wrong? Why are you crying?'

'I'm not crying,' Kathryn sniffed, brushing her face with the back of her hand.

'Something has upset you. Tell me, Kathryn!' She shook her head. 'Are you crying for your uncle and aunt?' She shook her head again. 'Then it is the Contessa…'

'She hates me!' The words burst from her.

'Do not be foolish, Kathryn. Why should she hate you?'

'She says that I have lost my reputation, that people will think I am your—' She broke off and turned away from him once more.

'Ah.' Lorenzo looked at her thoughtfully, seeing the pride and anger, and the despair. 'I understand. There was always the risk that this would happen, but the damage is done, Kathryn.'

'I know. There is nothing anyone can do.'

'No…unless you become my wife.' He smiled oddly as she whirled round, her eyes wide with shock. 'Forgive me. I know the idea cannot please you, but it would stop the vicious tongues before they can start.'

'But you do not want to marry me!'

'It is a matter of indifference to me,' Lorenzo said with a shrug of his shoulders. 'I have no wish for a wife, but it would be a marriage of convenience only. You have told me that though you may marry one day, your heart belongs to the man you lost so many years ago. Therefore it can make no difference who you marry. As well me as another. Indeed, I may be the only chance of marriage you will have.'

'That is no reason for marriage!' Kathryn did not know whether to rage at him or weep. 'Why should you want me? How does this benefit you?'

'Did you not tell me you were an heiress? This war is likely to cost me a small fortune. A wealthy wife would be no bad thing.'

Was he teasing her? There was a glint in his eyes, though he was not smiling.

'It is not a huge fortune…' She stared at him uncertainly. A part of her wanted to refuse his offer, for it was almost insulting in the manner of its making, and yet she could not help feeling that as Lorenzo's wife she would be safe. 'You cannot want me?'

Kathryn could not know how vulnerable and uncertain she looked or that the appeal in her eyes touched something in Lorenzo that he had thought long dead.

'Believe me when I say I have my reasons,' he told her, a smile upon his lips now. Surely he was teasing her! 'You know that I never do anything without profit, Kathryn—

believe that I want you. You are beautiful and a man should have a wife, after all.' He had her fast so that she could not escape. As she gazed into his eyes her heart raced and she longed for him to kiss her, to tell her that he was marrying her because he cared for her.

'Then…if you truly mean it, I shall accept,' she said, finding it difficult to breathe. Surely this was but another of the dreams that came to plague her when she slept? 'I shall try to be what you would have me be.'

'Do not worry about what I would have of you,' Lorenzo told her, a faint smile on his lips. 'We shall be married and then I shall leave you. Only He that they call God—whether he be Christian or Muslim—knows whether I shall return. If I do not, you shall be a rich widow, Kathryn. Choose your next husband with more care, I beg you.' Again his eyes were bright with mockery and she did not know what to make of him.

'Lorenzo…' Kathryn looked at him wordlessly. How could she tell him that she did not care for his wealth, that she wanted him to return to her? He said that he had his reasons for marrying her, but she could think of none—unless she had led him to believe that her father was richer than he really was?

'I told you not to worry,' he said, and then, moving towards her, he touched her face, lowering his head to kiss her softly on the lips. A wave of desire coursed through her, making her feel as if she would melt into him, become a part of his very body, though his next words brought her back to her senses. 'We did not choose this, Kathryn, but it seems that it is our fate. Let fate take its course and we shall see.'

Kathryn wore the gown she had borrowed for the night of the masque, which had been packed in her trunk with the rest of her things. She did not know why she chose it, except that that night Lorenzo had seemed so different, and she wanted him to be the man she had glimpsed then. She wanted him to laugh and tease her, to love her—but of course he did not. She looked at her reflection in her hand mirror, and then decided to let her hair flow on her shoulders, wearing only a small cap of silver threads on the back of her head.

She was still at the Contessa's house, for Lorenzo had begged her to be patient until he could arrange for the wedding and her removal to a villa he had taken for her stay in Rome. When she went downstairs the Contessa was waiting. She looked at Kathryn with dislike, her eyes moving over her with disapproval.

'Do not imagine that he loves you,' she said coldly. 'No one woman would ever be enough for a man like that. He is marrying you because he feels pity for you—and he will be unfaithful within a year.'

Kathryn held her tongue, for what could she say in answer? The Contessa might be speaking the truth for all she knew. Lorenzo was marrying her for reasons of his own, reasons that he had not chosen to divulge to her. She did not think that he was in love with her, but perhaps he might want her in his bed. She had been told many times that she was beautiful, and she believed that she was comely enough. Perhaps that odd look she had seen in his eyes sometimes meant that he wanted to make love to her.

It was evident that the Contessa was angry as she almost ordered Kathryn from the house, and she suspected that the older woman wanted him for herself. She thought that perhaps they had been lovers in the past and that the Contessa had hoped he might marry her now that she was a widow. Her husband had been dead for six months, and it must have seemed to her when Lorenzo first came that he had come for her, which made it easy to understand why in her disappointment she had felt so hostile towards the girl he had brought with him.

Lorenzo was waiting for them at the small church. Michael was to give her away, and a man she did not know stood up with Lorenzo as his witness. The Contessa was Kathryn's only attendant, and she left immediately after the ceremony, refusing to attend the small wedding feast. Kathryn could only be pleased.

Michael and the stranger, who told her that his name was Paolo Casciano, and that Lorenzo was a friend of many years, accompanied her and Lorenzo to a villa in the hills overlooking the city. It was not as large as the Contessa's home, but pleasant with lovely gardens.

'This will be your home until we can return to Venice,' Lorenzo told her. 'I have engaged servants to care for your needs and a lady who will bear you company while I am away.' He beckoned to an elderly woman with a sweet face, who came forward to curtsy to Kathryn. 'This lady is Madame Veronique de Bologna. She was born in France, but has lived in Italy since her marriage, and is now a widow.'

'May I welcome you to your new home, my lady,' the widow said and smiled. 'I was so happy to be of service to you when Signor Santorini asked me to come and bear you company.'

'And I am very grateful for your presence, *madame*.'

'I beg you to call me Veronique,' she said, 'for I hope we shall be friends.'

'Yes, of course. I hope so too.'

'Come,' Lorenzo commanded, 'our guests are waiting to see the bride.'

'Our guests?' Kathryn looked at him in surprise.

'Did you imagine I had no friends?' Lorenzo's violet-blue eyes were laughing at her as he drew her out into the garden where a feast had been laid out on boards over trestles, covered with white cloths and laden with platters of wonderful food.

Several ladies and gentlemen were gathered there and they burst into a spontaneous round of applause as Lorenzo drew her forward.

'My friends, I give you the lady who has been brave— or foolish—enough to become my bride this day.'

His introduction brought laughter and then the guests gathered round, giving her kisses and smiles, presents of money, silver, jewellery and objects of art. Kathryn was overwhelmed by this unexpected kindness—she had not expected anything of the sort.

She looked at them shyly, her throat caught with emotion. 'I do not know what to say…you are all so very kind.'

'They are curious,' Lorenzo said, a sparkle of amusement in his eyes, 'for they wonder that any woman would wed such as I.'

'No, I do not believe that,' she said. 'You are not so very terrible, Lorenzo.'

Her remark brought much laughter and she found herself swept away by a group of smiling women who chattered away to her in a mixture of Italian and English, wanting to know all manner of things about her.

'How did you meet Lorenzo?'

'Where do you live?'

'How did you come here?'

'I lived in Cornwall and journeyed to Venice with friends.'

'Cornwall? I have never heard of such a place!' one rather pretty woman with a lively manner cried.

'Do not show your ignorance, Elizabeta. It is in England!'

The questions came so thick and fast that Kathryn's head was spinning by the time Lorenzo came to rescue her. The laughter continued throughout the feast and the traditional toast to the bride and groom, and then music began to play and everyone demanded that they should dance.

Kathryn trembled as he took her into his arms, but found that it was easy to follow his steps as they danced on the tiled patio. Glancing up, she saw that he was smiling and her heart fluttered. Surely he did care for her a little or he would not look at her that way.

The merriment continued throughout the afternoon, but as the sun started to dip over the sea in a flash of fiery orange, their friends began to take their leave. The ladies kissed Kathryn and promised to call on her soon, and the men clapped Lorenzo on the back and told him he was a fortunate man.

At last only Lorenzo, Veronique and Kathryn were left. They went into the house and the servants came out to begin the task of clearing up the debris.

'If you have no need of me, my lady, I shall leave you alone.' Veronique smiled at Kathryn and curtsied to Lorenzo. 'Good evening, *signor*.'

'Goodnight, *madame*.'

Kathryn felt a little shiver run down her spine at the sound of his voice. They were alone at last and she was nervous, because she did not know the man she had married. She did not know what he expected of her. Her heart told her that there was nothing to fear, but still she could not help the trembling she felt inside.

'Let us take a cup of wine together,' Lorenzo said, pouring some of the sweet white wine she liked into a glass and handing it to her. He poured another for himself and sipped it, before setting the glass down. 'Did you like my friends, Kathryn?'

'Yes, of course. How could I not when they were so kind to me?'

'You were surprised to find so many here to welcome you?'

'I did not know what to expect.'

'That is hardly surprising, for we know nothing of each other's lives,' he said, looking thoughtful. 'Perhaps that will change when I return, Kathryn. I have never considered marriage, but a man may acquire new ideas. Now that you are my wife, I would have you content. However, should you be unhappy, I would consider taking you back to your father.'

Kathryn did not know how to answer him. 'I shall try to please you, Lorenzo.'

'You mistake my meaning,' he said. 'My life will be much as it has been, for I shall be often away. However, when I am at home I shall do what I can to make you happy.'

'Thank you. You have already done so much for me.' He had given her back her reputation and her pride. She could ask nothing more of him—unless he wished to give it.

'You must try not to worry too much about your friends,' Lorenzo said. 'If you wish to write a letter to your father, Paolo will see it on its way for you. I shall leave money with him, for you will need to run the house and to buy things for your own use. You may address any accounts to him and he will pay them for you. And when I return we shall talk again.'

Kathryn felt the emotion rising inside her. She swallowed hard, determined not to let him see that she was so affected. She wished that he did not have to leave her, but he had made his position clear. He had married her to keep her safe and would try to be a kind, considerate husband, but he had no use for a wife. She meant nothing to him.

She took a deep breath, controlling her voice as she said, 'When must you leave?'

'We put to sea in the morning. I have business that I must attend this night. I am sorry to leave you so soon, Kathryn, but we are at war.'

'Yes, I know.' Was she to spend her wedding night alone? 'Shall I see you again before you leave?'

Lorenzo hesitated, then shook his head. 'I think there will not be time. Besides, I shall make no demands of you this night, Kathryn. You must learn to think of me as your husband, and then, perhaps…but we shall see if we suit each other.'

Kathryn felt as if he had slapped her. She knew that he did not love her, but she had imagined that he would claim his right as a husband to sleep in her bed that night. Surely any man would do as much? It could only mean that he did not find her desirable enough. She swallowed her hurt pride, refusing to show him how she felt at being so summarily abandoned.

'As you wish. I pray that you have a safe journey, Lorenzo.'

He hesitated for a moment, then took two steps towards her and stopped, looking down at her with such a strange expression. She thought that he would take her in his arms and kiss her and her heart beat wildly, but then he seemed to change his mind. He moved away from her, as if deliberately putting distance between them.

'If anything should happen to me, you will be taken care of, Kathryn. You have nothing to fear. And now, forgive me, I must leave.'

Kathryn nodded, feeling miserable as he walked from the room. He did not find her desirable enough to want to lie with her. She was a bride, but not a wife, and the pain of humiliation at his rejection twisted inside her like the blade of a knife. She had longed for him to kiss her and make her his own, but he did not want her.

Tears stung her eyes, but she refused to let them fall. She would never, never let him see that she was fool enough to love him.

Lorenzo found the endless meetings and discussions tedious beyond bearing. It was now early autumn and the Sicilian squadron had gathered at Oranto. Many of the galleys were neither as well equipped nor manned as adequately as his own, including those of his countrymen. Venice had boasted that they had the finest fleet of all, but it was seen to be a hollow boast, for many of the galleys had lain idle for too long and were in need of repair. The papal fleet itself was weak, which meant that the Spanish had most of the power.

A man called Marcantonio Colonna had overall command of the fleet, but, despite his skill at diplomacy and his personal courage, it was proving almost impossible to hold the different factions together. Colonna wanted to go after the enemy at once, but another commander, Gianandrea Doria, had so far resisted. As one of the principal galley owners, he was concerned for the fate of his ships.

'We are not yet strong enough,' Doria said at one of the eternal meetings. 'We must wait.'

'I believe they will argue for ever,' Lorenzo said to

Michael, his patience exhausted when he learned that the decision to disperse for the winter had been taken late in September. 'What of our people on Cyprus? Are we to abandon them to their fate?'

Doria had decided to take his ships to Sicily for the winter, but Lorenzo would take his fleet to Rome.

'I see no point in wasting months in idleness when we might be more profitably employed,' he said. 'There are repairs to be made and they will be better done in Rome than Sicily.'

'So we return to Rome at once?'

'Yes, to Rome.' Lorenzo's eyes were distant, his thoughts clearly far away.

Michael returned to his own command to give the orders. Lorenzo frowned as he stood staring out to sea. Would he have chosen to winter in Sicily if it were not for Kathryn?

His thoughts had been with her these past weeks, and he felt a deep, instinctive pleasure at the prospect of her waiting for him, a sharp desire forming in his loins as he anticipated their meeting. He had not forced her to submit on their wedding night for it would not have been right. She had married him because she had no choice, but he would teach her not to fear his lovemaking. In time he believed that she would welcome him to her bed.

A shout from one of his men alerted him. 'Six galleys to the leeward, sir!'

Lorenzo looked in the direction the man was pointing. As yet there was some distance between them, but he could see that the oarsmen were pulling hard as they tried to catch up to him. He needed no one to tell him that they were the galleys of his enemy. He had been thwarted in his desire to beard the Turks in their den, but at least the chance of revenge was in sight. Rachid meant to attack them. His personal galley was at the forefront of the small fleet. It was the first time that Lorenzo and his enemy had met like this and they were evenly matched, for Lorenzo had five galleys with him. What Rachid did not know was that another six were not more than half an hour behind him.

He felt a sense of exhilaration, of destiny. It was the confrontation that he had always known must come one day, and it seemed that luck was on his side.

The battle lasted for two hours or more, but the Corsairs were outnumbered when the rest of Lorenzo's fleet caught up with them, and now, at last, it was over. Two of Lorenzo's galleys were damaged, but still afloat and able to limp home. Two of Rachid's galleys had been sunk, another three were crippled. Rachid's own galley had left when the battle was at its hottest, abandoning the rest of the galleys because it was clear that the Venetian was winning.

'Shall we take prisoners?' Michael asked as they saw that the flags on the Corsair ships had been hauled down and the men had surrendered their weapons.

'One of the galleys—that most of need in repair—may be left to those who wish to continue in Rachid's service,' Lorenzo said. 'They may save themselves if they can and we shall not hinder them. We shall take the other two as our prize. Any men aboard any of the galleys who wish to serve with me may transfer to the ships we take with us. Any who resist will be killed.'

'Yes, sir.' Michael was about to leave to see that his commands were carried out when they became aware of a commotion on board one of the captured galleys.

'See what that is about,' Lorenzo instructed, frowning.

Michael shouted to their own men who had boarded the

stricken pirate galleys and then came back to report. 'It seems that Rachid's oldest son Hassan has been taken prisoner. What shall we do with him?'

'Bring him to me.'

Lorenzo felt a strange excitement. At last he had the means to punish his enemy for all that he had suffered at his hands. He could repay Rachid for his cruelty a thousand times over by taking the life of his son. Coming on top of the loss of five of his best galleys, it might be a blow from which the Corsair would never recover.

He had his back turned when they brought the prisoner. Lorenzo tensed, then swung round to look at the son of the man he hated, his eyes moving over the youth. He let his eyes dwell on Hassan's face for some minutes, discovering to his surprise that his overriding emotion was pity rather than hatred. The youth could be no more than sixteen and was plainly terrified.

'Down on your knees, dog!' one of Lorenzo's men growled.

'No,' Lorenzo said. 'Let him stand. He is a man, not a dog, whoever his father may be.'

'Kill me,' the youth said, trying to act bravely, though he was shaking with fear. 'Let death come quickly, that is all I ask.'

'I shall not take your life, for it would not profit me,' Lorenzo said, his eyes narrowed, cold. 'Your father is my enemy. I do not make war on boys or innocents. You shall be ransomed.' He turned to Michael, giving him his instructions.

Michael looked surprised and then nodded. 'It shall be as you command, Captain.'

Lorenzo glanced at the youth again, for he had spoken to Michael in Italian and the Corsair did not understand. 'You are to be exchanged for the captive woman Maria, daughter of Don Pablo Dominicus. My captain Michael dei Ignacio will rendezvous with your father off Sicily and the exchange will take place at a given time. If Rachid brings more than one galley to escort him, you will die.' He nodded to Michael. 'Take him with you.'

'And the girl?'

'Bring her to me in Rome. Her father owes me for Kathryn's abduction. He shall pay a ransom to have his daughter back.'

Michael smiled, understanding the cleverness of his captain's mind. 'It is good,' he said. 'A life for a life and still we have our prize.'

'We need more galleys,' Lorenzo said. 'This war with the Turks has been delayed but it will come—and it will cost us much.'

He watched as the men took Rachid's son away. Many of them would have killed him without a second thought, but they would not disobey their captain, and when they learned of the ransom they would smile and see the logic of their commander's thinking. There was no profit to be had from a dead Corsair.

Despite the damage to his own fleet, this had been a good day, Lorenzo thought grimly. He would repair one of the captured galleys and paint it with his own colours. The other would be sold and the money shared between his men. The captive slaves would be given the choice of serving as free men or, in some cases, questioned before being either ransomed by their families or given their freedom. Any who betrayed their surrender terms would be killed at once. The first thing that Lorenzo demanded of any man was loyalty.

However, he had not forgotten his promise to Kathryn. He would continue to question all those who were taken, seeking information about the long-lost Richard Mountfitchet. It was possible that Lord Mountfitchet had been killed on Cyprus, but Kathryn was still alive and he would keep his word no matter what.

As for the dreams that had begun to haunt his sleep of late, he would dismiss them as nonsense. It mattered little who he had once been. He was Lorenzo Santorini and his purpose in life was… He frowned as he realised that he was no longer certain of his purpose.

He had spared the son of his enemy out of pity for a youth who surely did not deserve a cruel death. Yet that did not ease the hatred he felt for Rachid or the bitterness that had burned inside him like a candle flame for so long, driving him on. It would be foolish to let softer dreams rob him of his purpose in life, for he could not change all that had been, all that he was. He had taken life ruthlessly in pursuit of his enemy, and though he acted for good reason it did not wash away the blood.

How could a man such as he love a woman like Kathryn? He knew himself unworthy and yet his body burned for her, his soul thirsted for the sweetness of a life spent at her side.

But he was what life had made him, and surely there was no changing what fate had decreed.

Chapter Seven

Kathryn laughed at something her companions were saying. Her grasp of the language had improved gradually during the months she had lived in Rome. Almost four months had passed since her wedding day. She had had no word from Lorenzo in all that time and did not know what had been happening, for there had been very little news.

'Elizabeta!' Adriana Botticelli cried. 'You are the most wicked flirt. If I were your husband, I should beat you.'

'If Marco were not so dull, Elizabeta would not need to flirt with Caius Antonio,' Isabella Rinaldi giggled. She was the youngest of the ladies present, and unmarried. 'If my father chooses an old fat merchant as my husband, I shall take a lover too.' She fluttered her fan artlessly, her face alive with mischief. 'I hope that he chooses someone like your husband, Kathryn. If I were you, I should die of happiness.'

'But poor Kathryn was married only a few hours before her husband left her,' Elizabeta said. 'Have you heard nothing from him, Kathryn?'

'Nothing. Lorenzo is always so busy. He will come when he is ready.' She looked up as her companion came into the salon where they were sitting. 'Is your head better, Veronique?'

'Much better, thank you, Kathryn.' She sat down by the window and picked up her embroidery and then, seeing someone approaching, said, 'Oh, I believe we have company… Why, it is Signor Santorini. Kathryn, your husband is here!'

'Lorenzo is here?' Kathryn's heart missed a beat. 'You are sure it is he, Veronique?'

'Yes, quite sure.'

Kathryn's impulse was to run to meet him, but she fought her desire, pretending to go on with her sewing. She must not betray herself. Lorenzo would not wish her to show too much emotion at his return. He had married her out of pity. He did not want a wife who demanded love.

'We should go,' Elizabeta said, sensing the emotion she struggled to hide. 'Your husband will want to be alone with you, Kathryn.'

Kathryn shook her head, but all the ladies had followed Elizabeta's example. They trooped out of the room with Veronique in their wake. Kathryn stayed where she was, her heart thumping painfully. She could hear her friends chattering and laughing amongst themselves and then the deeper tones of a man's voice.

Her heart jerked as Lorenzo came into the salon. His eyes went over her, seeming to search for something, some sign, though she knew not what he wanted from her.

'Are you well, Kathryn?'

'Yes, sir. I am happy to see you back. I was anxious for your safe return. We have heard little news of the war.'

'That may be because there is little to tell. The Turks have taken Famagusta and Nicosia. The League talked of blockading Rhodes, but once Cyprus had fallen the plan was abandoned. Doria has decided to winter at Sicily. I preferred to return to Rome, for there are galleys to be repaired and provisioned and I can do that better here.'

'I am glad that you did.'

'Are you, Kathryn?' His expression was serious, intent on her face.

'Yes. You must know that.'

'It will be good to be here with you for a while. We shall be a long time at sea once we leave again in the spring.'

She stood up and went over to the table where a tray with glasses and jugs of wine and fruit drinks had been set out for her guests. She took a deep breath to steady her fluttering nerves, then turned to look at him.

'May I serve you some wine?'

'Yes, thank you.' He stood watching her as she poured the wine and brought it to him. 'What have you been doing while I was gone?'

'I have made friends with the ladies you saw here. They take me shopping with them and invite me to their homes.'

'So you have not been unhappy?'

She had missed him dreadfully, spending many lonely hours in the villa and gardens, crying herself to sleep for several nights after he left, but she would not tell him that. He did not want a wife who clung and wept for love of him.

'No, I have not been unhappy.'

'I am glad of it, for I have some news for you, Kathryn.'

'Of Lady Mary and Lord Mountfitchet?'

'No, I am sorry to tell you that as yet no news of them has come my way, though I have heard that some did escape the onslaught and reached other islands, before and since the invasion. Even if your friends are still alive, Kathryn, it will take time for letters to reach us. My news was of a possible sighting of Richard—one of the prisoners we took told us of a blue-eyed slave who works in the gardens of a wealthy merchant in Algiers. He was a youth when taken and, though he is apparently physically strong, has the mind of a child.'

'That is very sad,' Kathryn said. Once that news would have devastated her, but now she could feel only sadness and regret. Another love had replaced that childish one she had felt for Dickon. 'Is there any way we can discover more?'

'I have arranged to make further inquiries. I thought you would want me to continue the search.'

'I know that Uncle Charles would wish it to go on,' Kathryn said. 'And I should feel happier if Richard could be rescued from slavery. If his father is dead, he is the heir to the Mountfitchet estate in England.'

'He would need to prove his identity, I think?'

'Yes—and that might be difficult if his father is dead. There will be other claimants, and those who matter would not listen to the claims of a slave who behaves like a child. If I believe he is Richard, my father will help him, but as for the rest…'

'Do not concern yourself,' Lorenzo told her. 'Something will be done. You have my word.'

'Thank you.' Kathryn looked at him shyly. 'Will you dine with me this evening, husband?'

'Yes, certainly. It is my hope that now I am home we may spend some time together—learn to know one another, Kathryn.'

'That would be very pleasant.'

How could she speak so calmly when her heart was hammering against her ribs? Kathryn fought her desire to be close to him. When he looked at her that way she felt as if she were melting and wanted only to be in his arms.

'Pleasant…' A wry smile touched his mouth. 'Yes, it will be pleasant, Kathryn.'

'If you will excuse me, I shall go to make sure that everything is in readiness.'

She had no need to bother, for the house ran perfectly and the servants would already have done all that was necessary, but if she stayed she might disgrace herself by falling into his arms. She might have begged him to kiss her, to love her.

What had he expected? Lorenzo frowned as he cleansed himself of the dirt of his months at sea. It was good to bathe after weeks when only the most basic of cleanliness was available. A douche in seawater every now and then was all that any of the men could expect. A man got used to the stench of the galleys, but he had been too eager to see her to delay even for that little time. Small wonder that she had kept her distance.

Yet was it only that he had come to her with the dirt of his journey still upon him? She knew what life was like on board ship and had not flinched from it when she was forced to travel with few comforts. Was she keeping her distance because she did not wish to become his wife in truth?

He had thought of this homecoming for weeks, dreaming of what she would smell like, how she would feel lying next to him in bed. Had he been mad to let himself imagine that she might welcome him once she had accustomed herself to the idea?

Most women he had wanted had been eager enough to fall into his arms, but he had never wanted one this badly before. All too often it had been he who had refused the offer of a lady's company, too busy and too caught up in his quest to want the bother of a love affair. His chosen

companions had been ladies who understood that he would
go sooner rather than later.

Dressing in black Venetian breeches and hose and a
doublet of black slashed with silver, the hanging sleeves
attached by silver buckles at the shoulders, Lorenzo looked
a true aristocrat. His hair was longer than usual for it had
not been trimmed in months, curling to his shoulders, his
skin a deep bronze. He glanced at his reflection in the
glass, wondering as he had so often who he really was. For
a moment his fingers strayed towards the leather wristbands, feeling the accustomed discomfort. All he knew for
certain was that he had been captured by the Corsair
Rachid and kept as a slave, chained to the oar until he was
abandoned for dead. Yet he must have had a life before that
day, a family, friends…perhaps a lover.

There had been no more flashes of memory recently. It
seemed that the curtain was back in place, shutting out the
past. Yet it did not matter—he knew that he was Lorenzo
Santorini, owner of a fleet of galleys, his mission in life
to destroy his enemy and others of his ilk.

Yet was his purpose as firm as it had been? Lorenzo
frowned as he tried to understand the change that had
come over him as he looked into the frightened eyes of that
youth. Had it been Rachid himself he would not have hesitated to kill him—or would he?

He cursed softly as he realised that he was not sure. He
had fed on hatred for so long. It was necessary to him, for
without it what would he have?

The answer was so shocking, so alien to all that he had
been and believed that he could not accept it. Dreams of
a wife and family were not for him. He would grow soft,
forget what had made him the man he was—become
someone else.

Surely that was not what he wanted? He realised that he did not know. He did not know who he truly was any more.

Kathryn had dressed in an emerald green gown that set off the colour of her hair and made her eyes glow like jewels. She had only a small strand of pearls that her father had given her as a present for her birthday just before she left England, but she wore them with pride, never guessing that beauty such as hers needed no artifice.

'You look lovely, Kathryn,' Lorenzo said when he saw her. She was standing in the open arches that led out into a paved courtyard, her face pensive, a little sad perhaps. 'Of what are you thinking, Madonna?'

'It is such a lovely night. I was thinking of my home and my father.'

'Have you written to him?'

Kathryn turned to face him. 'I wrote to him when we reached Venice, but thought it best not to write again for the moment. Until we have more certain news of our friends I would not worry him.'

'Do you not think you should tell him that you are married?'

'Perhaps.' Kathryn took a step towards him. 'Lorenzo…'

She hesitated as a servant came to tell them that a meal had been served.

'You must be hungry?'

'Yes,' he agreed. 'Let us eat, Kathryn. We have all the evening to talk.'

Her heart began to race as she saw the look in his eyes. All these weeks she had convinced herself that he did not want her, but the way he looked at her now made her think that perhaps she had been mistaken.

Perhaps he had left her on their wedding night because there was no time, just as he'd told her. And now he was home and there was plenty of time before he must put to sea again…

'Tell me what you like to do with your days, Kathryn,' Lorenzo invited as they sat down to enjoy their meal.

'Oh, I walk in the garden. I shop with friends and visit their homes. Sometimes they visit me—but there is one thing I miss here, Lorenzo.'

'And what is that, Madonna?'

'Books,' she said. 'My father has a library at home and he allows me to read his books. Here there are no books.'

'Why did you not buy some for yourself? I left money enough for your needs.'

'I did not like to spend too much,' Kathryn said. 'And I did not know if you would approve of such purchases.'

Lorenzo smiled. 'I must show you my library when we go home, Kathryn.'

'When shall we return to Venice?'

'Not for some months,' he said. 'I have made arrangements to winter here—and you have friends, Kathryn. You would have to begin again in Venice. I thought it would be better to wait until we can return together.'

'Yes, you are right,' she said. 'I have not been bored, Lorenzo—but you asked what I like to do.'

'We shall buy you books,' he told her. 'But now I would hear about your life in England, Kathryn. Tell me what you did there.'

She told him of her home overlooking the sea, and the long walks she liked to take when the weather permitted, and then, somehow, she found herself telling him of the day Dickon was stolen by Corsairs.

'You say it was your idea that you should go down to

the cove to investigate?' He was looking at her thoughtfully. 'And you have felt guilt because of it ever since?'

'Had I not suggested it, he would not have gone.'

'Can you be so sure of that? Most men would be curious
and you were so much younger.'

'But Dickon always tried to please me. He was so kind,
so generous—always laughing and teasing me...' Her eyes
grew dark with remembered grief.

'Is that why you still love him?'

'I...am not sure that I do,' she confessed, not daring to
look at him. 'We were but children. How do I know that
we would still have loved each other when we grew up?
Besides...' Her voice tailed away. 'I am your wife now,
Lorenzo. And...and I would be a good wife to you...'

'What do you mean by that?'

Kathryn looked at him, her breath catching in her
throat. How could she answer, how could she tell him
what she meant without betraying her feelings? If only he
would give her some sign, show that he at least desired her,
wanted her in his bed.

She was saved from answering by the arrival of a servant.

'*Signor,*' the woman said, 'Captain dei Ignacio is here
to see you. He has brought someone with him—a woman.'

'Michael is here?' Lorenzo got to his feet. 'Excuse me,
Kathryn. I must attend to this.'

She stared after him as he walked from the room. She
had come so close to confessing her love, but the interrup-
tion had saved her. She wondered why it was so important
that Lorenzo must speak with his captain immediately—
and who was the woman Michael had brought with him?

Lorenzo's eyes went over the woman standing at
Michael's side. She was wrapped in his cloak, and from

the slippers on her feet and a glimpse of the harem pants she wore beneath it, he understood why.

'Donna Maria,' he said, speaking kindly, for he understood that she must be bewildered and perhaps frightened by all that had happened to her since she was taken from her father's ship. 'Welcome to my house. I trust that Michael has told you—you are to be restored to your father on payment of a ransom?'

'Please…' Maria looked at him with tear-drenched eyes. 'Do not tell my father where I have been…' Tears fell from her eyes and trickled down her cheeks. 'He would disown me—send me to the nuns.'

Lorenzo glanced at his captain. 'Perhaps you should tell me the whole?'

'Stay here, Donna Maria,' Michael said and moved a little aside with him. 'She has been kept in Rachid's harem. I am not sure whether she was sent to his bed, but she has been with his women.'

'And she believes that her father would disown her if he knew?'

'It is what she says.' Michael frowned. 'I brought her to you as you bid me—and now I ask leave to return to Venice for a while. I have had news of my father. He is unwell and asks for me.'

'Yes, of course you must go to him,' Lorenzo said at once. 'I hope you will return to me here as soon as you can?'

'You have my loyalty as always,' Michael said. 'But for the moment there is little here that cannot be done by others.'

'Go then with my blessing,' Lorenzo said and frowned. 'But the girl—how did she seem to you? Has she been mistreated? You understand my meaning—has she been subjected to rape?'

'I am not certain what to think,' Michael told him. 'It is true that she has been kept in the harem, but I do not think she was ill treated there. She asked me several times to let her return to her friends.'

Lorenzo nodded. 'I shall keep her with us for a while, and then we shall decide what to do about her father.'

'If you will excuse me, I would leave at once.'

'Of course. May your god go with you, my friend.'

'And with you. Give Kathryn my good wishes.'

Lorenzo inclined his head. His eyes moved to the Spanish girl. She was very beautiful, her hair black and thick, her eyes dark and her mouth soft and sensuous. Something in the way she looked at him made him vaguely uncomfortable, a knowing, calculating expression that he disliked and thought immodest in an unmarried girl.

'I am sorry for what has happened to you, Donna Maria,' he said. 'I shall ask my wife to take care of you. I am not sure what to do about you—though in the end you must be returned to your father. However, it may be that you would prefer to stay with us for a time?'

'Yes, please.' She came quickly towards him, catching at his hand, her eyes pleading. 'I do not want to go home.'

'Lorenzo…' Kathryn came into the hall at that moment, in time to see the girl clutching at his hand. She stopped, frowning and uncertain. Who was this girl? 'Has Michael left already?'

'He brought Donna Maria Dominicus to us,' Lorenzo said. 'We have managed to ransom her from Rachid, and she will stay with us until we can restore her to her family. Will you look after her, Kathryn?'

'Yes, certainly,' Kathryn said, feeling remorse for her suspicions and pity for the girl, who she knew must have suffered dreadfully. 'How did you manage this, Lorenzo?'

'I shall tell you later,' he said. 'Donna Maria needs clothes. You may have something that she can wear until we can have something made for her.'

'I think we are much of a size,' Kathryn said readily. 'If you will come with me, Donna Maria, I shall take you to the room that will be yours. I think you must want to bathe and rest, for you have had a terrible time.'

'You are so kind.' The girl's tears fell readily. 'I have been so very unhappy…'

'You are safe now,' Kathryn said, her heart touched by the girl's plight. 'Come, we shall go upstairs where we can talk and you may ask me for anything you need.'

Maria glanced at Lorenzo, but, finding no softness in his face, she clung to the hand Kathryn offered, her head bent as she allowed herself to be led away.

Lorenzo watched them leave. His instinct told him that the Spanish girl was not as upset as she seemed. There was something about her that he could not like, but, having ransomed her, he was honour bound to look after her until she could be restored to her family.

'I was made to wear these things,' Maria told Kathryn when they were alone and she had shed Michael's cloak, revealing the flimsy harem pants and tunic. 'I feel so ashamed.'

'It is not your shame,' Kathryn told her, angry that the girl had been subjected to such humiliation. 'You were a captive and had to do as your cruel masters bid you. I have heard that Rachid is one of the worst of the Corsair captains, a ruthless man. We must thank God that you have been rescued before it was too late.'

'They told me I was to be sold to the Sultan,' Maria told her, her eyes lowered. She wiped her hand across her face. 'Perhaps I was fortunate that Rachid did not want me for himself.'

'Yes, I am sure that you were,' Kathryn said. 'It must have been a terrible ordeal for you.'

'I wish that I had died rather than become a slave. My father will disown me or send me to a nunnery.'

'Surely not, Maria? He will be glad to have you home.'

'I do not think so. I have disgraced him.' She turned her luminous eyes on Kathryn. 'Could I not stay with you— as your companion? I promise I would be no trouble to you.'

'It is my husband who makes these decisions,' Kathryn said, her heart wrung with pity. 'But I believe you worry too much, Maria. Your father was desperate to have you back.' She explained what Don Pablo had done to try and trap Lorenzo. 'That must make you realise that he loves you?'

'Perhaps.' Maria drew a sobbing breath. 'But he did not know that I had been kept in a harem with…' She shook her head. 'You cannot know what they did to me to make sure that I was…'

'Do not distress yourself, Maria,' Kathryn said. 'I shall speak to my husband and see if he will keep you with us, at least until we can be sure what your father feels. I promise you that, if he says you have disgraced him, I shall not let you go back to him.'

'Oh, you are so kind!' Maria seized her hand and kissed it. 'I would do anything you asked of me, my lady.'

'No, no, you must call me Kathryn as my friends do. I promise you that you shall not be ill treated for something that was not your fault.' She smiled at the girl. 'Our servants will bring you water to bathe in and clothes, also food. You will want to rest this evening, but in the morning we shall talk again. The clothes you are wearing shall be burned.'

'May I not keep them to remind me?' Maria said. 'I must keep them to remind me of my modesty and that it was once lost. Please do not make me give them up.'

'Surely you do not want them?'

'Please!'

'As you wish, but you must not think of what happened to you as your shame.'

Kathryn left the girl to the ministrations of the servants and went downstairs to join Lorenzo. He gave her a look of inquiry.

'She is going to bathe, eat and rest. We shall see her in the morning.'

'I am sorry that I brought her here,' Lorenzo said. 'It was not my intention that she should stay with us, Kathryn. I had intended to send her to her father almost at once.'

'She is so distressed. Would it not be kinder to keep her with us for a while? At least until she can become accustomed to what has happened to her? She feels ashamed and it must have been awful for a young girl.'

'There is something I cannot like about her.'

'Lorenzo! You are too harsh,' Kathryn said. 'She has been through a terrible ordeal.'

'It would seem so and yet...' He frowned, uncertain why he felt that it would be best to be rid of the girl at once.

'Please, I ask you to be kind to her—for my sake.'

'For your sake?' Lorenzo's eyes narrowed. He moved towards her, gazing down into her eyes. 'I might do much for your sake, Kathryn.'

Her eyes widened as she saw the hot glow in his, and she swayed towards him, wanting him to take her in his arms, to kiss her.

'Why…' she asked, 'why do you say that?'

'Because you are my wife—because I care for you. Surely you know that, Madonna?'

'I thought that you left me because you did not want me. I thought you did not find me attractive enough to want to lie with me on our wedding night.' Kathryn gazed up at him, her eyes filled with an innocent appeal. 'Was that not so?'

Lorenzo laughed, the sound of it making her heart race as he reached out, drawing her into his arms, his eyes dark with some deeply felt emotion.

'Can you be so foolish, my love?' he asked. 'How could you think it was for my sake that I did not stay that night?'

'Was it not?'

'You married me because you had no choice. I would not force you to lie with me, Kathryn. I wanted you to become accustomed to the idea of a husband before you were forced to your duty. I want you warm and willing in my arms—not out of wifely duty.'

'I do not think I should mind my wifely duty so very much,' she said, her cheeks pink as she saw the laughter in his eyes. 'I think it might be pleasant…'

'Pleasant?' Lorenzo shook his head at her, wickedness in every line of his face. He seemed to her then a man she had never seen before, the man he might have been had life been kinder to him. 'It may be wonderful, exciting and passionate, but I do not think pleasant is a word I would use concerning my feelings for you, Madonna.'

'Then would you please kiss me?'

'Sweet Kathy,' Lorenzo said and pulled her into his arms, his mouth taking hungry possession of hers. The kiss was long and sweet and demanding, and it left her breathless. She stared at him in wonder as she began to understand what loving a man might mean. 'Shall I come to you tonight?' She nodded wordlessly, and he smiled at her, touching her hair. 'My red-haired witch. I never meant to let you beneath my skin, Kathryn. You have taken root inside me and I find I cannot live without you.'

'Oh, Lorenzo,' she breathed. 'I am so glad you have come home.'

Kathryn turned in the arms of her husband, lifting her face for his kiss. She had never expected to discover such pleasure in loving as he had given her and she curled into his strong, lean body, compliant as a sleepy kitten.

'Are you happy, Madonna?'

'You know that I am.' Her cheeks were warm, for she knew that she had behaved with shameless abandon as he loved her, crying his name aloud. Her hands moved on his shoulders and encountered the thick welts of old scars. She had been aware of them during their loving, but now she traced them with her fingers.

'Do they distress you, Kathryn—the scars?'

'Only because I know you must have suffered.' She leaned up on one elbow to look down into his face. 'Who did this to you, Lorenzo? Was it Rachid? Is that why you hate him?'

'I was a slave in his galley for three years.'

'Oh, my love,' Kathryn cried, not caring that she betrayed herself. 'How you must have suffered—but you never told me. No one told me.'

'Only Michael and my father ever knew,' he said, his voice husky with emotion. 'It is not something I care to have told, Kathryn.'

'I shall never speak of it without your permission—but how did you escape?'

'I was left for dead on the shores of southern Spain. A sick galley slave is worthless. They left me on the beach, threw me into the shallows, and I should undoubtedly have died if Antonio Santorini, a merchant of Venice, had not chanced to come ashore that day to provision his ship. He found me, took me aboard his ship and brought me to Venice.'

'You are not his son?'

'He was childless; his beloved wife dead some years before. He gave me his name, adopted me and made me his legal heir. As much as I was able I loved him, for he was a truly good man. He had suffered at the hands of the Inquisition himself; because of it, he devoted his life to helping others. I helped to restore his fortune, much of which he had given away to those who needed it. And when he died I mourned him.'

'You were lucky that day, Lorenzo.' She kissed his shoulder, which tasted salty with sweat after their loving. 'I am so sorry for what happened to you.'

'Do not be,' he said. 'For years I lived on hatred and that sustained me, giving me strength. It was only my hope of revenge that made me determined to live.'

'Lorenzo…' She bent over him, her hair brushing his face as she kissed him on the lips. 'I love you.'

'My sweet Kathy.'

He rolled her beneath him in the bed, his mouth plundering hers as the desire flamed between them once more. His hands stroked and caressed her, making her moan and move beneath him, her body arching up to meet him as he thrust deep inside her. Deep, deeper, into the inviting moistness of her femininity, her legs curling over his hips as they reached the heights of pleasure together. She screamed his name as he buried his face in the intoxicating softness of her hair.

'No other woman has pleased me as you do, Kathryn,' he murmured huskily against her throat. 'If you ever left me…'

'Hush, my love,' she said and there were tears on her cheeks. 'I shall never leave you. I want only your love.'

'My love, Kathryn?' His voice was harsh, his body suddenly stiff with tension. 'I am not sure that I know how to love—but all that I have I give to you.'

Kathryn clung to him in the darkness, her heart aching. She had begun to understand the man she loved. He had suffered things that no man should and the scars had gone deep, much deeper than those he bore on his shoulders and back. All the natural feelings, the softness and pleasures that others knew had been denied to him, and it had taken its toll. Perhaps he would never love her as she loved him, but he desired her and she pleased him—and for the moment she must be content with that.

It was only later, when Lorenzo lay sleeping beside her, that she realised he had not told her who he really was. If he was not the natural son of Antonio Santorini, then who was he?

Was it possible that her senses had told her truly the first time they met, when she had looked into his eyes and believed she knew him? He had strongly denied it once, when she had told him that he might more likely be Richard Mountfitchet than the man he had named William.

Surely he would have told her if there was any possibility that he could be the man they had been searching for? Of course he would. She was being foolish. Kathryn dismissed the idea as she drifted into sleep, curled into the body of her husband, warm and safe, protected by his strength.

Lorenzo had told her much this night. When he was ready he would tell her anything else he wished her to know.

When he was sure that Kathryn slept, Lorenzo left her bed and removed his clothes to the adjoining room, dressing before he went downstairs. He had feigned sleep so that she might rest; he could not sleep beside her for fear that the dream might disturb her. Although it had not happened of late, when he woke, screaming a name, his body covered in a fine sweat, he sometimes struck out with his fists or feet. Better that he should not risk injuring his wife. Besides, he would not have her see him that way.

His fingers sought out the leather wristbands, rubbing at the old injuries. Sometimes the irritation was almost more than he could bear. He wondered if a part of it was caused by the wristbands themselves, but he could not bring himself to remove them, to reveal to the whole world the badge of his shame. Kathryn had not recoiled from the scars on his back, but he hated them, hated what they stood for. He hated the memory of his slavery, of the humiliation of knowing that he must obey his masters, of the sharp stinging pain of a whip lash.

How long would it be before Kathryn asked him who he really was? He could give her no answer, for his past was still a mystery to him, though since the dreams had begun again he had wondered.

Was it merely his imagination playing tricks on him— or could he truly remember being taken by Corsairs when he was a youth of barely fifteen? If that were so, he must be six and twenty now, and yet he knew that he looked older. His years of slavery and the hardships at sea had taken a toll of him as it must of any man.

No, it was madness to let his thoughts take him down that road. Already, he had let Kathryn inside his head and that had changed him. Because of her he had let Rachid's son live and exchanged him for a girl who was like to cause them trouble, if his instincts proved true.

He frowned as he thought of the girl sleeping in his guest room. She was young and he ought to feel pity for her, but somehow he could not. She had looked at him in the same way as the harlots who plied the streets for their trade and he did not trust her.

Maria claimed that she had been kept in the harem and was to be sold to the Sultan's harem, but Lorenzo had seen something in her eyes—a knowledge that was not often in the eyes of an innocent virgin. Perhaps he wronged her, but he suspected that she had been one of Rachid's concubines—and that she had liked the experience. He suspected that she had resented being taken from him, and that was the reason for her distress.

She had pleaded with them to keep her in their home. She said that her father would send her to a nunnery because she had shamed her family. She could not be blamed for what had befallen her, unless… If she had enjoyed the position of favourite in Rachid's harem, that would explain her fear of being rejected by her family.

He would have to watch her carefully, Lorenzo decided as he left the house. And he would find another home for her before he put to sea again—either with her father or someone else.

Chapter Eight

'I do not like that girl,' Elizabeta told Kathryn when they were walking together a few days later. 'There is something about her—a slyness in the way she looks at you and Lorenzo, particularly Lorenzo. Be careful of her and trust nothing she tells you.'

'Oh, you are too hard on her,' Kathryn said with a smile to soften the words, for Elizabeta was perhaps the friend she liked to be with the most. She could not explain what had happened to Maria for she did not wish to ruin the girl's chances of making friends and she might be looked down upon if people knew that she had spent some time in a harem. 'She has been…ill. We are looking after her for a while, but she will go home to her family soon.'

'The sooner the better,' Elizabeta said. She took hold of Kathryn's arm as they approached the silk merchant's shop they had planned to visit that morning. 'Do look at that lovely green material! It would look so well on you, Kathryn.'

'Yes, it is very lovely,' Kathryn said. She turned and beckoned to Maria, who was walking behind with Isabella Rinaldi. 'Come and look at these silks, Maria. We shall buy material for you today; you must be tired of wearing my old gowns.'

'Oh, no,' Maria said, her eyes downcast. 'You have been so kind to me, Kathryn. How could I be so ungrateful as to resent wearing your things?'

'Well, you shall have a new gown,' Kathryn said. 'Come, look, and choose the silk you prefer.'

'Oh, I do not know what to choose,' Maria said, her hands fluttering over the bales of beautiful silks that the merchant had spread on trestles before his shop. 'There are so many…that blue is lovely, and yet so is the green.'

'Kathryn was thinking of buying the green for herself,' Elizabeta said, her dark eyes narrowed and hostile as she looked at Maria. 'The blue would suit you much better—or that grey.'

'I do not like dull colours,' Maria said and for a moment her eyes met Elizabeta's in an expression of such hatred that the older woman gasped. 'I shall have the blue if Kathryn prefers the green for herself.'

'No, indeed, I do not need any more gowns for the moment,' Kathryn said. 'We shall take both the green and the blue, Maria. You shall have two new gowns and then you need not wear my old ones at all.'

'You are too generous,' Elizabeta said. 'That green was perfect for you.'

'It does not matter. There will be other silks,' Kathryn said. She turned away, speaking to the merchant and directing him to send both bales of silk to her at the villa. 'Shall we have something to drink at the inn or go back to my home?'

'We are nearer to my house,' Elizabeta said. 'Come, we shall go home once I have ordered the silk I want for myself, and my servants will bring us refreshments. It is too warm to shop any more today.' She smiled and linked arms with Kathryn.

Kathryn agreed that the sun was very warm and they all returned to Elizabeta's house, which was situated not far from the Campo de' Fiori, one of the streets of beautiful Renaissance buildings begun by Pope Nicholas in the fifteenth century.

The house was large, almost a palace, for Elizabeta's husband was wealthy, though some years older than she. She took her guests through the echoing rooms, which were cool after the heat of the sun, into the courtyard garden, then left them to talk while she went to order the refreshments served to them.

Kathryn and Isabella sat down on one of the small stone seats, which had been set with cushions and placed in a shady spot, but Maria wandered off alone to explore the garden, which she had not seen before.

'She is a strange girl, is she not?' Isabella said, frowning a little. 'She boasted to me that she has a lover and that he has promised to wed her. I thought you told me she had been ill?'

'Yes, she has,' Kathryn said. 'I think she meant that she will be betrothed to someone when she goes home.' She thought Maria foolish to talk of such things, for it would do her reputation no good.

'She asked me if I had a lover,' Isabella said. 'I am sure she meant that she had…well, you know…'

Kathryn shook her head at her as Elizabeta came back to them, her servants carrying out extra chairs so that they might all be comfortable. Maria joined them as they sat down and the drinks were served.

For a while they sat talking about the things they had seen while they were out shopping, and Isabella told them that her father had said he was taking her to Venice in the spring.

'He says that there is a family he wishes me to meet,' she said. 'I think he means to make a marriage contract for me. I hope the man he has chosen to be my husband is as handsome as yours, Kathryn.'

'That is unlikely,' Maria said, having been silent for some time. 'There are not many men who look like Lorenzo Santorini. He is more likely to choose a rich man than a handsome one, for that is the way of fathers.'

'Kathryn's husband is very handsome,' Isabella agreed with a little secret smile. 'But I like his friend, Michael dei Ignacio. I would be happy if my father chose him.'

Maria pulled a face and then reached for her drink, knocking Elizabeta's into her lap so that she jumped up, brushing at her skirts as the liquid soaked through the material.

'Oh, forgive me,' Maria apologised. 'I am so clumsy.'

'Yes, you are,' Elizabeta said crossly. 'You should take more care. This silk was expensive and it is ruined.'

'I dare say your husband will buy you another,' Maria said with a little shrug of her shoulders. 'He must be very rich to own a house like this. One gown means nothing.'

Kathryn saw that Elizabeta was really angry, and poured her another drink from the jug on the table. 'Let me dry it for you,' she said. 'Come inside, Elizabeta.'

'No, no, it does not matter,' Elizabeta said and shook her head at her. 'I am sorry. It was an accident, of course. Do not worry, Maria. I have plenty more gowns—but this was a favourite.'

Maria lowered her head, her hands working in distress. 'I did not do it on purpose,' she said, but somehow not one of the other ladies present believed her. Her action had been quite deliberate and was meant to punish Elizabeta for some of her remarks earlier that day. It was a small spiteful thing, but somehow it made the other ladies join ranks against her. She was not one of them and they all thought it would be better when she went home to her family.

Kathryn was disturbed by the small incident at her friend's house. The ruin of an expensive gown was not so important, for it could be replaced, but if it was done out of spite it was quite another thing. She felt uncomfortable as they returned to the house, for if Maria was capable of doing something like that, what more might she do?

She tried not to let it make a difference to her manner towards the Spanish girl. Maria was in a difficult position and she felt sympathy for her, but as the days passed, she could not but be aware of something in Maria that she did not quite like.

The girl had a way of looking at Lorenzo that Kathryn found disturbing. She seemed to hang on his every word, and to follow him about the house and gardens. It was almost impossible for Kathryn to be alone with her husband, other than when they were in their bed.

The time they spent in bed together was very special. Lorenzo's loving made Kathryn so happy that insignificant things could not really upset her. She wished that he might love her, but there was still a strange reserve in him at times, and she had woken twice to find the bed cold and empty. It seemed that he left her once she was asleep, and that caused a small hurt inside her, for she wanted to wake and find him still beside her. Yet it was but a small thing, for he did everything he could to make her happy, giving her costly presents and encouraging her to spend money when she went shopping with her friends.

'I want you to be happy, Kathryn,' he had told her several times. 'You must tell me if there is anything you want.'

'I have all I need,' she said, for how could she ask for the one thing he was incapable of giving her? She loved him, but he could not return that love—something inside him had created a barrier between them. He was good to her and she knew that he wanted her with a fierce, needy passion, but she did not have his heart.

Even so, she was content with her life. They entertained their friends, visited them at home and were seldom without company.

Lorenzo was often busy, for the galleys were being cleaned and made ready for the next spring when it was thought that a new and much larger campaign would begin. Lorenzo had mentioned a man called Don John of Austria who would lead the enlarged fleet in the fight against the Turks, a man respected by all the factions of the League.

'There was too much argument and indecision last time,' Lorenzo told her once when they lay thigh to thigh in their bed, his hand idly tracing the silken arch of her back. 'If we are to strike a blow that will break the power of Selim, we must bind together and put our differences aside. I have no love of the Spanish, Kathryn, but I will fight with them if it defeats our common enemy. The Turks have become too predatory, too greedy, and we must stop them before it is too late.'

He had made love to her with such sweetness that night that she felt her inner self reach out to him and it seemed that they were one, their hearts, minds and bodies joined so sweetly that they could never more be separate beings. And yet still he had not told her he loved her.

Kathryn saw them walking together in the gardens that morning, her husband and the Spanish girl. It had happened before, but this time Lorenzo was laughing at something Maria had said to him, and she looked up at him as they walked, her smile inviting.

Maria was wearing the new gown of green silk that Kathryn had commissioned for her. She looked very beautiful and for a moment Kathryn was jealous. She felt the pain of it strike her. Lorenzo was not in love with her, his wife, and a man might desire many women. Was he becoming interested in the Spanish girl? Would she lose him to her rival? For she sensed that Maria was trying to arouse his interest in her.

Elizabeta had warned her against trusting Maria, and later that day there had been the incident of the spilled drink. Kathryn had never thought it an accident, because she had seen the look of triumph in Maria's eyes before she lowered them, pretending to be distressed. And what was it Isabella had said—something about Maria having had a lover who had promised to marry her?

It was not true as far as Kathryn knew, which meant the Spanish girl had lied. And now she was doing her best to capture Lorenzo's attention…

But this was mere foolishness, an irritation of the nerves. She would not let jealousy poison her thoughts, against her husband or the other girl!

Kathryn lifted her head and went outside to meet them. Immediately, Maria let go of Lorenzo's arm and moved away from him, pretending to be interested in one of the shrubs in the garden.

'Kathryn, my love,' Lorenzo said. 'Maria was telling me how happy she is here with us—and how kind you have been to her. I think we should give a dinner for our friends to celebrate the coming of Christ's birthday. It will be expected of us and it will be our farewell to Maria—I have written to Don Pablo and he asks that Maria may be taken to him in Granada.'

'You are sending me home?' Maria whirled round, looking at him. Her dark eyes blazed with anger. 'But you promised—Kathryn promised that I should stay with you.'

'For a while, until you had recovered your spirits,' he told her. 'I think you will find that your father is only too pleased to have you home, Maria. There is no need to be afraid that he will send you to a nunnery.'

'Kathryn…' Maria looked at her, eyes wild with such a mixture of emotions that it was hard to tell which was uppermost—fear or anger. 'Do not let him do this to me, I beg you.'

'My husband does what is right for you, Maria,' Kathryn said, hardening her heart against the girl. Elizabeta was right. Maria was sly and deceitful and it would be best for all of them if she returned to her father. 'I am sorry if you are distressed, but I am sure that it must be best for you. Perhaps your father will arrange a marriage for you—'

'No! I will not be sent back to him,' Maria cried and her eyes blazed with anger. 'You will be sorry for this—both of you!'

She ran from the courtyard, leaving Kathryn and Lorenzo alone.

'Do not judge me unkind,' Lorenzo said, misjudging Kathryn's silence. 'She is no true friend to you, Kathryn. Another man might have found her tempting, but she wasted her wiles on me. She might cajole many a man for she is comely enough, but I have never trusted her. Nor do I desire her.'

'She has been through so much,' Kathryn said, ashamed now that she had been jealous even for a moment. 'Who knows what such an ordeal may do to anyone? How can we know what she has suffered?'

'Be careful of her, Kathryn,' Lorenzo said. 'I warn you because I must leave you for two days. When I come back we shall arrange our special dinner—but until then do not trust Maria. If my business were not important I would not leave you, but I think she cannot harm you if you give her no chance. You have Veronique and your friends to keep you company while I am gone.'

'I shall miss you,' Kathryn said, 'but do not worry for my sake, Lorenzo. Maria may be capable of small acts of spite, but I do not think she would seek to harm me. Why should she? I have been kind to her.'

'For some people that means nothing,' Lorenzo said. 'Indeed, she may despise you for your weakness. It is a pity that I did not send her to her father immediately. However, the arrangements are made for two weeks hence. We shall have our party and then she shall go.'

'It must be as you say,' Kathryn agreed. 'But I shall still be kind to her while she is with us, for she has suffered much.'

He nodded, drawing her to him, gazing down into her face. 'I would expect nothing else from you, Kathryn, but be careful. I would not have harm come to you while I am away.'

She smiled, lifting her face for his kiss. 'Do not worry, Lorenzo. I promise you I shall be careful. Besides, what harm could she do in such a short time?'

* * *

'What is the matter, Veronique?' Kathryn asked as her companion came to her in the little salon where she had chosen to sit and read her book later that morning. 'You look upset.'

'A letter has just been brought to me,' Veronique said. 'My sister has been taken ill and wishes to see me. It will be a day's journey for me and I would be away at least three days.'

'You are anxious about her, are you not?'

'Yes—but I do not like to leave you, Kathryn. I know that Signor Santorini will be away for two days…' Veronique was clearly uncertain and anxious, worried by the letter she had received.

'You must go,' Kathryn said. 'Do not fear that I shall be lonely. I have Maria for company—and Elizabeta has promised that she will come this afternoon.'

'Are you sure that you do not mind?'

'You must go,' Kathryn insisted with a smile. 'Tell me, have you money for your journey?'

'Yes—Signor Santorini has been more than generous. I shall return as soon as I am able, Kathryn.' Veronique was upset, clearly torn between her sister and her duty to Kathryn.

'Take a few days to stay with your sister,' Kathryn said and kissed her cheek. 'Go now, and do not feel guilty. I shall be perfectly all right.'

She smiled as the older woman hurried away. She liked the kindly Frenchwoman, but she would not be lonely. Maria and Elizabeta would keep her company until Lorenzo returned. Besides, she had many new books to read and she enjoyed walking in her garden.

Kathryn was sitting alone in the salon that looked out to the garden when Maria came to her a little later that day.

She looked at her awkwardly, standing with her hands clasped in front of her, an expression of contrition on her lovely face.

'I have come to beg your pardon,' Maria said. 'What I said to you earlier was unforgivable. You must know I did not mean it.'

'I know that you did not,' Kathryn said with a smile of forgiveness. She understood what it was to be unhappy and could feel Maria's distress. 'Sometimes we all say things that we do not mean. I am sorry that you must return to Spain, Maria, but I am sure that once you are home you will be much happier. Your father will not be ashamed of you—why should he?'

Maria looked down at her shoes. 'He is so strict and not always kind to me, Kathryn. I have never been as happy as I am here with you. Please do not send me away. If you asked it of him, Lorenzo would not make me go home.'

'My husband is right,' Kathryn said, knowing that she must be firm. Maria could not stay with them for ever. 'It would not be kind to keep you with us for always. If you return home you will find a husband to—'

'I do not wish to marry!' Maria's head came up and for a moment her eyes blazed with anger. 'But if you say I must go, then I have no choice.' Her eyes filled with tears. 'Only let me stay with you until after Christ's birthday, I beg you.'

'I shall ask Lorenzo if you may stay a little longer,' Kathryn said, 'though I cannot promise that he will relent. Now, sit with me and I shall order refreshments for us both. It is a lovely day and we should not waste it in argument.'

'Let me order them for you,' Maria said. 'If I try harder to please, perhaps you will allow me to stay.'

Kathryn frowned over the book she had been reading as Maria went into the house. Was she being unkind to let

Lorenzo send the girl home to her father? If he was very strict, he might make her life miserable if he considered that she had disgraced him. And yet, would he have gone to so much trouble to get her back, only to shut her in a nunnery? It did not seem likely and Kathryn could not truly understand why Maria did not want to go home. Had she been in her position she would have wanted to be restored to her family.

For a moment she thought about Lady Mary and Lord Mountfitchet. As yet there was no news of them and she could not help worrying that they might have been killed when the Turks invaded the island of Cyprus. Surely if they were alive they would have found a way to let Lorenzo know? Yet she would cling to hope for a little longer, for, as Lorenzo said, it took so long for letters to be delivered in these dangerous times.

She looked up as Maria returned, carrying a tray of drinks and the little almond cakes that Kathryn was so partial to and which their cook made so well. Maria set the tray down and then poured a drink for herself and Kathryn, offering her the plates of sweetmeats.

'I love these sweetmeats,' she said, taking two for herself and popping one in her mouth. 'We had them in the harem, or very similar ones, and they were always so delicious.'

Kathryn took the cake nearest to her and bit into it. It was very sweet, but the whole almond on top seemed to be bitter. She placed it on the table and took another, which was much nicer.

'Was something wrong with that one?' Maria asked.

'The almond was bitter,' Kathryn told her.

'Oh, yes, it does happen sometimes,' Maria said. 'But do have another, Kathryn. They are so delicious—try this sort, they are softer and very sweet.'

Kathryn tried the one she indicated, biting into the soft sweetmeat and chewing it with some pleasure. Just as she swallowed it she tasted a little bitterness and took a long drink of her wine to wash it down. She pushed the plate of cakes away from her. Something must be wrong with the almonds the cook had used for these cakes.

Maria's hand hovered over the cakes, choosing with care. She ate three more with every evidence of enjoying them and finished her wine.

'Would you mind if I went to Isabella's house this afternoon?' she said. 'She asked me to visit her yesterday and I said that I would if you did not need me.'

'Of course you may go,' Kathryn said. 'Elizabeta said that she might call so I shall stay here—but you should take one of the servants with you. It is safer if you do not walk alone, Maria.'

'Yes, of course,' the Spanish girl said. 'You must not worry about me, Kathryn. I shall be perfectly all right.' Her face was pale but proud, as if she were struggling to be brave.

'And you must not worry, Maria,' Kathryn said. 'I am sure your father loves you and he will be only too pleased to have you home.'

'Perhaps you are right,' Maria said and lowered her eyes. She stood up, keeping her head downcast. 'If you will excuse me, I believe I shall go up and get ready for my visit with Isabella.'

'Yes, of course,' Kathryn said, watching as the girl walked away, her head still downcast. Was she being unkind to let Lorenzo send her home?

It was when she was sitting with Elizabeta that afternoon that Kathryn felt the pain in her stomach. At first it was slight and caused her to flinch, but then, as it struck again, she gave a cry and doubled over.

'What is wrong?' Elizabeta asked. 'Are you ill, Kathryn?'

'Pain…' Kathryn gasped. 'I feel terrible…' She got to her feet, hurrying to the shrubbery where she vomited. Her head was spinning and she swayed as the ground seemed to come rushing up to meet her. She might have fainted if Elizabeta had not come to her, steadying her as she vomited twice more. 'I am so sorry…'

'There is no need to apologise,' Elizabeta said, looking at her anxiously. 'Have you been feeling ill long?'

'I felt well first thing this morning, but it has been building up since then—not pain, just an uncomfortable feeling in my stomach.'

'What have you eaten?' Elizabeta asked as Kathryn moaned and clutched at her stomach again. 'I think we should send for the physician at once. Where is Lorenzo?'

'He had to leave for two days on business,' Kathryn replied as Elizabeta helped her back to her seat. 'I do feel very ill—perhaps I should go up to my room?'

'I shall help you,' Elizabeta said, looking at her anxiously. 'And the physician must be summoned. I do not like this, Kathryn. I think you must have eaten something that disagreed with you.'

'I have eaten very little today other than bread, cheese and fruit,' Kathryn said. 'Oh, there were also the little cakes that Maria brought out for us as we sat in the garden this morning. One of them tasted quite bitter.'

'Did she eat any of them?' Elizabeta asked, eyes narrowing with suspicion.

'Yes, most of them,' Kathryn said. 'I hope she is not ill, for if they were the cause she would be much worse than I am.'

'Where is she this afternoon?'

'She went to visit Isabella.'

'That is strange. I am sure that Adriana told me Isabella and her father were invited to their house for the day.'

Kathryn was feeling too ill to argue. Perhaps she had made a mistake? Her head was spinning and she could hardly put one foot in front of the other as Elizabeta helped her to her room. Once there, she vomited into a basin, and then collapsed on the bed, feeling too weak and ill to know what was happening around her. She lay with her eyes closed, unaware of the anxious faces of the servants or that Elizabeta sat with her, bathing her forehead until the physician arrived.

She told him what she feared and he examined Kathryn carefully, checking for signs of poison, and then, after careful consideration, giving his verdict.

'She may have eaten something that made her ill,' he said. 'But I do not think it was poison. Had it been, she would probably have been dead by now—and some poisons leave a smell on the breath and a blueness about the mouth. I believe she has taken a small dose of something that might in larger doses be dangerous, but I think she will be well enough when whatever upset her has passed through. It may be that something she ate was not quite fresh.'

'Kathryn told me that she ate only cheese, bread and fruit.'

'It must have been the cheese,' he said. 'It was most unpleasant for her, but I have given her something to settle her stomach and I think you will find that she will sleep now.'

Elizabeta thanked him, but she was not satisfied with his explanation. The vomiting had been violent and she suspected that something had been put into the cakes to cause Kathryn to be ill. Perhaps she had not eaten enough to make her ill enough to die, but the results were harmful. Maria was spiteful enough to play such a trick; she had proved that when she knocked Elizabeta's drink into her lap—but had she meant to kill Kathryn?

The poison must have been something she had taken from the garden, for it was unlikely she could have access to the poisons sometimes used by physicians and apothecaries in their work. And that, of course, would make it more difficult to judge the amount needed to kill, if it had been her intention. She might only have wished to make Kathryn ill out of a spiteful impulse.

Kathryn was resting for the moment. Elizabeta got up from the chair beside the bed and went out into the hall. She knew that Maria's room was at the far end, and she hesitated only a moment before making her way there. Perhaps it was wrong of her, but she needed proof before she could accuse the Spanish girl of trying to kill her hostess, and she might find what she sought amongst Maria's things. It was wrong of her to go through the Spanish girl's private things, but Elizabeta quashed her scruples and began to search the various chests and cupboards.

Her search took only a few minutes, and at the end she found nothing incriminating. What puzzled her was the flimsy harem costume hidden at the bottom of one of the chests, and a beautiful necklet that looked like a huge ruby surrounded by pearls. She turned it in her hand, wondering if it opened somehow for the gold backing was thick and might hold a secret. Then, as she heard a sound behind her, she turned to find that Maria had come in.

'What are you doing with that?' Maria came towards her, snatching the necklet from her hands. 'That is mine! You have no right to touch it. You have no right to be in my room.'

'Kathryn has been ill,' Elizabeta said. 'The physician says that something she ate must have made her so—but perhaps something in the food should not have been there.'

'You are accusing me of poisoning her!' Maria cried, her dark eyes flashing with temper. 'You have always hated me! You tried to turn Kathryn against me!'

'I do not hate you,' Elizabeta said calmly. 'But neither do I trust you. You made eyes at Lorenzo from the start—and if you could get rid of Kathryn, you think he might turn to you.'

'That is all you know!' Maria cried. 'I have a lover who wants me—he gave me this.' She was smiling now, her eyes bright with triumph. 'If Kathryn has been ill, perhaps it was you who poisoned her. I was not here—besides, if I wanted her dead, she would be dead.'

'But you made her ill,' Elizabeta said. 'I know that you did it, Maria. If anything happens to her—if she dies of a mysterious illness—I shall see that you are hung for murder.'

'Get out of my room,' Maria cried. 'You are a liar. I did nothing to harm Kathryn. She is my friend. You can prove nothing. Besides, I shall be leaving very soon now.'

'The sooner the better,' Elizabeta said. She did not believe in Maria's protests of innocence. 'I intend to stay with Kathryn while she is ill. If I find you in her room I shall have you confined to yours—and if anything happens to her, I shall make sure that you are punished for it. Kathryn may be deceived in you, but I know you for the evil wretch you are.'

'One day you will be sorry for your unkindness to me,' Maria said, her eyes flashing with anger. 'The man I love is very powerful. You will suffer for this, believe me.'

'I do not fear you or your threats, whore,' Elizabeta said. 'I do not know where you got that ruby or the harem

costume you hide in your chest—but I know you for
what you are. And when Lorenzo returns, I shall tell him
to be rid of you at once.'

Kathryn's head was aching terribly when she woke to
find Elizabeta sitting by her side the next morning. She
stared at her in bewilderment for a moment as she tried to
remember, and then, as the memory of her illness returned,
she said, 'Have you been here all night?'

'I was worried about you,' Elizabeta said and squeezed
her hand. 'You were so very ill that I was anxious—and I
would not leave you while Lorenzo is away. I do not trust
that Spanish girl.'

Kathryn pushed herself up against the pillows. Her
stomach ached, as did her head, but she was feeling much
better now the sickness had gone.

'You should not have sat up with me all night,' she said.
'I am sure Maria was not the cause of my sickness. How
could she be?'

'Perhaps she put something into the almond cakes—or
your drink,' Elizabeta said. 'I do not know, Kathryn, but I
am sure that she had something to do with what happened
to you. I am not sure if it was just a spiteful trick to make
you ill—or something more sinister.'

'Perhaps.' Kathryn sighed. She did not feel well enough
to think about Maria. 'Lorenzo had told her that morning
that she was soon to go home. She begged me to persuade
him to let her stay—but to tell you the truth, I do not really
want her here.'

'And why should you? There is something sly about
her—and she tells lies.'

'Yes, I think she does.' Kathryn hesitated. She could not
tell Elizabeta that the Spanish girl had been imprisoned in

a harem for some months, for that would be unfair. 'You may be right about her being spiteful enough to make me ill, but surely she would not try to poison me?'

'It was not a deadly poison or you would have died,' Elizabeta said. 'Yet I think she intended to make you very ill. Be careful of her, Kathryn. She might be capable of anything.'

'Yes, I shall,' she promised. 'And now you must go home, for your husband will worry about you.'

'But then you will be alone…'

Kathryn shook her head. 'I am glad that you were here when I became ill, and that you called the physician—but I do not think Maria intends to kill me. As you said, if she had wanted me dead I would be already. Besides, I shall not eat anything she brings me in future.'

'If you are sure?' Elizabeta looked at her doubtfully.

'I have a house full of servants, who will come if I call,' Kathryn said and smiled at her. 'I shall be perfectly all right. I promise you.'

'Very well, if it is your wish that I go.' Her friend smiled ruefully. 'I dare say my husband will be imagining that I have left him. It is foolish of him to think it, for he is kind and generous, and my little flirtations mean nothing. I have never been unfaithful, though I believe he fears it.'

'Please tell him that I am very grateful for what you did for me.'

After Elizabeta had finally been persuaded to leave, Kathryn rang for her maid and asked for water to be brought so that she could bathe. She had sweated a great deal while she was ill and she felt in need of a bath. The hip-bath was brought to her chamber and filled with warm, scented water. Kathryn's maid helped her to disrobe and to step into the water.

'Do you wish me to wash your back, my lady?'

'Not just for the moment,' Kathryn said. 'I am feeling very tired and I would like to relax in the water for a while—but stay within call, for I shall need you in a little while.'

'I shall be in the next chamber, my lady,' the girl replied. 'I am going though your gowns to see if any of them are in need of the services of the seamstress.'

'Thank you, Lisa,' Kathryn said. 'I shall feel better if I know that you are near by.'

She did not think that Maria would do anything to harm her, and she had only Elizabeta's suspicions to make her believe that her illness had been caused by the other girl's spite. Yet for the moment she would be very careful.

She lay back in the warm water, closing her eyes and feeling sleepy. Whatever had made her ill was most unpleasant, for her whole body had begun to ache and she felt drained. She would not want to go through an experience like that again.

Kathryn wondered where Lorenzo was and if he was thinking of her. She wished that he was with her—she would have liked to tell him what was on her mind, and she would feel much safer if he were with her. She was on the verge of sleep when she heard the slight sound behind her.

'Is that you, Lisa?' she asked and then something struck her on the back of her head. Just before she lost consciousness she smelled the heavy perfume that Maria had been wearing the day she first came to the house.

Lorenzo ran into the house, feeling that odd sense of anxiety that had hung over him throughout the night. It was his unease that had prompted him to cut short his business and return a day sooner than he had anticipated. It was foolish, of course, but he had the feeling that Kathryn was in danger.

As he entered the villa, he heard a cry from the direction of Kathryn's room and ran towards it, his heart racing. Entering, he saw that the maid Lisa was struggling with someone—Maria! As he hesitated, he saw that Maria had a heavy iron candlestick in her hand, which Lisa was trying to take from her. He rushed in, capturing Maria from behind, holding her as she struggled uselessly against him.

Glancing towards the hip-bath, he saw that Lisa had rushed to drag her mistress upright and was now set on pulling her from the bath. Kathryn had a slight wound to the back of her head, but even as he pushed Maria away from him with a cry of anguish, he heard a faint moaning sound from Kathryn and went to help Lisa lower her to the ground.

'Who did this to her?' he demanded.

'It was her!' Maria screamed. 'The maid. I came in and found her. I was trying to help Kathryn.'

'No…' Kathryn's lips moved with difficulty. 'Maria…'

'Call for more servants,' Lorenzo said. 'She is not to leave this house! I shall deal with her later.'

Maria backed away from him, then turned and ran from the room. Lorenzo let her go. If she succeeded in leaving the house, she would be found. For the moment all that mattered to him was his wife.

He lifted her gently in his arms, carrying her towards the bed and laying her down. Bending over her, he smoothed the hair from her face.

'The physician shall be called,' he said. 'I should never have left you alone with her. I knew she was not to be trusted.'

Several servants had responded to Lisa's call. Lorenzo asked for towels and dried Kathryn's body himself, turning her carefully to look at the wound to her head, which was slight.

'There is only a small cut,' he said. 'She could not have hit you hard.'

'I moved and the blow was deflected,' Kathryn said and caught back a sob. 'But it hurts, Lorenzo.'

'Yes, my love,' he said. 'I am sure that it is painful. She shall be punished for what she has done.' He glanced around the room. 'Where is Veronique? Is she not here?'

'She had a letter to tell her that her sister was very ill just after you left, Lorenzo. She asked if she might go to her and of course I told her that she had my permission…'

'And that wretched girl took advantage of her absence and mine.' Lorenzo looked furious. 'She will be very sorry when I have finished with her, Kathryn.'

'Send her away,' Kathryn said. 'I do not want her punished—but she cannot stay here any longer. I think that she tried to poison me yesterday, but she did not know enough about the substance she used and it served only to make me sick.'

'She tried to poison you?' His face darkened. 'The evil bitch! I should kill her—but it will serve well enough if we send her back to her father.'

'Yes.' Kathryn smiled at him. 'I think she fears he will discover the truth—that she has been Rachid's woman. I think she must have loved him, for she has spoken of having a lover who would marry her.'

'You suspected that too?' Lorenzo nodded. 'It must be the reason she tried to kill you. I think she was angry because he exchanged her for his son—and she wanted to punish us. It is strange, but some women do fall in love with their masters, despite their captivity. She resented being sent away from him and took her spite out on you.'

Kathryn nodded, too exhausted to say more for the moment. She thought that Maria's plan might go deeper— that she might have been following someone else's orders. It might be that Rachid had promised to marry her if she could find some way of destroying his enemy. She would tell Lorenzo about it later, but for the moment all she wanted to do was sleep.

'Yes, sleep, my dearest,' Lorenzo said in a voice that she had never heard from him. 'I shall stay by your side. I shall not leave you until that evil woman has been taken…'

Chapter Nine

A week had passed and there was no sign of Maria, though Lorenzo had men out searching. Kathryn was now recovered both from the stomach upset and the blow to her head, which had not been serious even though it had rendered her unconscious for a moment.

'Had Lisa not been there, she might have drowned you,' Lorenzo said, his face dark with anger. 'She hoped to make it look like an accident, for she wished to deceive us all.'

'It seems that she did want me dead.' Kathryn sighed. 'It grieves me to think that she would act in such a way, Lorenzo. We were not her enemies. You had rescued her from Rachid…'

'Evidently she did not wish to be rescued,' Lorenzo said, frowning. 'If he had chosen her as his favourite…it might be that she enjoyed her position in the harem.'

'She is very beautiful and what you say may be true,' Kathryn agreed. 'When I offered to burn the clothes she was wearing when she arrived, she begged to keep them. And if she did not want to leave the harem, it may be that she hoped to return if…' She hesitated, for it seemed unlikely that Rachid would use a woman against his enemy.

'If I were dead or captured?' Lorenzo nodded. 'Yes, I had thought of that as a possibility. Had I been attracted to her, she might have managed to lure me into a trap. And yet she attacked you—why? You had shown her nothing but kindness.'

Kathryn was thoughtful. 'Perhaps she was jealous because I had the man I loved while she had nothing? She must have known that you had no interest in her, and she may have thought it would grieve you if I died.'

'Yes, perhaps,' he agreed. 'We shall forget her, Kathryn. She is not worth wasting our breath or our thoughts on. When she is found, she will be dealt with appropriately.'

'You will not be too severe?' Kathryn looked at him anxiously. 'She has done terrible things, but I would not have her punished beyond what is right.'

'Her punishment according to the law would at the least be imprisonment, and perhaps a flogging.'

'No! That is too harsh,' Kathryn said. 'Can you not simply return her to her father?'

'Is that what you want?'

'Yes, I think so. I know what she did was wrong, but I am well again, and I could not live with her death on my conscience.'

'Very well,' Lorenzo said. 'It seems that I must give way, my love, though against my better judgement. Yet she shall be returned to her father and he shall be her judge, for I shall tell him of her behaviour while our guest. And now we shall talk of her no more. She is not important.'

'Tell me where we are going this evening?' Kathryn said. It was the first time that she had been out in a week and he had not told her where they were going, only that it was to be a surprise.

'You must wait in patience, Madonna,' he told her and bent to kiss her lightly on the mouth. 'You will see in a few hours and until then it shall be a secret.'

The secret turned out to be a huge masque ball, given in her honour and attended by all their friends. When Kathryn prepared for the evening she was given a new gown in a beautiful green silk; it had full panniers over a petticoat of a pale ivory silk, which was embroidered with appliqué and brilliants. Her cloak was of matching velvet, her mask a delicate silver thing that made her mouth look soft and kissable.

Lorenzo was wearing his customary black, though the sleeves were slashed with green silk to match her gown. He kissed her before they left, giving her a necklet of beautiful emeralds that sat like a little collar on her slender throat.

'It is lovely, Lorenzo. You spoil me.' She gazed up at him and he thought that the shine in her eyes put the jewels to shame.

'You have become very precious to me,' he told her in a voice that made her tremble inside. 'When I thought that I might lose you I realised that my life would be empty without you. I have not wanted to care for you so much, Kathryn, but I believe that I do…perhaps more than I had thought.'

'My love…' Kathryn's eyes were bright with tears, though she blinked them away. She had never thought to hear such words from him and they filled her with emotion. She had been content enough to be his wife and love him, but to have his love would be wonderful.

He smiled at her, kissing her hand, and then leading her out into the warm night. 'Come, Kathryn, our friends will be waiting for us.'

It was a perfect evening. Everyone was so kind to her, kissing her and telling her how much they loved her and how distressed they had been by what had happened to her. It seemed that none of them had truly liked Maria, and most had not trusted her.

'Lorenzo should never have let her stay,' Elizabeta said. It was at her house the party was being held, and she made a great fuss of Kathryn. 'I hope we shall remain friends when you return to Venice,' she told her. 'Perhaps you will invite me to stay with you sometimes.'

'I should like that very much,' Kathryn told her. 'I do not think Lorenzo can spare the time to take me home yet, but of course we shall go one day.' She thought she would miss the friends she had made in Rome, but she would make more in Venice and Lorenzo was talking of buying a summer villa in Rome so that they might spend some time here each year.

It seemed to Kathryn that night that she had never been as happy as she was then. She danced every dance, and most of them with Lorenzo. He seemed a different person, the grave looks and cold eyes banished as if they had never been. Indeed, several of his friends remarked on it to Kathryn, telling her that marriage must suit him for he had never been as relaxed and apparently happy as he now was.

'I think that you have worked a miracle, Kathryn,' Paolo told her. 'Or perhaps it is love?'

Perhaps it was love. Kathryn could not have wished for a more attentive or generous husband, and the evening passed in a haze of pleasure. It seemed that she had everything that she had ever dreamed of, her happiness complete.

It was very late when they left the celebrations. The torches had burned low in their sconces and there was very little light for clouds obscured the moon. As they emerged into the street, they met a man who was about to knock at the door and Lorenzo gave a cry of pleasure.

'Michael! It is good to see you back, my friend. How is your father?'

'Much better,' Michael said, smiling oddly. 'He lectured me about finding myself a wife—and that means he is well again.'

Lorenzo laughed. 'We have missed you. Will you not return to the house with us? We have much to discuss.'

'It was for this purpose that I came here tonight,' Michael said and he looked at Kathryn, smiling at her. 'I have good news, Kathryn. A letter from Lord Mountfitchet.'

'From Uncle Charles?' Kathryn felt the sting of tears behind her eyes. She had thought her happiness could not be bettered, but this news was wonderful. 'Oh, that is good news indeed. Is he well—and Lady Mary?'

'Yes, they are well. I thought it best to open the letter, though it was addressed to you, Lorenzo. It seems that Lady Mary was taken ill on the journey and Lord Mountfitchet ordered his ship to put into Sicily. They never got as far as Cyprus. When they heard of the invasion they decided to stay where they were for the time being. Because of the war, it was difficult to send letters, and Lady Mary was quite ill for a while. When Lord Mountfitchet was able to send a letter, he was not sure where you would be, so he sent it to Venice.'

'That is truly good news,' Lorenzo said. 'I am so pleased to—'

'My God!' Michael cried and suddenly gave him a great shove to one side. 'What do you think you are doing?'

Kathryn screamed as she realised that Michael had seen what neither she nor Lorenzo had noticed. A woman had come up upon them out of the shadows and she had a knife with a long thin blade, which she had attempted to plunge into Lorenzo's back. Because of Michael's swift action she had missed her target, but she was screaming wildly, out of control as she turned her vicious blade on the man who had thwarted her evil intent.

'I shall kill him!' Maria screamed. 'He took me from the man I loved. I was to have been Rachid's wife. When he is dead, Rachid will take me back again.'

Michael struggled with her, but somehow her blade struck him in the chest and he gave a cry of pain, staggering back as the blood spurted. Lorenzo caught Maria's arm as she attempted to strike again, twisting it back so that she screamed with pain this time and the knife fell to the floor. He kicked it away, jerking her arm up so that she was unable to fight him, and she went limp in his grasp.

Kathryn was bending over Michael as he clutched at his chest, and now people were spilling out of Elizabeta's house, alarmed by the noise and Maria's screaming.

'Take the bitch,' Lorenzo commanded as some of his men came running out of the shadows. 'We shall deal with her later. How is he, Kathryn?' He looked down at Michael as she cradled him in her arms.

'I fear he is in a bad way,' Kathryn said, her cheeks pale from shock. 'The wound went deep and he is bleeding badly.'

'Bring him into the house,' Elizabeta's voice commanded. 'My servants shall go for the physician at once and we shall do what we can for him.'

Kathryn watched as Michael was lifted and carried into the house. Lorenzo followed as she did, feeling bewildered amongst all the consternation. Everyone was shocked. It had been such a lovely evening and now a man was wounded, perhaps fatally.

How could it have happened? Kathryn heard the shocked whispers, for Michael was popular with many of the assembled company. People were saying that Maria must be punished, that she deserved to hang for her crime—and there were some who suggested burning, for she must surely be in league with the devil to have done such wicked things. Her attempt to murder Kathryn, and then Lorenzo—who would have been her victim if Michael had not acted so swiftly.

Kathryn followed Elizabeta as they carried Michael up the stairs to one of the many guest chambers. Together they prepared the bed for him, and made him as comfortable as was possible. He was still living, though he had lost consciousness as he was carried in, the blood soaking through his shirt and doublet.

'Help me remove his things,' Elizabeta instructed. 'We must try to staunch the flow of blood until the surgeon can tend him.'

Kathryn obeyed her, for it was obvious that she knew what she was about. Between them they cut away his doublet and shirt, leaving only his hose. Servants had brought linen and water, and Elizabeta cleansed the wound. Kathryn helped her to bind it tightly. In all this time Michael had not opened his eyes.

'That bitch will pay for this,' Lorenzo said when they had finished their task. Grief was working in his face. 'Damn her to hell for this night's work! She has killed one of the best men that ever lived.'

'No, no, my love,' Kathryn said. 'Michael is strong. He has every chance of recovery.'

'You have not seen men die,' he said his voice harsh. 'I do not believe in miracles. If Michael dies, so shall she!'

'Lorenzo…' Kathryn's throat caught, for she knew that beneath the anger was a terrible grief. Michael was as a brother to him, his closest friend. 'Please do not…' She meant only to comfort him, but his eyes glittered with anger.

'Do not plead for her life, Kathryn,' he said coldly. 'She is an evil woman and she deserves her fate. I would see her dead for what she has done this night.'

'Where are you going?' she asked as he turned to leave the room.

'Stay here, Kathryn,' he said. 'Elizabeta may need your help. I shall return later.'

Kathryn stared after him. How could such a terrible thing have happened? It had been such a lovely evening. Lorenzo had been so pleased to have his friend back, and Michael had brought her good news—and now it looked as if it might all end in tragedy.

Why had he ever traded Rachid's son for the Spanish girl? Lorenzo cursed himself as he left the house. It would have been better to have given Hassan the swift death he had pleaded for and left the girl to her fate. It was his fault for allowing himself to feel compassion. He had always known that to become soft was to invite disaster. Only a hard man could exist in the world he inhabited and he had been a fool to imagine he could change.

His feelings for Kathryn had made him soft, and he had relaxed his guard. He had not been aware of Maria. His instincts had let him down. In a mood of exhilaration and excitement, he had allowed a woman to murder his best friend.

Ransom Bride

It would not have happened at any other time! It would be his fault if Michael died. He should have been more aware. Instead of letting the girl live as a guest in his home, he should have kept her a prisoner and sent her back to her father immediately.

His love for Kathryn had made him weak. He had always known that he could not afford to love a woman, and now Michael lay close to death because he had betrayed his own rules.

His fists clenched at his sides. It would not happen again. He must be on his guard in future for, if a woman could come so close to destroying him and all he cared for, his true enemies would succeed where she had failed. Next time it might be Kathryn who paid the price.

Michael lay close to death for three days and nights. Kathryn stayed at Elizabeta's house to help nurse him. She saw Lorenzo only a few times, briefly, just to report on his friend's progress. Yet she sensed that an icy barrier had formed between them. Lorenzo was deliberately shutting her out.

What had she done to deserve this? Did Lorenzo blame her because Maria had attacked his best friend? She had asked that the Spanish girl might be allowed to stay with them at the beginning—but how could she have known what Maria was capable of doing? Surely he could not blame her for Maria's crime? And yet it seemed he must, for he had withdrawn from her. She had never known him to be so cold, so remote. Even at the beginning he had liked to tease her—now she felt that he had shut her out of his life.

After the third day, Michael's fever began to abate. He woke once when Kathryn was tending him, smiling at her as she bathed his forehead and gave him cool water to drink.

'You are very kind.'

'You saved Lorenzo's life. I would not have you die for it, Michael.'

'He is my friend—my brother.'

'Yes, I know.' She smiled at him. 'Sleep now. You have good friends to care for you.'

Michael closed his eyes. Kathryn turned to see Lorenzo watching her from the doorway. She thought his expression very odd, for it was a mixture of remorse and…she was not sure what else.

'How is he?'

'A little better, I think.' She moved towards him. 'I have stayed here for his sake and because we cannot expect to leave everything to Elizabeta, generous as she is. Once Michael is well enough, we can arrange for him to come home to us.'

'You think he will recover?'

'I pray that he will, Lorenzo.'

'I have no faith in prayers.' His expression hardened.

'Yet sometimes they are answered.'

'Perhaps.' His gaze narrowed. 'I am sending a ship to Sicily. What message would you have me send to your friends?'

'Tell them that we are married and that I am happy.'

'Very well.' He hesitated, then, 'What would you have me do with Maria?'

'If Michael had died, she must have been punished by the laws of Rome,' Kathryn said. 'Perhaps she should be. I do not know. I would wish to send her home, and yet perhaps she should be punished.'

'Her father is expected here tomorrow. I could let them

go—take the ransom and be rid of her. Her father shall know what she is and that shall be her punishment. Is that what you wish?'

'You must do as you think best.'

'You do not beg for leniency?'

'She might have killed you,' Kathryn said. 'And she has sorely harmed Michael. She deserves some punishment…'

'For myself, I would have her cast into prison to rot.'

'Lorenzo! I would not have you speak so harshly.'

'Life has made me harsh, Kathryn.' An odd, wintry smile flickered in his eyes. 'Yet it seems that Michael will live, because of you, I suspect. Perhaps I shall let Maria's father deal with her, as he thinks best.'

'If she has lost the man she loves, I dare say she will suffer enough.'

Lorenzo inclined his head. 'I am summoned to an important conference. It may be some days before I return.'

'Take care, my love.' Kathryn went to him, putting her arms about him. He did not take her into his embrace, and she felt him stiffen, as if resisting. 'Lorenzo—have I angered you?'

'You have done nothing wrong,' he said. 'But I was at fault in marrying you, Kathryn. You deserve so much more than I can give you.'

'I love you. You must know that?'

'Unfortunately, I cannot afford to love you,' he said and drew away from her. 'It was a mistake to think that I could be a true husband to you, Kathryn. Forgive me. I should have sent you home to your father when we thought Lord Mountfitchet lost.' He put her from him. 'Everything I own is at your disposal, but do not expect me to love you.'

The hurt welled inside Kathryn. She could not answer

him for he had wounded her beyond bearing. Tears were close. He must not see her weep for her pride's sake. She moved away from him, bending over Michael, bathing his forehead. When she looked round, she saw that Lorenzo had gone.

How could he reject her now? His loving had been so sweet and tender—how could it have meant nothing to him?

On the night of Elizabeta's masque she had been so sure that he loved her, but now…what had changed him? Michael had saved his life at a terrible cost to himself, but with God's help he would recover. Why had Lorenzo set his face against her?

Kathryn could not know of the agony it had cost him to take the decision. She only knew that her heart felt as if it were breaking.

Michael's recovery was slow but sure over the next week. By the end of the week he was well enough to be moved to Kathryn's home.

'Are you sure you wish to have me?' he asked as she moved about the room, making him comfortable. 'I could go to an inn now that I am so much better. You do not need to nurse me for I am almost myself again and would not wish to be a trouble to you.'

'You will do no such thing,' Kathryn said. 'Veronique will have returned from her sister's by now and she will help me to care for you. Besides, Lorenzo is still away and you may bear me company.'

'He will be making preparations to put to sea soon,' Michael said and frowned. 'I should be with him…' He groaned as he tried to get up from the bed. 'No, it is no use. I am too weak. I should be of no help. I fear he will have to do without me for some weeks.'

'You must not strain yourself,' Kathryn scolded. 'Lorenzo would rather have you stay here in Rome until you are well again.'

'I fear I have no choice.'

'You will be better soon,' Kathryn said and smiled at him. She felt comfortable with him, for they had become good friends of late.

Lorenzo returned a few days after Michael was moved to the villa. He spent some time sitting with his friend, who had been brought out into the garden to enjoy the sunshine, and afterwards thanked Kathryn for caring for him so well.

'I had plans for Christ's birthday,' he told her. 'But I fear I must leave you again, Kathryn. I have a gift for you— and you will not be lonely. You have your friends, Veronique and Michael to bear you company.'

It was almost as if those nights of passion had never been, as if he were a stranger, a distant relative who was bound to care for her comfort, but found it a burden. She wanted to cry out that she would always be lonely without him, that she loved him and her heart was breaking, but she said nothing. Her grief was still too raw, and it was pride that kept her from weeping and begging him to let things be as they had been before that terrible night. Yet she held back her tears.

She loved him so much, but he did not love her. The knowledge was almost unbearable and yet she bore it bravely, refusing to shed the tears that burned behind her eyes. She would not beg him to love her.

Over the next few weeks, Lorenzo's visits were brief, and Kathryn thought that each time he seemed to withdraw from her more. It was as if they were strangers, as if he had never held her in his arms and kissed her. The ache in her heart grew harder to bear and sometimes she did not know how she could live with it. Perhaps it might be better if she had died when Maria tried to kill her, better than this life without Lorenzo's love.

One morning, after a brief visit from her husband, Kathryn was alone in the garden and unable to hold back her tears. Why had Lorenzo turned from her? What had she done to make him look at her so coldly?

'Why are you crying, Madonna?'

Michael's voice made her turn in surprise. She had thought herself alone and was embarrassed to be caught giving way to her grief.

'Oh…' she said, wiping her face with the back of her hand. 'I did not hear you coming, Michael.'

'I am sorry to intrude,' he said. 'But will you not tell me what is wrong—or can I guess? I do not know how Lorenzo can treat you so coldly. He is a fool and so I shall tell him next time I see him.'

'No, you must not,' she cried. 'He has done nothing that should make you cease to be his friend. It is simply…' The hurt welled up inside her. 'He does not love me.'

She felt the touch of his hand on her shoulder. 'I am sure that Lorenzo does love you,' Michael said, his voice deep with emotion. 'It is just that he is afraid of his feelings— afraid to let go of the hate inside him.'

'But he was so loving to me until…' Her voice died away. 'He seems so angry, so cold.'

'Do not despair, Kathryn,' Michael said and his voice was soft, concerned. 'You know that I would do anything to make you happy.' As she turned to look at him, the warmth in his eyes sent a tingle down her spine.

'Michael…'

He placed a finger to her lips. 'Do not say it, Kathryn. I know that you love Lorenzo. But I wanted you to be aware of my feelings for you. If in the future you should need a friend, I shall be there for you.'

Kathryn's eyes filled with tears. He was kind and good and generous, and she had grown fond of him—but her heart was given to Lorenzo.

'Damn you!' Lorenzo said as Michael finished speaking. Three weeks had passed since his last visit to the villa, and Kathryn's eyes had grown sadder with the days. 'Who gave you the right to meddle in my affairs?'

'Kathryn is your wife and she deserves better from you,' Michael said. 'As for what right I have—we have been friends for years. If anyone has the right to tell you that you are throwing away something precious and good, then it must be I, deny it as you will.'

'You are in love with her yourself,' Lorenzo accused, feeling a prick of jealousy as he saw the truth in Michael's eyes.

'If she did not love you—if you had not married her—I should have asked her to be my wife,' Michael admitted.

'She would be better as your wife, Michael. I was wrong to marry her—selfish. I cannot give her what she needs. I cannot, dare not, love her.'

'Will you waste your life in bitterness?' Michael asked, his eyes narrowed and angry. 'I know that you suffered at that monster's hand, but nothing can change that. It is over. You are rich and powerful. You have a chance of happiness with Kathryn—throw it away and you will live alone with your regret.'

'You do not know what you ask,' Lorenzo said. 'If I love her…if I let go of what is inside me, I am nothing.'

'Then you are nothing,' Michael told him. 'And I am sorry for you.'

Lorenzo watched as he walked away, going into the house. Anger raged inside him, but with the anger was remorse, for he knew that Michael was right, and he knew something more. The path he had chosen was the coward's path. He was afraid to love Kathryn, afraid of what his life would be without her if he allowed himself to love her.

The stroke of an assassin's knife could take her as it had almost taken Michael. And yet, what was his life now—was it worth the living?

Lorenzo faced the truth at last. The hatred had gone, driven out by Kathryn's love. He had fought against her, but she was there inside him. It was love for her that had made him send Rachid's son back to him—a love that he could no longer deny, try as he might.

But had he destroyed her love for him?

Kathryn was in her chamber going through her gowns with Lisa. She looked round as the maid suddenly bobbed a curtsy and left the room, her heart beating wildly as she saw him. It was odd, but he had lost that cold angry look which had haunted her for weeks.

'Lorenzo?' She looked at him, her throat tight, unable to trust her senses. 'Is something wrong?'

'Have I made you hate me, Kathryn?'

'I could never hate you. Do you not know how much I love you?' She looked at him, her heart in her eyes, no pleading or reproaches, but simple love.

'You should hate me for the way I have treated you these past weeks,' he said. 'But I beg you to forgive me.

It was because of Michael. I did not sense that Maria was there that night. Always, I have known when I was in danger of being attacked. It was a sixth sense, an awareness that has saved my life many times. I felt that in letting myself love you I was losing that part of me—and I was afraid. It might have been you whom Maria attacked. I have enemies, Kathryn. There may be others who would seek to harm me through you—and I was afraid that if I loved you, if I let myself soften, I might become weak and be unable to protect you.'

'Lorenzo…' Tears sprang to her eyes as she moved towards him. 'I thought you blamed me—had turned against me…'

'I do love you,' he said. 'But it is not easy for me to admit it or to show it. You accused me of being harsh, and it is true. I have had to be hard, to be ruthless. It is the only way I could live. But perhaps I could change, perhaps there is another way to live. I must keep my promise to fight with the Holy League, but I think…I have no heart to continue my feud with Rachid. It is not that I have forgiven him, but…it no longer seems important.'

'My love.' Kathryn moved closer, putting her arms about him. She laid her head against his chest as after a moment's hesitation, his arms closed about her. They stood in silence for several minutes, just holding each other, his lips against her hair. 'We could go home to England. My father would welcome us there. You could begin a new life.'

'Yes, perhaps,' he said and smiled oddly as she looked up at him. 'Once the Holy League has fought its battle with the Turks, these seas will be a much safer place. I might perhaps continue to trade in fine wines, Kathryn—but I do not think that I shall need to be constantly at war as I have been these last years.'

'I am so glad that you have told me what was in your heart,' she said, lifting her face for his kiss, which was sweet and tender, concealing the fires beneath. 'I have been so unhappy—I thought that I had lost you.'

His eyes were dark with self-condemnation. 'Forgive me, Kathryn. I was a brute to you...'

She placed a finger to his lips. 'No more. I understand. I have always understood what drove you, my love. Come, let us go down and walk in the gardens. We must make the most of our time together, for Michael tells me that you plan to leave soon.'

'I fear I must,' Lorenzo said. 'The fleet is gathering and my galleys are a big part of what is to happen—but we have a few days, my love.'

She held her hand out to him and he took it. 'Then I am content,' she said, looking up at him with eyes that told their own story. 'Your love is all I want, Lorenzo.'

Kathryn turned in her husband's arms, feeling the warmth and strength of his body. He had hurt her so desperately, but she was ready to forgive and to love, for she understood that he had been in turmoil. She would never quite understand what drove him, for only someone who had suffered as he had could know what he felt, but she loved and that was enough. She was his wife, his woman, and at last, she believed his love. From the first she had sensed that they belonged together, and it was this deep instinct that had carried her throughout the uncertain days. She belonged to Lorenzo and, whatever came between them, that bond would always hold her.

His arms went round her, drawing her close, his hands stroking the slender arch of her back, caressing her, arousing her to passion. She gave herself up to the urgency of their loving. So much time had been wasted and they had so little left. His kisses brought her to a sweet ecstasy that consumed them both in the fires of love, and then at last, satiated and content, they slept in each other's arms.

And when Lorenzo woke with the dawn, he lay looking down at her lovely face, drinking in her beauty, absorbing every detail into his mind so that he would carry it with him in the weeks and perhaps months ahead when they would be apart.

Kathryn kissed Lorenzo, a long, sweet, lingering kiss that almost tore her heart from her body, and then stood back, letting him go. She knew that it might be many months before she saw him again, but it was the price she had to pay.

Lorenzo had paid his own price in loving her. He had fought his battle and come through it for her sake, and she could do no less for his. She would let him go with a smile.

'Promise me that you will take care of yourself, Kathryn.'

'I shall do nothing foolish,' she said. 'Veronique is here to bear me company, and my friends will visit me often. When I go shopping, it will be with them and a servant to watch over us.'

'I do not think Rachid will attempt to abduct you in Rome,' Lorenzo told her. 'I asked Michael if he would stay and guard you for me, but he says that he wants to fight by my side and I must accept his will. I am leaving men you can trust to watch over you.'

'You must not worry for my sake.'

'Nor you for mine,' he said and smiled in the old, teasing way. 'I shall return to plague you again, my love.'

'See that you do,' she said and tossed her head proudly. 'And now you must go. You have your duty to the League.'

'Yes,' he said. 'May God watch over you, Kathryn.'

'And over you, my love.'

She watched as he walked away, her heart aching. Her nails were turned into her palms and it took all her strength of will to let him go. He had come to her in love at last and it would break her heart if she should lose him now.

Chapter Ten

Their ships were sailing in precise formation. After weeks of talking and delay, Don John of Austria had given his orders and a mood of elation had spread throughout the fleet.

'At last we shall have some action,' Michael said to Lorenzo, when he came on board for a meeting. I had begun to think we should spend the autumn in wasted argument again.'

'This venture has been blessed by the Pope and we have a very capable commander in Don John. I believe that this time something good will happen.'

'I pray you are right,' Michael answered, looking thoughtful.

'There will be no more talk of turning back. If our information is correct, the Turks are settled for the winter at Lepanto.'

'Unless they retreat to Constantinople.'

It was a question their spies had been unable to answer for certain as yet, but if luck was with them they would catch their quarry at Lepanto.

'I must return to my own galley,' Michael said when their meeting had finished. He looked at his commander, noticing the shadows beneath his eyes. It seemed to him that Lorenzo had suffered some sleepless nights and he wondered what had caused them, for he knew that Lorenzo did not fear battle. However, he was wise enough not to mention it. 'God be with you, my friend.

'And with you,' Lorenzo replied. 'God protect us all if it comes to a battle.'

It was the first time he had ever replied in that way. There *was* a difference in Lorenzo. Michael had noticed it more often of late, though as yet he was uncertain as to what it meant.

Lorenzo woke from the dream with the images still fresh in his mind. At first he had been in a house—in a room. It was a room he knew well and filled with things he admired, in particular a banner of gold and a suit of black armour.

He had not dreamed of the house before. Always his dream was of a beach and a youth struggling against the men who finally succeeded in capturing him. Yet perhaps that particular dream was real. Perhaps it was a memory of the day he had been taken. If that were so, then all the other things he half-remembered might also be true.

Shaking his head to clear away the lingering thoughts, he left his cabin to join the men. It was a calm clear night and the news had come earlier that day. Their information had proved true. The enemy was at Lepanto, and it was said that they were in some difficulty. There were stories of plague aboard their ships and large numbers of dead, which had left them short of slaves at the oars. If this too was true, it would give the League the advantage they needed against the superior numbers of the Turks.

Lorenzo was eager for the battle to begin. Like all those who lived and sailed under the banner of Venice, he was angry at the way the enemy had attacked and pillaged Cyprus, but more than this was his desire to have an end to this conflict. Only then would he be free to return to Kathryn.

Kathryn awoke, got up and went over to look out of the window of her bedchamber. It was a beautiful sunny day, the sky a perfect cloudless blue. She had promised to spend it with her friends, and she knew it would be a pleasant day. The only cloud on her horizon was the lack of news from Lorenzo.

He had warned her not expect any messages from him. 'We shall be moving constantly,' he had told her, 'and there will be no way of sending you letters, my love—but you will know that you are always in my heart.'

Kathryn wondered if he was thinking of her now. She had dreamed of him, but the dream had been the old one, where she was swept away from him by an unstoppable tide of water, and she did not want to remember it.

If only she knew what he was doing, and if he was safe! If anything should happen to him now…but she would not let herself dwell on such things. Lorenzo had promised to come back to her and she would hold fast to that thought.

Lorenzo was in command of his own fleet. It was his condition for joining the League and it gave him the freedom to manoeuvre as he would. He had decided to stay close to Don John's personal ships, for he believed the overall commander to be not only a man of sense, but also a brilliant strategist.

On most of the galleys the men were chained to their oars, lashed by the bosun's whip to make them work.

Lorenzo's men were free to choose. They had been trained to obey his orders to the letter, and though they could be punished for disobedience, they were more likely to be rewarded for bravery. Any prizes they took would be sold and divided amongst them.

A mass had been held throughout the fleet and everyone accepted that the battle was near. The Turkish fleet had been sighted and the nearest guess they had was that there were some three hundred vessels, the majority of them fighting galleys.

'They are spread out across the gulf,' Lorenzo said to Michael just before he returned to his own galley that morning. 'It will be a hard-won fight, my friend.'

'But we shall prevail!'

'If we have faith in our own ability.'

'Listen to that!' Michael said as the sound of strange music floated across the sea from the enemy ships.

By contrast, the combined fleet of the League was silent. The atmosphere was intense, dedicated, as if every man was prepared to die for the cause.

'Go to your men,' Lorenzo said his expression set. 'This day shall be remembered for all time.'

They were closing on the enemy now. The decks of the Turkish galleys were packed with men in rich clothes and wearing jewels; they were Janissaries and served the Sultan. Amongst them crouched the archers, their deadly weapons poised and ready to inflict the maximum harm.

The League was heavily outnumbered and no one knew better than Lorenzo what fierce fighters the Turks were. Amongst them, he did not doubt, were the ships of his enemy Rachid.

On board the Turkish ships the Janissaries were

shouting and screaming, crashing cymbals and firing as the two fleets converged, hoping to confuse and scatter the League's ships. But the League held firm, waiting for the signal from their commander, which came in the end along with a change in the wind.

Suddenly the odds had altered. Now they were in favour of the League. It seemed that God was with them.

Kathryn could not rest. She had heard no news of Lorenzo for weeks and the waiting was at times unbearable. She had always known that it might be months before he returned to her, but she had hoped that there might be some news before this.

'It is the uncertainty I find so distressing,' Kathryn said to Elizabeta as they sat together at their sewing. 'Every day I expect that we may hear something, but there has been no word.'

Elizabeta nodded, stretching to ease her back. She was in the early stages of childbearing, though as yet it was hardly noticeable.

'My husband has contributed to the League's funds, as all men of conscience must,' she said. 'But I must tell you, Kathryn, that I am relieved he takes no part in this war. I know it must be very worrying for you.'

'I try not to be anxious,' Kathryn told her. 'Lorenzo promised that he would return to me and I must believe that.'

'Yes, of course,' Elizabeta said and smiled. She showed Kathryn the exquisite embroidery she was doing for her baby's shawl. 'I am sure he will return to you in time. After all, this is not the first time your husband has fought his enemies.'

'No, that is true.' Kathryn laid her sewing aside as she

heard voices in the hall and then Veronique came into the salon with their visitor. 'Paolo,' she said and stood up to greet him. 'It is good to see you.'

'I knew you would be anxious for news,' he said. 'I came as soon as I heard—it seems that the League has won a great victory over the Turks.'

'A victory!' Kathryn could not keep the delight from her voice, her eyes lighting up from inside. 'I am so very pleased. But what else have you heard?'

'There have been casualties on both sides,' Paolo said carefully. He had heard that they were heavy, but did not wish to frighten her. 'They say that Don John's strategy was brilliant, but there was hard fighting. It was not won easily, surging this way and that, but the Turkish commander was killed and that helped to carry the day. Also, it is said that, on board the Turkish ships, the galley slaves broke free of their chains and joined in the fighting against their cruel masters.'

'You have no other news...for me?' She looked at him eagerly.

'I cannot tell you that Lorenzo is safe, Kathryn, for I do not know. But some of our ships may return soon and then we may learn more.'

'Yes, I understand,' Kathryn said. She was on fire with impatience to discover more, but knew she must control her feelings. 'It was good of you to come and tell me.'

'I knew you would be anxious,' he said. 'As soon as there is more news I shall tell you.'

Kathryn thanked him. She invited him to stay and take some wine with them, but he said that he had other calls to make.

'Well,' Elizabeta said after he had gone. 'Paolo brought good news, Kathryn. If the Turks are defeated, it means that the war is over, and that means Lorenzo should soon be on his way home to you.'

'Yes.' Kathryn smiled, her heart racing with excitement. 'I do hope so, Elizabeta. I cannot wait to have him home again.'

The battle against the Turks was won for the moment. Lorenzo did not doubt that they would grow strong again in time, but it had been a fierce fight and for the moment the enemy could do nothing but slink away to lick its wounds, which meant that these seas would be that much safer.

Lorenzo had lost three of his galleys in the battle of Lepanto. Crews from other ships had rescued some of the men, though inevitably some had been lost. At least his crew had chosen to fight of their own free will, which was not the case for all. However, they had captured several rich prizes, and that meant the men would be well rewarded for their work.

'What will you do next?' Michael asked as he came on board Lorenzo's personal galley. 'Are you returning to Rome at once?'

'Those galleys that have sustained damage should head for Sicily and make what repairs they can before returning home,' Lorenzo said. 'It is my intention to escort them there and to visit with Lord Mountfitchet for a few days before I return to Rome.'

Michael inclined his head. 'And what would you have me do?'

'Take the rest of the fleet back to Rome. Stay there until I return if you will, Michael. I shall be a week or so behind you. When I come, we shall discuss the future.'

'Is it in your mind to change things?'

'I am not yet certain of my plans. I will know more when I have spoken to Lord Mountfitchet. I may return to England, at least for a while.'

'Return to England?' Michael looked puzzled. 'Was that country once your home?'

'Did I say that?' Lorenzo frowned. 'I meant that I might take Kathryn to her home for a visit.'

He spoke with Michael for a little longer, and then they parted company. He was thoughtful as he gave the order to the stricken galleys. It would be safer if they travelled as a group, for they were vulnerable. However, his own galley was not damaged and he would be their escort to Sicily. And then…

What did he expect to learn from Lord Mountfitchet? Lorenzo was uncertain, but his dream had haunted him for a while now. In it he saw two young people on a beach. The youth told the girl to run and fetch help while he fought the men who sought to capture them…and there was also a picture of a house and a man the youth had called father. There were other things coming to him now, things that seemed so real that he could not think them dreams, and yet he was afraid to call them memories.

Was it possible that Charles Mountfitchet was his father? Or had Lorenzo simply taken things that Kathryn had told him and made something from them? Were these flashes that came into his mind at times true memories or merely imagination? It seemed unlikely that he could be Richard Mountfitchet, and yet of late something had been telling him that he must speak of his thoughts.

Kathryn would be waiting for him in Rome, but it would mean a delay of no more than a week or so, and he had a feeling that it was important for both of them that he should speak to Charles.

* * *

Kathryn was in the garden, picking flowers to take into the house, when she heard the ring of booted steps behind her and turned eagerly. Her heart took a flying leap as she saw her visitor.

'Michael!' she cried joyfully. 'I am so glad to see you back. Are you well? Is Lorenzo with you?'

'I am well,' he told her. 'I thank you for you inquiry, Kathryn—and I am happy to tell you that Lorenzo was well when I last saw him. He escorted some of our wounded galleys to Sicily, for they needed urgent repairs and were vulnerable. I believe that he intended to speak to Lord Mountfitchet before returning to Rome.'

'I had a letter from Lady Mary only yesterday,' Kathryn said. 'They have found land and a house in Sicily that suits them and they think they may stay there. It was Lord Mountfitchet's intention to speak with Lorenzo and ask for his advice, so it may suit him if Lorenzo calls there to see him.'

'Lorenzo has asked me to remain in Rome until his return.' Michael frowned. 'I think it is in his mind to take a trip to England, though he said his plans were not yet formed.'

'Yes, he did speak of making changes,' Kathryn said. 'I think he believes that it will no longer be necessary to have so many galleys to protect his ships in future, but we must wait and see what he decides.'

'Yes, of course. If you will excuse me now, I have other calls to make.'

'Will you dine with me this evening?' Kathryn asked. 'I have invited Elizabeta, her husband, Paolo, Isabella and her father and a few others. We should be pleased to have you join us. Perhaps you could tell us more of the battle, for we hear so many conflicting stories. It would be good to hear from someone who was there.'

'I should be delighted to do so,' Michael said, hesitated, and then added, 'It is in my mind that I might ask Isabella Rinaldi to marry me.' His cheeks became slightly pink. 'My father is most insistent that I take a wife. I have resisted it, for it would mean that I should have to change the way I lead my life. Perhaps, if Lorenzo intends to make changes, it is time I did so also.' He looked at her oddly. 'Do you think there is a chance that Isabella would look kindly on an offer from me?'

'I do not know,' Kathryn said. 'But I think she likes you.'

He nodded and smiled. 'Then I shall think seriously about making the offer. I shall see you this evening, Kathryn.'

'We shall look forward to having you with us.'

Kathryn stood for a while after he had gone, a rosebud in her hand. She would be pleased if Lorenzo was serious about taking her home, for she would be glad to see her father. But she was not sure that she would wish to make her home there for she was happy here in Rome.

She had written to her father many months ago to tell him of her marriage and assure him that she was well, but there had been no reply. At first she had thought that he must be too busy to write to her or that he was perhaps angry she had married without consulting him, but now she had begun to wonder if he had received her letter. It was strange that there had been no reply of any kind.

'It is good to see you again,' Charles said, offering his hand to Lorenzo. 'My sister wrote to Kathryn some weeks back, telling her that we were thinking of staying here in Sicily. We have found land we like, and a house—but I wanted your advice before I made the purchase.'

'It is one choice,' Lorenzo agreed. 'I believe it might

be a good idea to buy land here, and establish vineyards of your own, but I thought you might consider living in Rome or Venice. I have plans to expand my wine-growing business, and perhaps to concentrate the shipping to England, Germany and France, where I have contacts. It was in my mind to ask whether you might consider being my partner? My business is expanding and I have plans to ship wines to more countries than before—but I shall need someone I can trust to help me in this venture.'

'Your partner?' Charles was surprised, but enormously pleased with the idea. 'I think I might, sir. Yes, I think I might. Had my son lived, I should have been content to sit back and let him take over my interests, but...' He sighed and shrugged his shoulders. 'I have reluctantly accepted that I may never see him again. And I am not sure that I would ever wish to return to England. I find the climate here suits me better. My only wish is that I might find some trace of my son.'

'He may be nearer than you think,' Lorenzo said, a sudden croak in his voice. 'Would you mind answering a few questions concerning Richard?'

Charles looked at him eagerly. 'Have you discovered something?'

'I am not sure. It may be nothing—but did you give your son a sword on his seventh birthday and tell him that it was time he learned to be a man?'

Charles looked shocked. 'I cannot remember if he was seven or eight—but it is true that I gave my son a sword on his birthday and I may have told him some such thing.'

'Tell me about the house you lived in then—has it a tower and a moat? Is there a room filled with armour from past times, and did Richard like to spend hours there?'

'Yes, all that you say is true,' Charles said and looked

at him intently. 'Richard liked one suit of armour particularly. My father wore it at the battle of—'

'When Henry VIII met Francis I on the Field of Cloth of Gold, and your father rode with Henry that day.' Lorenzo's eyes narrowed. 'And did your son have an unusual pet—one that you did not approve of?'

'A pet…' Charles wrinkled his brow in thought for a moment and then laughed. 'Good Lord, yes! I had almost forgot. He brought home a wretched fox cub and…' His voice died away as he saw the look in Lorenzo's eyes. 'What happened then?'

'He took it up to his room and fed it with food he had stolen from the kitchens, and you found out and beat him for it…'

'I made him take it back to the woods where he found it.'

'But he did not,' Lorenzo said and smiled. 'He kept it in a part of the stables and saved food from his own plate to feed it until it was old enough to be released.'

'I never knew that.' Charles looked at him oddly. 'Only Richard could know all this…'

'I have wondered if it was a dream or imagination,' Lorenzo said. 'But when you spoke of the special suit of armour I knew that it was true.' His voice was hoarse with emotion. 'Forgive me, I do not know how to say this to you. When we first met I felt an affinity that I have seldom known with another man, but I would not believe in what my heart was telling me. I thrust it from me, but the dreams started to haunt me. I cannot tell you that I am your son, for I have no proof—but I believe that it may be so.'

'God help me!' Charles staggered back, falling into a chair. For a moment he sat with his head in his hands, and when he looked up at last the tears were running down his cheeks. 'I felt it too, but I did not believe it could be true.'

'Then you believe…you would own me as your son?' Lorenzo felt humbled, closer to tears than he had ever been in his life. 'I can give you no proof…'

'I think you have given me enough,' Charles said and stood up, moving forward to embrace his son, his body shaking with the sobs of emotion he at least could not hold back. 'Since we met it has been in my mind that if I had a son I should want him to be much like you. Indeed, though I had not made a conscious decision, I had come to think of you as my son.'

'Then I shall do my best to make you proud of me, Father,' Lorenzo said. 'It does not mean that I shall honour Antonio Santorini the less, for without his love and care of me I should have died many years ago. But in my heart I do believe that you are my true father, and I hope that if we return for a visit to England with Kathryn I may recover many more memories.'

'Then it is settled,' Charles said. 'We shall look at the land I thought to buy here and make our decision, and then we shall return to Rome and from thence to England.'

'We shall make our decision about the land, but I may go on ahead while you settle things here, Father. Kathryn will be anxious. Besides, my stricken galleys will be a few days making repairs, and they will escort you. The seas are much safer for the time being, but I doubt that we have rid them of all the Corsairs who have plagued us. I would have you make the journey in safety.'

Charles smiled at him. His heart was overflowing with love for this son new found, and he would have agreed to anything that Lorenzo asked of him.

'Kathryn…' Veronique came into the salon, looking flustered. 'You have a visitor…'

'A visitor?' Kathryn's heart raced. What could her companion mean? Was it Lorenzo? A man had followed close on the heels of Veronique and as she saw him she got to her feet with a glad cry. 'Father! Oh, I am so glad to see you. How came you here? I had no word…'

There was anger in his face as he looked at her. '*You* have had no word from me? I have waited months for a letter from you, Kathryn. I travelled to Venice, to the home of Signor Santorini, and learned there that you have married. What is this? Why have you behaved so ill towards me? I do not think I have deserved this from you, daughter.'

'Forgive me, Father,' Kathryn said. 'I would not have hurt you for the world. It is a long story and I must ask you to sit down while I tell it.' She looked at her companion. 'This gentleman is my father—Sir John Rowlands. Would you please order some refreshments for us, Veronique?'

'It is a pleasure to meet you, *madame*,' Sir John said. 'Forgive me if I was short with you earlier, but I was angry and anxious for Kathryn.'

'There is no need to be angry,' Kathryn told him as her companion smiled and left the room. 'I am sorry that you did not get my letter, for it would have explained all. Lorenzo married me because there was some question of my good name having been besmirched.' She shook her head as he fired up. 'No, no, listen to my story, I pray you, before you judge. Lorenzo has done nothing that should make you angry.'

'Tell me it all, then,' Sir John said. His anger had been caused by months of frustration and anxiety, but now that he was here and could see she was well, his feelings were a mixture of relief and pique.

As Kathryn's story unfolded his emotions ran the gamut between fury and distress. That his child should have been kidnapped! He was grateful to Lorenzo Santorini for rescuing her, but blamed him for having brought it on her in the first place. But when he heard that his old friend had been thought lost and Kathryn had been alone, he began to understand that she had been lucky. Had Santorini been another kind of man, her fate might have been very different.

'I see,' he said as she finished her story. 'And where is your husband, Kathryn? I should wish to meet him before I give you my blessing.'

'He has been fighting, Father. You must have heard tell of the terrible battle that took place more than two weeks ago?'

'Yes, I heard of it in Venice. I was delayed because of it, but surely he should be home by now?'

'One of his captains came to see me,' Kathryn said. 'Lorenzo went to see Lord Mountfitchet in Sicily. Michael said he would not be long. I am expecting him any day now.'

'Then I must wait in patience I suppose,' her father said. He smiled at her. 'Well, come, kiss me, daughter. I was angry, but now that you have told me all, I am prepared to forgive you.'

'Two galleys to the leeward, sir,' Lorenzo's second-in-command came to inform him as he was looking at some papers in his cabin. 'I'm not sure—but I think they are Corsairs.'

'Damn it!' Lorenzo buckled on his sword as he prepared to go outside and investigate for himself. The galleys were closing on them fast, and as he looked he saw that they were flying Rachid's flag.

Cursing himself for being caught off guard, Lorenzo gave the order for battle. It was two to one and it was his own fault, for he had been impatient to return to Kathryn. Had he waited another few days they might all have sailed together.

He had imagined that the Corsair's galleys would have gone back to Algiers to rest up for the winter and lick their wounds, but it looked as if they were hungry for a fight. Well, they would get one. He was outnumbered, but his men were loyal and, if need be, they would fight to the death.

Kathryn and her father were sitting in the salon drinking wine and eating biscuits when they heard the sound of voices in the hall. Kathryn jumped to her feet as Michael walked in, followed closely by Lord Mountfitchet.

'Kathryn.' Lord Mountfitchet's expression made her heart catch with fright. 'Forgive me, but I fear I have terrible news.'

'Lorenzo?' Her face was white and she might have fallen if her father had not been by her side. 'Something has happened to him…'

He put out his hand to steady her. 'Damn it, Charles! What is it?'

'John—I did not know you were here,' Charles said. He looked grey in the face, clearly much distressed. 'The news is the worst imaginable. Lorenzo insisted on setting out alone, for he was impatient to see Kathryn. He imagined the seas would be safe enough after the recent battle but…' He put a shaking hand to his face. 'I can scarce believe it. To have found him and then to lose him…'

'What are you talking about?' Sir John barked. Veronique had helped Kathryn to sit down and was giving her a drink of restorative wine. 'What has happened to Kathryn's husband?'

'We found the wreckage of his galley,' Charles said. 'It had been severely damaged and abandoned, though there was a man clinging to wreckage in the water. Somehow the poor devil had survived for two days. He was half out of his mind and is still in a fever, but he told us that the Corsair had taken prisoners—and that Lorenzo was either dead or a prisoner of his enemy.'

'No!' Kathryn cried, terror sweeping through her. 'No, not Rachid. He will surely kill him.' Tears trickled down her cheeks. 'There is such hatred between them….'

'Do not despair, Kathryn.' Michael spoke for the first time. 'I have already sent out ships to make contact with Rachid. We shall offer a ransom for him. I shall go myself to Algiers. I promise that we shall leave no stone unturned in the effort to find him.'

'Lorenzo…' Kathryn bowed her head as the pain of her grief almost overwhelmed her. 'This is my fault. I made him love me and…' It was what he had feared. Because of his love for her, he had thrown his natural caution to the winds. He had been impatient to see her. 'Oh, my love, forgive me!'

'What nonsense is this, Kathryn?' Her father looked bewildered. He rubbed at a spot in his chest as if it bothered him. 'How can it be your fault?'

'Excuse me,' she said, tears blinding her eyes. 'I would be alone.'

The men stared after her as she fled, but Veronique followed.

'What was all that about?' Sir John asked. He rubbed at his chest again. Sometimes he hardly felt the pain, but at others it became severe. He needed to take one of the powders that his physician had given him, but for the moment it must wait.

'Lorenzo told me his story recently,' Charles said. 'Please allow me to tell you what he related to me—and then perhaps you may begin to understand what this means.'

'I must go,' Michael said. 'There is no time to waste if we are to find Lorenzo alive. Please tell Kathryn that I will do everything I can.'

'Any ransom,' Charles said. 'I will give every penny I possess for his safe return.'

'I shall do what I can,' Michael promised and left them.

Kathryn stood at the window, staring out at the night sky. She was in too much distress to think clearly, but her heart felt as if it were being torn in two. She could almost wish that Lorenzo had died in battle; at least that would have been swift. To think of him at the mercy of his enemy was unbearable. She knew what it had cost him to put the past behind him, the agony of mind he had endured—and now he was once more a prisoner of the evil Corsair who had nearly killed him once before.

'Lorenzo…' she whispered. 'My love, my love—what have I done to you?'

It was her fault, for Rachid would not have caught him off guard before he fell in love with her. She had given him her love, but it was a poisoned chalice—it had led to his death.

Tears trickled down her cheeks. She let them fall. Her grief was so sharp that it was almost unbearable. If Lorenzo was gone from her for ever…

What must he be suffering? To find himself a prisoner of his enemy once more would be humiliating and soul-destroying. He knew what it was like to serve at the oar for three years, and, unless Michael was successful in his attempts to ransom him, he might die this time.

No, no, he must not die, for she could not bear to live without him. She was his woman, his wife, and her heart belonged to him alone. He must live—she did not know what she would do without him.

Lorenzo explored the tender spot at the back of his head carefully. He had been unconscious for some hours after he was captured, for he had been taken from behind and received a heavy blow to the back of the head, but he knew immediately that he was in the cabin of the Corsair galley. Why had he not been cast down into the pit with the other captives?

Did the pirate who had captured him know who he was? It was almost certain that he did—so was he being held for a ransom? Or had Rachid reserved a special fate for him? Yes, of course, that must be so. It was the only reason he had not been chained up with the other prisoners.

They had been enemies for a long time now and Rachid had not earned his name for nothing. He was called the Feared One because of his barbarity. It was unusual for his men to take prisoners unless they needed more galley slaves or captured someone they could ransom for a large sum of money. As a rule they killed ruthlessly, plundering the captured ships and often sinking them afterwards unless they considered them worth selling.

Lorenzo's head was throbbing as he lay considering his likely fate. He could either be sold as a slave, put to the oars, or held for ransom. But Rachid had good cause to hate him and it was probable that he was being kept alive so that he could suffer some form of torture before his death.

He had been a youth when he had been taken the first

time, powerless to fight the ruthless men who had captured him. Finding himself chained to an oar with no memory of his life prior to his captivity, he had survived by instinct—an instinct that had served him well these past years. It would be different this time, for he knew exactly who he was and what had happened to him.

He knew that he must remain alert, while allowing his captors to think him still suffering from the blow to his head. Only if they believed he was ill and incapable of escaping would they give him the chance to make his break.

But he would do so when the chance came. He would rather die in the attempt than be a slave—or allow his enemy to humiliate him. The strongest man could break under torture, and he would rather die quickly and cleanly.

For a moment he thought of Kathryn. If he waited, perhaps Rachid would ransom him and he might be returned to Rome. He might see her again. A part of him wanted to take that chance, to put his faith in God and those he knew would even now be trying to arrange his freedom—but there was another part of him that refused to be sold.

Somehow he would fight free. If he died in the attempt, then Kathryn would be a widow. She was beautiful and she would be rich, for he had left much of his wealth to her in a will he had made before the war—and she would find someone else to love in time.

'Kathryn, Kathryn, my love…'

His heart cried out to her as he whispered her name, but even for the sake of his love for her, he could not simply wait for rescue or death. He must try to save himself if he died for it.

'You. Infidel dog!' A rough voice spoke from the doorway. 'Do you want food and water?'

Lorenzo moaned, but made no answer. He sensed the man coming nearer and forced himself to lie still. To attack one man would do no good. He needed to wait for the right time.

The Corsair muttered something and slopped some water into Lorenzo's face. He had been waiting for it, because he had seen it done often enough. He muttered and jerked, but did not open his eyes. The man grunted and moved away, closing the cabin door after him.

Lorenzo ran his fingers over his face, sucking the few drops of moisture he managed to acquire by this method. He was thirsty and hungry too, but he needed to keep up the pretence for as long as he could manage.

Kathryn woke with tears on her face. She had dreamed of Lorenzo, dreamed that he was ill and in pain, and that he had called her name.

'Oh, Lorenzo,' she whispered as she got out of bed and went over to the window, gazing out at the night. 'Lorenzo, do not die and leave me. Come back to me, my love. I need you so…'

He was not dead. She would not let herself believe it, for if she did there would be an end to all hope. No, she knew that he was alive. He was out there somewhere and thinking of her—and somehow he would come to her. Surely he would find a way to come back to her? He must because she loved him.

It was no use, she would never sleep. She dressed and went out to the courtyard, welcoming the cool night air. Her heart ached for the man she loved, but there was no comfort to be had.

'Lorenzo…' she whispered. 'Please do not leave me, my love.'

* * *

Lorenzo knew that they had reached a port. The ship was no longer moving and he could hear shouting from the deck, the ragged cheer that comes from the throats of weary oarsmen who knew that they would at last be allowed some rest.

He was tempted to get up and look out of the porthole, but wary lest someone come and find him clearly recovered from the blow that had rendered him unconscious. He must wait for the right moment before attempting his escape.

It was a few minutes before someone came into the cabin and stood looking down at him. Then he felt someone kick him in the side.

'Get up, infidel dog,' the voice said. 'Rachid requests your presence.' Coarse laughter and then the sound of other men entering the cabin followed this command. 'We shall have to carry the dog,' the man said. 'Rachid will have our heads if he dies.'

Lorenzo let his body flop loosely as he was lifted bodily and carried out on to the deck. It was good to feel the fresh air on his face. He was very thirsty and it took all his strength of purpose to lie still as he was dumped unceremoniously on to the deck.

He sensed that the men had moved away from him and cautiously opened one eye. To his amazement, they had all walked to the prow of the galley and were staring at something happening on shore. This was his chance!

Lorenzo moved cautiously, crawling on all fours to the stern. He glanced over his shoulder but the Corsairs were all intent on watching whatever was happening on shore.

He thought that they were getting ready for someone to come on board—possibly Rachid. The thought of coming face to face with his enemy lent Lorenzo wings.

He stood up swiftly, putting a leg over the side and finding a foothold, his other leg following just as the alarm was roused. Someone had seen him and shouted a warning. It was now or never.

He paused for a brief second before diving into the sea, but even as he hesitated he heard something just behind him and then a shot rang out. The ball embedded itself in his shoulder and he pitched face down into the sea.

Chapter Eleven

Kathryn was walking in the garden when Michael arrived later that day. She saw him talking with her father and Lord Mountfitchet and went quickly into the house to ask if there was any news.

'Have you found him?'

'No, Kathryn,' Michael said. His eyes begged for pardon for he knew that his words must bring her grief. 'Forgive me, I have no news at all. I made contact with one of Rachid's men, but he claimed to have no knowledge of an attack on Lorenzo's galley or of any captive.'

'But it was six weeks ago,' Kathryn said. 'Surely there must be some word by now? If he was taken back to Algiers—'

'My men and I visited the slave markets,' Michael told her. 'There was no news of him—they all denied having seen him.'

'Someone must have seen him…if he is alive…' Kathryn caught back a sob of grief. She was trying so hard to hold on to her hope to believe that he lived, but it was very hard.

'Do not give up hope yet,' Michael said. 'I have sent an envoy to Rachid, and if there is to be an answer it will come here to his father—but I shall go now to Granada to speak with Lorenzo's friend Ali Khayr. It is possible that he may have heard something—or that he may have contacts who could discover the truth of this.'

'But we have only one man's word that he was captured by Rachid's galleys,' Kathryn said. 'Supposing it was another pirate or…' She shook her head. 'No, I shall not believe he is dead. I am sure that he lives.'

'You always gave me hope when I had none,' Charles Mountfitchet said, a gleam in his eyes. 'And now I shall tell you that I believe he is alive, Kathryn. Lorenzo is not a green youth. He is a strong, resourceful man who has known suffering and survived, and I believe he will find a way to survive this time—no matter who his captors were.'

'I do hope you are right, sir,' she said, smothering a sob. Inside her head she was praying, begging for his life. 'I pray that he is alive and that we shall have him back with us soon.'

Sir John watched her anxiously, feeling her pain as if it were his own. He had experienced more pain in his chest of late and he knew that his time here was short. He must return home, for there were things he needed to do, yet he could not leave while Kathryn was so distressed.

Lorenzo opened his eyes. The woman bending over him had soft hands and a kind voice. She had been tending him for a long time now, though he did not know how long he had lain here in his fever.

'Are you awake at last?' the woman asked in her native tongue and smiled at him. 'Allah be praised. We all thought that you would die. You were as good as dead when my husband fished you out of the sea.'

'Where am I?' Lorenzo understood her, for it was a language he had learned of necessity long ago. He wrinkled his brow and tried to remember what had happened to him, but for the moment his mind was confused. He felt too weak to think, but he swallowed obediently when the woman put a cup to his lips.

'My name is Salome,' the woman told him. 'My husband is a fisherman—we are but poor folk, sir. When my husband found you, you had been wounded and he thought you dead. He knew that someone was looking for you and he thought to claim a ransom for your body, but when he discovered that you were alive, he brought you to our home. Khalid would have given you to the Feared One had you been dead, but he would not give any living man to that monster.'

'I am very grateful,' Lorenzo whispered, his voice hoarse. 'You shall be rewarded. I have friends who will pay for my safe return.'

'I told my husband it would be so,' Salome said and smiled encouragingly. 'I have tended you for many days and nights, sir. Even when your wound began to heal your mind did not. You have been wandering in the past I think, for you spoke of being a child…of your father…'

'My father.' Lorenzo's face creased with grief as the memories flooded into his mind and it all slotted into place. 'He will be so distressed, and Kathryn…' Kathryn would think him dead. He tried to sit up, but the pain struck him and he fell back against the cushions.

'You are not yet ready to get up,' Salome said. 'Rest and wait, impatient one. When you are better we shall send a message to your friends and then you shall go to them. We are not greedy people, sir, but we are poor. A small sum for our trouble is all that we ask.'

Lorenzo smiled at her as his eyelids fluttered. 'I shall make you rich,' he murmured and then he slept.

'I must return home soon,' Sir John said as he found his daughter walking in the garden. His heart ached as he saw her so pale, her eyes dark with unhappiness. She was even more distressed now than she had been when Dickon was taken from her. 'I want you to come with me, daughter.'

'I cannot leave Rome,' Kathryn cried in sudden alarm. 'I must stay here in case…he is found.'

'Two months have passed now since Lorenzo was lost,' her father told her, his expression grave. 'I know you loved him, Kathryn, and if what Charles says is true—if he is Richard—then this is the second time you have lost the one you love most in the world. You will grieve for him, it is natural that you should—but I cannot stay here much longer. I must return home almost immediately. And I would have you safe at home with me.'

'No, I must stay here. I must wait for my husband.'

'I think that you should do as your father suggests.'

Kathryn turned as she heard Charles's voice. He had come into the garden and overheard them talking. 'I must be here if Lorenzo returns.' Her eyes filled with tears. 'Please do not make me leave him—please, I beg you. I must be here when he comes back…'

'I shall remain in Rome,' Charles told her. 'When I have news I shall write to you. Lorenzo will know that you did not wish to leave. I shall tell him, Kathryn—but you would be safer at home with your father. Mary chose to stay in Sicily. She has kept poor William with her and has recently met a gentleman she likes and may marry. Had she been here, it might have been different—but I do not wish to leave you alone and I may have to travel elsewhere.'

'Then give me another week,' Kathryn begged. Her throat was tight with grief and she could hardly bear the pain. 'If there is no news of him by then, I must do as my father says…'

She turned away from them, controlling her tears with difficulty. Perhaps they were right and it might be better if she left Rome. It was for her sake that Lorenzo had travelled alone, because he had been impatient to be with her. He had feared that loving her might cause him to become soft—and it was that which had led to his capture or even his death.

Lorenzo had married her because she was distressed at losing her good name. She believed that he had loved her, but perhaps she was an evil omen to him. Had she not prompted Dickon to go down to the beach when they were children, pirates would not have taken him. Had she not made Lorenzo fall in love with her, he might even now be safe. The thought was like a dagger striking deep into her heart and made her stagger as she realised what love of her had done to Lorenzo not once, but twice.

'Forgive me, my love,' she whispered. 'But perhaps it is best.'

She raised her head, fighting her grief and the longing deep inside her. 'Very well, Father,' she said. 'If there is no news within a week, I shall go back home with you.'

Lorenzo was resting when Salome came hurrying into the room. The pain in his shoulder was much easier now, but he was still too weak to do much more than walk about the house. He could not go out into the gardens for fear that someone might see him. He had already stayed too long and his presence in this house might mean danger for the good people who had nursed him back to health.

'Is something wrong?' he asked as he saw Salome's anguished look.

'They are looking for you,' she said, a frightened expression in her eyes. 'Men came to the village earlier asking for a man of your description. My husband fears that someone will betray us. They are offering money for news of your whereabouts, *signor.*'

'Then I must leave your house,' Lorenzo said, 'for I would not bring harm to you. I fear I have nothing to give you for your kindness, lady, but you shall be rewarded as soon as I return to my home.' He thought of a small gold ring on his finger and slipped it off. 'Take this as a token of my good will. I owe you much more and, God willing, I shall live to repay you.'

'My husband had no thought of repayment when he took you from the sea, but he grows old and soon will be able to work no more.'

'You shall be rewarded,' Lorenzo promised, 'and now I must leave before they come looking for me here.'

'You must wear my husband's clothes,' Salome said. 'I have brought you something to darken your skin, else you will be noticed at once for your skin has the pallor of ill health. If I do not offend you, lord, you should keep your head down lest your eyes betray you.'

Lorenzo thanked her again for her advice, slipping on the long, shabby robe she offered over the remnants of his own clothing. The sea had taken most of his garments, leaving only his breeches.

He left Salome's house through a small gate at the back of the garden, avoiding the main street of the fishing village. It was late in the afternoon, the sun dipping over the sea in a blaze of gold, and he knew that dusk would soon cloak him in darkness.

He had not been idle these past weeks and he believed that his best chance of escape was to reach Algiers, where he might mingle with the crowds frequenting the waterfront. It was a busy port and there might be merchant ships from Portugal or Holland. With luck he could find work. If he could reach Spain, he had friends who would help him.

Lorenzo had been walking for some half an hour or more when he was alerted by the sound of hoofbeats coming fast up the lonely road. He realised at once that it could only be the men who had visited Salome's village earlier, and looked about for somewhere to hide.

The rocky hillside offered no protection. Perhaps he could simply bluff it out by pleading ignorance. He must remember to keep his head bent, and to act in a humble manner befitting his lowly status.

As the riders came nearer, Lorenzo moved to the side of the road. Perhaps they would simply ride by and ignore him.

His hopes were short lived as the leading horseman reined in and shouted to him. 'You there—dog! Have you seen anyone passing this way? A man not of our people?'

'No one has passed this way, sir,' Lorenzo kept his head bent humbly, thankful for the shabby robe that covered his hair. With luck they would ride on by thinking him merely a poor fisherman.

'How long have you been on this road?'

'All day, sir.'

The man looked back at his companions, who had brought their mounts to a halt, and an argument began between them. Some were for returning to the village, others for going on.

'The old woman lied,' one of the horsemen said. 'We should return and persuade her to tell us the truth. Perhaps if we split her lying tongue the fisherman will speak. The beating you gave him did not break him—but it may be different if you turn your attention to her.'

Lorenzo listened in horror. He could not condemn Salome and her husband to the kind of torture these beasts might inflict. His sense of honour would not permit him to escape while others suffered in his place. Throwing back his hood, he looked up at the leader.

'I am Lorenzo Santorini,' he said. 'I am the one you seek.'

For a moment the man stared at him in stunned disbelief, then a gleam of greed came to his rascally face.

'We have searched for you many weeks,' he said and grinned. 'Rachid has promised much gold to he who finds you.'

'Then you are a rich man,' Lorenzo said, his face cold with pride. 'Do not waste time with the old ones. I have friends searching for me. They are only a few leagues distant from us.'

An expression of consternation came into the man's eyes. He turned to his companions, some of whom had already dismounted and were eyeing Lorenzo warily. They clearly expected him to put up a fight, but he stood unresisting, letting them take him. Their greed for Rachid's gold would save Salome and her husband from further suffering.

Lorenzo offered his wrists for binding. He expected to be led behind the horses as in a Roman triumph, and was surprised when a mount was provided. Their leader took the reins of his horse, but he was neither abused nor insulted.

'Rachid wants you alive,' his captor told him. 'You do well not to struggle, for I have no wish to harm you.'

Lorenzo inclined his head but said no more. His pride would keep him strong. Most men broke under torture. All he could hope for was a quick death.

'Goodbye, Kathryn,' he murmured softly. 'Forgive me, my love. I would have come to you, but the price was too high.'

Kathryn watched as the cliffs of her homeland came into view. Soon they would be home and her heart was breaking. She had been forced to admit that Lorenzo was dead, for if not he would have found a way to contact his friends these past weeks.

Charles was remaining in Rome. He had refused to give up hope and Michael had promised to continue the search, but she knew that neither of them truly believed that he would be found. There had been no trace of him since his capture.

'Lorenzo, my love…' Kathryn blinked back her tears as her father came to join her on the deck, looking towards the shore and the foaming water as it rushed against a coastline that could be treacherous and had sent many a sailor to a watery grave.

'We shall soon be home, my dear,' he said, noting her pale face and sad eyes, purpled by shadows that robbed her of the carefree beauty which had been hers. 'Perhaps then you may feel better.'

'I do not believe that I shall ever feel better. I loved him, Father. I loved him so much that…' She left the words unfinished. In truth, she wished that she might die, but she did not want to hurt her father.

'I understand your grief, Kathryn. When your mother

died I thought that my world was at an end, but I learned
to live without her. I took solace in my children.'

'I have no children.'

'But you are young enough to marry again. Lorenzo left
you a fortune, so the lawyers tell us, though as yet we have
no details. You will have no trouble in finding another
husband, Kathryn.'

She did not want another husband, and talk of the
fortune Lorenzo had left her was anathema to her. No
money could ever heal the hurt inside her!

'Please do not speak of it,' she begged. 'Money means
nothing. I shall never marry again.'

'I pray you will not speak so foolishly,' her father said,
a note of anger or distress in his voice. 'Your grief is
natural, daughter, but it will pass in time. Believe me, you
will be happy again.'

Kathryn turned away. Her father did not understand.
She had given her whole self to Lorenzo. Without him she
was only half a woman. She could never love again and
she did not wish to marry without love.

Sir John saw the grief in her face and wished that he
had never allowed her to travel with Charles Mountfitchet.
He cursed the ill luck that had caused her to marry a man
he thought unsuitable. Charles was a fool to believe in Santorini's tale. No doubt it was a ploy to inherit the estate and
the title. Santorini had money, but to be an English lord
was something many men might aspire to, he imagined.
And the man had lost many ships during the war. He had
probably thought that it was a way to restore his losses.

Having never met Kathryn's husband—something that
rankled in his mind—he had no way of knowing whether
Santorini was wealthy enough to bear those losses. He had
taken a dislike to the man he considered had stolen his

daughter. In his opinion, it was for the best that Kathryn should be left a widow. He did not like to see her grieving, but she would get over it in time. And he did not have much time left to him. Before he died, and he knew that it was coming slowly, he must see his daughter safe—even if it meant forcing her to obey him.

Kathryn could not read her father's thoughts, but she sensed that he did not sympathise with her love for Lorenzo. At the moment she felt too distressed to argue with her father. As time passed he would surely accept her decision, for she could never remarry.

Her heart had died with Lorenzo, for she felt that he must be dead. Only death would have kept him from returning to Rome.

Lorenzo could not believe that he was still alive. Two weeks had passed since he was captured and as yet he had not been ill treated, nor had he been summoned to Rachid's presence. He had expected it would happen immediately and that he would first be humiliated and then tortured, but thus far his jailers had given him food, water and a grudging respect.

He was confined to a room that had bars at the windows and the door was kept locked at all times, other than when his jailer brought him food. Yet it was not the filthy dungeon he had expected to be cast into and he wore no chains about his wrists or ankles. Indeed, he had been given all he needed for his comfort, including water to wash, clean clothes and a soft divan on which to sleep. He had everything he needed other than his freedom.

What was in Rachid's mind? Lorenzo wondered. Was his enemy being fiendishly clever, lulling him into a state of acceptance before inflicting some terrible torture?

He paced the room restlessly. Thoughts of escape were constantly in his mind and yet he hesitated. Rachid was planning something. Perhaps he was like a cat toying with a mouse, daring Lorenzo to try and escape.

He tensed as the door opened. His guards were always regular with his meals, but this was the middle of the afternoon. Something was about to happen.

Lorenzo was fully alert. This might be his only chance to escape. He resolved to try if there was any slip on the part of his guards. Salome and her husband were no longer involved. It was merely his own life at stake now and he would prefer a quick death.

A man entered the room, surprising Lorenzo as his body tensed. It was not the guard who had been bringing him food and water, but a much older man, richly dressed with a bright gold turban.

'My master requests the pleasure of your company, lord.'

Lorenzo smiled grimly. So the summons had come at last.

'Requests?' he asked, a wry twist to his mouth. 'And supposing I choose to decline your master's invitation— what then?' A gleam of defiance was in his eyes, for if he must die he would prefer that it came swiftly.

'That would be a cause of much regret to my master, sir.' The old man smiled oddly. 'I believe you will find this meeting to your advantage. You have nothing to fear.'

'Do you expect me to believe that?'

'You have my word. I am Mustafa Kasim and I am guaranteeing your life—and your safety.'

Looking into his eyes, Lorenzo was puzzled. This was not what he had expected from Rachid. However, life had taught him to be a fair judge of character and somehow he believed this man, believed in his honesty.

'Very well, I shall accept your word, sir.'

'Thank you,' Mustafa Kasim said. 'Please follow me if you will. My master is waiting.'

Lorenzo followed in his wake, walking through what seemed the endless rooms and passages of Rachid's palace. The walls were built of thick grey stone, the floors tiled with a dull grey marble. Even on the warmest summer day this place would strike cold into the bones, but Lorenzo held himself erect, refusing to shiver.

He could not know what would happen when he finally came face to face with his enemy, but clearly he was not to be tortured or executed just yet. Perhaps Rachid had decided to hold him for ransom.

Until this moment Lorenzo had expected his enemy to be ruthless in exacting payment for all the ships sunk, the slaves rescued and given their freedom. He had believed that Rachid must hate him, for he had waged a merciless war on his enemy and could expect no less.

Mustafa had stopped outside an impressive door, which was fashioned of heavy carved wood studded with iron. He rapped on it once with a metal wand he carried and the heavy panels swung back, manipulated by two huge black slaves dressed in rich clothes. The room they were about to enter was very different from the rest of the fortress. The walls were hung with an array of dazzling silks in vibrant colours and the floor was covered with thick silk rugs. Several divans stood about the room, but there were also tables made of alabaster and silver, statues of marble and of gold, a veritable fortune of small items that were of immense value everywhere, almost as if a magpie had gathered them together. Clearly Rachid was very rich.

'My lord,' Mustafa said and bowed respectfully. 'He you have commanded is here.'

Lorenzo glanced towards what appeared to be a kind of throne. Rachid lived, as a king might, in his own little empire. The throne was made of solid silver and decorated with precious jewels. He knew a desire to laugh at such ridiculous opulence, but controlled it as the man, dressed in the robes of a caliph, rose and came towards him. Looking into his face, he was surprised. This man was not the enemy he had fought for so many years but his son: the young man he had exchanged for the Spanish girl.

'So we meet again.' The younger man smiled oddly, pleased by Lorenzo's confusion. 'You look surprised, Signor Santorini. You did not expect to see me?'

'I expected your father.'

'My father?' Hassan laughed. 'I am sorry to disappoint you, *signor*. My father cannot greet you. He died two weeks ago, on the day of your arrival here.'

'Rachid is dead?'

'Have I not said so? You must forgive me for keeping you waiting so long, *signor*. My father's death was unexpected and caused me a few problems.' He waved his hand to indicate the wealth in the room. 'There were others who wished to share in these things, which are rightfully mine. They have been dealt with, but it took a little time.'

Lorenzo repressed a shudder. For a moment he saw something in the younger man's eyes that made him go cold. At that moment there was no doubting he was Rachid's son.

'However, you wish to know why you are here?'

'I believed I was brought here at Rachid's command?'

'He intended to have you killed…very slowly I believe. You forced him to exchange a woman he wanted for me— a poor exchange, in his opinion, but one he was obliged to make.' Hassan's eyes glinted with anger, and he seemed to be waiting for Lorenzo's reply, but when none came he went on. 'However, I am not my father. I like beautiful things, as you see. Women, jewels, silks—all these things please me. I do not like blood. My father forced me to command one of his galleys, but now he is dead.' Something in Hassan's eyes told Lorenzo that he was pleased rather than distressed at the fact of his father's death. 'You could have killed me when you took our ships. Will you tell me why you spared me?'

'I thought that you did not deserve to die. You are not your father, his sins are not yours.'

'No, I carry my own sins, not his.' Again Hassan's eyes glittered. 'You were merciful when your men would have killed me. Now I shall be merciful. You gave me my life, I give you yours. You may leave my house when you choose. One of my galleys will take you wherever you wish to go in safety, that is my promise to you.'

'If you mean that, I would go to Rome.'

'Ah, yes. You have taken a wife.' Hassan nodded. 'I too am about to take my first wife. We have much in common, Signor Santorini. You will do me the honour of dining with me this evening. Tomorrow you may leave.' He indicated one of the divans. 'Please sit, *signor*. Tell me about your wife.'

Lorenzo sat, thinking furiously. He did not yet quite believe in his good fortune. This might be some deceit that was intended to lull him into a false sense of security so for the moment he must be very careful. Hassan was Rachid's son and might be capable of the same cruelty as his father. It seemed that he was sincere, but Lorenzo would remain alert until he was safely back in Rome. Rome meant Kathryn. He smiled and looked at the younger man.

'It is because of my wife that I sent you back to your father…'

* * *

'Do we really have to have such a large gathering?' Kathryn asked. She had no desire to sit down to a banquet with thirty or more guests, nor did she wish to dance and make merry.

'We are celebrating your brother's betrothal,' Sir John said, giving her a severe look. 'You would not wish to appear lacking in your good wishes towards Philip and Mary Jane?'

'No, Father, of course not. Mary Jane is a sweet girl and I have told Philip how happy I am for him, but—'

'I shall hear no excuses, Kathryn. I have forgiven you for your earlier neglect of duty towards me, but I insist you oblige me in this matter.'

Kathryn turned away, feeling his harshness like the sting of a whip. She had never known her father to be so stern and it hurt her deeply. He did not seem to understand that she was suffering terribly. She loved Lorenzo so much that sometimes her grief was almost impossible to bear.

Leaving her father, she fetched her cloak and went out walking. It was bitterly cold, the wind whipping about her slight body, tugging at her clothes as if it wished to tear them away. Kathryn shivered, her face pinched and white. It was so much colder here on this Cornish coast than in Rome; there the winds had been warm, the air perfumed by sweet flowers, and she longed to be back there. She shuddered as she felt the icy wind touch her face, glancing up as the storm clouds gathered overhead.

Such grey skies! How could she bear to go on living in this cold grey world without Lorenzo? It would be so much easier to die, for if there was an afterlife, as the priests promised, she might be with her lover.

Her footsteps took her beyond her father's estate, to the cliffs above the cove where her beloved Dickon had been stolen from her so many years ago.

Was it possible that Lorenzo and Dickon were the same person? Charles Mountfitchet certainly believed it was so and Kathryn recalled the way her heart had recognised him the first time she gazed into his eyes—eyes so blue that no others compared. Yet she had rejected the thought, believing him a highborn Venetian, the true son of Antonio Santorini. She had not been willing to accept that such a man could be her lost love, and yet now…

It seemed that she had lost her love for the second time. But why should she go on alone? Why should she bear this pain another moment? She had only to take two steps forward and she would go crashing down into that swirling venomous sea, where she would be instantly crushed against the jutting rocks.

'Kathryn? Kathryn! No, you must not!'

She turned as she heard the voice, her face suddenly alight with hope. For a moment she thought the man hurrying towards her was Lorenzo, but then she saw that it was Michael and she went to meet him, her heart racing. Perhaps he had news!

'Kathryn!' Michael said, his face anguished by concern. He had thought she meant to jump. 'I thought for a moment that you meant to…'

'Have you news?' she asked, her hand reaching out to him in supplication. 'Have you heard from him?'

'I am sorry.' He looked at her sadly, devastated that he must tell her what would hurt her. 'I have been told that he was shot while trying to escape and fell into the sea. I believe our search is at an end.'

'No…' Kathryn moaned and swayed as the despair swept over her, engulfing her senses. 'Lorenzo, no!' She had known it must be so, but to hear the details was unbearable. 'My love…'

Michael caught her to him lest she fall. He held her as she sobbed out her grief against his chest, his lips murmuring words of comfort against the perfume of her hair.

'My sweet love,' he said softly. 'Forgive me. I know it is Lorenzo you love, but I am here. I would love and protect you, heal your hurts.'

'I cannot…' She looked up at him, her eyes dark with grief. 'I shall never love another. Never marry again.'

'Hush, Kathryn. I do not ask it. I ask only to be your friend and perhaps one day you will look on me kindly. When your grief has healed.'

Kathryn could not answer him. Her heart felt as if it had been cleaved in two. Everyone spoke of her grief healing one day, but they did not understand. No one knew how she felt. Michael was being kind, and she loved him as a friend, but he could never take Lorenzo's place in her heart. It was impossible.

'Come,' she said, lifting her head, pride battling with the urge to give way to this pain inside her. She must try to put off this heavy grief. She must make an effort for the sake of her friends and family. 'We must go back to the house, sir. My father will wish to speak with you.'

Charles was at dinner when he heard a flurry outside the door. The sound of voices raised in excitement and disbelief alerted him and he was on his feet, expectant as Lorenzo walked into the room.

'Praise be to God!' he cried, his voice husky with emotion. Tears stung his eyes and spilled unchecked as he went to embrace his son. 'I feared I might never see you again, my son. They told us you had been shot while trying to escape in the port of Algiers.'

'And so I was,' Lorenzo told him, his eyes bright with

devilish laughter. 'But it seems that God must have been looking after me, for I was plucked from the sea more dead than alive by a poor fisherman and nursed back to health by that man's good wife.'

'We shall reward them,' Charles said. 'They shall never know poverty again.'

'It is as good as done,' Lorenzo said. He looked long and deep into his father's face. 'You have suffered for my sake, Father, but I shall try to cause you no more worry. Rachid is dead and I have no quarrel with his son. Hassan and I have made our peace. We shall make war on each other's ships no more.'

'Come, share the meal I was about to eat and tell me the whole story.'

'Yes, of course.' Lorenzo glanced about the room and frowned. 'You are alone. Where is Kathryn?'

'Her father came to Rome, looking for her. He had not received her letter telling him that you were married and was angry, I think. When the news came that you had been lost he was convinced that you were dead and insisted that she return home to England with him. Kathryn did not wish to go, Lorenzo, but she felt she must obey her father.'

Lorenzo's eyes glinted with anger and frustration. 'She should not have gone with him,' he said harshly. 'Her place was with you at this time.'

'Do not be angry with her, my son,' Charles pleaded. 'I know that she grieved for you terribly. It broke her heart when she learned what had happened to you.'

'And yet she did not wait to see if I would return.'

Lorenzo had been on fire to see Kathryn and his frustration made him harsh.

'I told you, her father made her go.'

'I might have expected more loyalty from my wife. She might have defied him if she had wished.'

'I swear to you that she did not leave willingly.'

Lorenzo nodded. 'At least you stayed, Father.'

'I had nowhere else to go. My one hope was that you would come back to me. I prayed for it, planned for it—and it seems that my prayers have been answered. You are alive and I shall thank God for it the rest of my days.'

'Yes, I truly believe that we have been blessed.' Lorenzo smiled. The bitterness from the past had disappeared with his doubts about his identity. He knew himself this man's son, remembered much of his lost youth. 'Do you recall when we used to go hawking in the woods at Mountfitchet? Sometimes I would follow the hawks for miles and you waited for me to return. I always did in the end, though you had thought me lost.'

'Yes, you always came back,' Charles replied and smiled at him. 'But you spoke confidently, as though you had remembered all?'

'I think it may have been the blow to my head when I was captured, or perhaps that the abduction brought back memories, forcing me to face the past. Perhaps I had forgotten because I did not want to remember.' His father nodded, understanding. 'Memories had been coming to me in drifts for a while, but always vague, seeming like dreams. I did not know I was Richard Mountfitchet before I was captured. I suspected it might be so, but now I know for certain.'

'I was certain in Sicily,' Charles said and looked at him steadily. 'I think when you were a boy I did not always show my faith and love for you, Lorenzo, but in future I intend that it shall be different. God has granted me a second chance and I shall make the most of it.'

'We have both been lucky. I see now that I might have fared far worse than I did. Something kept me alive and perhaps that was God's love.'

Charles nodded, but said no more—Lorenzo must find his own way back to the faith he had lost. 'So what will you do now, my son?'

'It was in my mind to return to England with Kathryn. I thought we should visit her father before settling in Venice. That is still my intention. My life is here now, sir. England does not have much to offer me— though it might be different if you were there. What are your own plans?'

'As we discussed them in Sicily. I believe I shall stay here in Rome until you return, Lorenzo. I have travelled enough of late and I like it here.'

'I shall leave my business affairs to you until I return, Father,' Lorenzo said. 'But before I leave I must speak to Michael about the future. If I am to make changes, I would have him with me.'

Charles hesitated, looking awkward. 'Michael is not here. He went to England. I believe it was his intention to see Kathryn. We heard that you were shot trying to escape and I think he means to tell her that there is no hope of finding you alive.'

What he left unsaid was his conviction that Michael was in love with Kathryn and would have her for himself if he could. It could not help matters, for Lorenzo was already angry enough. He just hoped that he would not arrive too late.

'Then I must not delay,' Lorenzo said, a brooding expression in his eyes. He needed no telling that Michael cared for Kathryn—he had observed it himself. 'I shall spend this evening with you and then I must sail for England.'

Chapter Twelve

Kathryn looked at herself in her hand mirror. She was wearing a gown of green silk that her father had presented her with as a gift especially for that evening. She had asked that she be allowed to wear the black velvet she had chosen for her mourning, but Sir John had given her a stern look.

'You will not come to your brother's betrothal wearing black. It becomes you ill, Kathryn, and would be seen as an insult by Philip's betrothed and her family. You are a young and beautiful woman. You should make the most of your beauty, daughter.'

'Do not forget that I am in mourning for my husband, Father.'

'You grieve for a man by the name of Lorenzo Santorini, daughter. If Charles is right, that man does not exist. Therefore, I am not certain that your marriage was ever a true one. However, you *are* my daughter and as such will not disgrace me by appearing before our guests as a black crow.'

'That is unfair!' Kathryn cried, hurt almost beyond

bearing by her father's unkindness. Why was he being so cruel to her? Had she not enough to bear without this hurt? 'Lorenzo married me in good faith. I was and am his true wife.'

'You wed without my blessing and I could dispute it if I wished,' he reminded her coldly. 'You will oblige me by forgetting that unhappy period of your life. It is my sincere hope that you may marry again soon.'

'I do not wish to marry.'

'It is my wish that you shall be properly settled, Kathryn. People will whisper behind their hands about this odd marriage, but if you marry again they will be silenced. It is in my mind that a marriage shall be arranged by the end of your official period of mourning, and the contract may be made before that if we choose.'

Kathryn did not answer him. She could not for fear that she might say something that would anger or hurt him and cause a wider breach between them. She was greatly upset by what she considered his harshness and his words had brought her to the edge of tears. How could he force her to think of marrying again when her heart was broken? It was a cruel suggestion and she could hardly believe that the father she had loved so much could do this to her.

But she must not let anyone see her tears this evening. It was to be a special celebration for her brother, of whom she was fond. Raising her head, Kathryn prepared to go downstairs to greet her father's guests. She must be brave and smile this evening, for Philip was to be betrothed to a girl he admired and liked.

'Do you love Mary Jane?' Kathryn had asked her brother earlier that day.

'Love her?' Philip had wrinkled his brow, giving her a strange look. 'I am not sure what you mean by love,

Kathryn. I have known Mary Jane all my life. We are friends and I think her a sweet, pretty girl who will make me a good wife and bear my children. She is of good family and will bring me a small estate as her portion. I do not think I can ask more of my marriage.'

Kathryn had not known how to answer that declaration. She could never be content with such an arrangement, though she knew that it was commonplace amongst men and women of her class. It was not for her, though if she had never known Lorenzo perhaps…but she had! Her heart contracted with the familiar ache. It might have been better if she had never met him. She would rather die now than live with another man as her husband. She belonged to Lorenzo and could never be another's.

The betrothal ceremony was over. Philip and Mary Jane were dancing while everyone else looked on, smiling in approval, feet tapping to the merry music the minstrels played.

'It will be your turn next, Kathryn,' said a lady standing to her left. 'Sir John will find you a husband, my dear, and you may put all this nonsense behind you.'

'I am still in mourning for my husband, Mistress Feathers.'

'Oh, you will soon discover that one man is very much as another. I have been married three times and there was nothing to choose between them. Money, power and children will bring their own content. Love is merely a myth.'

Kathryn felt her throat closing and the tears were close. This insufferable woman knew nothing of love! She could feel the grief welling inside and knew she could not stay in this room another moment.

She turned and left the hall, which echoed with laughter

and music. Snatching a cloak that lay carelessly on a chest in the anteroom, she went out into the chill of the night air and began to walk, tears trickling down her cheeks as the grief spilled over.

'Lorenzo, my love,' she whispered to the night. 'Come back to me…oh, please, come back to me. I cannot bear this life without you.'

'Kathryn! Please wait!'

She turned as she heard Michael's voice calling to her. She had hoped to be alone, but the one person she could bear to be near at the moment was Michael. He had been with them in Venice and in Rome. He understood her better than any other, and he cared for her—which it seemed her father did not.

'You should not be out here on this bitter night,' Michael scolded her. 'It looks as if it will snow before morning. If you continue like this, you will become ill.'

'If I am ill, my father cannot force me to marry a man I neither know nor love.'

'He would surely not be so unkind!'

'He has spoken of it. Everyone tells me I must forget Lorenzo and put the past behind me, but I cannot. I love him. I shall always love him.'

'But to force you into marriage…' Michael hesitated. He had not intended to speak so soon, for he knew that Kathryn was suffering. But he had fallen deeply in love with her during the time she had nursed him back to health, and he could not bear to see her so unhappy. 'Your father has been courteous to me. Do you think he would accept an offer for your hand from me?'

'I cannot marry you. It would not be fair to you, Michael. I like you very much. You are a good friend— but my heart is with Lorenzo. I fear it always will be.'

'I meant only to save you more unhappiness. I would take you back to Rome, to your friends. You were happy there, Kathryn.' He moved towards her, looking into her face, her eyes, his hand reaching out to touch her cheek. 'It would not be a true marriage at first. I would be patient, Kathryn. I would wait until you felt able to be my wife in truth.'

'Oh, Michael,' she said brokenly. 'You make me ashamed. You are so good, so kind—but if I accepted your offer I might ruin your life. Supposing I could never love you, could never give you what you wanted?'

Tears were trickling down her cheeks. She could taste their salt on her lips. Michael put his arms gently about her, not imprisoning her but holding her in a comforting embrace, his lips moving against the fragrance of her hair.

'I love you, Kathryn. I would wait for ever and count it a blessing to be of service to you.'

She gazed up at him, tears hovering like crystals on her lashes. 'But you spoke of asking Isabella Rinaldi to be your wife?'

'My father wishes me to marry and I must oblige him, for he grows old and it is important to him. Isabella is pretty and I like her—but I love you. I have loved you since I first saw you, but I knew you saw only Lorenzo. I did not imagine that there was hope for me then…' He left the rest unsaid, for to remind her would only cause her more distress.

'Oh, Michael.' Kathryn wiped away her tears. 'I pray you, give me a little time to think. Perhaps…I do not know.'

She could not bring herself to say she would marry him, and yet she would rather it was Michael if she must marry again. Yet was it fair to take what he was offering her, knowing that she would never be able to give him more than second best?

'Say no more for the moment,' Michael said and smiled, taking her by the hand. 'Come back with me now, dearest one. I cannot let you walk alone in this bitter chill. Lorenzo would not demand that your life be sacrificed to grief, Kathryn.'

'I wish I was in Rome.' Kathryn sighed. 'It was so much warmer.' She smiled, feeling better than she had in weeks, allowing him to lead her towards the light and heat of the great hall.

The music had stopped quite suddenly. People had started talking, whispering excitedly one to another. She sensed that something had happened to change the mood of the evening. Kathryn's nerves tingled, feeling a prickling sensation at the back of her neck as Michael led her into the room. Everyone seemed to be looking in the same direction, at something—someone! Her heart stood still as heads suddenly turned towards her and Michael, and then the guests were parting, like the sea for the Israelites departing from Egypt, suddenly silent. She gasped as she saw that a man dressed all in black was walking towards her.

She felt as if she were in a dream, her head spinning as she saw him clearly. Her senses were reeling. Could it be— or was she in some kind of feverish nightmare? Her face had drained of colour and suddenly the ground came zooming up to her. As she fainted, two men moved to catch her.

It was Lorenzo whose arms surrounded her, sweeping her up as she would have fallen, lifting her effortlessly. His face was grim, eyes dark with anger as he looked at Michael and saw the jealousy that the other man was unable to hide.

'She is mine. Do not forget that.'

'We thought you dead. Kathryn has grieved enough.' Michael was defensive, angry in his disappointment, for he knew that he had lost all chance of her. 'I merely sought to comfort her.'

'We shall speak later.'

Lorenzo turned away, carrying Kathryn's limp form in his arms. He had such an air of command, such burning anger in every line of his face that when he demanded Kathryn's chamber, servants hurried to conduct him there.

Sir John watched the little scene from across the room. He had hoped for a match between Michael dei Ignacio and his daughter, but one look at Lorenzo's face had told him that it would be both futile and dangerous to attempt to deny him. He had come to claim his wife and nothing would stop him.

Sir John moved to confront him as he strode from the hall. 'My daughter, sir?'

'Is safe enough with me.'

'You wed her under a false name.'

'Not so. Antonio Santorini adopted me. I am legally his heir and bear his name. My father has agreed that I shall keep it at least until I inherit his title—which I pray will be many years in the future.'

Kathryn moaned and fluttered her eyelashes.

'Take her to her chamber,' Sir John said, a hint of bitterness in his voice. 'She has made herself ill with her grief.'

Lorenzo inclined his head. He followed the servants up the stairs to Kathryn's chamber. Servants fluttered ahead, clearly impressed by this stern-faced, aristocratic man who had declared himself her lawful husband to an astounded company. Covers were pulled back so that he might deposit his precious burden on clean linen. But when they lingered, their eyes large with curiosity, he dismissed them with an imperious wave of his hand.

Kathryn was stirring. Her lashes were wet. She had been crying earlier—and yet she had been holding Michael's hand when he first saw her enter the hall. He felt a surge of murderous jealousy against his friend. Had Michael stolen her love from him? For a moment as he saw them together in the hall he had contemplated murder.

Kathryn's eyelids moved. She opened her eyes, gazing up at him for a moment in bewilderment as though she did not believe what she saw, closing them once more as a tear squeezed from beneath her lashes.

'I am sorry that the sight of me made you faint, Kathryn.'

She opened her eyes again. 'Is it truly you, Lorenzo? They told me there was no hope—that you were dead.'

'And if I had been?' His voice was made harsh by anger. 'Would you have married Michael?'

'No!' She edged herself up against the pillows. The faintness had gone now, but she had a nasty taste in her mouth and her head ached. 'Why are you looking at me like that? You know I love you. You must know it!'

'Do you? You had been somewhere with Michael—in the midst of your brother's betrothal feast you slipped away with him. Why would you do that if you were not lovers? It is some months since you thought me lost, but I had hoped you would not have forgotten me so soon.'

'You cannot think that I would betray you so easily?' Kathryn was shocked, hurt. He had looked at her this way once before, as if he hated her. He blamed her for what had happened to him. 'My father said that I must marry again. I did not wish to—but Michael said he would be patient…'

She faltered as she saw the fury in his eyes. He was so very angry! 'He did ask me to marry him—a marriage in name only for the moment. I told him I needed time to consider.'

'You could not believe he meant that?' Lorenzo's voice lashed at her like a leather thong. 'He would take you any way he could, but he wants you the way a man wants his woman. The way I want you, Kathryn.' His hot eyes scorched her, making her tremble all over.

'I did not wish to marry again.'

'Yet you would have let them persuade you had I not returned. I thought your love stronger, Kathryn.'

'It is,' she said. He must believe her! She gave him a pleading, desperate look. 'You know I love you. I have always loved you.'

'Even when we were children?' he asked. 'You forgot your poor Dickon when you fell in love with Lorenzo—and you would have forgotten him as easily again once Michael was your husband.'

The reproach in his voice stung her, but he was unfair. 'That is not true! You know it isn't, Lorenzo. I am yours. I have always been yours...'

'Yes, you are mine, that much is true.' He rose from his seat on the side of her bed, causing her to look alarmed.

'Pray do not leave me!'

'You need to rest. We shall talk another time, for now I shall call your women to attend you. In the morning we leave for Mountfitchet.' His eyes were cold, remote. 'We are married, Kathryn, though your father would have had it otherwise. You will come with me. I do not give up what is mine, nor do I easily forgive.'

Kathryn stared after him as he left the room. He was insisting that she go with him and yet he was angry with her. He blamed her for his capture, because his love for her had made him careless, and he had decided to withdraw from her again.

She had longed, prayed for his return, hoping that he was alive despite all the odds, yet now that he had come to her, he had closed the door, shutting her out once more. It could only mean that he no longer loved her.

The journey to Mountfitchet Hall took only half a day's journey by horseback. It was bitterly cold, little flurries of snowflakes drifting into their faces, but not yet settling on the hard ground. Kathryn rode by her husband's side, glancing at the stern cast of his features from time to time. Two of her women and ten of Lorenzo's own men accompanied them.

When they reached Mountfitchet, she noticed that Lorenzo seemed to know exactly where he was going and wondered if he had been to the estate before coming to her father's house. They were greeted eagerly by Lord Mountfitchet's servants, who treated him respectfully as their master and seemed delighted to see him.

'Did you call here before you came to us?' she asked him when the greetings were over and they were alone in the private parlour that was situated to the right of the Great Hall.

'No, I came straight to you. Why do you ask?'

'You seem so at home here.'

'It was my home for fifteen years, Kathryn.' His eyes were intent on her face, though not as cold as the previous evening.

She opened her eyes wide in surprise. 'Have you recovered your memory? Charles told us that you had some vague memories, but you seem so sure…'

'I remember everything, Kathryn. Just as it happened.'

'You recall that day on the beach—the men who took you?' He nodded. 'Do you hate me for what happened to you?'

'Why should I hate you?' He looked puzzled.

'Because it was my fault. I dared you to go down to the beach to see what they were doing.'

'I was old enough to make up my own mind, and I knew the dangers better than you.'

'You told me to run away and fetch help while you fought them, but by the time the men looked for you it was too late. I have always blamed myself for not staying to help you fight them.'

'You were a child. What could you have done against such men? Would you rather I had let them take you too? Can you imagine what might have been your fate—where you might be now had you lived?'

Kathryn turned her head away so that he should not see her eyes, should not see the hurt he inflicted. 'Do not mock me, Lorenzo. I cannot bear it.'

'You mistake me. I do not mean to hurt you—but I should not have wished such a fate for you, that is all.'

'If you will excuse me, I should like to go to my chamber and rest.'

'Of course.' He inclined his head, respectful, cool—almost a stranger. 'I have things I must do while we are here. My father left the business of the estate for me to order as I thought fit.'

Kathryn glanced at him. 'Do you think of living here?'

'Would that please you?'

'I was happy in Rome.' She raised her head proudly. 'At least, I was happy for some of the time.'

'What does that mean, Kathryn?'

'Whatever you would like it to mean,' she said, a flash

of pride in her eyes. She was suddenly angry. She had mourned him sincerely and he had no right to treat her this way! 'Since you think so ill of me I shall not try to explain.'

She turned and walked away from him, leaving the room. Her heart was racing wildly and she wondered if he would follow her, compel her to answer him, but he did not.

Why should he? He did not want her love. He found it a burden. In Rome he had told her that he had never wanted to love her. Somehow he had conquered his emotions. He had claimed her because she belonged to him, but he did not truly want her.

Alone in the room Kathryn had just vacated, Lorenzo was haunted by the scent of the perfume she had left behind her. Throughout his captivity the memory of her scent, her softness, her sweetness, had made him determined to live, and now that he was with her he could not break down this barrier between them—a barrier he knew was of his making.

Had his jealousy driven a wedge between them? He had noticed her silence on the journey, her pale face, the accusation in her beautiful eyes, and knew it was his fault. In his first anger at seeing her so close to Michael, he had been too harsh. He cursed his ill temper. He had learned to be harsh of necessity. Once, he had been a very different man. Could he be as he had once been again? Could he learn to laugh and be happy?

He must and would try to make Kathryn happy! He could not know if it was too late to recover the brief happiness they had known in Rome, but he would try to win her.

And if that was not possible? Lorenzo asked himself if he would be prepared to give her up.

No! His mind rejected the idea instantly. She was his! He would not give her up. Somehow he would make her love him again.

Kathryn was walking in the gardens when she heard her husband's voice calling to her. She stopped, waiting for him to come to her. She had seen him only at mealtimes or a brief moment in the evenings, for he had seemed to be working ever since they had arrived at Mountfitchet.

'Kathryn,' he said as he joined her, 'is it not too cold for you to be walking?'

'It is a little chilly,' she agreed. Her restless mood had driven her outside, but she would not tell him that.

'Shall we return to the house?' he said, offering her his arm. 'I have some news. A letter has come from Queen Elizabeth of England. It seems that she has heard of us and some of what has befallen us. She wishes to know more about the battle of Lepanto.'

The letter had expressed curiosity about Lorenzo too, for the Queen had heard that Corsairs had captured him from her shores, and she always took an interest in such matters. Indeed, it was said that the Queen liked to have bold and handsome young men about her.

Kathryn felt a chill about her heart. Was he going to leave her once more? 'Are you to visit the court, then?'

'We shall go together, Kathryn. It is time that I gave a little time to my wife's pleasure. We shall buy you some pretty things in London. Perhaps you would like a ring or a rope of pearls? I have given you few gifts. There was never time for such things.'

Kathryn gazed into his eyes, trying to understand this new mood. Did he not know that his love was the most precious gift he could give her? She wanted for little else.

'You were always generous, Lorenzo. I never wanted for material things when I was in Rome.'

'But I gave you nothing more. Is that what you are saying, Kathryn?'

'Sometimes you gave me more.'

'Kathryn…' He was interrupted by the arrival of a servant who came hurrying towards them, clearly the bearer of an urgent message.

'Yes, what is it?' Lorenzo was impatient, for he had believed he was at last breaking through the barrier she had been keeping in place these past days.

'A message for the lady Kathryn, sir,' the servant said. 'Sir John, her father, has been taken gravely ill and would fain speak with her once more before he dies.'

'Before he dies?' Kathryn looked at her husband in alarm. 'What has happened? I did not think him ill before we left.'

'We shall return at once,' Lorenzo said as he saw her concern. 'Do not worry, my love. I am sure this seems worse than it is.'

He had called her his love, and in such a voice! Kathryn's heart beat wildly—but for the moment she could not think of herself. Her father was ill and she must go to him.

Tears were in her eyes as she let Lorenzo hurry her into the house. She had not been happy in her father's house these past weeks for he had seemed unlike the loving father she had known and loved, but she could not bear that he should die with bad feeling between them.

Sir John was lying with his eyes closed when Kathryn entered the room. As she approached the bed, he opened them and looked at her.

'Kathryn, my dearest child—forgive me.'

'Father…' The tears were very close though she struggled to hold them back. 'There is nothing to forgive. I love you.'

'I have been harsh with you,' he said, his voice little more than a whisper as she went to his side, reaching for his hand to hold it gently in her own. 'It was only because I wanted to make sure you were safe when I was gone. I was fearful for you if I should die before you were wed.'

'You must not die, Father. I love you. I do not want you to die.'

'I have known for some months that I could not live many years, my dearest child. It is the reason I made you come home with me. I could not leave you alone and defenceless in Rome and I believed if I could see you safely wed to a good man I could die in peace. You might have lived in your brother's house, but that would be no life for you. Now that you have your husband to protect you, I may die easily—if you will forgive my unkindness to you, daughter?'

Kathryn bent to kiss his lips. 'I love you,' she said. 'You have always been a good and loving father to me. It hurt me when I did not understand your harshness, but now…' She bit back the sob that rose to her lips. 'If my forgiveness will ease you, you have it, my dearest father.'

'Thank you, Kathryn,' he said and smiled. 'Sit here by my side for a little. It is good to know you are near.'

Kathryn's eyes stung with the tears she would not allow to fall. She had felt estranged from her father because of his apparent intention to force her to marry against her will, but now that she understood his reasons, all she could feel was grief that he was dying, and regret that she had not seen the signs of illness in him.

She sat with him for most of the night, leaving his bedside only when her brother came to take her place, insisting that she must rest for a few hours.

'Lorenzo says you must get some sleep,' Philip told her when he came to take her place. 'I shall call you if need be.'

'I had no idea he was so ill.'

'Do not blame yourself, Kathryn. He hid it well, even from me in the beginning. I begged him to let me come to Venice and find you, but he insisted on making the journey himself. I think it took the last of his strength. He has been failing ever since you returned.'

She had been too caught up in her grief for Lorenzo to notice! Regret mingled with her grief as she went to her bedchamber. She had hoped that Lorenzo might come to her there, for she needed his arms about her, but he did not. For a while she lay sleepless, tossing and turning in the feather bed, and then at last she slept.

Lorenzo came to her the next morning as she was dressing. Her heart caught with fright as she saw his grave expression.

'Is he worse?'

'He is certainly no better. I have spoken with the doctors and they do not hold much hope of his recovery. I am sorry, Kathryn. I know this must cause you pain.'

'Yes, it does,' she admitted. 'We had not been on the best of terms of late, and that makes it harder somehow.'

'You had quarrelled with him because of me?'

'Yes…' She smothered a sob. 'I did not understand why he wanted me to marry again so soon. He thought it would make me safe when he was gone.'

'I am sorry to have been the cause of anger between you.'

'There is no need,' she replied. 'I was grieving for you and because of that I did not notice that he was ill.'

'Did it hurt you so much when you thought I was dead?' His eyes were on her face, seeking out the truth.

'Yes, of course,' she said, looking steadily into his eyes. 'It broke my heart. I thought it would have been better if I had died. One day I walked to the top of the cliffs where…I think I might have thrown myself into the sea then if Michael had not come.'

'He saved your life, then?'

'He stopped me from committing a sinful act, for it is a sin to take one's own life—but still I had nothing to live for until you returned to me.'

'Kathryn…' His voice was hoarse with emotion, remorse strong in him. 'And then I was harsh to you. Forgive me if you can. When I saw you enter the hall holding Michael's hand I thought the worst, and—'

He was prevented from continuing by the arrival of a servant.

'You are wanted, Mistress Kathryn,' the girl said. 'Sir John is dying and asks for you.'

'Oh, no!' Kathryn cried and Lorenzo caught her hand, holding it tightly. 'Come with me, please?' She gave him a look of such appeal that it almost tore the heart from him.

'Of course,' he said. 'I shall always be there when you need me, Kathryn. We shall not be parted again in this life if I can help it.'

She smiled at him, but her eyes were filled with tears. They hurried to Sir John's bedchamber. It was obvious that he was failing, for he looked deathly pale as he lay with his eyes closed, and Philip was kneeling by the bed, head bent in prayer. Sir John opened his eyes as Kathryn approached.

'My dearest child,' he said. 'Come, kiss me one last time.'

She went to his side, bending over him and pressing her

lips to the papery softness of his cheek, her tears spilling over.

'Ah, do not cry, my dearest,' Sir John said. 'I am ready to die now that you are safe.' He looked beyond her to Lorenzo. 'You, sir. I pray that you love my daughter as much as she loves you.'

'I love her more than I have ever loved anyone.'

'Then I am content.'

Sir John closed his eyes. He had been holding Kathryn's hand, but his fingers lost their grip and fell away.

She gave a little sob as she realised he had stopped breathing, but then Lorenzo was there beside her. He drew her gently to her feet and into his arms, holding her as she wept against his shoulder.

'He is at peace now,' he said to comfort her.

'He is with our mother,' Philip said. 'I think it was what he wanted.' He bent over his father, closed his eyes and placed coins over them, and then drew the sheet over him. 'We should leave him to the women now.'

Her husband and brother led Kathryn from the room. She was glad of Lorenzo's arm about her waist, supporting her, but for the moment she wanted to be alone. The tears were draining her and she had no strength to fight them.

'Would you excuse me for a little?' she asked. 'I need to be alone for a while.'

'Yes, if it is your wish.'

Lorenzo watched her walk away from him, her back straight, head high. His heart ached for her and would have offered comfort if she had asked, but it seemed that she preferred to be alone.

She had told him that she loved him still, but he felt very alone at that moment. Perhaps in her heart she had not quite forgiven him.

* * *

Kathryn wept until there were no more tears left in her. She felt drained, exhausted, and fell into a deep sleep. When she woke again it was night. A fire had been lit in her chamber and someone had placed a coverlet over her, but the bed was empty beside her.

Suddenly, she wanted Lorenzo here with her. She had needed to be alone to let go of her grief, but now she longed for the comfort of his strong arms about her. He had not come to her, but she would go to him.

Throwing back the covers, she got out of bed. She went across to the fire to light a taper and touched it to a candle in her chamber-stick. She was approaching the door when it opened and Lorenzo entered. He stared at her in silence for a moment.

'I thought you were sleeping.'

'I was.' She drew a deep breath, then continued, 'But when I woke I wanted you. Will you not lie beside me, Lorenzo? It is a long time since we were together as man and wife.'

'I was not sure you wanted that.'

'How could you doubt it? Have I not always welcomed you to my bed?'

'I would not blame you if you hated me,' he said, his deep blue eyes intent on her face, his expression grave but questioning. 'It was because of me that you were kidnapped. I was unkind to you in Rome when I feared to let myself love you and then I was the cause of an estrangement with your father…'

'Hush, my love.' Kathryn moved towards him, her perfume seeming to surround him, capturing his senses. She put her fingers to his lips, smiling up at him so tenderly that he caught his breath. 'I have sometimes been angry with you, and sometimes I have broken my heart for the loss of you, but from the moment I first looked into your eyes in Venice I have loved you. My heart knew you as Dickon then, though my mind would not have it so. But Lorenzo Santorini or Richard Mountfitchet, I shall love you all my life.'

'Kathryn…' His eyes gleamed as he moved to take her in his arms, holding her pressed against him. 'I do not deserve such love from you. I am not worthy of you.'

'Perhaps not,' she teased, a wicked expression on her lovely face. 'But you may strive to be so for the rest of our lives.'

'The rest of our lives?' There was laughter in his face as he gazed down at her, his hold tightening, hot eyes devouring her with a passion that made her breathless. 'For this life and the next,' he murmured huskily. 'I love you, Kathryn. I love everything that is you—your smile, your laughter, and your scent…your lips that haunt me when I sleep.'

'You are no longer afraid that loving me will make you weak?' she asked anxiously. 'You said that it was the reason you withdrew from me in Rome and I have wondered—'

'That was a fool's notion,' he replied hushing her with the softest of kisses. 'Your love made me stronger, Kathryn. I was determined to live for you. Besides, it was because of that love that I am here with you now.'

'What do you mean?' she asked, feeling puzzled.

'The man I was before I loved you would not have spared Rachid's son. It was Hassan who spared my life after his father's death. He is a Corsair and I think there is something of his father in him, but when we talked I discovered that he is a very different man. We have made a truce. Neither of us will attack the other's ships. It means that I may carry on my trade without the need for so many war galleys.'

'Do you trust him? Will he keep his word?'

'I believe so. For years Venice had a similar treaty with the Turks. Before I left Rome I heard rumours that the Doge may make some sort of pact again. A tribute of gold so that we may trade in peace. Some would think it a betrayal of the League and all that it stood for, but Venice grew strong on trade and without it we would be nothing.'

'And shall we live in Venice?'

'You were happy in Rome,' Lorenzo said. 'Venice is the base of my wealth, Kathryn, and I must continue to trade from there. Yet I do not see why we should not have a home in Rome. My father will live in Rome for he likes it there, and I shall spend much of my time there.'

'And when you go to Venice I shall go with you,' Kathryn said, 'for I would not be parted from you again.'

'Nor I from you,' he said and drew her closer. 'I do not think life would hold me if I lost you, my love.'

She looked up at him then, a naughty sparkle in her eyes. 'Then lie with me, Lorenzo. I want to feel you close to me, holding me, loving me.'

'You are sure?' The heat was in his eyes, testament to his burning desire, but still he hesitated. 'You wanted to be alone…'

'Only for a little,' she said. 'I have wept for my father, but I shall put my grief aside now. There have been too many tears. I want to be with you, Lorenzo, to be happy and loved.'

'You are loved, my dearest one, and I shall do all I can to make you happy.'

'If I have your love, I shall be happy.' She smiled and took him by the hand, leading him to the bed.

Their loving was sweet and tender, a sealing of the promises they had made each other. Later, they made love again, a hot, hungry coupling that made her cry his name over and over as he thrust himself deeper into the warm moistness of her welcoming femininity. And when it was over at last, there were tears on her cheeks.

Lorenzo wiped them away with his fingertips. 'Did I hurt you, my precious? I wanted you so much…'

'Never,' she said, kissing away his doubts. 'You have never hurt me when you love me. My tears were because you gave me so much pleasure.' She smiled up at him. 'Perhaps we have made our son this night, Lorenzo.'

'When children come they will be welcome,' he murmured against the silky perfume of her hair. 'But it is you I adore, my Kathryn.'

She sighed with content as his lips nuzzled against her throat. She was safe and happy in his arms, and something told her that a child would be born of such sweet loving.

Chapter Thirteen

'I think you are bigger than I was with my son,' Elizabeta said, laughing as Kathryn pouted and placed a hand to the small of her back. 'Poor you. These last few weeks seem for ever, do they not?'

'Not as long as the time we spent at Queen Elizabeth's court,' Kathryn said and frowned. 'She seemed delighted with Lorenzo and demanded his attention day and night. I believe she would have kept him with her for ever if she could. I thought that we should never get away.'

'Well, now you are here, and I am pleased that you will stay in Rome for the birth.'

'Yes.' Kathryn sighed. 'I long to give Lorenzo a son, but I cannot wait to be back to my normal size again. I feel so huge!'

'It is always the same,' her friend agreed, 'but Lorenzo thinks you are beautiful, so do not worry. He never looks at another woman.'

Kathryn smiled. She did not need to be told that her husband was faithful to her. He had shown his love for her in so many ways these past months that she no longer doubted him.

She believed he had still been a little jealous of Michael when they first returned to Rome, but now Michael was married to Isabella and living in Venice. He had Lorenzo were still friends, though Michael had his own fleet of ships now. Lorenzo no longer needed so many galleys, for his ships sailed without fear of attack from his old enemy. It seemed that the seas of the Mediterranean had become much safer since Lepanto.

Lorenzo was out on business, which continued to take much of his time, though he had promised he would not leave Rome until after their child was born.

'I shall be near when you need me,' he told her. 'And we shall stay in Rome so that you have your friends about you.'

Kathryn was glad of Elizabeta's company that morning. She stood up, walking about the walled garden, stooping to smell a beautiful red rose. It was as she straightened up again that the pain suddenly struck her.

She gave a cry of mingled surprise and alarm, looking at her friend in consternation. 'I think…oh…' She gasped as she felt another strong contraction. 'The baby…' Her eyes reflected fear as she looked at Elizabeta. 'I thought there were another few days left…'

'I am not surprised if you are coming early,' Elizabeta said. 'You have been carrying low for the past week or more. Some babies do come a little early, Kathryn. There is no need for alarm.'

'Oh…' Kathryn breathed hard as the pain ripped through her, much stronger now and more urgent. 'I think I should go to my room.'

As she went into the house, she met her father-in-law. Charles looked at her white face and realised what was happening. He summoned a servant as Kathryn bent over with the pain.

'You must go to bed, my dear. I shall send for the physician—and a message will be delivered to Lorenzo. You need him to be here with you at this time.'

'Thank you.'

Kathryn bit her lip, refusing to give into the fear and pain, which was coming often now. She was glad of the assistance of her maids. They helped her to undress and to lie on her bed, packing pillows at her back to try to make her comfortable, and bringing towels when her waters broke.

Elizabeta came to sit with her, holding her hand as the pains racked her body, making her writhe in agony and cry out.

'You are doing well,' she said. 'Your pains are much stronger than mine were at this early stage. I think your labour will be shorter.'

Kathryn could not answer. She had never felt such terrible pain and could not stop herself screaming as it became intense once more, and she experienced a strong desire to push.

'It is coming,' Elizabeta cried. 'Oh, my dear friend, I can see the head. Push harder now and it will soon be over.'

Kathryn did as she was bid. The pain then made her scream long and loud, and it was this sound that Lorenzo heard as he entered the house.

His father met him, restraining him, as he would have gone to Kathryn. 'Wait a little, my son. She has her women and Elizabeta.'

'She needs me. I must go to her.'

At that moment they heard a wailing sound and looked at each other in relief. 'It is over. Kathryn…'

Lorenzo broke from his father's hold and started towards his wife's room. As he reached it another terrible scream broke from her.

'Kathryn?' He looked towards the bed and was met by a warning look from Elizabeta. 'We thought the babe was born?'

'Your son was impatient to make his way into the world, sir—but it seems there is another child. And this one may take its time.'

'Another child? Twins…' Lorenzo turned pale, for such births were more difficult for the mother. He went to the bedside, reaching for Kathryn's hand as she writhed in agony. 'My poor love, forgive me.'

Kathryn shook her head to deny his fault, but the pain was too intense for her to speak to him. She clung on to his hand, her fingers digging into his palms as the pain struck again.

'Our son. Call him Dickon,' she whispered hoarsely. 'If anything should happen to me…'

'Nothing will happen!' He looked about him impatiently. 'Where is the physician? Has no one sent for him?'

'He was sent for at once,' Elizabeta told him, 'but your son came quickly.' She showed him the babe wrapped in soft swaddling. 'Is he not beautiful?'

'Yes, but I would to God he had been the only one,' Lorenzo said, his face white with concern. He watched as Kathryn moaned and writhed, frustrated that he could do nothing to help her. 'Damn the man! Where is he?'

'Here, Signor Santorini, at your service.'

The physician entered, a small, dapper man dressed in dark clothes and carrying a wooden box, which contained the instruments of his trade.

'She is in such pain,' Lorenzo said. 'Do something to help her!'

'If you would please leave the room. Only one lady should remain while I examine your wife, *signor.*'

Lorenzo seemed as if he would refuse, but Elizabeta gave him a speaking look. 'I shall stay with her. You can trust Signor Viera. He was very good when I was in labour. Kathryn will do well now that he is here.'

Lorenzo bent to kiss Kathryn's forehead, which was damp with sweat. 'I shall return soon,' he promised.

Outside the bedchamber he found his father waiting anxiously for news. 'Is all well?' he asked.

'Kathryn has given birth to a healthy boy, but there is another child and this one does not come so easily.'

'God have mercy!' Charles crossed himself. 'At least the physician is with her now.'

'For what good it may do us,' Lorenzo snarled. He had little faith in doctors and was consumed with fear that he might lose the woman he loved more than life itself.

It was several minutes later that the doctor came out to them.

'The second child has turned the wrong way. I must turn it and perhaps use my instruments to bring it out. If I do, the child may be damaged. It is a risk, but unless I help your wife she may die in the struggle to give birth.'

'Save Kathryn,' Lorenzo said. 'I pray the child will not suffer too much harm—but you must save my wife.'

'It shall be as you say.'

Lorenzo stared as the door closed behind him once more. He belatedly tried to follow, but Charles stopped him.

'The birthing chamber is no place for you, my son.'

'Kathryn needs me.'

'I know how you feel, but you must leave this to Elizabeta and the doctor. When your mother died giving birth to a stillborn child, I wanted to be with her, but she did not want me near her. Go to Kathryn as soon as it is over, Lorenzo.'

Lorenzo was torn by his desire to comfort his wife and the wisdom of his father's words. He paced the hall outside Kathryn's chamber like a caged beast, each minute seeming like an hour. And then, at last, when he thought he could bear it no longer, the door opened and the doctor came out to him.

'Your daughter is very weak, *signor*. She may not live the night. Your wife is well, but will need to rest. She has suffered some damage and it may be that she will not be able to have more children.'

'But she is well? She will live?'

'She needs rest, but she will live,' the doctor told him. 'You may go into her now, *signor*.'

Kathryn lay with her eyes closed as he approached the bed, but she opened them and smiled as he bent over her to kiss her softly on the lips.

'We have a son and a daughter. Is that not clever of me, Lorenzo?'

'You are wonderful, my darling,' he said and looked at her with love. 'Thank you for my son, Kathryn. He is a most precious gift.'

'And your daughter? Are you not pleased with her?'

'Of course…' He hesitated, but thought it best to be honest. 'Doctor Viera told me that she is delicate. We may lose her, Kathryn. But you will live and so will our son.'

'She shall live too,' Kathryn said. 'And we shall call her Beth.'

'I pray that you are right, my darling.' Lorenzo kissed her again. 'You should sleep now, Kathryn. I love you and our babies and I shall come to you again soon.'

He watched as she lay back against the pillows, dark shadows beneath her eyes, worn out by the fight to give birth, and whispered a silent prayer. He gave thanks for her life and that of his son.

'If you are merciful, God,' he murmured aloud, 'watch over our Beth this night, I pray you.'

Elizabeta beckoned to him and he crossed the room to gaze at the face of the tiny girl she held for him to see.

'Is she not beautiful?'

'Very. She is like her mother.'

'And as such, she is a fighter. I think the doctor is wrong,' Elizabeta said. 'She was sucking my thumb strongly just now. I shall summon the wet nurse to attend her and then we shall see.'

Lorenzo felt a wave of tenderness as he bent to kiss the tiny scrap of humanity that was his daughter. 'Live, my little one,' he said. 'Live for yourself, for your mother and for me.'

It seemed to him then that the child smiled at him, and he felt her little fingers curl about his heart, binding him as surely as he was bound to the woman who had given this tiny scrap life.

It was a beautiful day and the first time that Kathryn had come down in more than two weeks. Lorenzo had insisted on carrying her to her chair in the garden, placing cushions at her back and a rug over her knees. She looked about her, catching the scent of a full-blown dark red rose, and lifting her face to the sun as a feeling of content surrounded her.

'I am quite well now,' she told him with a smile.

'You are still a little tired,' he replied. 'You must rest for three weeks as the doctor told you.'

'He makes such a fuss,' Kathryn said and pulled a face at him. 'Did he not tell you that Beth would not live through the night? And does she not thrive?'

'Thanks to our good friend Elizabeta and the wet nurse.'

'I should have liked to nurse her myself,' Kathryn said

wistfully, 'but Dickon is so greedy there would not be enough milk left for her.'

'She thrives as she is,' Lorenzo said. 'And you make much fuss of her when you hold her. She will learn to know that she is loved, Kathryn.'

'She likes you to hold her,' Kathryn replied with a tender smile. 'She stops crying instantly when you pick her up. I think she knows you are her devoted slave, Lorenzo.'

'She is so like you,' Lorenzo said and laughed ruefully, knowing that the babe had him curled about her little finger. 'I cannot resist spoiling her, because she is so beautiful.'

Kathryn sighed with content as she looked up at him. He was so different now to the man she had married, always laughing and teasing her, making up stories to entertain her, just as he had when they were children. She knew that Dickon had come back to her at last. He was Dickon and he was Lorenzo, the two now blended into one whole, a man she could love, respect and lean on in the years to come.

'We are so lucky,' she said, 'to have each other and our children.'

'God has blessed us,' Lorenzo said. 'Once I thought he did not listen to our prayers, but now I know that I was wrong.'

Kathryn reached out for his hand. Her fingers moved to the hard welt of scarred flesh, tracing it gently. Lorenzo no longer wore his wristbands. He had no secrets to hide. The past was gone, if not entirely forgotten.

'I love you,' Kathryn said.

'As I love you,' he replied. He looked up and smiled as his father came out to join them in the courtyard. 'I have everything that any man could want.'

* * * * *

The Pirate's Willing Captive

ANNE HERRIES

I thank all my readers for their continued support.

Prologue

Spring 1557

The man walked away from the hostelry on the water-front deep in thought. He had booked passage on a ship bound for France and it might be many years before he returned home. He was filled with regret and anger for he had parted from his father with bitter words.

'You take the word of others above mine, Father—you would believe a stranger above your own son.'

Justin Devere's blue eyes had flashed with pride, making Sir John snort impatiently. 'You were a damned fool, Justin. By God, sir! There is no excuse for what you have done. You are the great-grandson of Robert Melford and a more devoted supporter of the Crown could not be found. Your grandfather was much favoured by King Henry VIII—and my own family has always been loyal. By becoming involved in this con-spiracy to murder Queen Mary and replace her with the

Princess Elizabeth you have let your whole family down. I am ashamed of you!'

'No, sir. You wrong me…'

Justin raised his head defiantly. He was a handsome devil, with pale blond hair and deep blue eyes; reckless, arrogant and dismissive of rules, he stood head and shoulders above most men, including his father. His grandfather said he was a throwback to Robert Melford in temperament and build, though not in colouring. He was also fiercely proud and it pricked his pride to hear his father call him a fool.

'You have spoken treason against the Queen and that cannot be tolerated.'

'It was no such thing, sir!' Justin declared passionately. 'I will grant that some hotheads have talked of such a plot in my hearing, but I am innocent of any conspiracy—as is the princess herself. She was gracious enough to grant me an audience; many of us wished her to know that we support her and if any attempt were made to disbar her from inheriting the throne when the Queen dies we should rise to her—'

'Be quiet!' John Devere thundered. 'Do you not realise that that in itself is sufficient to have you arrested for treason?'

'I shall not be silent, sir. I am as loyal an Englishman as any, but I cannot love a Catholic queen who puts good Englishmen to the fire in the name of religion.'

'It is not so many years since we were all Catholic and proud of it,' Justin's father reminded him. 'King Hal saw fit to break with Rome and we were all forced to follow or lose our favour at court, but that does not mean—' He broke off, for the anger was writ plain on Justin's face. 'While the Queen lives 'tis treason to speak of her death and well you know it.'

'We did not plot to murder her, merely to protect our own Elizabeth.'

'Surely it is enough that talk of your conspiracy has reached her Majesty? The Princess has herself faced questions from the Queen regarding treason and was lucky that her Majesty was in good humour because her husband has promised to visit her soon. Had it not been for that fortunate circumstance, she might have found herself in the Tower once more.' John placed a hand on his son's shoulder. 'Go to France or Spain, Justin. I know that though you have done wrong your heart was good. You have my blessing. Send me word of your situation and as soon as I think the coast clear you may return.'

'You would have me flee like a coward?' Justin's face reflected his disgust.

'I would have you live, sirrah! Stay and I may have no son to inherit my estate—and that will break your mother's heart.'

Lost in the memory of the bitter quarrel with his father, Justin did not notice the shadows behind him. Not until it was too late did he realise that he had been followed from the hostelry. Even as he turned, about to draw his sword, a crashing blow to the back of his head sent him to the ground and he lost consciousness as he was carried aboard a ship, not as the passenger he had paid to be, but to serve before the mast.

Chapter One

Spain—autumn 1558

'No, Father, please do not ask it of me.' The girl faced the tall man with iron-grey hair defiantly. He was a man of wiry stature, elegantly dressed in black with only one jewel of note, which was a ring made from gold and black agate to denote his mourning for his late wife. 'I am not ready to marry again. I know you are grieving and you wish a better life for me, but I would rather stay at home with you.'

'It is nearly a year since Don Pablo died.'

Don Miguel Sabatini's face was cold as he looked at his beautiful daughter. With her dark hair dressed in ringlets in the Spanish way, she reminded him of his first wife, whom he had come to hate after learning she had played him false with a lover. Her eyes were those of a temptress, a wanton wretch who had betrayed him, leaving a scar that would never heal. When he looked at Maribel's face he saw the pride of her English mother, a pride he had never been able to break despite his treatment of her, and the hatred burned cold and deep within him. His first wife had been a wanton, deceiving him with a man he had believed his friend. He had never forgiven her and his unkindness had driven her to the decline that led to an early grave. She swore that Maribel was his child, but he had never been certain and because of it could not love his daughter.

However, his second wife Juanita, a gentle kind-hearted woman, already past thirty when he wed her, had loved the motherless babe, and, unable to bear a living child herself, had taken the girl as her own, forcing him to show acceptance of a child he despised. It was she who had arranged Maribel's marriage to her young cousin. Unfortunately the bridegroom had died at the hands of bandits while riding in the hills a few months after the wedding, and Juanita had insisted her much loved stepdaughter return to live with them. Maribel had been grieving for her young husband ever since.

'You must marry, daughter. It is a woman's duty and her destiny.'

'But I cannot put aside my feelings for Pablo so easily, sir. I loved him truly and I do not wish to marry again.'

'I have written to a gentleman in England with whom I have business. He imports wine from our vineyards and a marriage between you would seal the alliance, make it stronger.'

'But I do not know this man…' Maribel protested, dark eyes flashing a protest. 'You have not even told me his name.'

'His name is not important, but since you will have it—he is Lord William Roberts of Helbourne.' He waved his hand as if to dismiss her.

Maribel refused to be dismissed so brusquely.

'An English lord?' Her gaze narrowed as she looked at him, saw the cold proud stance and felt again the hurt he had inflicted so often. Why was he so often unkind to her? What had she done to make him hate her, for she felt that his feeling went deeper than mere dislike? 'How old is he? What manner of man is he? Please tell me, Father.'

'What can his age signify?' Don Miguel demanded with an icy stare. 'He is of good character and rich—what more could you wish for?'

'A man such as Don Pablo. He was young and handsome and I cared for him,' Maribel said proudly. 'He left me a fortune—so why should I marry for wealth when I do not need money?'

'A woman alone cannot properly care for her estates. I have done what I can for you, daughter, but you should think of marriage. It is the right and proper course for you to follow. Surely you wish for a husband and children?' His voice softened, took on a persuasive note. 'You cannot wish to spend all your life in mourning for a man you hardly knew? He would have wished you to be happy.'

'Yes…perhaps,' Maribel faltered. When her father spoke softly to her she almost believed that he truly cared for her, and yet in her heart she knew that it was Juanita who had always stood between them, sheltering her from his anger. She thought sometimes that he had hated her from the moment she was born. However, Juanita had told her that he was a good man despite his stern ways and she believed her stepmother. If he felt she should marry this English lord, it might be for the best. To openly disobey him at a time when they were both grieving for the woman they had loved would be to show disrespect to Juanita's memory. 'I beg you will allow me time to consider this marriage, sir. I should like to meet the gentleman before making a commitment.'

'I will write and invite him to visit. He is a busy man. He may send someone in his stead—perhaps a portrait would ease your mind?'

'I should like to see his likeness.' Maribel moved forwards, her hand outstretched. 'Please, give me a little time, sir. I have not yet recovered from my stepmother's death. I loved her dearly.'

'As did I, God rest her soul,' Don Miguel said piously. 'For Juanita's sake I shall grant you a further few months, but I want you to make yourself ready, Maribel. It is my wish that you should marry soon.'

Maribel inclined her head. From the tone of her father's voice she knew herself dismissed. He had no more to say to her and considered the matter settled. No doubt he would invite Lord Roberts to visit them and arrange the wedding without further reference to her wishes.

Going outside to the shaded courtyard, Maribel blinked to stop her tears. She had no wish to leave Spain for England, which was a country of which she knew little. Her mother had been an Englishwoman, but Maribel could not remember her, though she had lived until past her child's second birthday when she had died of a fever after giving birth to a stillborn son. It must be because she was half-English that her father had decided she should marry this English lord.

Maribel's throat caught as she thought of her handsome young husband. He was but sixteen when they married, her own age at the time, and beautiful to look upon. Pablo Sanchez had a gentle nature. He was loving and kind, and he had treated Maribel as a sister. They had had fun riding together and playing foolish games. Something that no one else knew was that their marriage had never been consummated. Maribel was as much a virgin now as she had been on the day of her wedding.

Perhaps if her father understood that she was still virgin he would have some sympathy for her, but she could never tell him for it would shame her.

The future loomed dark and forbidding before her. She had been granted a few more months, but she knew the time would come when her father would force her to marry the man of his choosing.

'Cut him down and carry him below,' Justin commanded of the sailors. He had just been compelled to order the flogging of one of the crew for disobedience and it had taken all his self-control not to snatch the cruel whip from the bosun's hand. 'We must tend his wounds.'

'Aye, that we must,' Higgins growled. ''Tis a wonder the poor lad bore it as well as he did.'

'I know it well enough.'

Justin did not remind the man that he had been lashed the first time he disobeyed the monster that was their captain. On waking with a crashing headache that first morning to discover that he was aboard a strange ship and bound for the east, Justin had at first refused to take orders from Captain Smythe and his bosun. However, a lashing at the mast had made him realise that he had little choice but to obey. It was entirely due to the first mate Higgins's care of him that he had recovered.

Gradually, over the months, Justin had found his sea legs and gained the respect of the rest of the crew. He knew that they looked to him for a lead, and that most of them were at the point of mutiny. The time was coming when he must act, but for the moment the injured lad was his main concern.

Once they were safely below decks, they laid the young sailor on a mattress of blankets and sacking and Higgins began to wash away the blood as carefully as he could. The sailor had fainted after forty lashes and was unaware as the man tended his wounds with a salve. When he had finished, Higgins looked up at Justin.

'The men can't take much more of this, sir. They are looking to you for a lead.'

'You are talking of mutiny?'

'Aye, sir—common justice, I call it. The captain and his bosun must be put overboard in the night. Some of the officers are ready to join us, but any that refuse will go with the captain. The men think you should be their captain. They will follow you, sir—wherever you lead us.'

'I have heard the whispers. I am honoured by your trust in me, Higgins. Do the men understand that if we do this we shall be outlaws—forced to earn our living by piracy? If we were taken, we should all hang. This ship sails under the Queen's flag. Some of you may have signed of your own free will. I was press-ganged against my will, but it would not save me. I should hang with the rest of you.'

'Aye, we'll all hang if they take us, sir—but some of us think it worth the risk. A year or two as privateers and we can live like kings for the rest of our lives.'

'We'll be pirates, make no mistake, Higgins. A privateer sails with the Queen's blessing and I think we shall not be granted such a dispensation.'

'Aye, sir. The men know it.'

Justin's gaze narrowed. 'If I agree to this, there must be as little bloodshed as possible. I shall not stand by and see old scores settled. If I am to be master then the men will obey my rules. I shall not flog a man for a petty offence, but if a man murders a comrade he will hang. I am no soft touch and it is best the crew understand it before we begin.'

'We'll sail by the laws of the brethren. We all know

what is involved, sir—and we're all behind you to a man.'

Justin hesitated, then, 'Very well. The men will wait for my signal. Do we know who is with us amongst the officers?'

'The bosun will side with the captain, and perhaps Mr Hendry—all the others are as sick of their brutality as the rest of us.'

'Mr Hendry has the keys to the arsenal. We shall need that if we are to succeed.'

'He may resist, sir.'

'Leave him to me,' Justin's eyes gleamed with excitement. A life of piracy was not one he would have chosen, but now that it had been thrust upon him he saw that it was his only chance. If he refused, the men would butcher the captain, officers and midshipmen, and he would receive a knife in the back. Besides, it offered an adventure and freedom from the tyrant who had made all their lives a misery. 'When Hendry comes on late watch I shall offer him the chance to join us. If he refuses, he will be made captive until we have the ship—and then we shall put the men ashore. We are not far from the coast of Venice. The captain and officers can stay there until an English ship makes port and takes them home.'

'They will tell their tales of us, sir—we shall be hunted across the seas.'

'We shall be the hunters, Higgins. We'll head for Cyprus and refit and rename the ship. She needs trimming down to make her faster. We might sell her and buy something more in keeping with our trade. Trust me, I have learned much these past months and my mathematics are good; I know what is needed to improve her speed.'

'Aye, sir, we all know it. You will make a good captain—and you'll have the men behind you. Willing hands make light work.'

Justin smiled—he knew that the men often disobeyed orders or deliberately took their time carrying out their tasks as their only means of revenge on a master they hated.

'Tell the men to be ready for my signal.'

'Aye, aye, Captain Sylvester.'

Higgins saluted and left him alone with their patient. Justin smiled. He had given a false name to the bosun when he was first ordered to report for duty. No one knew his true identity and he would never reveal it. He was Sylvester and would now be the captain of a pirate vessel; for he had no doubt that they could take the ship. Justin was not sure that first officer Hendry would be prepared to sail with them as pirates, but he would be given his chance. If he could achieve it, the mutiny would take place with no loss of life, but he accepted that there might be casualties. Facing reality, he understood that he could not ply his trade without some bloodshed, but he would offer a safe passage to the crews of the ships they took. If they refused… Justin's expression hardened. They would do what was necessary and no more.

He had not asked to be brought on board this ship.

Injustice and prejudice had forced him to flee from England, and a press gang had robbed him of his liberty. In time he would part company from the ship and its crew and make his way to France, as he'd planned, but for the moment he was committed to leading the men to the fortunes they all hoped to make.

'I have had word that Lord Roberts is to send his cousin to escort you to England, daughter,' Don Miguel Sabatini said. 'You have had time enough to grieve. Captain Hynes will be here within days. You are to have your possessions packed and be ready to leave.'

'But am I to have no choice? Supposing I do not like him?' Maribel's head went up, her expression defiant.

'You will obey your husband, as you obey me. I have made my decision, Maribel.'

'What of my lands here in Spain?' Maribel had hoped that he had forgotten his plans for her marriage these past six months, but it seemed he had not.

'You may trust me to administer them for you. Once you are married, they will belong to your husband. He may wish to sell them and I shall await his instructions.'

'They belong to me. Pablo left them to my care. I do not wish to sell them.'

'Pablo has no son to inherit. Your new husband will instruct you in his wishes. Perhaps if you please him he will allow you to keep them and send his agents to inspect them.'

Maribel stared at him, mutiny flaring. She was angry that he refused to listen to her plea, but uncertain what she could do. Had Pablo's father lived, she might have applied to him for help, but her young husband had had no family. She was quite alone and had no influence with anyone; instead, she was at the mercy of her father's will.

As she left him and went out, wandering to the crest of the hill to look out over the sea, her thoughts were heavy. Even if she denied her father he might send her to England. There was little she could do; her fortune was in her father's hands. The lawyers had told her it was for the best and she had foolishly signed—but Juanita had been living then and her father had not been so stern...so unforgiving.

Hearing a muffled sound out to sea, Maribel shaded her eyes. The ships were too far out for her to see them properly, but she believed that one was firing on the other. What was going on? She had heard her father complain of the pirates that often attacked merchant ships in Spanish waters. Could it be a pirate vessel— and whose ship was being attacked?

'We found a rich haul in the holds.' Higgins grinned at Justin as he swung aboard the *Defiance*. 'The captain would not tell us from whence he came, but we found chests of unrefined silver...'

'From the New World, you think?'

'It would seem so, Cap'n.'

Justin nodded. Since he had taken command of the ship, putting its master and most of the officers ashore, they had been fortunate and had already taken three rich merchant ships, all of whom had surrendered when the first shot was fired across their bows.

'They surrendered the ship without a fight. Johnson told me that the crew have no love for the owner of this vessel. They were ordered to kill the slaves who mined the silver for them before they took it aboard and it hath sickened some of them.'

'That is beyond forgiveness!' Justin was angry. 'By God, the man responsible deserves to be taught a lesson!'

'Don Miguel Sabatini is the owner of the *Juanita*. He has men whose job it is to run the mines and they do not treat the slaves well. I have heard of him before from crew I met when we went ashore at Cyprus. His name is feared. Once he knows we have attacked his ships we shall be marked men.'

'We are faster than any Spanish ship, be it man of war or merchantmen,' Justin said. 'I do not fear Don Miguel nor yet any Spanish merchant. Only an English fighting ship can challenge us—and thus far we have outrun them all.'

'Aye, the luck has been with us,' Higgins agreed. 'The men think you are their lucky charm, sir.'

'We have been fortunate so far.' Justin laughed, feeling a surge of elation. 'This is the third rich prize we have taken. One more and we shall sail for Cyprus to re-provision and give the men a chance to spend some of their booty.'

'On wine and women,' Higgins agreed. 'For myself I'll be saving it to invest, perhaps in land in the New

World. I had a wife once, but when I returned from a long voyage I found her in bed with her new lover. She wanted a man who was content to live ashore. I needed to feel the wind in my face and the waves beneath me so I left her to it and signed on for a decent master. I'm in no hurry to retire, but when I do I'll find me a good woman and become a man of property.'

'A goodly ambition.' Justin's eyes revealed no secrets. The austere life at sea had hardened him in body and in mind. Thoughts of his quarrel with his father no longer tortured him. Though he'd not chosen his new life he had become accustomed to it and even relished it at times. 'Make secure the ship, Higgins. We'll find shelter in a quiet cove for the night. The look of that sky tells me that there will be a storm before long…'

As the first mate went out, Justin looked at the small chest he had taken from the captain of the captured ship. It was locked, but he prised it open with his knife and looked at the contents. Realising just what he had found, Justin hid the parchment inside his jerkin. If this fell into the wrong hands, it might cause mutiny and endless arguments, even some bloodshed. The map might be worth a fortune, but it would be more trouble than a little. He would keep it hidden for the moment while he decided what he ought to do with the unexpected discovery.

'Will you not relent and let me stay in Spain, Father?' Maribel asked one last time before she departed for the ship. 'I could go to my husband's house and you need not see me again.'

'To draw back now would cause offence to Lord Roberts and default on our contract,' her father said. 'Go with Captain Hynes. Your future husband has entrusted you to his care and you must forget all that you knew here. Your husband is a man of some stature in England. You should thank me on your knees for arranging such a marriage for you.'

Maribel understood that there was to be no reprieve for her. 'Very well, sir. I shall obey you.'

She turned away, her face proud and cold. Since there was no help for it she must accept her fate. Samuel Hynes was in the courtyard, waiting for her with the horses. He approached, offering his hand as if he would help her, but she gave her hand to her groom, Rodrigo, and let him put her up on her horse. There was something about Lord Roberts's cousin that made her distrust him; he had a sly, lascivious gleam in his eyes that made her uncomfortable and she would not have him touch her.

She saw him frown as he turned away. Her maid, Anna, who was to accompany her to England, was taken up behind the groom. They had both chosen to accompany her to her new home for they loved her dearly. It was Anna who had held her when she wept after Juanita's death, and Rodrigo who had taught her to ride as a child. Knowing that they were with her gave Maribel courage. She was not completely alone. She had people who cared for her—and perhaps in time she would learn to love the man she was to marry.

It was but a short ride to the cove where the ship had anchored. Maribel knew that her father had received bad news about one of his ships recently. The *Juanita*, which was his flagship, had been attacked and robbed of its cargo by pirates. Having sustained damage, it was in port being repaired. She was to travel on an English ship belonging to Samuel Hynes and understood that the *Mistress Susanna* was not as large or as well armed as the *Juanita*.

'Welcome aboard my ship,' Samuel Hynes said as he helped her step on deck. 'I am honoured to have you as a passenger, Donna Maribel. My cousin is a fortunate man. Had I been in his shoes, I would have made the journey myself.'

'I dare say Lord Roberts has much to concern him with the welfare of his estate and people.'

'Yes, perhaps. He is often at court. Yet I believe I should have spared the time for a bride as lovely as you, Madonna.'

Maribel lifted her head proudly, her eyes conveying her feeling of scorn. She would not accept his compliments for she did not like or trust him.

'I believe I shall go to my cabin, sir.'

'As you wish. I have given up my own so that you may be comfortable, Donna Maribel.'

'You will address me as Donna Sanchez, if you please.' Maribel said coldly. 'I have not yet married Lord Roberts and am still the widow of Don Pablo Sanchez.'

'Indeed you are, lady.' Samuel inclined his head respectfully, but there was a glitter of anger in his eyes. 'Forgive me. One of my men will show you the way.'

He signalled to a cabin boy, who came at a run. He grinned at Maribel and beckoned to her.

'Come, lady, I will take you to your cabin.' He hesitated as Maribel did not immediately follow. 'I don't speak Spanish, *señorita*...but you must come or he will be angry...'

Maribel smiled at him, because she sensed his concern. 'I understand English very well. My mother was English and Juanita thought it right I should speak it as well as my father's language. As a child I had an English nurse.'

The lad looked at her, but said nothing, glancing back at Captain Hynes as if he feared him. Only when they were in the cabin did he speak again.

'He would punish me if he heard me say it, lady— but be careful of the captain. I don't trust him. If what I've heard is true, he has tricked you and your father...'

'What do you mean? How hath he tricked us?'

'I heard as Lord Roberts lay close to death when this voyage was begun. If 'tis true, Captain Hynes will inherit the estate from his cousin—and you mayhap?'

Maribel turned pale, her head swimming for one terrible moment as she realised what this might mean. She had seen the look of lust in Samuel Hynes's eyes and felt sick, because she knew that she would be alone in England, apart from her servants, and at the mercy of an unscrupulous man. Hearing the sounds on deck, she understood that they had already begun to cast off.

It was too late to go back, and even if she were to return to her home she was not sure that her father would believe her.

As the cabin boy left, Maribel fell to her knees. She began to pull her rosary through her hands, her lips moving in prayer.

'Save me from this wicked man,' she whispered. 'Please God, do not allow me to fall into the hands of such a man—for I believe I should prefer to lie in my grave...'

'She is an English ship,' Justin said as they saw the flag flying proudly. 'We do not attack English ships.'

'The *Mistress Susanna* belongs to Samuel Hynes.' Higgins growled. 'I've served him and he was a worse devil than Captain Smythe knew how to be. He is a merchant and fair game. We've seen no Spanish ships for three days and the men are restless. I think we should take this prize. Besides—look at the second flag. That is Sabatini's pennant...'

'Why would an English ship fly the pennant of a Spanish Don?' Justin's gaze narrowed. Since discovering what kind of a man Don Sabatini was, he had determined to single his ships out whenever possible. 'There is something odd here. Mayhap Sabatini thinks to fool us into believing it is an English ship. Put a shot across their bows and run up the skull and crossbones. I would discover what kind of trick the Spaniard plays here.'

Justin was thoughtful as his men sprang into action. He knew they were restless and eager to return to their island to turn some of the booty they had taken into gold so they could spend it in the taverns and with the whores that plied their trade on the waterfront. His instincts had been to let the ship pass, but seeing Sabatini's pennant had changed his mind. The Spaniard was obviously trying to sneak one of his ships through under an English flag, and was possibly carrying a rich prize.

The men he commanded were loyal to a point, but wild and reckless. If he denied them such a prize, they might turn against him as easily as they had Smythe. Justin did not intend to continue as a pirate for longer than necessary. Once he had amassed enough gold, he could buy his own ship and become a merchant adventurer, which would suit him better than his present trade. Perhaps one day he might be able to return to England. He was not certain of his welcome, for his father would feel that he had disgraced the family by becoming a pirate, but his mother would always welcome him with open arms.

Justin had sent no word to his home. Better that his family think him lost than that his gentle mother should know what trade her son followed. Before he could return he must redeem himself in some way.

The *Mistress Susanna* was lowering her flag in surrender. She had given in without a fight—why? What cargo was so precious that the master was willing to surrender rather than risk being sunk?

Maribel rushed to the porthole as she heard the first shots fired. She could see that another ship was closing in on them fast—and it was flying the skull and cross-bones. They were going to be boarded by pirates!

'Donna Maribel, you must hurry…' Anna came bustling into the cabin. 'The captain bid me tell you to hide somewhere. He says he did not dare to fire back lest the ship was badly damaged and harm came to you—but he would have you hide for he says these men are scum and they will kill us or worse.'

Maribel's face drained of colour. Her knees felt weak and she was frightened by all the shouting and noise on deck. The ship's captain had surrendered, but it seemed that not all the crew were willing to obey him. Some were putting up a fight and there were screams as men were injured.

'I shall not hide,' she said. 'There would be no point for they will search the cabins and I will not be dragged from beneath the bed. It would not be dignified. I am the wife of Don Pablo Sanchez!'

'You could hide in your trunk, lady.'

'Do you think that would stop them?' Maribel's head went up proudly. 'These men only want money. If I tell them who I am, they will hold me for a ransom. My father is in charge of my fortune and he will pay if my life is in danger.'

Maribel's face was white, but she was proud and stubborn. She was the widow of Don Pablo Sanchez and a rich heiress. Her father would surely pay to have her returned to him safely. He had forced her to take this voyage, but he would not allow her to die at the hands of pirates for what could that gain him?

He had arranged the marriage because he wanted an alliance with Lord Roberts. Nothing had changed. He would pay the price these rogues demanded.

Maribel resisted her maidservant's attempt to make her hide and stood proudly in the centre of the cabin. When the door was suddenly thrown open, she looked at the man who stood on the threshold, facing him angrily.

'Who are you, sir? How dare you enter a lady's cabin without permission?'

The man stared at her for a moment. He was tall, handsome, with long pale hair that looked windblown; his was a strong face, arrogant and bold. His blue eyes seemed to burn her flesh as he stared at her in a way that challenged her. His gaze made her flush and tremble inside, but she did not allow her fear to show. She was a proud Spanish lady and would not show fear in front of a pirate dog!

'A thousand pardons, my lady,' the pirate said and swept her a bow to rival any courtier. A smile played about a mouth that looked sensuous, one eyebrow arched in inquiry. 'And who might you be, Madonna?'

'I am Donna Maribel Sanchez, widow of Don Pablo and daughter of Don Sabatini—and soon to be the wife of Lord Roberts of Helbourne.'

'That old roué? He was on his last legs before I left England,' the pirate said and grinned. His smile made her heart leap in her breast and insensibly some of her fear evaporated. 'Nay, lady, you are wasted on such a husband. I believe we have rescued you from a fate worse than death—the man is riddled with pox and steeped in vice. We shall take you with us to save you from this evil.'

'No!' Maribel stepped back as he approached her. She raised her head, her ringlets tossing as she trembled with indignation. 'My father will pay a ransom. I am wealthy in my own right…' A little gasp escaped her as she saw the gleam of mockery in his eyes.

'Indeed? Then Fate was with us this day, for we have a richer prize than we thought. A cargo of wine is one thing—but the widow of a rich man and daughter of Sabatini is another. Your father hath much to atone for, Madonna—and now we have the means to make him pay.'

'What do you mean? My father is a good man…' Maribel caught her breath as she saw his stern look. 'What is it? Why do you look at me that way?'

'I shall not offend you, lady, for I believe you may be innocent.'

'Tell me! I command it!'

'You command?' The pirate's teeth were white against the tan of his skin as he smiled and then bowed to her. 'Very well, I shall obey you, lady. Your father is a thief and a murderer. He allows his captains to mistreat the crews that sail for him—and he forces the natives of the New World to mine their silver for him and then has them murdered so that they cannot reveal the whereabouts of the silver to anyone else.'

'No! I do not believe you! You are lying!'

Maribel flew at him as he tried to take her arm to drag her from the cabin. She raised her hand to hit him, but he pulled her arm behind her back, catching her against his body, and holding her pressed hard to him. Maribel stared up at him fearfully, sucking in her breath as he lowered his head and took possession of her mouth. His lips demanded where Pablo's had softly whispered; his arms were strong, his body like iron and the heat of his manhood burned her. She felt the press of his desire through the silk of her simple gown and her heart raced. No man had ever treated her thus, and she did not understand why her heart was beating so fast. She should despise him, yet her body felt as if it were drowning in pleasure and a part of her wanted to stay in his arms. It took all her control not to moan and press herself against him for she had never felt such sweet sensation.

What was she thinking? He was a pirate, a barbaric rogue! She placed her hands against his chest and pushed; his strength was such that he could have taken full advantage, but to her surprise he let her go.

As he drew back, she saw the hot glow fade from his eyes and a cold disdain replace the lust that had for a moment seemed to have him in its grip.

'You are proud lady and lashed out in temper. Perhaps that will show you the error of your ways. Attempt to strike me again and I shall not stop at a kiss.'

'You are a pirate and an ignorant barbarian.' Maribel had recovered her senses. Perhaps because she felt ashamed of her weakness in not fighting him sooner, her voice was laced with scorn and she was every inch the haughty lady.

'The barbarians were not as ignorant as you might imagine, Madonna. In some ways their culture out-strips our own.' Justin grinned, more amused than angry. 'Think yourself fortunate that I am not what you think me. Had I been the ruthless devil you would have me, you would this night be warming my bed before I gave you to my men for their sport.'

Maribel drew back in shock, her eyes wide with horror.

A smile touched his mouth. 'Nay, I shall not treat you so ill. You may be a shrew, but you are a lady and I shall treat you as such. You will not be harmed while we hold you for ransom.'

'How can I trust your word?' She would be a fool to believe him for an instant, but something inside her responded despite herself.

'Because I give it. Behave yourself, lady, and I shall restrain my hand—but cause me trouble and I may just put you across my knee and teach you a lesson.'

'You would not dare!' Maribel stared at him. She saw that he was laughing and realised that he was mocking her. Her cheeks flushed; she knew that he might have done exactly as he wished with her, yet she could not accept her fate so easily. Her tone was more moderate, but still cool as she said, 'You are a rogue and a thief and—and no gentleman, sir.'

'I believe you are right. I was once a gentleman of sorts, but life has taught me that I must take what I can from it.'

'Do you give me your word that I shall not be... ravished and despoiled if I come with you?'

'If any man lays a finger on you I shall hang him. You have my word on it.'

'And my servants? My maid and groom?'

'Your maid may attend you and she is also safe from my men—but your groom returns to Spain with the ship, unless he cares to join us and become one of the brethren.'

'You do not intend to keep the ship? Surely it is your prize?'

'We have the cargo and you. The captain will deliver my message to your father. If he sends the gold we demand, you will be returned to him.'

'And if he does not?'

'Then he will never see you again.'

Chapter Two

Could this pirate truly mean his threat? Maribel's heart was beating wildly. She hardly knew how to breathe as he took her arm and steered her from the cabin. Yet firm as his grip was, he was not hurting her and he seemed to mean her no harm, at least for the moment. As they went on deck she saw that his men had surrounded and disarmed the crew. Some of the men were bringing up wine from the hold and transferring it to the pirate ship, which she saw was called *the Defiance*. As far as she could tell only a few men had resisted, but there had been some fighting and one or two men had been wounded, but it appeared that none had been killed. She saw Samuel Hynes on his knees, a knife being held at his throat; it was obvious that he had not surrendered immediately.

'What do you intend to do with Captain Hynes?'

'My men are of a mind to hang him, but I think we may send him back to Spain this time.'

Maribel did not like Captain Hynes but she hated brutality. 'You should not treat him so disgracefully.'

'Why, pray, should we not?'

'He deserves your respect.'

'Indeed? You have known the man a long time, perhaps?'

She flinched beneath the pirate's dark mockery. 'I know little of him—but I believe that all men should be treated with dignity.'

'Then perhaps you should know that Captain Hynes has men flogged for being in the wrong place at the wrong moment and sometimes just because it amuses him.'

Maribel gasped and lowered her eyes, because against her will she believed him. She had always felt something was not right when Samuel Hynes smiled and bowed to her, sensing that he was hiding his true nature.

'He may be a cruel man—but if you allow your men to ill treat him you are his equal.'

'You think so?' Justin arched his brow, his manner icy cold. 'I shall remember your words, lady. Now you must go aboard with your woman and those of the crew that have chosen to serve with us.'

'Are there many?'

'A cabin boy and a few others…'

Maribel turned to Anna as she joined her. The pirate captain had moved away. He was talking to the pirate who had a knife at Samuel Hynes's throat. Another man, older, with a scar on his cheek and a red band around his brow, had come to help them cross the plank that had been placed between the two ships to make it easier for the women to cross from one to the other.

'Give me your hand, lady,' Higgins said gruffly. 'You, lad, help the lady down there.'

Maribel felt a hand on her arm steadying her. She looked round to thank whoever it was and saw the cabin boy who had spoken to her when she first came aboard the *Mistress Susanna*.

'They have taken you too?'

'I came willingly, lady,' he said and smiled at her. 'It can't be worse than my last berth. 'Sides, I've never had more than a few silver coins in wages, and if I do my work well for the brethren I shall be rich.'

Maribel looked at him doubtfully. 'Do you not know what could happen to you if the ship is taken? You might be hung as a pirate.'

'I'd as soon hang as starve on the streets of London, lady—and the life at sea is hard for every man jack of us. I could die of the typhoid or the pox any day.'

Was life so harsh for a young lad? Reared to the privileges of birth and wealth, she had not realised what others suffered. She felt humbled and a little ashamed.

'What is your name?'

'I'm called Tom, lady. 'Tis as good a name as any for I know not my own. I was born in prison. Me ma died and I was brought up by the parish until I ran away to sea.'

'Why did you run away?'

'Because they made me work for nothing and gave

me scraps to eat. I was better off at sea, and if I'd stayed with my last berth I shouldn't have left the captain—but this one is a monster.'

Maribel reached out to touch his hand, her heart moved to pity by his plight. She had not realised there was so much suffering, for as unhappy as she had been after her stepmother's death, she had never known what it was like to go hungry or go in fear of a cruel master.

'If I am ransomed, I shall ask to take you with me. As my servant you would be fed and paid a wage—and I should not beat you.'

'I thank you, lady,' Tom said and lifted his head with a touch of pride. 'Here on this ship all men are equal. We sail by the laws of the brethren and share in the spoils. I reckon I'll be a servant to no man or woman in future—though if I were I could not want a better mistress.'

Maribel inclined her head, uncertain whether she had been rebuffed. Did servants dislike working for their masters? She had never considered it before. For the first time, Maribel was aware of the sheltered life she had led, protected, kept apart—but not loved, at least by her father.

The older man with the scar on his face was ushering her below deck. She obeyed, moving towards the hatch, but lingered for a moment looking about her. Tom seemed to think he had made a change for the better and somehow her fear had evaporated.

Of course their captain was a wicked, arrogant rogue and she disliked him, even though she had felt something very odd when he kissed her. She would do her best to avoid his company, but it would appear that for the moment she had little to fear from the pirates. They were not as wild as she had feared, and, as she looked back and saw that the captain was coming aboard, she understood that he was in complete command of his ship. The men jumped to obey his orders as he indicated they should disengage with the other ship, but they did so willingly. She had seen no sign of fear or resentment in their faces.

Her gaze went beyond him to the deck of the *Mistress Susanna*. She saw that Samuel Hynes was tied to a mast and that his men were beginning to cut the ropes that bound him…but they were taking their time. She had seen both fear and resentment on board that ship—as she had seen it in some of the men who served her father. Why was it different here?

'You should not linger on deck, lady.'

Maribel jumped guiltily as she heard the pirate captain's voice.

'I see that you have allowed Captain Hynes to live.'

'Against the will of some of my men.' Justin's gaze narrowed. 'Have you some affection for this man?'

'None, sir. I merely regret any bloodshed.'

'It is necessary at times, but we are not monsters. We kill only when we must.'

'Then why are you pirates? Could you not find an honest trade?'

'You ask too many questions, Donna Maribel.'

'You know my name—may I not at least know yours, sir?'

'Captain Sylvester, at your service.'

'Do not mock me. If you were at my service, you would not have kidnapped me.'

'I saw no force used, lady. You walked aboard my ship willingly.'

'Because I was given no choice! What would you have done had I refused?'

'Ah…' His eyes gleamed with mockery. 'I should then have had to carry you on board myself, for I would have no other lay their hands on you. As Captain I have first choice of the spoils—and you are my share, lady.'

'You promised to ransom me…' Maribel's heart raced as she looked into his eyes. They were so blue that she thought of a summer sky and for a moment she was drawn to him, but there was ice at their centre and she shivered, sensing his anger.

'Perhaps I shall…' Justin did not smile. 'Yet there is something about you that I think might be worth more than mere gold. So perhaps you should not tarry; I have work to do and you will be safe in your cabin.'

What did he mean? Her heart jerked with fright and yet her body tingled, making her feel more alive than she had for a long, long time. He might be a pirate and a rogue, but there was something compelling about Captain Sylvester—something that made her heart beat faster.

She turned and hastened towards the open hatch. Her pulses were racing as she climbed down the ladder taking her to the cabins below. She squashed the feeling that she might like him if she allowed herself to judge him fairly. No, she would not give in to weakness. The pirate captain was a devil! An arrogant, wicked, mocking devil and she hated him! Yet at the back of her mind a little voice was telling her that he had saved her from a fate that might have been far worse than her present situation.

Maribel stared out of the porthole at the calm sea. They had been at sea for two days and she had not left her cabin. She turned her head as her maid entered. Anna brought her food and wine each day and already knew her way about the ship.

'The captain says you may come on deck for some air, my lady—but that you should keep your head covered for the sun is hot and he would not have you take harm.'

'You may tell Captain Sylvester that I have no wish to come on deck or to mix with rogues.'

Anna looked at her oddly. 'Do you think it wise to send such a message, my lady?'

'How would you have me address him—as a friend?' Maribel knew that her maid's counsel was wise, but something inside her would not allow her to give in so easily.

'We have not been treated ill…'

'Indeed?' Maribel's dark eyes flashed. 'If you do not think it *ill* to be abducted and forced aboard a pirate ship, I do. Sylvester had no right to take us captive.'

'He had the right—'tis the law of the sea. He might have sunk the vessel and all with it, but only those that resisted were harmed, and I think none killed. It is not always the case with pirates. Had we been taken by corsairs we should be dead or on our way to a slave market, where we should be sold to the highest bidder.'

Maribel wrinkled her brow. She knew that her maid spoke the truth; they could have fared worse. However, she had no intention of relenting towards the pirate.

'You will please give my message to the captain, as I bid you.'

'Yes, my lady—but should you not like to go on deck for some air?'

'Not with rogues!'

Maribel turned back to her view of the sea. She was longing for some fresh air, tired of being cooped up in her cabin, and yet her pride would not let her give in.

After Anna had left her, Maribel ate a piece of bread and a mouthful of cheese. The bread was coarse and harder than she was used to, but the cheese tasted good. She sipped her wine, then put it down and began to pace the cabin. How long would it be before they made land? Where was the pirate taking her—and what would happen next?

'Forgive me, sir. My mistress is proud and bid me answer you in her own words. She is angry because she was forced to come aboard your ship.'

'Do not look anxious, Anna,' Justin said, a wry smile on his mouth. 'I shall not blame you for your mistress's words. I shall leave her to her own devices for a few days and then we shall see.'

'She needs to come up for some air or she will be ill.'

'Is she unwell? Does she suffer from sickness?'

'She is well enough, but I know she is fretting.'

Justin inclined his head. 'I shall speak to the foolish woman myself.'

He spoke to his first officer and then left the bridge. The Spanish woman was proud and ill tempered. When he first saw her she had taken his breath with her exotic beauty. Her hair was dressed across her forehead and caught in ringlets at either side of her face in the Spanish style, her clothes heavy and ugly compared with the gowns his mother had worn, for Lady Devere's gowns had come from France. Donna Maribel Sanchez was proud, cold and disdainful, as were most of her kind. Clearly she considered no one but herself and was furious at finding herself a captive. Her maid was concerned for her and would bear the brunt of her sickness if she fell ill. She deserved to be taught a lesson and yet he had seen spirit in her, something fine and lovely. He would not have her become sickly from lack of fresh air.

Outside her cabin door, he paused and then knocked. There was a moment's hesitation and then the word 'enter' spoken in a way that made him smile inwardly.

'Donna Maribel,' he said as he entered the cabin, 'I understand you are frightened to come on deck because you think us rogues and murderers.'

'I am not afraid, sir!' Maribel's head came up with a flash of pride. 'I simply do not wish to consort with murdering rogues…pirates.'

'I shall not deny that we are pirates, for 'tis clearly our trade. However, my men are not wicked rogues.

They were driven to mutiny by a cruel master and must now earn their living by roaming the seas in search of rich merchant ships to plunder.'

'You do not consider that makes you rogues?' She looked at him scornfully.

'Did you see anyone murdered aboard Captain Hynes's ship?'

'No…' She looked at him uncertainly. 'You said your men wished to hang him.'

'Yet I did not allow it. Some men in my position would have taken the ship as well as the cargo and hung or marooned those who would not join us.'

She was forced to acknowledge that he spoke the truth. When he spoke softly to her, she found herself drawn to him against her will, but she was not ready to admit defeat.

'Very well, not murderers, but still thieves, for you took what was not yours.'

'We are adventurers. We take what we need, but we do not harm innocent women and children; men are given the chance to surrender and join us or go on their way. Your maidservant has not been harmed and you may walk safely on our decks. I give you my word that not one member of my crew will lay a finger on you.'

'The word of a pirate?'

'My word is as good as any man's.' Justin moved towards her. She gasped and stepped back, her eyes widening as if she thought he would repeat the punishing kiss he had given her before. 'You are quite safe, as long as you behave yourself, lady. I have never yet taken an unwilling woman…' He laughed mockingly. 'Most come willingly enough to my bed.' His voice had a deep, sensual timbre that sent shivers down her spine. 'I shall not deny that I think you desirable, but I shall never force you to lie with me. You must come to me of your own free will…as you may one day.'

'If you imagine that I would lie with you willingly…' Maribel's manner was one of disdain, but underneath her heart was hammering wildly in her breast; the picture his words conjured up was disturbing. She suddenly saw him bending over her as she lay in silken sheets, his mouth soft and loose with desire, his breath warm on her face, and her throat closed as she was pierced with desire. She gripped her hands at her sides, controlling her feelings, as she had been taught from childhood. A high-born lady did not allow herself to be seduced by a pirate, despite his undoubted charm. It was a picture too shocking to be contemplated. Turning away, she used anger to hide her confusion. This was madness! She was beginning to like him and she must not. 'You are a mocking rogue, Captain Sylvester. I shall never come to you in that way.'

'So be it…but still you are free to take the air every day for an hour or so. If you stay here in your cabin you may become ill and we have no time to spare for nursing a sick woman. I shall not force you to come up, but if you are not sensible I may have to persuade you.'

'What do you mean?' Maribel's heart raced and she caught her breath as her senses whirled and she imagined what he might do. 'You wouldn't dare…'

Justin moved in closer, towering over her. 'I dare anything, lady—but I mean you no harm. We shall soon reach a secluded cove on the island of Mallorca, where I mean to go ashore and replenish our water supplies before we set sail for Cyprus.'

His words banished the foolish thoughts, making her angry once more. 'Cyprus? No, I shall not go with you, sir. You promised you would ransom me to my family! How dare you take me to Cyprus? I demand to be returned to Spain!'

'I believe I made no promises.' Justin's gaze narrowed. 'I have learned that you know nothing of your affianced husband—or his cousin. You would not go so gladly to your wedding if you knew what manner of men they were, believe me.'

'I do not go gladly, but I must obey my father. He controls the fortune my husband left to me and I have no choice…' Her throat closed and the tears stood on her lashes. She looked at him with an unconscious appeal in her eyes. Could she trust him? If he spoke the truth, it seemed her father had betrayed her. She had never felt more alone in her life. 'Is Lord Roberts truly the monster you told me?'

'When I knew of him he was steeped in vice and, I believe, riddled with the pox. I would not have expected him to live long enough to take a bride. If you lie with him, he will infect you with some foul disease—a disease that will cause you great suffering, perhaps even your death.'

Maribel's face was ashen. 'My father could not have

known he was so evil…' Her voice broke on a sob. 'My first husband loved me. He loved me…' The tears slid down her cheeks, her pride forgotten for the moment. 'I would rather die than become the wife of such a monster.'

Justin moved in closer. 'Do not weep, lady. I would not see you break your heart. Perhaps the future holds more than you might think.' His hand moved out to touch her, but fell without doing so. 'For your own sake, come on deck for some air—or I may have to fetch you!'

Maribel looked up at him. Something about him then made her long to trust him. For some foolish reason she wanted to go to his arms, lay her head against his shoulder and weep, but pride made her raise her head once more. She was so alone and he seemed to offer comfort, yet how could she trust a pirate?

'You swore none of your men would lay a hand on me,' she said and even as she spoke saw his frown and regretted that her words broke the tiny thread that had held them.

'Aye, I did—but I said nothing of myself.' Justin glared at her. ''Pon my soul, lady, you could do with a lesson in manners—and I've a mind to give it! Think yourself fortunate that I have much to do on deck.'

He went out, letting the cabin door close behind him with a bang. Maribel caught her breath—she knew that she had pushed him hard. If he lost patience with her, he could make her very sorry for daring to challenge him. She sat down on the edge of the bed, her thoughts whirling in confusion. Her upbringing had taught her that men of his kind were not to be trusted, and yet her instincts told her that he was a man she could turn to in times of trouble. There was no reason why he should help her, and yet a little voice in her head told her that if she asked for help he might give it.

Maribel knew that the ship was no longer moving. She could see the coast of an island a short distance away and understood that they had anchored in the bay. Although she had never been there, she believed they were close to the island of Mallorca. Don Sabatini had estates here, brought to him by his second wife Juanita, who had come from the island. Maribel wondered if there might be cousins or relatives of her stepmother living here. Would they know her if she managed to get ashore? Would they help her to escape from the pirates who had captured her?

Yet if she did escape, what would happen to her? Would her father still force her to marry Lord Roberts? She doubted that he would believe her if she told him that the man was a disease-ridden monster. He would never take the word of a pirate captain, and perhaps she should ignore it—and yet why should Captain Sylvester lie about such a thing? How could it benefit him?

Maribel jumped as the cabin door opened. She swung round, half-expecting another visit from the captain since she had ignored his advice to go on deck, but it was only Anna.

'We are to go ashore this evening,' Anna told her. 'The pirates will provision the ship ready for the voyage to Cyprus and it is the last chance for us to go ashore before we reach our destination.'

'We must try to escape,' Maribel said. 'Juanita came from Mallorca. My father has estates here. If we could reach them…'

'I have given my promise not to try to escape in return for being allowed ashore, and you must do the same. It is the only way, my lady.'

'A promise to a pirate? Would you put that above your duty to me?' Maribel asked, feeling piqued that her maid had seemingly given her allegiance to the enemy.

Anna looked uncomfortable. 'Please do not ask me to break my word. I swore that you would not try to run off, my lady. I think they would punish us both if you did—I might be beaten…'

'No! I should not allow that,' Maribel said. 'If we were caught, I should take the blame.'

'We have not been treated ill, my lady. Why do you not simply wait for the ransom? It might be dangerous to escape. We could fare worse at the hands of others. Remember we have no money to buy a passage home.'

'I am not sure I wish my father to ransom me.' Maribel frowned. 'If my stepmother's relatives would take me in, I might recover control of my fortune—and then I should not have to obey my father. I could marry when I chose.'

'Do you think Don Sabatini would allow that? Do you not know why he is sending you to England?'

'What do you mean?' Maribel's gaze narrowed.

'Your father covets Don Pablo's estates. It was the

reason he allowed you to marry him. I have heard it whispered that it is the reason your husband was killed.'

'That was bandits…' Maribel felt sick and shaken. She moved her head negatively. 'No! You cannot believe that my father…would have had Pablo killed.'

'I do not know, my lady. I have heard these whispers. But why would he send you to such a man if it were not so? Perhaps he anticipates your death…'

Maribel turned away from her, unable to look into her servant's face. She thought of her sweet young husband. She had always believed he was killed by bandits, but if her father… No, she could not believe that of him, even though he had disregarded her wishes in the matter of her marriage. Yet if the servants were talking of these things, there must be some truth in them. Her determination to escape hardened. If she could reach Juanita's family, they would surely take her in and help her…

'I am pleased that you have decided to be sensible,' Justin said, a wry smile playing about his mouth as she came on deck later that day. 'We shall sleep under the stars this night, lady, but a bed shall be prepared for you so that you may lie comfortably.'

'How long do you intend to remain here?'

'A day or two to replenish the supplies of fresh fruit and wine, also meat and water. We have taken on supplies here before and the people are friendly. They do not condemn us, as your people do, as heretics and pirates, but trade with us for gold and silver.'

'When will you send word to my father that you wish to ransom me?'

'Captain Hynes will have carried the tale to him. I said that he might arrange a meeting through an agent in Cyprus. We shall do the exchange there…if one is made…'

'What do you mean—if?' Maribel studied his face, trying to read what was in his mind. She was not sure why his nearness made her feel so odd, as if her chest was constricted and she could scarcely breathe. She drew away, suppressing her feelings. She must not begin to like him. If she once let down her guard… Impossible thoughts filled her mind but she banished them.

'I thought you might prefer your freedom?'

'You would let me go without ransom?'

'I might take the ransom and still keep you.' Justin's teeth flashed white as he smiled in the moonlight.

'You do not mean it?' She was not sure if he was teasing her.

'Would you prefer me to hand you over to a man who would sell you to the devil?'

'I should prefer it if—' Maribel stopped. She had been about to tell him of her stepmother's family and beg him to let her go to them, but something held her tongue. He was persuasive, but she must not trust him. She had only his word that Lord Roberts was diseased and evil, though she could see no reason why he should lie to her.

'What would you prefer, lady? Tell me. Perhaps I might grant your wish.'

Maribel hesitated. His voice was soft; it seemed to promise much and a part of her longed to confide in him. He was so strong and she wanted someone to help and protect her from the things she feared, but he was a pirate. How could she believe the man who had abducted her? Her mind told her it would be foolish and yet her instincts were telling her something very different. Despite herself she was beginning to like him.

'No…' She shook her head, because she could not be sure he would help her. 'I should prefer it if you had never taken me captive.'

'Would you, Madonna?' He smiled at her and her heart missed a beat. 'I am not sure that I believe you. Come…' He held out his hand. 'You must climb down to the boat and be rowed ashore.' She gave him her hand and his fingers closed about it, strong, cool and somehow comforting. 'I have your word that you will not try to run away?'

'I believe Anna already gave you surety?'

'Yes, she did, but I would have it from you.'

'Very well, you have it.' Maribel glowered at him. She looked down at the rope ladder. 'I am not sure I can manage that.'

'Fear not. I shall go before you. I shall steady your feet so that you do not miss a rung—and if you fall I shall catch you.'

'I shall not fall!'

Maribel did not miss the gleam in his eyes. She watched as he went on to the ladder. Tom came forwards to help her place one foot on the ladder and then she was over the side and seeking the next. A strong hand caught her ankle and placed her foot on the next rung, sending a shock running through her that made her gasp and almost lose her balance. How dare he touch her in such an intimate manner? She had almost begun to trust him, but this was too much! She would have liked to vent her fury on him, but it would be undignified to rage at him in this position. She glanced down indignantly and saw the gleam of mischief in his eyes.

'Thank you, but I need no help of that kind.'

'I would not have you fall on me, lady.'

Maribel caught the mockery in his voice and fumed inside. Oh, what a rogue he was! How dare he laugh at her? She would have liked to reprimand him, but all her concentration was on negotiating the ladder without treading on her skirts or lifting them high enough to give him a view of her thighs.

As she reached the bottom he helped her to step down into the boat, steadying her as she found a seat and sat down. She sent him a look of scorn, but refused to speak, because the expression on his face told her that he had enjoyed her predicament.

Maribel watched Anna descend nimbly into the boat and scowled. Her maid had managed easily alone and she might too if that oaf had not grabbed her ankles every time she took a step. How he must have enjoyed that!

She would not look at either of them, sitting stony-faced and staring at the shore as they were rowed closer.

When she realised that she would have to wade through water to get to the beach, she was dismayed. She must either lift her skirts high enough to avoid getting them wet and thus reveal her legs in front of the pirates or suffer a wet gown for hours.

She stood hesitating, unsure of how best to go about it, but then became aware that Captain Sylvester was in the water beside the boat.

'Come, lady, let me carry you.' He held out his hand.

'I can manage…'

'You will get your gown wet and it will not be pleasant.'

'I can manage.' Maribel tried to put one leg over the side of the boat, but he grabbed her waist, swinging her up and over his shoulder. She gave a scream of anger, beating at his back.

'Put me down, you brute! Put me down at once.'

'You tempt me, lady. You sorely tempt me to dump you in the water,' Justin said but carried her up the beach and then set her on her feet. Maribel immediately took a swing at him, but he caught her wrist in an iron vice, his expression stern and forbidding. 'Be careful, Madonna. Try my patience too often and you will regret it.'

'You are arrogant and I hate you!'

'Arrogant? Yes, perhaps I am,' Justin said. 'But I do not believe that you hate me. Tell me you are sorry.'

'No. I shall—' Maribel caught her breath as he suddenly crushed her against him. She lifted her gaze and something in his face made her gasp. He was so powerful and strong and she was playing with fire. 'I take it back. You are arrogant, but I do not hate you.'

The strong feeling he aroused in her was not hate, but a mixture of annoyance and frustration, because he seemed to enjoy provoking her. She was used to politeness and respect and this man—this man had cut through the layers, stripping away all that she had known and accepted as her due.

'That is better.' Justin laughed and let her go. 'Forgive me, lady, but you tempt me almost past bearing. I have seldom seen such delicious ankles and beautiful legs. I could not help myself. You are a siren sent to lure me to my death, I dare say.'

Maribel tossed her head, protecting herself in the only way she knew. 'You are impossible. Would that I were a man! I would run you through with my sword.'

'You might try.' His eyes seemed to flash blue fire, making her hold her breath. 'Tantrums will avail you nothing. We of the brethren are equals. You will be required to work, as is everyone else. You may help Tom fill the barrels with water from the well at the hacienda. It is a job for boys and women.'

Maribel threw him a look of disgust, but held her breath. He had made her very aware of his strength and power over her. She could only obey him for the moment—but when everyone was sleeping she would rouse Anna and together they would escape into the interior of the island. Someone would tell her where she could find Juanita's family.

Justin watched the woman struggle with the heavy pail, tipping it into the barrel, which would be loaded on to the ship with others for their journey. She had made her dislike of him plain enough, but she had not shirked from the job he had given her, even though she must find it hard after the life she had led.

He frowned as he wondered just what kind of life she had led as Don Sabatini's daughter. Everything he knew of the man had led him to feel nothing but disgust and anger, but the girl was different. Yes, she was proud and arrogant, but anyone might react that way when taken captive by pirates. No doubt she had feared for her life or worse at the start, and indeed if it had been one of the other pirate vessels that roamed the seas in search of ships to prey on she might have fared much worse. Had Corsairs taken the ship she could have been sold as a slave in the markets of Algiers.

She was proud and spoiled, and at first he had thought she might in truth be her father's daughter and not to be trusted, but he had realised almost at once that she was innocent. Indeed, had he not known she had been widowed, he would have thought her still an untouched girl.

Her beauty stirred his senses, and had he been another kind of man he would have taken her when she defied him in her cabin, but her courage in defying him had amused him. She was Sabatini's daughter and as such could mean nothing to him save for the ransom she would bring, but there was something about her that made him smile.

Maribel's teeth sank into the soft meat of the suckling pig that had been slow roasted over a fire for hours. It was very strange, but she had never eaten anything quite as delicious. At first she had been inclined to refuse such fare when the succulent thigh was offered her, but the smell was so good and she was hungry after her work.

She wiped the grease from her mouth, then hesitated before rubbing it into her hands. The water buckets had been heavy and her hands felt sore from carrying them from the well to the barrels that the men had then transported to the ship; the grease would act like a salve and ease the stiffness.

The owner of the hacienda had come to greet them. He seemed on friendly terms with Captain Sylvester and more than ready to supply them with all the food they needed for their journey. It was he and his wife who had supplied the feast they had just eaten. Maribel wondered if he might know of her stepmother's relatives.

Getting up from the bench where she had sat to eat her meal, she wandered over to where the farmer's wife was ladling soup into wooden bowls.

'Good evening, *señora.*'

'Would you care for some wine, Donna Maribel?'

'Thank you, but I have eaten well of your suckling pig. I was wondering if you might know some friends of mine who live on the island?'

'I know everyone who lives on Mallorca, lady.'

'Would you know the family of Donna Juanita Sabatini? Her family name is Mendoza.'

'I knew Donna Juanita, a lovely lady.' The woman smiled at her. 'I worked for her family as a young woman. There is only an elderly cousin left now and he lives alone.'

'Where can I find him?'

'At the other side of the island, a journey of some hours on foot—but I would not go there if I were you.'

'Why?'

'He is a peculiar, lonely man. He might not welcome strangers.'

'Juanita was very dear to me…' Maribel hesitated. 'Could I borrow a horse from your stable? I would return it.'

'You will have to ask my husband, lady. Perhaps if Captain Sylvester stood surety for you…'

Maribel hesitated. It seemed these people trusted her captor, but not her. She might have to make her journey on foot—and she could not be sure of a welcome. She had hoped that Juanita might have a sister or female cousin, but when she thought it over, her stepmother had never talked of her family.

It was a risk, but one she must take. She could not go with the pirates to Cyprus and she would not return to her father to be sent to England like a package he had sold.

One thing the pirate captain had done for her was to make her question her father's motives. It seemed that there might be more behind his determination to marry her to an English lord than met the eye—but surely Juanita's cousin would help her? She would pay him once she had control of the fortune left to her by her husband.

Surely someone somewhere would be willing to help her?

* * *

The crew had been drinking and singing for a long time. They were obviously enjoying their time on shore, but at last they had quietened. She believed that most were asleep now.

Maribel sat up and looked about her. She could see no sign of movement. It seemed that the pirates felt secure enough not to set a guard. She reached out and shook Anna's shoulder. The woman snorted and grunted, but would not wake.

'Anna!' Maribel whispered, bending close to her ear. 'It is time for us to leave!'

Anna snored on, giving no sign that she had heard. Maribel hesitated. If she shouted at the girl, someone else might wake. Perhaps it was best to leave her and go alone. Beneath Maribel's gown was concealed a pouch containing all the gold and jewellery she possessed; her clothes and other valuables remained on board the pirate ship, but she must leave them behind if she wanted to escape. She could only pray that Juanita's cousin would be prepared to take her in and help her recover her fortune. If he would not…

Maribel was not certain what she would do then. She only knew that she did not want to remain as the pirate's captive, nor did she wish to return home.

Anna could stay where she was; it seemed she was happy enough under the pirate's rule. Maribel stood up, taking her blanket with her. It was cooler now, though during the day it would be hot. The blanket would keep her warm and if she had to spend more than one day in the open she would have something to lie on at night.

She deliberately put the farmer's wife's warning from her mind. Juanita's cousin would surely help her. Why should he not?

Creeping from the campsite, Maribel slipped away into the trees that fringed the beach. She had only a vague idea of where to find Juanita's family, but she could ask someone. The people at the hacienda had been friendly and she had money to ease her way.

She had been walking for only a few minutes when she heard a twig snap behind her. Her heart beating wildly, she turned but could not see anything.

'Who is it?'

No answer came. Maribel took a deep breath and walked on. She began to climb the ridge that led away from the beach. She could hear rustling sounds behind her and her pulses raced. It must be some kind of animal. Perhaps a pig turned loose in the woods to forage…

Suddenly, the noise came from a different direction. Spinning round, she saw a man's figure through the trees and caught her breath.

'I thought it was you. Where do you think you are going?'

Maribel hesitated. He had followed her! She might have known that escape would not be as easy as it seemed!

'I needed to relieve myself.'

'So far from the camp? Why did you bring a blanket with you? Are you sure you were not trying to escape?'

'Why should I? Where could I go?'

'To the house of Don Vittorio Mendoza, perhaps?'

'She told you…' The farmer's wife had betrayed her!

'Señora Gonzales told her husband and he told me. He warned me that I should not let you go there for Mendoza is not a good man—he is bitter and lives alone since his family died of a fever.'

'He is the only one I can turn to. He will help me because of Juanita.' Tears stung her eyes. 'You must let me go. You must…'

His manner was stern. 'I have given my word that you will not be harmed, but I cannot let you go there.'

'Why? My father will probably refuse to pay the ransom. Why should he pay for my return if he wants my fortune?'

'I think he will pay, for his pride's sake, and because if you married your estates would belong to your husband. Under the law, he could not keep them from you then. Unless your future husband agreed to give them up…'

'Do you think Lord Roberts agreed to give them up? Why…?' Her gaze narrowed. 'Why would he agree to such a bargain?'

'Perhaps because he has little chance of finding a young and beautiful bride of good birth in England. Besides, once you were his wife, he could have reneged on the deal had he wished.'

'Then my father knew what kind of a man he was sending me to.' Maribel felt sickened. 'I will not marry him. I shall never marry, for who could I trust if even my own father would use me thus?'

'You may not have a choice.' Justin's eyes were on her. 'Would you rather go to England with Captain Hynes or take your chance with me? I promise that I will help you find freedom. I shall not let your father sell you to that man or anyone else.'

He was asking her to trust him. It was a huge step, but she was not sure she had a choice, and there was something about him that reassured her…something that made her insides melt and she longed to feel safe and secure within his arms. Her father would call him a rogue and hang him if he had the chance, but her father had sold her to a man she must despise and fear. This man seemed honest and something was telling her to give him her trust for all he was a pirate. Once again she experienced a desire to be held in his arms, to give up the struggle to be free and let him dictate her life.

'Do you swear it?'

'I swear on all I hold sacred.'

'Then I shall believe you.' She felt close to swooning; if he had taken her into his arms then, she would not have resisted.

'Come back to the camp—and give me your word that you will not try to run away again?'

Maribel stared at him for a moment, then inclined her head. 'Very well. I give you my word.' Her eyes sparkled with tears. 'I do not know why I have resisted you. You have been kinder to me than my own father.'

'Maribel…' Justin moved towards her, gazing down at her face in the dawning light. Her heart pounded in her breast and she found it difficult to breathe as she caught the fresh masculine scent of him. She swayed towards him, her will to fight almost gone. 'Will you give yourself into my care? I promise I shall not force you to do anything against your will.'

'I believe you. I think that I…' Maribel hesitated, looking into his eyes. Even as she would have spoken, they heard a booming sound from out at sea. Looking down at the beach, she saw the pirates were awake and yelling something as they dashed down to the water's edge. 'What is happening? Are we being attacked?'

'No, the ship is mine—one that I took captive some weeks ago. It is bringing a message from your father.'

'But you told me you were to meet on Cyprus…' Her eyes widened and she drew away from him, feeling hurt. 'You lied to me. You were planning to sell me to my father all the time!'

'At first, yes, I thought of a ransom.' Justin frowned. 'When I spoke to you of Cyprus I planned to leave a message here for my other ship, but it has arrived sooner than I expected.'

'How can I believe you?' Maribel felt betrayed. 'You are the same as my father—you care only for the money I may bring you.'

She turned from him and began to run back down the hill to the beach below, the tears stinging her eyes. He had looked at her in such a way that she had begun to trust him, to believe that he would treat her fairly—but he would use her for his own purpose like every man she had ever met, except her Pablo.

Chapter Three

Maribel sensed that someone was watching her. She turned her head in the direction of Captain Sylvester and the man who had brought the second pirate ship into the cove. He was older, dark of hair and pale complexioned; his eyes had a strange piercing quality.

'Who is that man with the captain?' she asked of Tom as he came up to her. 'There is something about him…' She shook her head, not knowing why the man's gaze made her uncomfortable.

'Higgins told me he is the acting captain of the *Maria*. The ship was taken a few weeks back and is a Portuguese merchantman. His name is Mr Hendry—or Captain Hendry, I suppose. Higgins doesn't like him; he thinks he is sly and not to be trusted, but Captain Sylvester put him in charge of their sister ship, because of his experience. He will sail with us to Cyprus.'

'Are we still to sail for Cyprus?'

'I have heard the men say that we may sail for the

pirates' island instead. There are many islands in the region that are uninhabited, some used by the brethren. We need a safe haven so that we can divide the spoils of the past months. I am to receive a share though I took no part in capturing them.'

'What is the name of this island?' Maribel looked apprehensive. 'I suppose it is a sinful place where pirates congregate to get drunk and frequent the tavern whores.'

'I cannot tell you the name—its location is a secret— but I believe it is much the same in any port, lady,' Tom told her. 'Men will drink and indulge themselves after a long sea voyage. It is natural for men who live as we do to spend their gold in such fashion. At least until the time comes to settle down.'

Maribel was silent. In her heart she knew she had no reason to condemn the pirates or their captain. It was true they had taken her captive, but she had been treated fairly since then. She wanted to believe in their captain, if only she could let go of her preconceived prejudices and accept his word.

She walked towards Captain Sylvester and Mr Hendry, wanting to know what was being decided between them. As he saw her approach, the captain left his companion and came to meet her.

'Your father has sent word that he wants a truce between us,' Justin told her, but there was an odd expression in his eyes. 'He asks that I meet him face to face. He will pay a ransom for your safe return and for safe conduct through these waters. It would mean an end to what has become a feud between us.'

'Do you wish for an end to it?' She held her breath as she waited for his answer.

'If Don Sabatini agrees to pay us for safe passage, we shall leave his ships in peace. There are plenty more vessels we might take and the Portuguese merchantmen are usually the most profitable.'

'So you will sell me to him?' Maribel's face was white and she felt the sickness rise in her throat.

'I thought it was what you wanted?' Justin's gaze narrowed. 'When I took you captive you assured me your father would pay to have you back—and it seems you were right.'

'I did not know then what manner of man he was.' Maribel was close to tears. 'I hate you… Why did you pretend to care what happened to me?'

She turned and fled down the beach, because the tears were close and she did not wish to shame herself before him.

Justin stared after her. He had not told her the whole truth, because he was uncertain what to believe. The Don's message was a little strange. It seemed that there was something he wanted even more than the return of his daughter.

Touching the package inside his jerkin, Justin frowned. Could the map of the silver mines, which he had captured from Don Sabatini's flagship, be the only one in existence? If the Don wanted the map more than his own daughter, it must be that he could not return to the mines without it. Justin had taken some chests of silver from the Don's ships, but the map to the mines might be worth vast sums—if a man were willing to risk all that it entailed.

Had Maribel been sent to sea as bait? Had he walked into some kind of a honeyed trap—and did she know about it? If she did not and her father truly desired the map above her, he must indeed be as evil as rumour would have him. If he were so evil, it would be wrong to send her back for she would be given to a man whose very touch would corrupt her. This was a problem that required some attention and could not be solved in an instant.

Justin was thoughtful as he stared out to sea. He knew that the Don was a brutal man who had murdered slaves—could he ever be justified in returning the map to such a cruel devil? Giving his daughter back was out of the question.

Maribel walked for some time and then found a rock to sit on. She stared out at the sea. Within hours she might be back with her father—and how long would it be before she was once more on her way to England?

She did not want to marry the English lord her father had found for her! Even if she discarded what Captain Sylvester had told her, she would not wish to marry a man she did not know. If the story of his wickedness were true…she could not bear that her father would send her to such a man. Tears trickled down her cheeks. She dashed them away and began to walk slowly back towards the pirate camp. When she saw Captain Sylvester coming towards her, she hesitated, wanting to run away again but knowing she could not avoid him for long.

'I am sorry if I made you cry,' he apologised as he came up to her. 'Forgive me, Madonna. I shall send word that you are not to be ransomed and there will be no truce. The men would be against it—some of the crew have served aboard his ships and they hate him.' His hand reached out to her, wiping her face with his fingertips. 'Will you forgive me?'

'I do not know what to do.' Maribel faltered, her heart pounding as he moved closer. He was so strong and handsome and powerful, his mouth sensuous and strangely compelling. She felt the pull of his magnetism, but still struggled against it. 'If what you told me is true, I can never return to my home. My father controls my fortune. I have nothing but the things I took with me when I left for England.'

'Have you no friends or relatives who would help you?'

'There is only Don Mendoza...and you say he cannot be trusted.'

'What of your own mother's family?'

'She was English and died when I was small. I know my uncle's name but I do not know if they would take me in.'

Justin cupped her chin in his hand, looking down into her face. 'If you will trust me, I shall try to find where your mother's family live—and if any are still alive I will make sure you get safely to them.'

'You would do that for me?' Maribel's eyes widened, her mouth parting slightly. Before she knew what was happening, she swayed towards him and he caught her against him, kissing her softly on the lips. For a moment she tensed, then allowed herself to melt into his body, giving herself up to the unexpected pleasure that flooded through her. For a few moments she floated away in a cloud of sheer ecstasy 'Oh…that was nice…' she said as he let her go.

Justin chuckled deep in his throat. 'Sweet lady, you tempt me to sweep you up and run off to a place where no one will ever find us, but I have given my word. I shall make every effort to find your English family and return you to them.'

'But how will you discover them? I can only tell you my uncle's name.'

'And that is?'

'Fildene…I think that is right. Juanita mentioned my uncle once—Sir Henry Fildene.' She saw his eyes gleam. 'What? Do you know him?'

'I have not met the gentleman personally, but I believe I may know where to find him—and, since my father purchased wine from him, I believe he must be honest.' He smiled at her in a way that made her feel safe and protected. 'There should be no difficulty finding your family, Maribel.'

'I do not have words to thank you.' She lifted her eyes to his. 'Where shall we go next? To Cyprus as you planned?'

'We shall go to our island so that the spoils of previous journeys may be divided between us. I shall ignore your father's request to return his property and forget the truce.'

'Supposing my father sends his ships to attack you?'

'I do not fear Don Sabatini or any other man.'

'But…I do not wish to cause trouble for you.'

Justin touched her mouth with his fingertips. 'Your father and I were born to be enemies, for he is all that I despise. Whatever may happen in the future it will not be your fault, Madonna.'

He smiled down at her, making her heart beat like a drum. When he smiled like that she felt that nothing could ever harm her again.

Maribel stood on deck watching as the ship sailed away from the island of Mallorca. She had come on board willingly this time, though she was still apprehensive about her future.

She turned her head to smile as Captain Sylvester came to stand by her at the rails.

'You look pensive. Are you thinking of your home— or your husband?'

'My husband was kind to me. We were childhood friends. Pablo always told me that he would marry me one day. For a short time we were happy in our way. I think we were still children and thought like children, but we could not have stayed that way for ever.'

'I am not sure I understand you?' Justin lifted his brows.

'Pablo was killed riding in the hills soon after our marriage—I was told by bandits, but I wonder now if my father had something to do with his death. Pablo was young to inherit such rich estates and he would never suspect my father of playing him false.'

'You think your father coveted his wealth even then?'

'Yes, perhaps. I did not suspect it then and when he asked me to return home after my husband died I was lonely and wanted the comfort of being with my step-mother. Juanita loved me. My father was much kinder to me while she lived.'

'He controlled your fortune. Perhaps he had no reason to be unkind.'

'My father is not a poor man. I do not understand, why would he seek to steal what belonged to Pablo?'

'Wealth is power and some men will do anything for power. There are men driven by sheer greed; he may be one of those men.'

'Supposing he tries to take me back by force?'

'He did not demand your return. There was something he wanted more.'

'Something he wants more than his own daughter?' Maribel was intrigued.

'I suspect that I have the only copy of the map leading to his silver mines in the New World.' Justin's eyes were on her face. 'It was the map he demanded in return for a ransom.'

'A map that reveals the location of rich silver mines?' Maribel was stunned. 'How did you come by such a thing?'

'It was in a small chest I took from the captain of the *Juanita*. No one but me knows of its existence. If my men learned of such a map, they might wish to exploit it, for there is a fortune to be made from these mines.'

'You could be rich beyond your wildest dreams.'

She saw his smile and bit her lip. 'Is that why you refused his truce?'

'You must know it was not my main reason for refusing?' Justin laughed softly as her eyes widened. 'Wealth is not my driving ambition. I am not sure what should happen to the map, but I was not willing to send you back to him once I understood what he intended for you.'

'Oh…' Her breath came faster as she gazed into his eyes. Was he telling her that she was more important than the treasure map? 'Will you keep the map?'

'Perhaps…' Justin's eyes were on her face. 'What do you think I should do with such a map? It must be worth a great deal for your father to offer a large sum of gold for its return but some would say the mine is stained with the blood of those that died there.'

'I…do not know what you should do,' she said and shivered at the thought of what had happened at the mine. 'But if my father wants that map, he may try to get it back. He may send ships and men to look for you.'

'He might try. I have refused his offer. I shall not return the map, at least until I have considered more. Captain Hendry was brave enough to say that he would take the message.' Justin suddenly grinned at her. 'I told you once before, I do not fear Don Sabatini.'

'Is there anything you fear—anything that causes you pain?'

His eyes clouded, his manner becoming reserved. 'If there were, I should not tell you, Maribel. Such things are best unspoken.'

She felt a withdrawal in him and was sorry. Did he have a dark secret that he kept hidden?

Justin frowned as he watched her go below. He thought that she had begun to trust him a little, but he was not certain how he felt about the beautiful Spanish woman. It was true that he found her desirable. From the first moment he saw her standing so defiantly in her cabin he had wanted to make love to her. Being close to her was enough to make him burn with the need to kiss and hold her, the need to feel her heart beating next to his, to have her in his bed—but there were so many barriers between them. She thought of him as a pirate and a rogue, and although she had accepted that he was her only hope of reaching England and freedom, he was not certain that she would ever like him.

He had told her about the map to gauge her reaction, but she had no interest in it, and he was sure she thought it should be destroyed—that the blood of the murdered slaves tainted the mine. At first he had looked for something of her father in her, for a sign that she would betray him if she had the chance, but the more he spoke with her the more certain he became that she was innocent. She was certainly proud and wilful, but now that she had stopped fighting him, he found her too attractive for his peace of mind. Something inside him wanted to take away the look of anxiety from her eyes, to hold her and comfort her, and assure her that nothing would ever harm her again.

A rueful smile touched his mouth. Justin had loved once with all his heart, but the girl he would have made his wife had died suddenly of a fever a few days before their wedding. He had vowed that he would never allow himself to feel that kind of love again, to feel the deep dark despair and the pain that had almost torn him apart.

It was because of Angeline's death that he had become involved with the wild friends that had talked of deposing Queen Mary and setting Princess Elizabeth in her place. His despair had led him to drink too much and become careless—and that was what had brought him to his present situation.

Justin could never ask a woman to marry him, because he was a pirate and he had nothing to offer a decent woman…a woman like Maribel Sanchez.

He should put all thought of her from his mind and make arrangements to restore her to her family as soon as he could. In the meantime it would be better to avoid her company. Being close to her made him think of what might have been—what might be in the future if things were different.

Hearing the knock at her cabin door, Maribel looked up in surprise as the captain walked in. For a moment her heart pounded, but in an instant, she saw that he had not come with seduction on his mind.

'I thought you might like this, to help you pass the time,' Justin said, and handed Maribel a small book. It was bound in leather and looked as if it had been much used. 'It is written in English, but I think you understand the language well enough to enjoy it.'

'That is kind of you,' she said. 'Sometimes the days are long on board ship.' Opening the pages, she saw it was a book of poetry and exclaimed with pleasure. 'Oh, how lovely. I shall truly enjoy reading this, Captain Sylvester.'

'I thought you might,' he said and smiled. 'I shall not keep you longer, but finding the book amongst my things made me think that it might please you.'

Maribel stroked the worn leather with her hands reverently. The book contained an anthology of poems by different poets, but as she touched it, she noticed that it fell open at one particular place again and again. Glancing at the poem, she was struck by the title.

'A Lover's Lullaby' by George Cascoigne, she read aloud in wonder, for she would not have thought that such a poem would hold the captain's interest time and again

Sing lullaby, as women do
Wherewith they bring their babes to rest;
And Lullaby can I sing too,
As womanly as can the best.
With lullaby they still the child;
And if I be not much beguiled,
For man a wanton babe have I,
Which must be stilled with lullaby.

Her eyes scanned the following verses, which told a sad but poignant tale, of a woman who, it seemed had borne children out of wedlock, and must pay the price.

It was a beautiful set of verses, and yet Maribel wondered why it had drawn the captain to it so many times.

Maribel had been taking the air on deck. The sun was very warm and she fanned herself lazily, looking out across the water. They had been at sea for several days now and the weather had remained fine all that time.

She saw Captain Sylvester coming to meet her and waited for him to reach her. Although she had decided to trust him, Maribel never sought him out herself. She tried to keep a little distance between them—she was afraid that if she once let down her guard she would not be able to raise it again, and she suspected that he did the same.

'Have we much longer to go until we reach the island?'

'Are you impatient to get there?' Justin raised his brows.

'I am just curious. Where is this island?'

'It is one of a group off the coast of Greece. You may know that there are thousands of islands in the Aegean? Some are inhabited, many are not. We have made it our own and a small community awaits our return.'

'And is your community known to the wider world?'

'The approach is through a channel of dangerous rocks that keep unwanted visitors at bay. One day we may be discovered, but for the moment it is a haven for us and others of our kind.'

'You could not have taken me to England first?'

'I must honour my word to my men. Once we have

settled our business there I shall do as you ask me, Madonna. You have my word that no man will touch you without your permission. You are under my protection until I can get you to your family.'

'I believe you,' she said. 'But I must ask, how long must pass before we can sail for England?'

'There are things I must do at the island. Besides, we must wait until Hendry joins us. He will have given my message to your father—and he will bring his answer back.'

'Are you certain of that?' Maribel gazed into his eyes. 'My father might decide to hang Captain Hendry and keep your ship.'

'Hendry understood the risks, but he volunteered to take the message. I wanted your father to understand that there will be no truce between us.' Justin frowned. 'In return Hendry will own his ship and may sail where he wishes under his own command. Whatever happens, I shall take you to England—and find someone to care for you. You have my word.'

'Why should you do so much for me?'

'My word is my bond,' Justin told her, a harsh note in his voice. 'I think you have had little reason to trust the word of any man, lady—but I have told you you can trust mine.' His eyes glowed with fire as he looked down at her, causing her stomach to spasm with nerves. 'You tempt me more than you will ever know, yet I shall not force you—nor yet persuade you. You are as safe from me as any other man of my crew. Only if you came to me of your own free will would I make you mine.'

'What do you mean?' she whispered, a strange mixture of fear and hope spreading through her.

'I am not in a position to offer marriage to any woman,' he said and a little nerve flicked in his throat. 'Since I do not wish to live alone for the rest of my life I may take a mistress…'

'Why can you not marry? Are you married—is there someone anticipating your return?' Her mouth was dry as she waited for his answer, which was a while in coming. 'Someone you love?'

'There was once a woman I loved.' He frowned and looked into the distance. 'That was long ago, before I became what I am now. No one waits for me and I have no wife. Love is something I cannot afford, Maribel. It softens a man and makes him weak—but I would be generous to any woman I took as my partner in life. She would have to be the right kind of woman, one who could share the hardships of the life I live.'

Maribel drew a deep breath. What was he saying to her—that she could be his mistress if she chose? Or was he telling her that she was the wrong kind of woman? She knew that he desired her, and suspected that it would be heaven to lie with him. Part of her yearned to tell him that she would rather sail the seas as his woman than be wife to any other man, but something held her back. She knew nothing of this man or his hopes and dreams. It would be foolish to imagine that she could be more than a temporary amusement to such a man.

'I accept your word that I shall be safe on the island,'

she said at last. 'It seems that there are some honourable men left. My husband was one such man and perhaps you are another.'

'You told me your husband loved you—but did you love him? Are you still grieving for him?'

'Yes, I loved Pablo. I did not wish to marry again, but my father forced me to agree.'

She had loved Pablo, but she was beginning to understand that perhaps she had only ever loved him as a brother. However, she could not admit the truth to this man.

'And you truly wish to find your mother's family?'

'Yes…' she whispered, though her heart spoke otherwise.

She could not deny the strong attraction he had for her, the way something deep inside called to him, but he had spoken of taking a mistress. He did not need or want a wife. She was sure that he had been warning her to keep her distance, for he felt the attraction too. He would take her as his mistress and treat her well for as long as it pleased him but then, when it was over, she would be truly alone.

At least he had been honest with her and she must respect him for that, but there could be nothing more than a wary friendship between them.

Justin inclined his head. 'You will excuse me, lady. I have much to do.'

'Yes,' she said and smiled at him. 'I must not keep you from your work. I know I must often be in your way when I come on deck…'

'You would never be in my way,' he replied, and for a moment the heat in his eyes seared her.

Maribel went below to her cabin, feeling restless. Sometimes when the pirate captain looked at her that way she had feelings that were hard to ignore. Without his realising it, he had lit a fire inside her and she could not ignore it no matter how hard she tried.

It was merely physical. The result of a marriage that had not satisfied the woman in her. She had not realised then how much she would have missed as Pablo's wife, but she was beginning to understand now. There was something inside her that craved the kind of love she should have known with her husband—but it was the bold pirate who filled her dreams and made her restless, not her gentle husband. Yet it would not be just physical for her, because if she gave herself she would give her heart and he wanted only her body. He had loved a woman once and he did not wish to love again. Could she be content with such an arrangement?

A part of her cried out that she would take what happiness she could, but her mind denied it. She might long for the kind of loving that she had never known with her husband, but to love and not be loved in return would break her heart.

'Forgive me, Pablo,' she whispered, saying goodbye to the memories she had treasured. No longer a child, she felt that she was at the threshold of becoming a woman—if only she had the courage to step over.

* * *

Justin watched the woman as she stood at the prow of the ship, her long hair blowing softly in the breeze. She had abandoned her formal ringlets and the new style suited her. There was pride in every line of her body. She was a true lady and it showed in all she did, in her every movement and her speech. Her smile was an enchantment, though it was seen seldom enough. Sometimes when, as now, she stood staring out to sea, there was an air of sadness about her that wrenched at his heart. He could only guess at the causes. Was she missing her home or her husband?

Justin was aware of a nagging jealousy. Pablo Sanchez must have been a true man to hold her heart beyond the grave. Given the choice she would remain faithful to her dead husband, but for how long? Anger stirred in him. She should not be allowed to waste her life in regret for a man who could no longer hold or love her. Such beauty should be for the living.

Seeing her day by day as they sailed, spending a few moments in her company, explaining the way the sails were worked and the tools that he used for reading the stars to guide them on their journey, had brought him to a closer understanding with her. Her eyes no longer held that faint hint of fear whenever he approached. He believed she was beginning to trust him, to respect his word—but did she like him? Did she feel anything more than respect?

Justin had given his word that she would be safe from him and his crew. He had told her that she must come to him willingly, but he did not believe that it would happen. It would have been better to have taken her to England, given her money and let her find her own family, but the crew might have mutinied.

No, he would not lie to himself. He could have found a way to persuade them, but he had not wanted to part from her too soon. She drew him like a moth to a flame, but he knew that he would be foolish to hope that a woman like Maribel Sanchez would look twice at a pirate. Her world was not the one he had chosen; there was too wide a divide between them and he did not see how it could be crossed, except in a way that would shame her.

His smile was wry. Of late she had spoken softly to him, but at the start there had been such contempt in her voice when she spoke of pirates. She had challenged him so proudly and her contempt stung. He had been born to a proud family. There were times when he thought of his home longingly, but how could he ever return? One day Queen Mary would die and, pray God, Elizabeth would reign in her stead. He knew that the charges of treason would then be dropped, but there might be others in their place. He had incited men to mutiny. He had preyed on merchant ships, and the ships of friendly countries, also the *Mistress Susanna,* which was an English ship. He could not shame his father by returning to a trial and a hanging.

At the start he had been carried along by his sense of fair play and justice. The men had been ill treated and Captain Smythe had deserved what happened, perhaps more. Had he left the men to their own devices and gone to France to his cousins, Justin might have been able to return home, but it was too late. In Maribel's eyes he had seen the disgust and contempt that his mother would feel if she learned what her son had become.

Justin had not sent word to let his parents know he was still alive. Better that they should think him dead than know what trade he followed…

Maribel sighed as she brushed her hair. The weather had been so hot these past days, and the ship had been becalmed for a short time, making a long journey seem endless. She was desperate to go ashore again, though nervous of what awaited her at their journey's end. The atmosphere on board ship had become increasingly excited and tense as the ship drew nearer to its destination. The men could hardly wait for the promised time on shore and the division of spoils.

She had heard that some of the islands in the Caribbean had been for some time the haunt of pirates, and the seas about them were said to be a lawless place, but she had heard nothing of this island in the Aegean. She knew however that Corsairs haunted the Mediterranean seas, many of them from the Ottoman Empire. Her father had dismissed all pirates as thieves and rogues and spoken of a need for the seas to be swept clean by a sufficient force of ships ranged against them.

'While that nest of rats is allowed to survive we shall none of us be safe from these rogues,' she had heard him say more than once.

However, she knew that it was easier to talk of gathering a force to move against the brethren of the seas than to actually do it. Rich merchants cursed the pirates that preyed on them, but to fit out ships for battle was costly and wasted time that might be put to better effect. In truth, it was unlikely that it would happen unless several countries banded together.

Getting to her feet, Maribel gazed out of the window. She could see a dark haze on the horizon and knew that it must be the island they had sailed so far to find. Her heart pounded and she could scarcely breathe. She had been lulled into a sense of peace on the long journey for she had been treated with respect, both the pirate captain and his men seeming to keep a distance between them and her.

It was not so for Anna, who spent most of her time talking with Higgins or Tom on deck. She still did her work, but there was a new attitude in her manner. Now she was less deferential and treated Maribel more as a friend than a mistress.

Maribel was not certain how she felt about the new order. Anna had moved on while she was in limbo, neither a part of the close community that made up the crew or a prisoner. The men looked at her uncertainly, but few of them spoke to her.

'At first they thought you were Sylvester's woman,' Anna had told her once. 'Now they are not sure what you are to him. They keep you at a distance because he has said that any man who lays a finger on you will be hung.'

'That was harsh.' Maribel frowned. 'Surely such words were not necessary?'

'Some of them would respect you as a lady, others would rape you given the chance.' Anna was brutally frank. 'Some of the men are honest enough, but Higgins said that many are scum and not to be trusted. It will be worse when we get to the island and mix with the other crews.'

'I see…' Maribel shivered. Yet Anna had told her nothing she had not sensed from the beginning. She was safe only because she was under Captain Sylvester's protection. 'Perhaps it would be best if I did not go ashore.'

'We shall all go ashore,' Anna told her. 'The ship must be cleaned and refitted. You could not stay on board while that was happening.'

'I see.' Maribel bowed to her superior knowledge. Higgins must have told her what would happen when they reached the island. Anna was one of them. Maribel was still an outsider. 'Then I must wait until Captain Sylvester tells me what I must do.'

Chapter Four

'We shall drop anchor in the bay this evening,' Justin commented as he came to stand by Maribel that afternoon. She nodded, but did not turn her head to look at him.

Her gaze was intent on the island, a feeling of doubt mixed with anticipation in her heart. It had been just a dark smudge for some time, but now she could see the crowded waterfront with its untidy huddle of buildings. Few of them were substantial, most built of wood, and to her eyes of poor quality. Further back there were houses and taverns of a better standard, larger and more what she might have expected in a port anywhere, but it was clear that the community was small.

'It is not what I expected.'

'The accommodation here is not what you are used to, Maribel. I have a friend whose house is further inland. I shall take you there. Peg will look after you while we stay here.'

'Who is he? I do not know the name? Is Peg an English name?'

'It is a nickname, a woman's name. I dare say she was once called Margaret.' Justin frowned. 'Peg was sentenced to hang for murder. She killed a man who tried to rape her. Someone rescued her from the noose; then she found a lover and went to sea with him, dressed as a man. She served before the mast for some months and was involved in a mutiny. Eventually, the crew landed here. She and her man ran the largest tavern on the waterfront. He died of a fever last winter, but she carries on. Everyone respects Peg and they know she would as soon stick a knife in a man as allow him to take liberties. If she takes you under her wing, you will be safe.'

'Thank you.' Maribel hesitated, then, 'Where will you stay?'

'I shall lodge at one of the taverns. I am building a house. I commissioned it when we were last here with what gold I had, not stolen but my own, which I had hidden about me when I was shanghaied aboard my first ship. It is expensive to bring in stone, though we have an abundance of timber, which is why so many buildings are made of it. Once the house is finished, I shall stay there when we visit the island.'

'You were shanghaied—does that mean you were taken on board against your will?'

'Yes. Why do you ask?'

'I know so little of you, where you come from—and how you became a pirate. I do not think that you were always the man you are now?'

'No, I was not always a pirate,' Justin agreed. 'It was never my intention to become one, but sometimes we have little choice in life. Had I not become a pirate, I and others might have died.'

'You are a powerful man. Others obey you. Could you now not go where you wish?'

'Perhaps this is what I wish for.'

Maribel turned to look at him, her eyes wide and intent. 'Is this what you intend for the rest of your life? To roam the seas in search of prey and then come back to this place?'

Justin's expression hardened. 'I know that it must seem a wretched place after your homeland. The cities in Spain are beautiful and your home was no doubt solid and well built, the house of a wealthy man, but you were not happy there. Even a palace may be a prison if it is not a place of freedom. This island has been a refuge for men such as I for a relatively short time. In years to come it will grow larger. As more settlers arrive the town will begin to look more prosperous.'

'It will always be a haven for pirates,' Maribel said and then realised that her words sounded harsh— harsher than she intended.

'Yes, I dare say it will—until someone decides to blow us all from the face of the earth.' Justin's face was expressionless, his thoughts hidden. 'Yet not all the men and women here are scum. Some like Peg were forced to the life by the unjust laws that would have hung her for defending herself against an evil man. Would you condemn her too? Your own father has done many evil things. He is wealthy, but more to blame than some here for they never had a choice.'

Maribel's eyes fell before his anger. 'Yes, I know. I did not mean to insult Peg—or you. I understand that something terrible must have driven you to this life. I suspect that you were once a gentleman…'

'You suspect that I was once a gentleman…' A gleam of humour showed in his face for a moment, then it faded. He made her a mocking bow. 'Thank you, my lady. What makes a gentleman in your eyes—fine clothes and wealth or a large house?'

'No, of course I did not mean…' Maribel's cheeks were on fire. 'I beg you will not mock me, sir. I did not intend to insult you. I believe you would not describe your present position as that of a gentleman?'

'Oh, no, believe me, I should not,' Justin said, his mouth grim. 'I am well aware that I forfeited all right to call myself by that title long ago. Yet still I have some honour. My word is my bond and you may rely on it.'

'I know and I do trust your word.' She lay a hand on his arm, feeling the hardness and strength of muscle and bone through the thin shirt he wore. He was a powerful man, and could, if he wished, break her with his hands. Yet she sensed that somewhere deep inside there was a different man, a man who knew how to be gentle and generous. It was that man she longed to see, that man she caught glimpses of now and then. 'Forgive me if I have offended you, sir. It was an idle question and not my business.'

'No, it was not your business—yet I shall tell you. I

led a mutiny against a man of such brutality that he drove his crew beyond all limits. After that, there was nothing for us but to make a living from piracy. For myself, I intend to pursue the career only until I can make a new life elsewhere.'

'Shall you return to England and your home one day?'

'I think not.' Justin's eyes were shadowed, giving no indication of his feelings. 'Enough questions, lady. 'Tis time to go ashore. Higgins will look after you and Anna. He will find transport and take you to Peg's, where you will stay until I come. Under no circumstances are you to venture on to the waterfront unless I am with you. Do I make myself clear?'

'Yes, sir.' Maribel was silenced. Why did he think it necessary to give her orders? Was he punishing her for what she had said? It was not necessary, she was not a child nor would she dream of straying to the port alone. 'I shall obey you, for I have no wish to mix with pirates or their whores!'

Justin gave her a searing look. 'Have a care, lady! Such language will earn you no friends on shore. Pride is all very well, but for the moment you are a guest in company that you may despise but should fear. I can command my own crew, but there are men on shore who would rape and hurt you if they found you wandering alone. You have been warned, so take care! I cannot always be there to protect you.'

'Then why have you brought me to such a place?' Maribel demanded, provoked by his attitude into retaliation.

Justin looked at her, seeing the pride but underneath the vulnerability. She was trying to hold on to her dignity but she was out of her depth and afraid of things she did not understand. She might no longer have her hair dressed in ringlets and she had left off her heavy panniers, but the pride of a high-born Spanish lady remained. 'You are asking a question I have asked myself a thousand times on the journey, lady. I should have sent most of the crew here and taken the *Defiance* to England—you are a burden we could do without and the sooner we are rid of you the better!'

Maribel felt the cut of his words like the lash of a whip. He was angry with her and it was her own fault. Captain Sylvester had proved himself a man of his word and yet she had done nothing but provoke him—and she did not know why.

Tears stung behind her eyes as she was assisted into the boat taking her and Anna ashore. What a fool she was to quarrel with the only man who could help her. She knew that he had been forced to keep his promise to his crew and sail them here. She was stupid to make so much fuss about being brought to this place. Captain Sylvester had done his best for her and she must endure whatever discomfort there was until he took her to England. She could only hope that she had not pushed him too far, for she shuddered to think what life would be like for her here if he abandoned her.

'So Sylvester sent you to me, did he?' Peg stood with her hands on her hips and looked Maribel over.

'Yer a lady, ain't yer? What are yer doin' in a place like this?'

'It is a long story. Captain Sylvester has agreed to take me to my family in England when we leave here.'

'Well, if he gave yer his word he will.' Peg laughed. She was a buxom woman, but still attractive though past her best years. 'He is a good man. I owe me life to him, but that is another story—and one yer won't hear from me. Yer can stay here if yer like. It may not be ter yer ladyship's liking, but it is sanctuary on this island. All the scum of the earth frequents that waterfront, believe me. There are a few honest men forced to the trade what retain a sense of fair play, but most would slit yer throat for a handful of silver.'

Maribel shivered. 'I have heard that the waterfront can be a terrible place.'

'Aye, it is that and more—but the brethren live by a code and most won't break it. They know what will happen if they do—either a trial and a hanging or cast off on one of the tiny deserted islands in these seas. We've trees, water and food enough here, but some of the islands are little more than bare rock. There's many a sailor been left to die on an island without a drop of water save the sea. It drives 'em mad in the end. Given the choice, most would rather hang than die that way.'

'I suppose it is a kind of justice?'

''Tis the only law we have. If there were none there would be no living at all—and 'tis as fair as many of the laws in England, and Spain, I dare say. I wouldn't like to be a prisoner of the Inquisition.'

'No, nor should I,' Maribel agreed and smiled. She had begun to like Peg even though the woman was coarse spoken and had killed a man in self-defence. 'Shall I be a trouble to you?'

'Lord 'ave mercy!' Peg shouted with laughter. 'Not the least, though yer'll have to give a 'and now and then. Share the chores we all do, for there are no servants here. Yer woman is free to come and go as she pleases. If it suits her to help yer she may, but she can't be forced to it. We are all equal here—though some of them think they can lord it over the rest of us…' Peg scowled. 'I don't mean you, dearie. That black-hearted scum Captain Pike is in port. He is a murdering devil and would split a man in two as soon as spit. My advice is to stay out of his way. If he sees your pretty face, he'll want yer. You may be under the protection of Captain Sylvester, but Pike is no respecter of property. If he wants yer, he'll come for yer and take the consequences after. He has fought and won more duels than any other man I know.'

Maribel felt sick. She shivered despite the heat of the day. It had been bad enough knowing she must marry against her will to an evil man who laid claim to the name of gentleman—but a ruthless pirate who cared for no man would be far worse! If he had taken her captive she would no doubt already be dead, for she would have taken her own life rather than let a man like that touch her.

Peg's words made her reflect on the treatment she had received from Captain Sylvester. He had given her his protection and shown her respect and what had she offered him in return? She regretted her quarrel with him more than ever. Supposing he decided to leave her to her fate? She would be a prisoner in Peg's house, for she would not dare to go anywhere alone while Captain Pike was in port.

Justin frowned. He knew that he had provoked Maribel to a sharp retort, but he had been annoyed with himself for bringing her to this place. He should have known that it was too rough and ready for a woman like her. She could never live happily on the island. He must see to his business here and leave for England as quickly as possible.

'So you're Sylvester...' The bulky pirate placed himself square in Justin's path, his narrow set eyes glinting with malice. Some of his teeth were black and rotten, and his breath foul. He wore a red scarf beneath a battered black hat and an overcoat with several pockets over his shirt; his breeches were salt-stained, his boots had never been polished and his hair hung on his shoulders in greasy rattails. 'I've heard you took a few prizes this trip—bagged yerself a mighty fortune, by all accounts.'

'We have done well enough,' Justin replied, keeping his tone civil though he disliked the man instantly. They had never met, but Pike's reputation had gone before him and Higgins had pointed him out earlier. 'My men are happy with the fruits of their labour. I trust you had similar fortune?'

'Trust, do you?' Pike spat on the ground, snarling in disgust. 'We took nothing but a poxy merchantman with a cargo of wheat and barley. It will fetch a few guineas here for flour is always needed, but we had no rich pickings. Seems that you had all the luck, Sylvester. Tell me, what be your secret?'

'We have no secret, just good fortune,' Justin said. 'Next time we may not fare as well.'

'I heard tell you took at least two of that devil Don Sabatini's ships?'

'We may have done. Excuse me, sir. I have business.'

The pirate made no attempt to move. His hand rested suggestively on his sword hilt. 'I took one of his ships last year…'

'I dare say you will again.' Justin's eyes glittered. His hand moved to the hilt of his sword. 'I believe there are plenty of merchant ships to go round. Perhaps you should try hunting in a different place—in the West Indies, mayhap?'

For a moment Captain Pike's hand hovered above his sword hilt, a snarl on his lips, and then, as Higgins and one or two others came to stand at Justin's back, it dropped to his side.

'As you say, there is plenty for all. It would be better if we do not tread on each other's toes in future, Sylvester.'

'I wish you luck wherever you choose to go.' Justin bared his white teeth in a smile. The other man glared at him, then pushed by and walked off.

'Take care with him,' Higgins warned in a low voice.

'He has a foul temper and picks a quarrel too often. More men have died duelling with him than we lost in a year at sea!'

'Captain Pike does not bother me.' Justin did not smile. 'He may not lay claim to the seas—they are for everyone to roam as they see fit.'

'I agree with you there and, if we meet at sea, we are more than a match for him. He has but the one ship while we have two…'

'Three—I intend to purchase another ship. We shall be strong enough to stand against anything Sabatini or any other man sends against us when we sail again.'

'The men expect to share the spoils of the last voyage. I am not sure they wish to purchase another ship.'

'They will have their share. I have enough put by from other prizes to buy her. My house takes little of what I earn and I need nothing more. The new ship will earn its price many times.'

'I thought you meant to gather what you could and start a new life elsewhere?'

'In time, perhaps.'

Justin dismissed the question. Once he had thought to make a quick profit and start elsewhere, but he could see no real future for himself. He had forfeited his right to the life of a gentleman. His father would rightly disown him if he returned with the profits gained as a pirate in his pocket—and he was not sure that his cousins would welcome him in France.

Maribel's scorn for his trade was proof if he had

needed it that no decent woman would want him as her husband. He had made his choice when he threw in his lot with the mutineers and assumed command of the *Defiance*. There was no point in trying to be something that he could no longer claim to be.

His mouth twisted wryly as he recalled her scathing words when she was first taken captive. Even recently she had told him that she *suspected* that he had once been a gentleman. Well, she was right. He had been once, the son of a respected landowner and cousin to men who stood well at court. Those days were over. He was a pirate and must live and die as one—though he would not compare himself to the scum he had come in conflict with a moment earlier.

Pike was the lowest creature to crawl on this earth. Justin understood that he had made an enemy of the man. He had not provoked the quarrel, but it had happened and he would have to take great care while the pirate remained in port.

He grimaced and put the incident from his mind. They would split the profits from their successful hunting trip once he had sold what he could for gold. Justin already knew what he meant to purchase with some of his share. He was smiling as he went inside the tavern to meet the man with whom he had arranged to do business. There was something he had it in mind to purchase…

Maribel had finished unpacking her trunk. Anna had offered to do it for her, but under Peg's sceptical eye she had refused, asking only that Anna would show her how to wash her undergarments and how to take the creases from her silk petticoats.

''Tis not fitting that you should do such work,' Anna scolded. 'Some of the linens will need to be held over a steaming pot and then spread flat with a heated smoothing iron. I am not sure that such a thing is to be found on this island, my lady. Leave your linens to me and I shall see what I can do.'

'I must learn to do these things for myself, Anna. Peg told me that there are no servants here.'

'She may say what she pleases.' Anna's eyes glinted. 'I know my duty to you, my lady, though it is so hot here that you may care to do as other women do and leave off some of your petticoats.'

'Leave off my petticoats?' Maribel was shocked. It was true that she was feeling the excessive heat, sweat trickling down her back and legs beneath the heavy layers she wore. She had already left off her heavy padded panniers, but she could not dispense with her petticoats! 'No respectable lady would appear in public without her petticoats.'

'You are not in Spain nor yet England,' Anna reminded her. 'I took off my petticoats days ago. Higgins advised me to go without them for comfort and I have felt much better for it.'

'But you—' Maribel stopped, ashamed that she had almost said the word servant. Anna had been a good friend to her, supporting her through the ordeal they had both suffered. She looked down at the stiff skirts that felt so wrong for her present situation. 'You are right, Anna. I have been very uncomfortable. Perhaps I should leave off two of the heavier ones and just wear a thin shift and one silk petticoat.'

'I am sure you will feel more comfortable, Donna Sanchez.'

'You should call me Maribel. It is best not to use my titles here, Anna.'

Anna looked dubious. 'I am not sure I could do that, my...*señorita.*'

'Yes, call me *señorita* if you will not use my name.' Maribel sighed with relief as she shed some of her layers of petticoats, then, feeling how much better it was, she took off the last of them and stood in just a simple shift and the gown she had chosen. 'This is my simplest gown, but still it is too costly for life here. Do you think you could purchase something simpler for me to wear, Anna? I am not permitted to visit the waterfront, but there must be merchants of a sort, I think.'

'I am certain there are, though they do not have shops to trade from, merely a stall or the window of their house. I shall ask Higgins where suitable clothes can be purchased, D—*señorita.*'

'Thank you. I will give you some gold pieces. I do not know how much you will need.'

'One gold piece should buy you at least two gowns of the kind you require,' Anna said. 'Do not give me more, for I might be robbed.'

'Is it too dangerous for you to visit the merchants?'

'I shall not go alone. Higgins will take me if I ask him.'

Maribel looked at her thoughtfully. 'Has he spoken to you—asked you to wed him?'

'We shall not marry in church, but it is agreed between us that we shall live together once he has built us a house.'

'And when the ship leaves? Shall you come with me to England?'

'We've talked about that,' Anna said. 'I shall look after you on the journey, but once you are in England I shall leave you and return with Higgins to the island. He says that when he retires from the sea, we shall set up a little trading station of our own. More people are beginning to settle here and we can buy from the ships that drop anchor and sell to those who live here.'

Maribel felt a pang of regret. 'I shall miss you, Anna. You have been a good friend to me.'

'You were always a fair and generous mistress. In England you will find others to serve you, perhaps better than I ever could.'

'They will not be better than you, Anna.'

'Well, it will be some weeks before we must part,' Anna said. 'I am to stay with you until Higgins has his house built—and there will be the voyage to England. He says we can buy goods there and bring them back to the island. When you leave to join your family, it will be time enough to say our goodbyes.'

'Yes…' Maribel turned away to tidy some of her things. She had set out her own brush, silver combs, perfume flasks, and a small hand mirror on the top of an oak hutch that served her as a dressing chest. Tears stung behind her eyes. She felt very alone. When Anna left her she would have no one in the world that cared for her. Her mother's relatives would be strangers and she was not even sure they would welcome her to their house. Especially if they knew that she had been living with pirates for some weeks.

Maribel spread the wet clothes on bushes to dry in the heat of the scorching sun. The steam immediately began to rise and she knew she must be careful not to let them dry too much or the creases would never come out. She had washed a few of her things while Anna was out buying things they needed from the traders on the waterfront. Her back was trickling with sweat and her hair felt sticky on her neck, falling into her eyes despite all the combs she had used to keep it out of the way. Anna had offered to help her, but Maribel felt that she must learn to manage these things for herself, and she had merely brushed her hair back and fastened it with combs.

'Well, well, what have we here…?'

The man's voice made her swing round. She stared at the tall man in dismay for he was a fearful sight. His clothes were salt-stained and looked as if he had never washed them, his hair long and greasy beneath the red scarf he wore beneath his hat—and when he grinned at her she saw a row of blackened teeth.

'Excuse me, sir? Were you looking for someone? I believe Peg is in the house. Your business must be with her.'

'My business with Peg can wait, sweet doxy. You will suit me for the moment.'

Maribel gasped and stepped back in horror as she read the look in his eyes. 'No, sir, you mistake things. I am not a whore. You have no business with me.'

'She thinks herself a fine lady!' The man laughed, clearly finding it amusing. 'Well, my lady, when Pike says he has business with you, you would do best to heed him.'

'Stay away from me!' Maribel gave a scream of fear as he lunged at her. 'Keep your distance, sir. I will have none of you!'

'You'll do as I bid you and keep your mouth shut…'

Maribel screamed again as he grabbed her arm. 'Let me go! Take your filthy hands off me, you pig!'

'I'll teach you some manners, whore…'

'I suggest you take your hands off my woman,' another man's voice said. 'Otherwise I shall slit your throat, Pike. The choice is yours.'

Pike swung round, his face shocked as he found himself at the wrong end of a wicked-looking sword. 'Sylvester…' he croaked, sweat beading on his brow. 'I didn't realise she was your woman.'

'Well, you do now.' Justin's eyes glittered with fury. 'Lay one finger on her and you are a dead man, Pike. No man touches my woman and lives.'

'I was just having a bit of fun…' Pike held his hands up, moving away from Maribel. 'Why didn't she say she belonged to you? I wouldn't have gone near her if I'd known.'

'She is a lady, unused to the ways of scum like you.' Justin's voice was like the lash of a whip. 'Stay away from her—and from this house until we leave. Do you hear? If you attempt to touch her again, I'll kill you.'

'I hear you. I'm on my way.'

Maribel watched the man slink away. She was trembling and she felt sick, but she managed to hold back the tears.

'Thank you. I do not know what I should have done had you not come.'

'In future tell any man who tries anything on with you that you belong to me. They won't molest my woman.' Justin's eyes went over her. The thin gown she was wearing was sticking to her, revealing the intimate contours of her body. Desire flared and he was tempted to crush her to him, his need intensified by the temptation she offered in such flimsy clothing. His voice was harsh as he rasped, 'I am not surprised he thought you were available in that gown. Where are your petticoats?'

'I took them off. It was so hot. Anna took hers off and I thought...' Maribel flushed as she saw the expression in his eyes. 'I didn't expect to see anyone.'

Justin was angry, because he wanted to do much the same things as Pike had, and he was disgusted with himself. She had given him her trust and he had no right to feel such hunger just because her air of vulnerability tempted him past bearing. So he deliberately chose words to hurt her.

'No lady would come out of the house without her

petticoats. I am surprised you let a servant tell you what to do, Donna Maribel. I am aware the heat is almost unbearable, but you need to keep a certain standard or you will not be given the respect that is your due. Especially amongst men like Pike.'

'I…' A dark flush stained her cheeks. She crossed her arms over her breasts defensively. 'You are right. It will not occur again. I shall wear petticoats if I come outside.'

'I shall not always be around to protect you.' Justin frowned at her. He knew that his words had hurt her and he was already regretting having spoken so harshly. She was not to blame, because he could not control his hunger for her. 'I know how uncomfortable you must feel, but you need to be careful on this island.'

'You are right.' Maribel hung her head. She saw that he was correctly dressed despite the heat and felt untidy and ashamed of her appearance. 'I was careless. Thank you for helping me.'

'I do not mean to be heartless, Madonna. I know this kind of heat can be suffocating. I speak only for your own good.'

'Thank you. You will not need to reprimand me again, sir.'

'Is Peg treating you well? You are comfortable here?'

'Yes, thank you. She has been kind.'

'My own house is almost ready. I am having it furnished. I had thought you safe here, but perhaps you should move in with me.'

Maribel was shocked, her heart hammering against her ribcage as she stared at him. What could he mean? He had told her he would not marry—was he now suggesting that she should be his mistress? A part of her longed to say yes, but a tiny part of her mind still retained its sanity.

'Captain Sylvester! You may have told that vile man that I am your woman to protect me, but it is not so. I cannot live under your roof, sir.'

'I shall provide a chaperon. Anna will live with us and there will be a woman to keep the place tidy.'

'Peg said there were no servants here.'

'I pay well for service and find willing hands. I think Peg was trying to put you in your place, my lady. There are always those willing to work for good wages—but I treat them decently. They are not servants, as you have known them in your father's house. I pay for their service, but I treat them as equals.'

'Then they are not at all like the servants in my father's house. My father's servants feared him. I do not think anyone would fear to work for a man like you.'

An odd smile touched his mouth. 'Thank you, Maribel. I believe you just paid me a compliment. As to the matter of the house, I have arranged for the furniture to be moved in today. I came to bring you a gift, but now I am asking if you will live under my roof— as my guest, no more and no less.'

'Everyone will think I am your woman…'

'And they will leave you alone as a consequence. You will be able to move freely on the island. If you stay here, other men may have the same notion as Pike. It is the only way I can be certain you will be safe.'

Maribel shuddered. 'I should never have come to this terrible place. I do not belong here. I see resentment in the eyes of those I meet. They hate me because of who I was.'

A nerve flicked in his throat. 'It is my fault that you are here, lady. I have put my mark on you for your protection—it is all I could do to protect you. However, when we leave here you will be as you are now. I shall not abuse the situation. I have apologised, but I cannot change what is done. You must accept it and wait patiently until I can take you to your family.'

Maribel hesitated, then inclined her head. 'Yes, I shall trust you to keep your word, sir. Thank you. I shall be happy to live under your protection.'

Justin smiled and moved closer. 'I will make your stay here as pleasant as I can, Madonna. I wish that it had been possible to take you to your family immediately. I was wrong to bring you here, but I thought it best.' A wry smile touched his mouth. 'Your family will never know anything of your stay here. I promise you that when I take you to them they will accept my story that I have merely been your escort.' He arched one eyebrow. 'You suspected that I was once a gentleman. I know how to play the part and will not let you down, Maribel.'

The way he said her name then made Maribel's insides curl with a feeling she knew was desire. His mouth was curving in a mocking smile. She longed to be in his arms and to feel that mouth take possession of hers, as it had once before. It was all she could do to stop herself swaying towards him. She wanted to give herself to him, to tell him that she would be his woman in truth, but pride held her back.

The expression in his eyes told her that he desired her but she knew that he did not love her. He had made it clear that a man such as he had no time for softness or love. Maribel was certain that to give herself to this man would mean loving him—the kind of love that would become a consuming flame. If she gave him her heart, he would crush it beneath his boots.

'You speak my name,' she said. 'But I know you only as Captain Sylvester. I do not think it is your true name.'

'I may not give you my family name—it would shame them.' His eyes were flinty, distant. 'They do not know that I have become a pirate and it would hurt them. However, my Christian name is Justin…'

'Justin…' she breathed. 'Justin…' A smile touched her mouth. 'Yes, I like it very well. It suits you, sir— for you are a just man.'

'Am I?' He moved in closer, gazing down at her. 'I retain some honour, Maribel, but a man may only be tempted so far. Be careful how far you tempt me—and wear your petticoats or I may not be responsible for my action.'

'Justin…' Her stomach clenched as his hot eyes scorched her. 'Forgive me. I did not mean to tempt you or any man. My gowns were so hot…but I shall be more sensible in future.'

'Be careful when out walking,' he said. 'I have purchased some lighter gowns for you with fine petticoats that will not be so heavy. I should have sent them immediately, but I was caught up with other things. I shall have them taken to my house. They will await you in your room—and now I shall take my leave of you before I lose all sense of honour.'

He turned and walked away from her. Maribel watched. She longed with all her heart to call him back, but her pride held. He spoke of honour and yet he mocked her. If he cared for her, he would surely have asked her to be his wife, but he did not want a wife—only a mistress.

She knew that she had only to say the word and she could become his woman in truth, for she had seen desire in his eyes and felt an answering need in herself. Yet if she were so lost to all pride and sense of what was fitting that she gave herself to him it could only bring unhappiness in the end.

A little voice in her head told her that it would be worth the risk to know the sweetness of lying with him, of being safe in his arms—but he did not love her. He had told her that he had once loved a woman and would not give his heart again. She could be his mistress if she chose, but not his wife.

Chapter Five

'Why didn't you tell me that you were Sylvester's woman?' Peg said when Maribel mentioned that he was sending someone to take her to his house and to fetch her trunk later that day. 'You would not have needed to help with the chores if I'd known you were special to him.'

'I did not mind helping,' Maribel said and blushed. 'It is good to understand what other people have to do.'

'Show me your hands.' Maribel held them out and Peg frowned as she saw the red marks on the palms. 'You should have told me that you had never done hard work. I should not have asked you to carry water from the well if I had known. I'll give you some salve for your hands.' Her eyes narrowed. 'It's the first time I've known Sylvester to take a woman under his protection. You must have made an impression on him! There will be some jealous females once 'tis known you've done what none other could.' Peg grinned suddenly. 'What is he like as a lover? I've thought many a time I would be happy to lie with such a man!' She threw back her head and laughed as Maribel flushed. 'I thought not! You have not lain in his bed, have you? He is protecting you from scum like Pike.'

'Why do you say that?' Maribel looked at her.

'You are innocent, child. Anyone with sense can see it in your eyes. Besides, I know his heart is in the grave of the woman he loved.'

'He has told you this?' Maribel felt as if a knife had entered her breast, because to hear it from Peg seemed to make the woman real instead of the shadowy person Justin had mentioned in passing. 'He has spoken to you of this woman—you know who she was?'

'That I cannot reveal without telling his secret,' Peg said. 'Before I came here I was a servant in a big house. When I killed the rat that raped me I should have hanged had it not been for Sylvester. He took me from the hellhole I was locked in and set me free. I escaped to sea with a man I cared for. I know that Sylvester's heart was broken when the woman he was to marry died of a fever a few days before their wedding…and if you tell him that I revealed so much I'll slit your throat myself!'

He had lost his love shortly before his wedding day. It was not surprising that he could never think of putting another woman in her place. Maribel felt a flow of sympathy for him, feeling his hurt and the pain it must have caused him. In that moment she wanted to put her arms about him and kiss away all the grief and pain, to make him whole again. She knew how it felt to lose someone you loved and she had loved Pablo as a brother. How would it feel to lose someone who meant so much more—someone who was a part of you?

'I swear I shall not reveal what you have told me.' Maribel said. Her heartbeat had returned to normal. Peg had told her something so revealing that she thought it had begun to explain the mystery that was Captain Justin Sylvester. Sylvester was not his true name. He had come from a respectable family, from what Peg had hinted, perhaps a great family.

The mystery was deep and she might never reach the bottom of it, but Maribel suspected that she might be falling deeply in love with the man himself. He *was* a gentleman despite his present situation. He was also a man of honour.

Why did he believe he could not return to his homeland? What had he done that was so terrible?

She knew that he could be harsh. It was necessary to discipline the men that served with him. Yet he could also be compassionate and honourable.

Maribel's heart ached as she saw to the packing of her own trunk for the move to Justin's house. Being here on the island had caused her to lose so many inhibitions that she had had before being taken captive. When she first left for England she had been very much the correct Spanish lady. She was not certain who she was any more. Maribel was not sure that she would ever be able to give orders to a servant in the way she once had, taking it for granted that they should obey her every whim, though she would be expected to do so once she was living with her English family.

If only there was another way to live! One that was possible for her. She did not think that she could be happy living on the island, because the pirates were dangerous, coarse men and she would always fear most of them. Yet to return to the kind of life she had known in her father's house would be hard.

She thought that she would like to live simply in a modest house, somewhere in the country—perhaps a farm—but with whom? One face filled her mind, but she struggled to push it away. To dream of such happiness was foolish.

Justin Sylvester was not looking to settle to a quiet life. He might desire Maribel, but he did not love her. He did not wish for a wife, merely a mistress to lie with when it suited him.

Blinking back her tears, Maribel dressed herself in a thin shift, one petticoat and the thinnest gown she possessed. She looked respectable, because her hair was disciplined into the ringlets she had worn at home. She had teased her comb into her tangled hair, curling it about her fingers. The effect was not quite as neat as when Anna dressed her hair, but she did not look like the wanton hoyden Justin had rescued from that vile man.

Lifting her head, Maribel glanced at herself in her tiny silver-backed mirror. She vaguely resembled the formal lady that had first set sail for England, though she knew that inside she was very different. She had been living inside a shell, in a cold dark place and barely alive. Now she was aware of her feelings, aware of pain and love and a need that she scarcely understood.

Maribel glanced round the room she had been given. It was furnished with an impressive tester bed of Spanish hardwood and hung with silken drapes. Other hutches made of a similar wood, a stool, and a cupboard on a carved stand had been provided for her comfort. She wondered where and how Justin had come by such fine items. They must either have been captured from Spanish vessels or brought here at some cost—perhaps both. A trunk with iron bands had been delivered and when Maribel opened the lid she discovered the gowns and undergarments she had been promised. They were of such fine silk that she knew they must have been extremely costly. Because of their light weight she knew that they would be much more comfortable than the heavier gowns she had prepared for her trousseau. She had deliberately chosen heavy materials because she had been told she would need them in the cooler climate of England.

She was finding herself more and more reluctant to complete her journey to the home of her mother's family. Yet what else was there for her? If she gave herself to Justin without marriage, she would indeed be a whore. What if he tired of her? Where would she go and what would she do then?

The questions weighed heavily on her mind. Her

heart was telling her that even a short time as his woman—to lie in his arms and experience his loving—would be worth losing her honour. However, her mind reminded her that she was a lady and gently born. Her father might be a tyrant and a murderer, but her mother was undoubtedly a lady. If she gave up honour for love, she could never return to the life she was meant to live. She would be an outcast and might one day be forced to earn her living on her back. Yet she was not even sure that she had a family who would take her in, though Juanita had told her that she had an uncle in England and named him. She had received no letters from him. Perhaps he would not wish to know her.

Maribel's tortured thoughts were scattered as Anna came into the room bearing clean linen for the bed.

'This is a fine house,' Anna told her. 'True it is built mainly of wood, but the foundations are set on stone. It should withstand the worst of winter storms.'

'Yes, it is stout enough.' Maribel gave a little shiver. 'I should not want to live here all the time. Are you sure you wish to settle here, Anna? If you change your mind, you will have a place with me—if my family can be found and will accept me.'

'I thank you, my lady, but in England I should always be a servant. Here I can be my own person.'

'Surely you and Higgins could have an inn or a shop of your own in England?'

'It would not be the same. You have always been a lady. You do not know what it is like for the people who serve you. The laws are harsh in Spain for such as us, and Higgins says it is the same in England. A man can be hung for stealing game from the woods, even if he only did so to save his family from starvation. Besides, Higgins would be hanged as a mutineer if he returned to his home country. If he cannot live there nor shall I.'

Anna's words struck home. Maribel had been spoiled in some ways, for she had been waited on and given fine clothes and good food, but in other ways she had been poor. She had never known her father's love or felt her mother's arms about her. Juanita had been good to her, but after her death Maribel had felt alone and at times unhappy. She would not wish to return to a life like that—in Spain or England.

She sighed. 'Is there no country on this earth where a man can be free from such harsh laws? I know you say there is freedom on the island, but the men here…' She shook her head. 'I do not care for men like Pike or pirates.' Save one, her heart said, but she would not voice her true feelings for the man she knew would never love her. Peg had told her that his heart belonged to the woman he had meant to marry. Justin had told her himself that he had no intention of taking a wife.

'Well, 'tis what I have chosen,' Anna said. 'The life may not be perfect, but I have no family waiting for me in England. I would not wish to return to Spain—I should have nothing to look forward to there.'

'You must do as you please, but I could not live here—even though this house is well enough for a short visit.'

Maribel said the words carelessly, though it was not

the house that she found lacking, merely the knowledge that she did not belong on this island.

Justin paused outside the open door and listened to the conversation between the two women inside. He had come to ask if Maribel had all that she required, but he had his answer. It had cost him far more than he had intended to spend to furnish the house to a standard he considered suitable for her use. In his foolish desire to please, he had imagined that she would understand that he had provided the best the island had to offer. It seemed that she found it lacking—as she had found him lacking.

He had given her his first name as a proof that he was willing to lower the barriers between them. Yet now he was glad that he had not revealed his other secrets to her. She did not care for pirates—or their captain presumably. It had seemed to him that she was warming towards him…that she felt something of the passion her beauty aroused in him—but it would seem that he had deceived himself.

She was willing to accept his hospitality for a short visit, because she knew that she would be safe beneath his roof. Clearly she could hardly wait for their stay on the island to be over so that she could continue her journey to England and the family that awaited her.

Frowning, Justin walked away. He had business enough to keep him occupied. His crew wanted only gold or silver that they could spend, which meant that he must bargain with the merchants and other captains for the best prices for the goods they had taken. The chests of silver had already been divided according to the rules of the brethren. He had spent much of his captain's share, which was the largest, but still only a portion of that taken. Each man was paid according to his standing, and even Tom the cabin boy now had more money than he could have earned in ten years before the mast. If he took care of his share, he could be a rich man in another year or so—they all could be if they continued to be as lucky as they had been this trip.

Justin had wondered if his share would buy him a new life somewhere. Not here on the island. The money he had spent here could be recouped when he left, or at least a part of it; he might not get back all for he knew he had spent recklessly to buy things of quality for Maribel. Yet where could he go to start this new life?

Maribel had asked where on this earth there was a country where the laws were fair to all men. Not a pirates' haven, but a land where a man could breathe and make a fine life for himself and his family.

Anna had not known how to answer her and Justin did not know either. He had left England under a cloud for speaking his mind. He had neither spoken nor committed treason. However, just for voicing his opinion that it was wrong to send a man to the fire simply because he followed a different religion, he could have been condemned as a traitor and executed. Perhaps if the old queen were dead he might have found a better life…but not with the stain of piracy hanging over him.

His father would not accept him. He would accuse him of bringing shame to their name and it was true.

So if he could not return to England, where would he find the life he craved? Not in Spain and perhaps not in France—his cousins might also think he had brought shame on them. Justin would have to think again. There must surely be a country where he could find the life and the freedom he craved...

Maribel saw him chopping wood in the yard at the back of the house. Justin had taken off his shirt and his skin glistened with sweat. His body was tanned and his strong muscles rippled as he worked. Her eyes fastened on him hungrily and she was aware of heat spreading through her from low in her abdomen. He was beautiful and she wanted to touch him, to run her hands over his back and touch the scars she thought must have come from cruel whips when he served before the mast. No wonder he had taken the law into his own hands. The master of that ship deserved to lose his position! Yet it had made Justin something he had no wish to be, an exile from the law and his home. For the first time Maribel began to understand why a man might become a pirate. She watched him a little longer from her window. Justin was working so hard, attacking the wood as if it were his enemy. She thought he must be angry for his actions seemed those of a man bent on spending his frustration in work and there was surely no need for so much kindling.

Picking up the hat with a wide brim that he had so

thoughtfully provided, Maribel put it on and fastened it to her hair with silver pins. She went out of the house, hearing the rustle of her skirts and relishing the feel of the silky material against her flesh. She had never worn anything as fine as this and thought that even her stepmother had not owned silk as costly as she was wearing now.

Justin looked up as she approached. He scowled at her, reaching for his shirt. 'Forgive me. You should not have come out. I am not properly dressed.'

'I saw you from the house. You were working so hard. I wanted to thank you for my clothes. They are so light and comfortable. I have never worn anything as fine.'

'I am sure you must have…'

'No, sir, I have not. My gowns were always heavier and thicker. Even my stepmother never had such fine silk as you have given me. I am grateful for your thoughtfulness…and for the room you have provided.'

'The furnishings are not what you are used to,' he growled. 'But all I could find here.'

'I thought it very comfortable. I am grateful for all you have done for me, sir.'

'I am aware that my house lacks the comforts you were accustomed to, lady. Well enough for a short stay, but not for long. I shall endeavour to see you safe in the arms of your family as soon as it may be done.'

'You heard me…' Maribel's cheeks burned as she realised she had been overheard. Shame washed over her, for she had been ungrateful and hasty. 'When I spoke to Anna it was not of you or your house, Justin.

It is merely that I do not find the island a pleasant place…' She saw his expression and stopped. 'I would not have offended you for the world, sir. I believe I owe you more than I can ever repay. It is just that I feel uncomfortable because of what happened with Pike—and what could happen if I left your house to go walking or visit the merchants.'

'Do not judge us too harshly, Maribel. It is true that men like Pike are to be avoided, but many of those who live here would not harm you, especially now they believe you belong to me. You have not seen the rest of the island. The port is a shambles, I grant you, but the community is young and the town is not yet built. The island has become a safe haven for pirates and their kind, but one day it may be something more. As people make their homes here it will become a proper community. I think it might be possible to have a good life here—if one were willing to accept it for what it is.'

'I should not have spoken so carelessly to Anna. I have received no harm at your hands, sir.' She turned away, walking back towards the house, her head down. A moment later she felt her arm caught and looked at Justin. He had put on his shirt and his expression had lightened.

'No, do not leave, Maribel. The other side of the island, away from the port, is beautiful…perhaps as paradise must have been before we humans spoiled it.'

'I should like to visit this paradise you speak of…if it may be arranged.'

'The interior of the island is hilly, covered in woods,

and you would not enjoy the walk in this heat. I could arrange for us to be rowed there—perhaps one day soon. There are other things to enjoy here. This evening there will be a feast and then the division of the spoils. Would you care to attend the feasting? I must do so and I would prefer that you be there so that I can watch over you.'

'I think I am a deal of trouble to you, sir.' She hung her head, feeling ashamed that she had given him cause to think her ungrateful. 'You have been generous... more so than I could ever have expected.'

'I have given you my word that I will deliver you safely to your family, lady. I shall endeavour to keep it. If you do not wish to attend the feasting tonight, I shall ask you to stay inside and lock your door.'

'Thank you, I should like to attend. I think I am safe enough if you are there, sir.'

'You know that I would never allow anyone to harm you while I live.' Justin hesitated, then, 'Would it be too much to ask you to call me by my name? I should like to think we had gone beyond the formality of sir...'

'I owe my life to you. If you wish it, I shall call you, Sylvester, as you are known here. You gave me your first name, but I think you may not wish others to know it?'

'I once had hopes of returning to my home, but I doubt it will happen.' Justin's eyes clouded, his mouth thinning. 'You owe me no gratitude, Maribel. Had we not attacked your ship the first time you might have been in England.'

'And perhaps wed to a man I hated.' She shuddered. 'I think I should thank you, Sylvester. I resented being your captive, but I was proud and foolish, and afraid. I misjudged you and I am sorry. Perhaps one day I may do something for you in return.'

'I ask for nothing.' He inclined his head. 'Excuse me, I have things I must do. You need not stay in the house; you are safe enough here in the garden, such as it is. I have been meaning to clear some of the undergrowth at the back so that a fruit garden can be planted, but as yet I have not had time. Be careful if you stray further. I do not think anyone will attempt what Pike did…but, as you know, these men are not always to be trusted.'

Maribel watched as he walked away from her. The barriers had come down as soon as she spoke of his name and reminded him of his home—and the woman he had loved. Clearly such memories pained him. He must have loved her very much…still loved her if it could cause the shadows to fall. He was a man and had a man's needs. He might desire Maribel, but his heart still belonged to a woman he had once loved.

She was foolish to think of him! He had sworn to protect her but that was all. Maribel began to realise something her heart had tried to tell her long ago. Justin was an exceptional man and she was beginning to feel things for him that she could scarcely understand. He had been kind to her, but she had rebuffed him and it would serve her right if he abandoned her to her fate.

Maribel knew that she must make the best of her stay here. She could only hope that it would not be too long before the ship was ready to sail. In the meantime, she would make herself useful in the house. Some large chests had been delivered earlier and she knew they contained things for Justin's house. He was so busy that he had no time to unpack them. She would do it for him.

Maribel spent an hour or more unpacking items of value from the sturdy oak trunks that had been set down in the living room. She discovered porcelain the like of which she had never seen and stared at the markings on the underneath, trying to make out the strange figures. Beautiful blue-and-white designs depicting figures dressed in clothes that seemed different to her. She imagined they must be very costly and thought that they rightly belonged in the chamber destined for the master of the house.

She sought and found Justin's bedroom, discovering that his bed was much plainer than the one he had given her. Here there were no fancy hutches or carved stools, but just his sea chest and a plain stool with three legs. She set the vase down in a corner of the room, looking round as she thought that something more was needed here to make it comfortable. Noticing some stained linen, she picked it up intending to wash it for him. She was about to leave when she heard a sound and turned to find Justin looking at her.

'What are you doing?'

'I unpacked the chest you had sent here. That vase was so beautiful I thought it belonged in your room. I have never seen its like. Where did it come from?'

'I believe China. It was taken from a Portuguese merchant vessel. I have been told that the Portuguese have trading arrangements with China that no other country has and vases such as these are rare—beyond price. It does not belong here and should have been left in the trunk to protect it.'

'Forgive me. I thought you would wish these things unpacked. I shall replace it…'

'No, leave it now. This room is bare. I dare say it will come to no harm.' He frowned as he saw the linen in her arms. 'What are you doing with those shirts?'

'I meant to wash them for you. It is little enough in return for all you have given me and I have time on my hands.'

'You will ruin your hands,' he said and took them from her, tossing them on to the bed. 'Tom will see to them for me. It is one of his tasks as cabin boy to care for the men's clothes.'

'I feel so useless. Everyone else has work to do.'

'If you wish for work, there is some mending. A lady's hands were not meant for menial tasks, but I believe needlework is acceptable?'

'Yes, of course…' Maribel was hesitant. 'I did not think it right that I should do nothing. I am sorry I unpacked the chest if you did not wish it.'

Justin reached out and caught her wrist, as she would have turned away. She raised her head, holding back the tears that would shame her, but he saw them and reached out to touch her cheek with his fingertips.

'Forgive me. It looks very much better in here. I did

not mean to be harsh to you, Maribel. We should try to deal more kindly with each other for the time we spend on the island. I know there are things here that you cannot like, but it is not such a bad place—is it?'

'No...' She blinked away the foolish tears and smiled at him. 'The view to the sea is breathtaking and some of the flowers are lovely. I should have asked before I touched your belongings, but I wanted to be useful. There is no place for a lady here.'

'I should have remembered that you would need some employment. I will purchase silks another day and then you may use your skills to mend or embroider some trifle.'

Maribel turned away. He thought her good for nothing but idleness or some embroidery! At home she had been used to many tasks—she had helped Juanita in the stillroom and with mending, as well as embroidering covers and hangings for the house and the church. There had always been a task of some kind, though she saw now that much of her time had been spent in idleness, either walking in the gardens, riding or playing her viola.

What had she ever done of real use? If her husband had not died, she would have been mistress of his house, but in her father's she had been nothing—just the daughter of a woman it seemed he hated.

What would she be in the house of her English relatives? Perhaps they would give her some tasks to perform for her keep?

Maribel was aware of a growing unease in her mind.

She was not sure of her welcome in England. Even if her mother's family accepted her, she could only be an outsider at best, for she did not truly belong with them.

Where did she belong? The answer was nowhere. Anna would be accepted here, because she shared the work they all did—but Maribel was too much of a lady to do hard physical work and so she could never belong.

Returning to her own room, Maribel spent the rest of the afternoon staring out of the window and watching birds flitting in and out of the trees. She had nothing to occupy her time and wished for some needlework or canvas and paint so that she might have something to make the hours seem shorter.

As dusk began to fall, she saw Anna at the well. She filled one bucket and left the other while she carried that back to the house. Maribel went out and tied the other bucket to the rope, letting it down until she heard the splash of water. She had begun to wind the handle to bring it up when Anna returned.

'You should not be doing that, my lady.'

'I am sick of being told what I should not do,' Maribel told her crossly. 'I have nothing to do but stare at the walls of my room, while you struggle to carry water, clean, wash my clothes and cook. In future I am going to help you with the chores.'

'Captain Sylvester said that you were to be treated with the respect due you as a lady.'

'He is not my father or my husband! He cannot command me. I shall do as I see fit. When I am in

England I shall be a lady for I shall have no choice, but here on the island I must do some work or go mad.'

'It is better to work,' Anna said and smiled. 'Let me carry the bucket, for you have filled it to the brim and it will be heavy. Tomorrow you can help prepare the food.'

'We shall carry the bucket between us,' Maribel said. 'And then I shall change my gown for the evening. It will be cooler when the sun goes down and I think it would be better to wear one of my simpler gowns this evening.'

Maribel looked around the beach. Bonfires had been built at intervals along the shoreline and tables made of rough planks set upon trestles had been set up. Some of them were covered with plates of food: bread and fruit and messes of meat cooked in wine and sauces. She caught the aroma of roasting pig and the smell made her mouth water. Already barrels of ale and sack had been tapped, and the men were drinking heavily.

On some tables goods were displayed for sale. Weapons of many kinds, boots, clothes, all manner of trinkets, from combs for a lady's hair to gentlemen's silk breeches; barrels of wine and ale, goblets and cooking pots were jumbled together to be haggled over.

'That is what is left of what we took,' Higgins told Maribel and Anna. 'The Cap'n sold the best stuff and we'll be dividing the money later. The rest is there for anyone to buy, but it will not bring much.'

'Is this the kind of thing you and Anna mean to trade?'

'Aye, something of the sort. But there are other things that are scarce here, like flour, salt, spices and sugar—and I mean to buy a cargo after our next voyage and bring it back,' Higgins replied. 'But you must be hungry. May I fetch you food, lady—and you, Anna?'

'I shall come with you.' Anna smiled at him. 'I know what my lady likes to eat.'

'You are not to wait on me. I shall come with you and choose for myself.'

Anna made a disapproving face, but did not try to stop her. Maribel followed behind them, taking one of the pewter platters and moving along the table as others were doing. She helped herself to some coarse bread and a yellow cheese, hesitating over the fruit; eventually she selected a peach.

'You should try the suckling pig,' a voice said close behind her and she jumped, swinging round to look at the man who had spoken. That evening Captain Pike was wearing clothes that looked cleaner than those he had worn the first time they met. His beard had been trimmed, but his hair was still greasy and nothing could disguise the foul smell of his breath. Maribel's flesh crawled; she found him repulsive. 'Let me bring you a slice, Maribel.'

She shuddered, feeling her stomach heave. The lascivious look in his eyes robbed her of the desire to eat and she moved away, going to stand by a palm tree, her back against it as she surveyed the scene. A group of men were dancing on the beach, arms crossed as they performed some kind of a jig. Others were eating or squabbling over the goods set out for sale. She saw one draw a knife and threaten another.

'Are you not hungry?'

Maribel turned her head as Justin addressed her. 'In a little while, perhaps.' She was aware that Pike was watching her still and suppressed a desire to run away.

'Has something upset you?'

'No, no, I am not upset.' She took a peach and bit into it. The flesh was perfectly ripe, sweet and delicious, and the juice ran over her chin. Before she could wipe it, Justin reached out and smoothed it away with his fingers. He ran his index finger over her lower lip and then put it to his mouth and sucked it, his eyes on her face. Maribel's appetite fled once again and she could hardly swallow even the small piece of peach in her mouth. She took a deep breath, her voice shaking, 'You must not worry about me, Sylvester. Please attend to your business. I am perfectly well.'

Justin's eyes flashed. 'I did not ask if you were ill. You are distressed. Was it something Pike said to you?'

'No, of course not,' Maribel said a little too quickly. 'He merely asked if I wished for some suckling pig. I said no…'

His mouth tightened. 'You must tell me if he accosts you, Maribel. I would kill him rather than let him sully you with his touch.'

'No…please, do not kill anyone for my sake. I am certain he will not try to touch me; I shall stay out of his way. Please, mix with your men. I am certain you must have more important things to do.'

'Nothing is more important to me than your safety.' Justin reached out to touch her cheek, caressing it and trailing a finger down her throat to the little pulse spot at the base. She swallowed hard, because the look in his eyes set her pulses racing again. His gaze was full of meaning, conveying a message if only she knew what he meant. Perhaps she did and that was why her heart was thudding so violently. He had told her once that he wished for a mistress, not a wife—was he letting her know she was his choice? 'I would kill anyone who tried to harm you. I shall keep you safe until you are with your family if it costs my life.'

Maribel caught her breath, for his voice throbbed with passion. She wished that they were alone at the house. Her body was aching for his touch. She wanted to tell him that she did not want him to fight for her; she wanted him to love her. The moment was broken by the sound of shouting on the beach. Justin turned to look. A fight had broken out, drawing a crowd to watch.

'I must sort out these fools before they kill each other,' he said grimly. 'I shall tell Anna to come to you.'

'No, let her have fun,' Maribel said, but he did not answer her.

However, as he walked away, Peg came towards her. She smiled, feeling relief as the older woman joined her.

'This is the first feast yer have attended,' Peg said. 'Do not be too alarmed, Maribel. Most of this is high spirits. The men will fight, but it is not often anyone is killed; they are like children at play.'

'Children do not have knives.'

'Perhaps not where you lived. On the streets of London children learn to defend themselves early. I carried a knife from the age of eight. Me parents died of the plague, but I survived. I had to steal to eat until I could find work—and the work I wus offered did not please me, for I would be no man's whore. Later, I found work as a servant, but men would not leave me be. When one of them raped me I used me knife to good effect to defend meself—and yer know the rest.'

Maribel saw the defiance in her eyes, but felt only admiration for her courage. 'Would you teach me how to protect myself, Peg?'

Peg's eyes narrowed. 'Yer have Captain Sylvester to protect yer. Besides, yer will not stay here long. Why should yer need a knife?'

'I should feel safer. You know what happened when Pike first saw me. I do not think he has forgiven me. Captain Sylvester cannot always be with me. If I had a knife, I might stand a chance against him.'

'Yer have spirit despite yer fine ways,' Peg said and grinned. 'Yer may be a lady, but I see no fool. I will come tomorrow and begin yer lessons—and I will bring yer a knife.'

'Thank you. I have some money. I can pay for my knife.'

Peg gave her a look of reproof. 'Have I asked for payment?'

'No. Forgive me. I did not mean to offend you.'

'No offence taken, luvvie.' Peg grinned at her. 'I

thought yer wus above yerself when yer first come to me, but I like yer. I wouldn't show everyone me tricks, but I reckon I can teach yer to protect yerself from scum like that Pike. I seen him lookin' at yer and I reckon he may try somethin' if he gets the chance.'

'Yes, I think he may,' Maribel said. 'I did not wish to say anything to Sylvester because I am enough trouble to him already, but that man frightens me. He is evil.'

'Evil he is,' Peg agreed, her eyes blazing, 'but he bleeds like any man. If I show yer how to defend yourself, yer'll be safe enough.'

'Thank you.' Maribel smiled. Someone had started to play a fiddle. The fighting had been stopped and men were dancing, some with their women and others together. 'Do you wish to dance, Peg? You must not stay with me if you do.'

'Aye, I'll dance,' Peg said and seized her hand. 'And you'll dance with me.' She arched her brow as Maribel hung back. 'Don't tell me yer don't know how ter dance?'

Maribel shook her head. Suddenly, she felt better. She was no longer the outsider, watching and feeling apart from the others. Peg was forcing her to join in the fun, and she discovered that she wanted to dance.

It was just a simple joining of hands. The dancers twirled, broke hands and then joined in a line skipping up to meet each other and then breaking off to dance with a partner once more. Maribel discovered that her partner was another woman instead of Peg, because everyone was changing partners. Next she danced with a man who grinned at her, but held her respectfully, clearly remembering that she was Captain Sylvester's woman. After that, she found herself being twirled by Tom and then she was back with Peg again. When she broke from the line again, her hands were taken firmly and she looked up into bold eyes that made her heart race.

'I did not know you liked to dance, Maribel.'

'You hardly know me, Captain,' she replied and laughed softly. 'We sometimes danced at home in the courtyard when the wine harvest was done. I enjoyed dancing in the sunshine with the people of the estate, but when my father held a banquet, Juanita and I did not dance, for he did not approve of it—though others did. My stepmother taught me even though my father would not allow it.'

'Then dance with me, Maribel…like this…'

He pulled her into his arms, directing her body so that she felt as if she were floating, thistledown in his arms. The music had changed, was slower now, and when he twirled her round and round he did not let go of her hand. Others swapped partners, but he kept her with him, gazing into her eyes as they moved.

Maribel hardly noticed they had moved away from the throng of dancers. When he took her hand and led her along the sandy beach her heart was racing, her breast heaving as she caught her breath. What was this feeling between them? Was it only physical passion, the need for release—or was it something more? Maribel felt that she was being drawn into a net from which she could never escape; her heart told her that this was love—but she was afraid that it was only on her side. Justin desired her and he was both generous and kind— but she wanted so much more.

'Are you feeling better now?' he asked, gazing down at her in such a way that she swayed towards him, wanting to be back in his arms, wanting to be kissed. 'I could not resist when I saw you dancing. You seemed to be so happy…'

'I was—I am happy,' she breathed. 'I am looking forward to seeing the other side of the island, away from—' She broke off as his eyes narrowed. 'Forgive me, I do not mean to criticise your men, but there is a wilder element amongst the pirates. I do not like men like Captain Pike.'

'Well, you need not fear him while I am with you. Besides, I believe he means to leave soon. He had little luck last time out and needs to find a good prize.'

'It would be a better place without his sort,' Maribel said. 'Though I have found friends. Peg is a friend. I like her.'

'You know that she was convicted of murder and should have hanged had she not escaped?'

'Yes—but she took revenge for what was done to her. I cannot blame her.'

'Yet some would say that murder is wrong even if the cause be just.' Justin's expression was serious. 'I shall return you to Anna. Higgins will take you back to the house. The serious business is about to begin and there may some fighting as the men drink too much.'

'Yes, we shall leave you to your business.'

Maribel walked away from him to join Anna and Higgins. She had thought as they danced that Justin wanted to make love to her. If he had taken her in his arms and kissed her she would not have denied him, but she had spoken of wanting to see the other side of the island and the spell had been broken.

Justin was keeping his promise not to take advantage of her while she was under his protection. Maribel knew that if she wanted him to make love to her she would have to show him that she was willing to be his.

While a part of her longed for it, her pride ruled her head. To become his woman meant that she could never return to her own world. If he loved her she would give it all up willingly, but she was not sure he felt more than a fleeting desire—and that was not enough for her. She wanted, needed to be loved. There was a lonely place inside her that only love could ease.

He had told her that he could not return to England for he might be hanged as a mutineer. Maribel would be willing to sail with him—or settle in another country if he truly cared for her. She was not sure she wished to be a lady again. The life she had found here was a fulfilling one. She enjoyed helping to prepare the food and other small chores that Anna allowed her to do. Perhaps the life of a country gentlewoman would suit her, with a maid to help her. Juanita had delighted in her stillroom and Maribel had found it interesting to help with the preserves and cures they made from herbs.

To be a fine lady and sit all day at her sewing would

not suit her. It was the life she would have had as the wife of Lord Roberts and perhaps in the house of her mother's kin. Surely there must be another way to live, something more worthwhile?

Here on the island she would always have to be on her guard, but a simple country life mixing with honest folk would be so much more satisfying than the life of a grand lady.

Maribel shook her head, smiling at her foolish thoughts. Captain Sylvester might want her, but he would not be prepared to give up his way of life at sea to pander to her foolish whims. His was a precarious trade but it brought him great wealth. The money he must earn from preying on merchant ships would be far more than he could expect from the existence of a simple farmer.

Her thoughts were nonsense! She must accept what the future had in store for her. She would be restored to her mother's family and then…her thoughts refused to think further; it seemed like a dark tunnel that she must follow with no turning or reward.

How much better it would be if she were like Anna, free to give her heart to a pirate and think nothing of it. Anna was prepared to live on the island and mix with the rough seamen that lived and visited here. Maribel did not think that she could settle for such a life, even though she longed to be with Justin.

She did not even know his true name! Maribel was restless as she lay in her bed that night. Who was he truly? What was his family like and how did they feel about his disappearance? Did they have any idea of what he had become?

It was very late when she heard him come in. His footsteps paused outside her door and her heart raced as she heard the sound of his hand upon the latch. The door was locked. She had turned the key as a precaution lest Pike should attempt to get into her room while Justin was occupied elsewhere. Now she wished that she had left it unlocked.

Would Justin have come to her? Would he have woken her, taken her in his arms to love her?

Her body cried out for him and she longed to feel his arms about her. Had she been less proud she would have left her bed and gone to him, but years of strict upbringing would not allow her to offer herself to a man.

If he loved her, surely he would speak? Maribel longed for him to give her a sign that he cared even a little for her, but her head told her that she could never expect him to love her.

It was no good, she could not sleep. The night was too warm and her mind would not let her rest. Getting out of her bed, Maribel pulled a thin wrap over her night-chemise and went through to the living room. It was still stuffy and warm in here so she unlocked the door and went down the little steps leading to the veranda.

The moon was full, making Maribel feel lonely. She walked a few steps to a position where she could see out over the cliffs to the ocean below. At night it looked dark and mysterious, the water strangely calm, un-moving. She sighed deeply for she longed for something…something she could not name.

'What are you doing out here at night?'

Startled, Maribel turned to face Justin. He was wearing just his breeches. His feet were bare and he had not put on his shirt. She could see a trickle of sweat running over his bare chest and guessed that he too had been unable to sleep.

'I could not rest. It is so hot and…I was thinking…'

'I often come out at night to think. The air is cooler and things seem simpler.'

'You must have many problems…regrets?' Maribel looked at him. 'You told me that you could not return home—do you miss your family?'

'I think of them sometimes. I know my mother must miss me.'

'Do you have brothers or sisters?'

'I had a younger brother, but he died when he was but a child.'

'Then your mother must miss you terribly.'

'Perhaps.' Justin frowned. 'Did you have no brothers or sisters?'

'My mother died giving birth to a stillborn child, at least that is what I have been told—but my father never spoke of her. I think they quarrelled.' She sighed deeply and turned away to look out over the sea.

'Were you sighing because you wished yourself at home?'

'No.' Maribel met his narrowed gaze. 'I do not wish

to return to my home ever. There was a time when I was happy. When my stepmother lived she made things better. I do not know if my father was always the cruel man you claim, but I remember that Juanita loved me. She was kind to me and I was happy then. I was happy when I married…'

'You loved your husband very much?' Justin's voice was sharp suddenly.

'He was my friend. He loved me. Yes, I loved him very much.' Maribel hesitated, then, 'You told me that you once loved someone?'

Justin was silent for a moment, then, 'There was once a lady I would have married. She was young and beautiful. I loved her and I would have married her, but a fever took her before our wedding day.'

'That must have hurt you terribly.' Maribel looked into his face, witnessing the pain he could not quite hide.

'Yes, it hurt me…' His voice grated, as if he found it difficult to speak of his lost love. 'It was a long time ago. I have learned to live again. A man cannot spend all his life in regret.'

'No, that is true.'

Justin moved towards her. She stood absolutely still, waiting. For a moment his eyes held hers, then he reached out and drew her to him. He lowered his head and took her mouth, kissing her softly at first and then hungrily. Maribel melted into his body, realising that this was what she had been longing for…this was what she needed. She was so alone and she needed to be loved.

'You are lovely. The moonlight becomes you, Maribel, but why are you out here alone?'

'I was restless and could not sleep.'

'Nor I,' he murmured, his hand moving to the small of her back. 'I was thinking of you. You haunt my dreams, waking and sleeping.'

'Justin…' she whispered, lifting her face for his kiss.

'Maribel…' Justin said hoarsely. He ran his thumb over her lower lip and she trapped it with her teeth. A shudder went through him and he pressed her closer so that she felt the hardness of his arousal and a thrill of desire shot through her. 'I vowed I would not.'

'I absolve you of your vow,' she said. 'Justin, I…'

What she might have said then was lost as they heard something and then a man came towards them through the gloom. Justin stood back from her, staring into the darkness for a moment, then he recognised the newcomer.

'Hendry,' he said, cursed beneath his breath and left Maribel to greet the newcomer. 'You are back. I thank God for it. I was beginning to wonder where you had got to and to fear that things might have gone wrong— that Sabatini had reneged on the truce.'

'All went well,' Hendry said and took the hand he was offered. 'The exchange was made and I have the packet for you.'

'Thank you,' Justin said. 'Come and have a drink with me. The ship is yours, as I promised. You may sail with us or go your own way.'

'I shall drink with you—unless you have unfinished

business?' Hendry glanced at Maribel, who was watching them.

'I was merely telling Maribel that she should not wander outside alone at night,' Justin said. 'Go in, Madonna. I shall see you in the morning.'

Maribel inclined her head, turning reluctantly towards the house. She shivered, feeling suddenly cool despite the heat. Captain Hendry had looked at her so oddly. She wished that he had not returned. He had brought the information Justin needed to find her mother's family but something in the way he looked at her had made her uneasy.

She had a feeling that something special might have happened with Justin had Hendry not arrived at just that moment. The barriers had come down between them and she had been on the verge of confessing that she was ready to be what everyone on the island already thought her—Sylvester's woman.

'Captain Sylvester asks that you forgive him,' Anna said the next morning. 'He has had to postpone the trip to the other side of the island, because he has business with Captain Hendry.'

'Oh…' Maribel's disappointment swathed through her. She had been looking forward to the pleasure trip and for a moment the day seemed long and empty, then an idea occurred to her and she smiled. 'I am going to clear some of the undergrowth behind the house. Captain Sylvester told me that he wants to create a fruit garden there, but has not yet found the time.'

Anna looked at her doubtfully. 'Do you know how hard that will be, *señora?* Your hands have never done hard work like that and they will blister.'

'I shall wear gloves,' Maribel said, determined not to give up her idea. 'Captain Sylvester has done much for me. I want to do this to thank him for his care of us, Anna.'

'If you must…' Anna sighed. 'I suppose I must help you.'

Maribel smiled at her. 'We can work together as friends, but I am not ordering you to help me, Anna. We shall clear more ground if we work together, but if you have something else to do I can manage alone.'

Anna gave her a look of grudging admiration. 'I would never have thought you could change so much, *señora.* You would not have dreamed of getting your hands dirty once.'

'I was another person then,' Maribel told her. 'I have been changing little by little, though at first I fought it—now I want to discover for myself what it is like to work hard.'

'We must begin by chopping down the grass and weeds, then we can make a start on the digging…'

Maribel's back ached and she was soaked in sweat when they decided that they had done enough for one day. A patch large enough to plant vegetables and soft fruits had been cleared at the back of the house and they had begun to dig a small part of it. The work had been even harder than Anna had warned, but Maribel was filled with a sense of pride as she looked at the results of their labour.

'I think we have made a good start,' she said to Anna as they walked back towards the house. 'I am thirsty and dirty. I must wash away the sweat and change my gown before we begin to make a meal for this evening.'

'You have done enough for one day. Let me bring water for you. You must be weary.'

'No, I am not tired,' Maribel said and smiled. 'My back does ache and I think I may be stiff tomorrow, but I feel so alive. I have enjoyed working with you in the sunshine. I feel as if I have done something useful for perhaps the first time in my life.'

'You used to have such soft hands and your needle-work was so fine,' Anna said. 'Even Donna Juanita said how lovely your work was—do you not remember?'

'Yes…' Maribel sighed. 'The girl who sewed pretty cushions was a different person, Anna. That world seems so far away. I have become someone different— a woman with a heart and mind of her own.'

Anna looked at her and nodded. 'Why do you not tell him how you feel? I have seen a look in your eyes.'

'I am not sure that he would care. I know that he desires me, but I cannot speak first.'

'You must forget your pride,' Anna told her. 'You must decide if you want to stay here with us.'

'I am not sure.' Maribel's throat caught with emotion. 'I would stay, but only if…'

She would stay if Justin loved her, but she knew that he still loved the woman he had once wished to marry, despite what he had said about moving on. She could have him for a while, but in the end he would tire of her and then she would be alone.

Maribel enjoyed the feel of the cool water on her skin. She had been so very sweaty and her hair had collected bits of twig and dirt. Anna had helped her to wash it in the yard, and now she was stripped of her clothes in her room, the shutters closed for privacy. She washed in the water she had brought into the house herself, drying her skin and pulling on a shift to cover her body. Her hair was still wet and she sat down on the edge of the bed to rub it dry on a towel, singing a little song that Juanita had sung to her when she was small. She looked up as the door opened, expecting to see Anna, but was shocked to see Justin standing on the threshold. For a moment he stared at her without saying anything, but she saw the pulse at his throat and the way his eyes fastened on her and became aware that her body was clearly outlined through the thin shift. Her nipples had peaked with the instant response of her body to his presence, aching with the need to be touched and caressed.

'Forgive me. I heard voices and thought Anna was with you.'

'I was singing.' Maribel reached for a silken wrap and drew it on over her shift. His eyes seemed to burn into her, making her breath catch in her throat. 'Did you want something?'

'The garden behind the house…who did all that work?' he asked, but his breathing was ragged, his voice hoarse. He looked at her like a man dying of thirst when he sees the oasis for the first time, his need writ plain on his face. 'Anna? Or Higgins?'

'Anna and I did it together. You said you had not had time and I wanted to thank you for—'

'Foolish woman!' Justin strode towards her. 'Show me your hands.' Maribel held them out and heard his indrawn breath as he saw the red welts across the palms. 'You should not have done such heavy work. Your hands will be sore in the morning.'

'I enjoyed it,' she replied. 'I shall rub some salve into them. Anna always packs some into my trunks…' She gasped as he caught her hand and carried it to his lips, licking at the redness in a way that made desire shoot through her. 'Justin…'

'Sometimes saliva will help,' he said huskily, but as her eyes met his he groaned and reached out, drawing her close. 'You were made for love, not hard physical work…'

For a moment she melted into his body, wanting his kiss to go on and on, wanting so much more that she could not name. Yet even as his hands held her closer so that she could feel the heat of his manhood pressing against her through the thin robe, she felt tears rise up to choke her. He said that she was made for love, but he did not love her—he only wanted her. As he gathered her up in his arms, her mind refused to work properly. She wanted him to kiss and touch her, to make love to her, but she knew that she might lose everything.

Justin placed her carefully amongst the sheets, bending over her to kiss her throat at the little hollow at the base. His hand moved aside her robe, exposing the open neck of her shift. He bent to kiss her, slipping his hand inside her shift to caress her breasts. His thumb caressed her nipple, making her gasp and tremble, her body arching towards his despite her fears.

'You are very beautiful, Maribel, and I have wanted this for a long time. Deny me now if you will, for I can no longer deny myself.' He raised his head to look down at her and then reached out to brush away the tear on her cheek. 'Crying? Have I mistaken the case? Last night in the moonlight I thought…but I see I was wrong. You do not want this, do you?'

Maribel could not answer, nor could she control the tears. She felt them slide helplessly down her face, staring up at him wordlessly. How could she tell him that she loved him, wanted to be his woman, when she knew he did not love her?

'Forgive me. I came to tell you we shall take our trip tomorrow and seeing you…I forgot myself.'

He turned and walked to the door. Maribel tried to speak, but could not make the words come.

'Do not leave me. Stay and make me yours,' she whispered, but the door had closed behind him.

Chapter Six

That morning was as warm as the one before it. Maribel rose early, dressed in one of her simpler gowns and went out to draw water from the well. She had carried both buckets to the house when Anna came sleepily into the kitchen. Hair was straggling down her back and it was obvious that she found it difficult to rouse herself.

'I stayed out drinking with Higgins after you retired last night,' she told Maribel, her cheeks flushed. 'I did not expect you to wake so early.'

'I was excited by the thought of the visit to the other side of the island.' Maribel smiled. 'It was no trouble to me to fetch the water.'

'I am still your maid—until you dismiss me.'

'I would never dismiss you, but I should like us to be friends, Anna. Now, I must change into one of the gowns Captain Sylvester bought for me.'

'I shall help you,' Anna did not meet her eyes.

Maribel sighed. She knew that Anna could not think of her as a friend, perhaps she never would. They had been mistress and servant and they would be parted when Maribel travelled to her mother's home.

Maribel was trying not to think of the moment when Justin had kissed her the previous night, the moment when her foolish tears had sent him away. What would have happened if she had not allowed herself to think of love? Would he have made love to her? Would he have accepted her as his woman? Did he care for her at all or was it just the sight of her in her shift that had made him take her in his arms?

When Maribel came from her room dressed in one of her best gowns, Justin was waiting for her. He greeted her with a nod, but gave no sign that anything had happened the previous night. She smiled at him shyly, her eyes going over him. He was so handsome clothed in black hose and long leather boots that reached to his thighs, his thin linen shirt open at the neck, revealing a sprinkling of dark hair on his tanned chest. His long hair had been caught back by a ribbon at his nape; he was wearing his sword and a leather belt across his body into which was thrust a long-barrelled pistol and a heavy knife.

'You look prepared for trouble,' she said, because she needed to say something or the silence between them would be unbearable.

'It is always best to be prepared,' he told her coolly. 'Higgins will help to row us to the shore, but he will remain with the boat while we explore.'

'Is Anna to come with us?'

'Would you like her to?'

'She would be company for Higgins while he waits for us.'

'Very well, she may come.' Justin's eyes were on her face. 'You are certain you wish for this outing?'

'Yes, of course. I am looking forward to seeing what Paradise looks like.' She did not add that the best part for her would be that she would be alone with him for a while, that perhaps she might find the courage to tell him what was in her heart.

'We should leave at once,' Justin told her, leading the way outside. 'The day looks fair, but the air is heavy. It is possible that there may be a storm before nightfall.'

'Surely not?' Maribel looked up at the cloudless blue sky and then out to sea. Several ships were anchored in the bay, though she could see no sign of the *Defiance*. It looked as if the *Maria* and Captain Hendry had already sailed, though Justin's third ship, the *Siren Eater,* which had joined them a few days before the feast, was still in port. 'Did you finish your business with Captain Hendry yesterday? I do not see his ship in port?'

'He told me that he had decided to become a merchant adventurer. I wished him well and we parted on good terms. I shall tell you more later, but the news he brought is good, Maribel. Your father seems to have accepted your decision not to return, though he has doubled his offer for the map. He sent you a letter. I intended to give it to you last night, but—' He broke off abruptly. 'You shall have it later.'

'Do not talk about it now,' she begged, suddenly wanting to delay talking of the future. 'It is a beautiful day and I see no sign of a storm.'

'They come suddenly at times. I would not be at sea in a small boat if a storm should strike. If that happens, we may have to stay at the other side of the island until the morning.'

Maribel's stomach caught. If they were stranded alone with no house or walls to separate them, who knew what might happen…?

'I do not think there will be a storm,' she said and smiled at him. 'But if there is we must make the best of it.'

Maribel watched as the two men pulled on the oars. It was a small boat and the blades cut through the water effortlessly as they rounded the point coming at last to a large, deserted cove. Here the beach was entirely fringed with trees that seemed to be thick for some distance inland; the sand was soft, unsullied by human habitation and beautiful as a glistening sea lapped against it. A few strokes more and the boat was beached. Higgins and Justin jumped out and hauled it into shallow water so that the hull scraped against the bottom.

Justin came to take Maribel's hand, then swept her up in his arms, carrying her through the water to where the sand was dry and silvery-soft beneath her feet. Her heart raced as she inhaled the spicy scent of him and felt her stomach spasm with desire. He was more to her than all the world and she must find the courage to tell him.

She looked about her. The sea was a deep turquoise, white crested with foam where the waves broke against the shore, sparkling in the sunshine like precious jewels. To each side of her was a wide expanse of sand, and behind her the dense woods that looked as if they might be difficult to penetrate.

'Why is this part of the island uninhabited?'

'There are dangerous rocks beneath the water and the ships would have to anchor further out. Until a harbour and a pier are built the only way to approach is in small boats, as we came today. In time I dare say the trees may be cut back and the harbour built—but the other side of the island was easier to settle—the water is deeper and the ships can unload much nearer to the beach if need be. As you know, we have built a harbour of sorts, though as yet it is primitive.'

Maribel nodded. She looked towards the trees, hearing the call of a bird and catching sight of its bright colours as it flitted between branches.

'It will be a pity if the woods are cut down to build houses.'

'Yes, perhaps, but men must have somewhere to shelter. If the island is to become a permanent settlement and not just somewhere for pirates to replenish their ships and enjoy some leisure on shore there must be some clearance in time.'

'Yes, I suppose it must happen. I think it would be pleasant to live where there is plenty of land and you could ride for a day and not find another settlement.'

'Would you not miss the company of others?'

'Yes, perhaps,' Maribel said and laughed. 'I am foolish. As you say, land must be settled and trees cut for wood if people are to live here—but I am glad that this place is unspoiled for the moment.'

Justin hesitated, then offered his hand. 'Come, I shall show you a place I discovered some months ago when I first visited this side of the island. I think you will like it. You may find the walk a little arduous but it will be worthwhile when we get there.'

Maribel took his hand. He did not look at her and she knew he was keeping a barrier between them, but her heart beat very fast. She had thought he might be angry after the previous night, but he seemed to have put it from his mind. Glancing back at Anna and Higgins, she saw they appeared engrossed in each other and envied them the uncomplicated nature of their relationship.

It was darker in the trees, but very warm despite the shade. The heat made the sweat run between Maribel's breasts, and her gown felt as if it were sticking to her. She had worn one of her best gowns for Justin's approval, but wished that she had a simple shift and skirt, as Anna was wearing. Long branches brushed against her face and hair. There were insects on the greenery and in the air, some of them settling on her arms and face. She brushed them away, feeling that the density of the trees was overpowering and unpleasant, and wishing they were still on the beautiful beach. Feeling hot and sticky, Maribel was on the point of asking if they could turn back when she heard the sound of water and her curiosity was aroused. In another moment the trees thinned out and then they were in a clearing.

The sound of water came from a little waterfall. It cascaded down over rocks, making a rushing noise. Clear and cool, it looked inviting and Maribel ran towards it, bending down to scoop water from the tiny pool at the base of the fall and splashing it on her face and neck. A stream wound away from the falls, and without thinking what she did, she sat on the bank, slipped off her shoes and dipped her feet into the stream, relishing the coolness on her flesh.

'This feels so good…' she said, arching back so that the sun was on her face while her feet dabbled in the water. 'This is a beautiful place, Justin. What are those flowers over there? They look like hibiscus but, I am not sure.'

'They are probably a different variety to those you have at home,' he said from just behind her. He sat down on the ground and hunched his knees in front of him. 'Was it worth the walk?'

'Oh, yes…' She looked round at him, her eyes alight, mouth slightly parted, an expression of such delight in her eyes that he caught his breath. 'Thank you so much for bringing me here. I think it is Paradise, though while we were in the trees I almost asked to go back. I was so hot and sticky.' She bent down to scoop water from the pool and splashed it once more over her face and neck. It trickled down her throat and disappeared under her bodice. The thin material clung to her, caressing the softness of her breasts where the water had soaked through. 'I did not think anywhere could be this beautiful…' Her eyes followed one of the birds that called from branches high above her. In the distance she could hear a faint booming sound, which she took to be the sound of the sea crashing against the rocky coasts further round the island. She turned her head to look at him and saw that he watched her.

'Last night…' Maribel sought and found the courage to say what must be said. 'I wept because I am a foolish woman, but after you had gone I wanted you to stay. I know you cannot love me, for you told me, but I…' The words caught in her throat as she saw the heat in his eyes.

'You are beautiful,' Justin said huskily. He reached out, taking her hand, pulling her to her feet. For a moment he hesitated, then his arms went round her, crushing her hard against him. His mouth sought hers, hungry and demanding, yet tender. 'You inflame my senses, Maribel. I vowed I would not do this, but you tempt me beyond bearing. Last night you wept and I thought—'

'Do not talk, kiss me,' she whispered and placed her finger against his lips. 'I want you to kiss me.'

'You know what it means if I kiss you?' His gaze was dark, intense as his eyes drank her in. 'I want more than a few kisses. I want…everything…you, your body, your mind, your heart.'

Maribel swayed towards him, her body melting into him as he kissed her, her mouth opening to his inquiring tongue, giving of her sweetness as she felt the desire race through her. This was what she had longed for.

What she wanted more than anything else in the world. His hand found and cupped her breast, his thumb caressing her through the thin material. She whimpered with need and pressed against him, feeling the hot desire curl inside her. As he bent his head and kissed her, sliding her bodice down over her shoulder, his tongue caressing the dark rose nipple, she moaned with need.

'Justin, I want…'

'What do you want, my darling? Say it is everything…say it is me you want, as I want you.'

'Take me, make me yours. Justin, I…'

Her words were lost as they heard the shot. She looked up at him, eyes wide and startled. Higgins had arranged that he would fire one shot if he needed them to return.

'Damn!' Justin let her go immediately. He looked back towards the shore, a pulse throbbing at his temple. 'Higgins would not summon me unless it was important. I am sorry, Maribel. We must go back.'

Maribel inclined her head. She wished that they could stay longer in this beautiful place, but Higgins would not have given the signal had it not been urgent. Taking Justin's hand, she let him hurry her back through the path they had cleared on their way here.

What could possibly be happening? Why had Higgins given the signal? As they heard a second shot, her heart started to pound. Something must be terribly wrong…

As they neared the beach Justin was ahead of her. He glanced back, signalling to her to slow down.

'Wait in the trees until I call you,' he warned. 'Just in case there is trouble.'

Maribel would have argued, but she could not catch up to him as he ran out on to the beach. She hovered at the edge of the trees, watching as Justin spoke to Higgins. The sailor appeared to be pointing agitatedly towards the other side of the island. Maribel turned her head and saw the smoke rising into what had been a cloudless sky. A cry from Justin alerted her and she left the shelter of the trees to join him.

'What is it?' she asked. 'What is happening?'

'Something is on fire in the port. We think there has been an attack of some kind.' Justin frowned. 'We must get back to the settlement, but you and Anna should stay here until someone comes to tell you that it is safe to return.'

'No!' Anna and Maribel spoke together.

'I would rather be with you whatever happens,' Maribel insisted. 'If we stayed here and you did not return, we might never reach the other side of the island. No matter what is happening, I shall come with you.'

'I'm not staying here without Higgins.' Anna said, her mouth set stubbornly.

Justin inclined his head. 'Very well. I have no time to argue. Into the boat with you.'

He was frowning as he assisted Higgins to push the boat into deeper water and then helped Maribel to climb in. She sensed that he was anxious for the crew and friends he had left behind. There were no words of comfort to offer for the smoke did not lie. Something terrible must have happened and she could sense the urgency and frustration in the two men as they pulled on the oars. They must be wondering what they were doing on a pleasure trip when their comrades were in trouble.

Maribel caught her breath as they rounded the point and she saw the ships blazing in the harbour. At least three were on fire and the smoke was thick, blowing across the sea towards the land.

'Damn it!' Justin cried. 'One of the ships burning is the *Sea Siren!* By the look of her she is finished.'

'What of the *Defiance?*' Maribel asked. 'I did not notice it in harbour as we left this morning.'

'Yesterday, I sent *Defiance* and a crew to fetch supplies from another island. We were running short of essentials like meat and milk and I bargained for live-stock that can be reared here.'

'Then *she* is safe?' Maribel said, thinking that if he had not sent his best ship for supplies that too might have been destroyed. It was bad enough that he should have lost the *Sea Siren,* because he had given his third ship to Captain Hendry as a reward for bringing the information about her family. Maribel felt relieved for his sake, but he misunderstood her question.

'You need not be concerned. A ship would be found to take you to England even if my ships were all destroyed.' His tone sounded scornful and she knew he believed she had been thinking of herself.

'I did not mean…' Maribel began but her words were lost as Anna cried out and pointed to the island

and they saw that some of the houses had been damaged by what could only be cannon fire. 'Who has done this terrible thing?'

The attack was clearly over; people were working frantically on shore to stop the fires spreading. The burning ships seemed to be done for, blazing too fiercely to be saved, but on land the people seemed to be winning their battle. Maribel's expression was puzzled as she looked at Justin.

'Why have these people been attacked?'

'We are pirates, hunted and hated by many,' Justin told her, white-lipped. 'The attack could have come from anyone. We may discover more when we go ashore. Whoever made the attack did as much damage as possible from the sea and then fled before they could be attacked in return—the cowards! May they rot in hell!'

Maribel flinched. Something in his tone made her feel that he blamed her for what had been done. She could hardly wait to be on shore. Terrible damage had been inflicted and people would be hurt. She wanted to help wherever she could, dousing the fires or tending injured people.

Everywhere was confusion and chaos. Maribel joined a chain passing buckets of water, asking the woman next to her what had happened as she took the bucket and gave it to the next in line.

'Three ships sailed into harbour. At first we took no notice, then we saw that some of our ships were on fire. The intruders worked swiftly and secretly, inflicting the most damage they could. When it was seen, the men manned the cannon that protect the harbour and started firing on the strange ships. That is when they fired on the buildings. Some of the men tried to swim out with pistols and swords, but the strangers fired on them. Then, sensing that the fires they had started might spread to their own ships, they sailed off.'

'I was on the other side of the island. Once or twice I thought I heard a muffled boom, but I thought it was just the sea,' Maribel said. 'Are there many hurt?'

'Several injured and some dead, those that were caught in the first blast—also men who tried to reach the swine that attacked us.'

'Where are the injured housed?'

'In the taproom of the Nag's Head, I heard.'

Maribel saw that the fire was almost out. She left the line and ran towards the inn where she had been told the wounded were housed. As she went into the taproom, she saw men and women lying on the floor. Some had been attended, others were moaning, begging for help. One man seemed to be in charge; by his instruments she guessed that he was a ship's surgeon. He was binding a man's head when she went up to him and asked if she could help.

'Have you treated wounds before?' Maribel shook her head. 'Give water to those that ask for it—and get out of my way.'

Feeling rejected, Maribel moved away. She found a barrel of water and a jug. Filling it, she took a pewter cup from the bar and began to move between the injured men and women, giving those that asked a few sips of water. Never in her life had she felt so useless, especially when she saw that Anna was washing away blood and binding wounds at the surgeon's direction. Why could she not have done that?

Maribel noticed that Anna was having some trouble holding a patient and trying to bandage his arm at the same time. She went to her and asked what she could do and was rewarded by a fleeting smile.

'Hold him for me. He keeps flopping over and I cannot bind him and hold him.'

'Like this?' Maribel put her arm about the injured man, supporting him while Anna bound his shoulder with clean linen. 'Let me help you with the others— please? I feel so useless.'

Anna looked at her for a moment, then nodded. 'You can give him a little of this mixture to ease his pain. Support him on your lap and spoon a few drops into his mouth, and then come to me. We need all the help we can get.'

'Yes, whatever you say. You are the mistress here, Anna.'

Maribel managed to spoon a little mixture into the man's mouth, then laid him gently down and made sure he was comfortable before moving on to help Anna with the next injury. She waited for Anna's directions and obeyed them implicitly, never asking why or deviating from her instructions. They worked together quietly and efficiently until all the wounded had been treated.

Maribel did not care that her beautiful gown had bloodstains on the skirt or that her face was smeared with it. She was moved to tears by the suffering of men, women and even one child who had received burns, but she held them back, knowing that she could not give way to sentiment.

At last Anna stood up and looked about her. 'We have done all we can here for the moment,' she said. 'We should go back to the house. I shall come back later to see what else may be done for them.'

'Then I shall come with you.'

'You are tired and hungry. We must prepare food for the men when they come back.'

Maribel followed Anna from the inn. She could see that the fires were out, but two buildings were burned to a shell and others were blackened and badly damaged by the fire. The stink of burning and thick smoke was in the air, as the two women left the waterfront and walked through the row of houses behind.

Maribel was too tired to notice the way people looked at them. She was thirsty and anxious now to be at home so that she could help prepare the food for Justin and Higgins when they had time to eat.

It was an hour or so later that Justin and his first mate came back to the house. Maribel had washed her face and hands, changing into one of her simple gowns before helping Anna to prepare food. The men were grim-faced and silent as they came in, both of them drinking water before seating themselves at the table.

'How bad is it?' Maribel asked. 'I know several were hurt—were many killed?'

'Three men and two women,' Justin replied. 'Two ships were lost, another damaged but not beyond repair. It might have been worse.'

'Was one of the ships lost yours?'

'Yes. Pike's was damaged, but it will sail again.'

'So you have only the *Defiance*?'

'I am fortunate to have that.' A nerve flicked in his cheek. 'It seems that my ships were what they were after. Pike's vessel and another caught the flames, but the fires were meant for us.'

'Meant for us?' Maribel's eyes widened. For a moment she did not understand, then the colour drained from her face. 'Are you saying…no, how could it be?'

'The ships that attacked us were Spanish. Pike saw the attack. He says that the pennant belonged to Sabatini…your father…'

'No! How could my father know where to find you?'

'Word of this place may have spread. I do not know that they came looking for us, but it was not mere chance that made them attack my ship.'

Her throat tightened. 'You think…you blame my father…and me?'

'No, I do not blame you,' he said, his voice hoarse. 'But I fear others will, Maribel. They will blame you— and me for bringing you here.' He frowned. 'It may be that I am to blame…'

'Why? I do not know what you mean.'

'If it was your father's ships, then I may have brought them here.'

'Surely not? My father could not have known you would come here—he could not!'

'You forget Mr Hendry. He had knowledge of our plans. It may be that he passed on his knowledge.'

'You think he betrayed the location of the island?' Her eyes widened. 'He sailed away before the attack. You think that he brought them here? Why would he do that? He took your message to my father and you gave him the ship, as you promised. Why would he betray you—all of you?'

'He may not have had a choice. Your father may have hoped to trap me. When I did not walk into the trap or send back the map, he decided to take another kind of revenge. I was told that he had doubled his offer, but that may have been just to lull me into a sense of security. Hendry may have agreed to show them the way here to save his own life…and a cowardly attack is something your father might try. He knows that our ships will beat his when we meet at sea, but with the ships anchored and a skeleton crew aboard…'

'What happened to those men?'

'Some managed to swim for the shore, some died.' Justin's mouth settled into a hard line. 'I care little for the ships. We began with one and we can rebuild our fleet, but…' His eyes were flinty. 'Tom was one of the crew on watch. He did not make it to the shore.'

'Tom is dead?' Tears welled in her eyes. 'No! Oh, no, I cannot bear it. He was so happy to be a part of all this and he was so young.'

'He knew the risks when he threw in his lot with us.'

'How can you say that?' Maribel was too distressed to think clearly or to notice that he was strained and tense. 'Tom was little more than a child.'

She ran from the room, feeling close to tears. In her own bedchamber she sat on the bed, covering her face with her hands. The tears she had held back as she helped with the wounded fell thick and fast. She had known that the pirates led precarious lives, but the cabin boy's death was shocking and painful. She looked up as her door opened and saw Justin standing on the threshold.

'You should not weep for him,' he said. 'We all run the risk of a violent death. It could have happened at sea. Ours is a precarious trade and death is common amongst us.'

'You speak so lightly of death.' Maribel's face was white as she stood up. 'I cannot help but weep for Tom. He was like a young brother to me.'

'Weep then, but accept it.' Justin moved towards her, looking down at her face. She believed she saw something like regret in his eyes. 'I thought perhaps we might have something, you and I—but this is no life for you, Maribel. You do not belong here. The life is too harsh for a woman of your breeding and you would sicken and die of a broken heart. The sooner I get you to England the better for all concerned.'

'I thought…' She choked back the words. Earlier that day he had held her in his arms and kissed her until she melted for love, but that was a different man, a man she could love and respect, the man he had been before he became a pirate perhaps. This man with the cold eyes

looked at her as if he despised her, thought her weak
and useless. 'Yes, you are right. Yet even if I do not
belong, I can do something to help. Anna and I tended
the wounded and we shall return to see what more we
can do in the morning.'

'No! You are not to go down to the waterfront. I
forbid it.'

'You forbid it? I do not understand. I am capable of
helping to nurse the wounded.'

'Now that the fires are out there will be plenty to
help the wounded. You are not needed—and Anna
would do well to stay away too. These people can
look after their own.'

His words struck her like the lash of a whip. 'You
are cruel, sir. I wished only to help.'

'You will do more harm than good. People are
blaming you for this attack—and me. They do not want
your help. Even I must watch my back when I walk
there—you would be too vulnerable.'

Maribel was silenced. He was so harsh and his words
were like a knife in her heart. He spoke of others
blaming her—but he blamed her too. The ships that had
wreaked so much damage on the island and its inhabitants were part of her father's fleet. She had tried to
change, to become like Anna and the others, but she had
never belonged here—and now she was hated.

'I would not have had this happen…' Her eyes were
wide, filled with tears. 'You know I would not…'

'What I know is nothing to the point. For your own
safety stay away from the waterfront. The *Defiance*

should return in a few days. As soon as it has unloaded its cargo and provisioned we shall leave the island.'

Maribel inclined her head. 'Very well, I shall be ready. As you said, the sooner I am on my way to England the better.'

Maribel slept little that night. She had wept until there were no more tears, but then she tossed restlessly, going over and over all the events of the past weeks in her mind. What could she have done differently? People believed that she had brought this cruel attack on them, but even if her father's ships had been responsible it did not mean that she had brought them here. Had they been looking for her they would surely have brought a party ashore and demanded her return? No, she could only think that the ships had come at this time by chance—and seeing so many pirate ships assembled had taken a swift revenge before retreating.

It was unfair for Justin to blame her!

In the morning she rose early and went out to fetch water. Anna came into the kitchen as she was washing some clothes. She looked tired and her hair was hanging down her back, as if she had not bothered with it.

'Did you not sleep last night either?'

'I went to the inn to see if I could help but I was told to stay away.' Anna looked at her sulkily. 'They are blaming us for bringing the trouble here. Higgins says that we may not be able to return to the island.'

'I am sorry. I know that you wished to make your home here.'

'Higgins says we may have to find somewhere else to set up our trading store. Some of the men told me that we are no longer welcome on the island. I think we must be careful, Maribel. There could be trouble.'

'Surely we are safe enough here?'

'Perhaps—but we must not go to the waterfront alone.'

'Captain Sylvester forbade it. Yet you still went last night—why?'

'I thought the resentment would not be for me, but it seems I am tarred with the same brush as you.'

'Do not hate me, Anna. Please. You know that I would not have had this happen. Besides, I do not think they came to look for me, because no one came ashore—though it seems they were my father's ships.'

'Perhaps they thought you were not here since the *Defiance* was not in the harbour.' Anna frowned. 'Higgins says people are wondering why it was not here.'

'They cannot think that Sylvester knew the attack would happen? If he had, he would have warned others and sent all his ships away.'

'When people are hurt and angry they do not think clearly.'

'This is so foolish,' Maribel shook her head. 'We were not even here when the attack happened.'

'That makes it all the worse... Do you not see what people think?'

'They believe he deliberately chose to be absent?

How foolish can people be? We rushed back as soon as we saw the smoke…we all helped as best we could!'

'Higgins says someone is stirring them up, making trouble.'

'Why? Who would do that?'

Anna shook her head. 'I do not know. I only know that things have changed. We must leave this island and the sooner the better.'

Maribel was about to reply when she heard a noise behind her. Swinging round, she saw Peg watching them.

'I did not hear you come in?'

'I wanted to creep up on yer,' Peg told her, unsmiling. 'Yer asked me for lessons to defend yerself and yer will need them. Folk are saying yer brought the trouble on us and they want yer gone—one way or the other. Some are fer hanging yer.'

'Anna has told me what people are saying. I knew nothing of this, Peg. I swear I would not have had it happen for the world.'

Peg looked at her in silence for a moment and then nodded. 'Aye, I believe yer, but others will not. They won't listen. Especially with Pike stirring them up. He says Sylvester sent his ship away to save it.'

'That is nonsense! You know he would not do that, don't you? He could have sent all his ships if that had been the case—so why didn't he?'

'Yer need not try to convince me, lass—but others will listen to Pike. Sylvester has been too successful. Some are jealous of him and need only a grievance to make them turn against him. He brought yer here and that's good enough for most.'

'Is he in danger?' Maribel asked. 'I have not seen him this morning. I do not know where he is.'

'It's yerself they hate most. Come outside now, and I'll show yer a few of me tricks with a knife so that yer can defend yerself, but it will be best fer yer all if yer leave as soon as yer can.'

'It is getting late,' Maribel said as the sun began to dip on the horizon that evening. 'Sylvester has been gone all day and Higgins with him. I fear that something has happened to them.'

'Someone would have told us,' Anna said, but was clearly worried. 'They are not all against us despite what happened. Sylvester's crew would stand behind him whatever others thought.'

'Would they?' Maribel eyed her uncertainly. 'Supposing they have been hurt? The crew might be afraid to send for us…Sylvester might forbid it if it meant danger for us.'

'There is little we can do. They might be anywhere.' Anna frowned. 'I do not think they would leave the island without us.'

'Of course they would not. Captain Sylvester would never desert us.'

Chapter Seven

Maribel's anxiety grew with every minute that passed. Justin must know that they would be worried. Why was he so late? It was almost dark and he had still not returned. Her instincts were to go and look for him, but he had forbidden her to go down to the waterfront.

She could not sit and wait. The house felt too small and confined to contain her and she needed some air. Anna called to her as she moved towards the door.

'Where are you going? It is nearly dark and too dangerous to go looking for them now.'

'I just need some—' Maribel broke off as she heard sounds outside. She rushed to the door and threw it open, staring in dismay as she saw Higgins and two of Justin's crew she recognised. They were carrying something between them—Justin's body. She saw blood on his shirt and clapped a hand to her mouth to stop herself screaming. 'What happened?'

'He was set upon by some ruffians.' Higgins

scowled. 'It was Pike's crew, ordered to it by him no doubt. The captain had been to see some of the wounded. He had promised to make good their losses and explained why our ship was not in the harbour. They listened to him and he left believing all was settled—then this gang attacked him. He fought them off and wounded or killed three, but they were too many for him. Had I and some of the crew not arrived in time he might have been finished.'

'Carry him through to his room,' Maribel said, hovering as they brought Justin's unconscious body into the house. Her heart was hammering and she felt sick with worry, but would not give way to her fear. 'He has lost blood—where is his wound?'

'He has a wound to his thigh and another to his shoulder—but he was knocked unconscious by a blow from one of those murdering devils. Fortunately, we drove them off before they could finish him, but he will need nursing. I've sent word to the surgeon and he'll be here soon.'

'Thank you for all you have done. I am so grateful.'

In the bedchamber, Anna had pulled back the sheets. Justin was deposited gently on his bed by the men; they then drew back to look at him in silence, not sure what to do next. Anna brought a knife and slit his breeches at the side so that they could see the wound to his thigh. She examined it and then looked at Maribel.

'It has bled a lot, but is not too deep. He should mend without too much help from the surgeon,' she said on a note of relief. She then slit open the sleeve of his shirt all the way to the shoulder. 'This is a little deeper, but I think neither wound will kill him—providing he does not take a fever.'

'It seems you were in time to save his life. Thank you,' Maribel said to Higgins. Tears trickled down her cheeks, but she brushed them away. She turned to Anna, an appealing expression in her eyes. 'Please tell me what to do. You know better than I how to help him.'

'We must cleanse and bind the wounds,' Anna told her. 'I do not know what more we can do, but the surgeon will tell us when he comes. It may be that he will cauterise the wound to Sylvester's shoulder.'

Maribel's face turned white and she swayed, clutching at a bedpost to steady herself. She had never been present when it was done, but she knew that to apply a hot iron to open flesh must be fearful and would cause terrible pain.

'I pray God that it will not be needed,' she whispered. 'I shall fetch water and clean linen.'

She was praying and crying at the same time, for she was afraid that whatever they did Justin might die.

The surgeon had closed Justin's wounds without cauterising them, cleansing the skin with a mixture of his own that smelled like alcohol to Maribel and binding him tightly to stop further bleeding. When he had finished, he turned to Maribel.

'Fortunately, they are both little more than flesh wounds. He should heal within a week or two if he rests, but you must watch for a fever. That blow to the head has rendered him unconscious. Such wounds can kill a man, but sometimes the victim recovers without serious harm. You must watch over him and wait. I will leave something to help him with the pain. If a fever develops, you must keep him cool, and if necessary send for me again.'

'Thank you.' Maribel's throat was tight as she held back her tears. 'Anna is very good. She will help me to nurse him and she knows how to prepare mixtures that help with a fever, if she has the herbs.'

'Send to me if you need anything and I will bring whatever Anna requires. It is best that she does not go looking for her herbs alone—the mood here is still uncertain.' He wrinkled his brow in thought. 'I do not blame you or Sylvester. I dare say the ships found us by chance, as was bound to happen one day. Had they been prepared for an attack, they would have done much more damage and probably sent a party ashore to look for you.'

'I think much as you do,' Maribel said. 'My father would have sent men ashore to look for me if he had planned this attack; I believe they must have found the island by chance. However, they may return with more ships and more men; my father is a vengeful man.'

'There is talk of setting up cannon on shore in case we are attacked from the sea again, though others talk of leaving the island, giving up the attempt to settle here. Most of the captains neglected to protect their ships; they felt safe here, but this attack will make them take measures to make sure next time we can at least fight back. However, some feel the island is no longer safe for us.'

He smiled as he took his leave. Maribel thanked him. She stayed by Justin's side, watching as he lay unconscious. He was breathing still, but had given no sign of coming to himself, though he had moaned once or twice as the surgeon treated his wounds.

'Please live,' she whispered. Her tears came freely now for she could no longer hold them back. One or two fell on his face as she bent over him, pressing her cheek to his. 'I love you, my own dear pirate. I would not tell you if you could hear me—but I love you as I have never loved anyone else.'

Bending over him, she bathed his forehead with a cloth wrung out in cool water, then slid it over his shoulders and arms. His body was so hot and he had been throwing his arms out of the bed.

'I love you so,' she said as the tears trickled down her cheeks. 'I know so little of you, but you are brave and generous, and I was luckier than I knew when you took me captive. Please get better, my dearest. If you died I should not want to live.'

Justin did not stir. She looked for a flicker of his eyelids, but there was none. Please God he would wake soon…she could not think of a future without this man.

As the night wore on he began to moan and move restlessly in his bed, calling out a name she could not quite catch. She lay a hand on his forehead and thought he felt too warm. The surgeon had told her to keep him cool. Maribel hesitated and then fetched water in a bowl; it was cold from the well and she dipped a cloth into the cool water bathing his face and neck once more. He was still hot, so she stroked her cloth down his arms, then drew back the covers to his waist and bathed his chest. He seemed to settle then and she replaced the covers.

His breathing was easier now and she thought that he seemed more comfortable than before. She settled down on a blanket beside the bed and after a little fell asleep.

When a sound awoke her light was beginning to creep into the room. She started up, giving a little moan as she felt the stiffness in her back from lying on the floor. Getting to her feet, she looked at her patient and saw that he was now awake and staring at her.

'That was foolish of you, Maribel,' he said, looking stern. 'You should have gone to your own bed—or had someone else watch me. Where is Anna?'

'Anna has enough to do. She helped the surgeon when he tended you—and she stopped the bleeding when you were brought back. It did not hurt me to watch over you for a while.' She reached out to touch his forehead, but he caught her wrist. 'You were hot last night. I thought you might have a fever.'

'I have a damnable soreness in my thigh and left shoulder.' His gaze narrowed. 'I remember fighting the rogues off, but then something hit me from the side.' He scowled. 'There were too many of them. It is impossible to guard against such a cowardly blow. What happened after that—how did I get here?'

'Fortunately, Higgins and some of your men arrived to drive the wretches off. You were unconscious when they brought you home. Anna tended you first and then the surgeon came.'

His eyes were on her face. 'You know what is being said of you?'

'That the attack was because of me. Do you believe that? Do you think I would want that to happen?

'I know you would not. That it was your father's ships is not in question. However, it may have been chance that brought them here—unless Hendry revealed the secret of the island and how to enter its waters. One reason this island was chosen from so many others is that there is chain of rocks guarding it. Only those that have visited know how to navigate the channel. If your father's ships got close enough to inflict so much damage, they must have known the secret—but if they came for you, why was there no attempt to rescue you?'

'I do not know—perhaps I was not important.'

Justin frowned and was silent for a moment. He knew, but would not tell her that her father cared so little for her that he had been willing to give her up for the return of his map. Sabatini was evil and it made him wonder if the man was truly her father. 'I think he came to show me what could happen to me if I do not return his map.'

'You think the attack was planned merely for revenge? Because you refused to give up the map?' She was silent for a moment. 'What will you do? Shall you send it to him?'

'The way he so callously destroyed property and life here tells me that he should never have that map. With it he will become even more powerful and I cannot condone what he did. He is an evil man.'

'But if you keep the map he may attack you again.'

'Do you think I should be safe from his vengeful spite if I sent him his map? He would see it as a sign of weakness.' Justin looked thoughtful. 'I had considered trying to find the silver mine myself, but it has cost too many lives already. I think it is cursed and I shall destroy the map. Better it is never found again than it should cost more lives.'

'My father will always be your enemy.'

'You need not worry yourself over my safety. In two or three days I shall be able to get up. As soon as the *Defiance* returns she will be provisioned and we shall sail to England. Once you are with your family you will be safe.'

'The surgeon said you need to rest.' Maribel felt that he was dismissing her once more and her eyes stung with tears she would not shed.

'I shall be well enough to leave when the *Defiance* is ready to sail.'

'What will you do next? Will you return to the island? You've built a fine house and furnished it—but you have lost one of your ships and people may turn against you because of what happened.'

'It can be of little interest to you what I do. I promised to keep you safe until you are with your family. After that you should forget me.'

How could he speak to her so? Was he deliberately trying to drive a wedge between them?

'I think you must be thirsty. I shall draw some fresh water from the well.'

She walked away from him, her throat closing with choking emotion. He was still determined to take her to her family and leave her. Did he blame her for the loss of his ships and the destruction here? She blinked away her tears. Maribel had wept when she believed he might die, but she would not weep now!

'If your father saw you now he would not know you,' Anna said as Maribel was drawing water from the well three days later. 'Your skin used to be a pale olive and was much admired, but now…you are as brown as a gypsy.'

'I cannot stay in the shade all the time here. There has been more work to do since Justin was injured. It would not be fair to expect you to do everything. You chopped the wood so that we can cook, so I draw the water and help with the washing and other chores.'

Anna stared at her in silence for a moment, then smiled a little reluctantly. 'You have learned to make yourself useful. Sometimes I almost forget that you are a lady and I am your servant.'

'You are my friend, Anna. The old ways are forgotten here.'

'But when you go to England you will be a lady again, and if I came with you I should be a servant.' She shook her head as Maribel was silent. 'No, do not deny it. That is the way of your world, the way it has always been. You cannot change it if you would, which is why I shall not stay in England.'

Anna was right, but Maribel did not want to admit it. Here on the island she had found a measure of freedom and she did not want to return to her old life—but what else could she do?

'Where will you go if you cannot return to the island?'

'Higgins thinks he shall go to the New World and I shall go with him. There is plenty of land there for settlement. If you have money for sufficient supplies to get you through the first year or two until the land begins to grow enough crops, it could be a good place to live.'

'The New World…' Maribel wrinkled her brow. 'I have heard it said that it is a land of savages. My father and men like him take silver from the mines, but to live there…I am not sure…'

'At first our people, men like your father, sought to conquer and take only silver and gold, but other people have begun to settle further to the north. Higgins has heard from men who have taken settlers to the New World. The savages are called Red Indians, because of the colour of their skins, and it is thought that there are many tribes. Some of them are thought to be friendly to the white man.'

'It sounds dangerous and the living will be primitive at first,' Maribel said, but she felt a tingle of excitement at the nape of her neck. 'Even here on the island there are often shortages of food, which is why Justin sent the *Defiance* to bring pigs and chickens here from one of the larger islands.'

'In the New World they say there is an abundance of game. Ships taking settlers to a new life will carry seed corn and other supplies to tide them over. A ship bringing in fresh supplies to be sold at a trading station could do well.'

'Yes, I see.' Maribel nodded. 'You would set up your trading station there instead of on the island as you planned, but—' She had questions concerning such trading, but she broke off as she saw a man coming towards them. Chills ran down her spine as she saw the look of hatred on his face. 'Go inside, Anna.'

'And leave you alone with that pig? I shall stay with you.'

Maribel faced the pirate. One hand moved to the place in her skirts where she had created a pouch to keep the knife that Peg had given her. Her heart was pounding wildly as he came closer.

'Why have you come here?' she asked. 'You tried to have Sylvester murdered. You are not wanted here.'

Pike's eyes narrowed to menacing slits, his mouth curved back in a sneer. 'I came only to tell you that the *Defiance* is back in the harbour. People are demanding that you leave immediately. I have some business with Sylvester that he might want to hear.'

'Do you imagine I shall let you near him after what you tried to do?'

'You?' He laughed harshly. 'What will you do, my lady? Kick me, perhaps, or scratch my eyes out—if you can?'

'Go away. If you have business, you may return

when Higgins is here…' Maribel gasped because she had revealed their vulnerability.

Pike grinned evilly. 'Oh, do not distress yourself for betraying your weakness. I saw Higgins on the water-front not twenty minutes ago. I know he is not around to save you or your precious Sylvester, whore.'

'I am no man's whore.' Maribel flashed.

'Are you not? Then I might as well amuse myself a little before I complete my business with…'

Maribel moved back a step as he came towards her. Then she stopped, determined to stand her ground. If she ran or showed fear, he would have the advantage. She could not let him into the house because Justin was not yet strong enough to fight him off.

Pike laughed mockingly and reached out to grab her. Whipping her knife out, Maribel struck his right arm, making him yell out in shock. His left hand moved to cover his wound. He stared in disbelief at the blood running between his fingers.

'You bitch! I'll teach you a lesson—and then I'll pay your lover a visit.'

'You will have to get past me first.'

Maribel held her knife in front of her the way Peg had taught her. She circled him warily, her eyes never leaving his face. He made a move to grab her once more and she flicked her wrist, stabbing him swiftly on his hand and darting back. He swore, looking at his hand as if he did not know what had happened.

'You asked for this,' he grunted and drew his cutlass. The sunlight glinted on the wicked blade as he advanced on her. 'I thought to have a little fun before you died, but it is not worth the bother. I'll be rid of you once and for all!'

Maribel held the knife in front of her, but she knew a knife could not compete with a cutlass. Peg had told her to keep the knife secret and wait until her target was close enough to stab him in the stomach, but she had struck too soon, inflicting only superficial wounds. The element of surprise had gone. She had wounded him, but not sufficiently to stop him. He would kill her and then Justin.

Maribel was vaguely aware that Anna had run into the house. She retreated slowly towards the house, her gaze holding his as he advanced on her, knowing that it was only a matter of time before he killed her.

'Stay away from her!'

Hearing Anna's voice, Maribel glanced round. Even as she saw the pistol in her hand, Anna fired. Her shot hit Pike in the chest and he fell, clutching himself. For what seemed like an eternity, he writhed in agony on the ground, his eyes wide and staring at them. Anna came towards them, her hand shaking. She looked sick and shaken as she watched the man twitching on the ground.

'Have I killed him?'

The twitching had stopped at last. Pike lay still. 'Yes, I think so,' Maribel said. Anna dropped the pistol. She was shaking, clearly upset by what she had done. 'Do not look so guilty. You had no choice. If you had not shot him, he would have killed us all.'

'I meant to stop him, not to kill him.' Anna looked

frightened. She turned away to vomit on the ground, then wiped her mouth on the back of her hand. 'Will they hang me?'

'No, they won't hang you.' Justin's voice spoke from the doorway. 'It was in self-defence, Anna—but no one will know, because we shall bury him out there.' He jerked his head towards the back of the house. 'I can't do much to help you. There is a spade in the lean-to at the rear. You will have to drag him there between you. I'll help to dig the hole.'

'No, you will not,' Maribel spoke decisively. 'You have told us what to do. Go back to your room and rest. We can do this between us.'

Justin set his mouth stubbornly. He took a step towards them, then hesitated, his face white.

'Go on, then. I will make sure there is no sign of the blood here—and I'll keep watch and warn you if anyone comes.'

'Yes,' Maribel agreed, because she knew that he would only follow them if she refused his help. 'As soon as it is done you must go back to bed and rest. Pike told us that the *Defiance* is in the harbour. When it is provisioned we shall leave as intended.'

Justin nodded, his mouth set in a grim line.

'Come, Anna,' Maribel said. 'You have to help me drag him. I can't do it alone. Take one leg and I'll take the other.'

Anna shuddered, then did as she was told. Pike was heavy and it took both of them to drag his body across the front yard and out behind the house.

Maribel chose a spot where the earth looked softer. A tree had been cleared to supply timber for the house and the earth had been disturbed, making it easier to dig. When Anna fetched the spade, Maribel started the digging. She dug out an oblong large enough to hide the body. After the first few cuts were made, Anna went to the lean-to and came back with a chopper. She used it to dig down into the earth and then scraped the dry earth out with her hands.

The women worked in silence for what seemed like an eternity. At last the hole was deep enough and between them they placed Pike in his grave and then started to scrape the earth over him. When they had finished Maribel looked at Anna.

'He was a wicked man, but I think we should say a prayer for him.'

'Yes…' Anna was pale and penitent. 'You are right, Maribel. I did not mean to murder him, only to stop him.'

'You did what you had to do—we both did,' Maribel said. She felt sick and a little faint, but forced herself to continue. 'God keep and forgive this man. He was not a good man, but we pray that his soul will find peace.'

'You can see the earth has been disturbed,' Anna said when the prayer was done. 'We should lay branches over it to hide it for a while. The grave may be found, but it will not matter once we are gone.'

'You will not be able to return here now.' Maribel remarked as they finished their work and returned to the house. 'But you should not feel guilty, Anna. You saved my life—and Captain Sylvester's.'

'And my own. He would not have let me live to tell the tale.'

'No, he could not have risked it, for Higgins would have demanded justice.' Maribel saw that Anna was still pale, still shocked by what she had done. She reached out and kissed her cheek. 'Forget what happened, Anna. You must put it behind you.'

'He was a bad man.' Anna met her eyes, seeking reassurance. 'I do not believe I shall burn in hell for what I did, do you?'

'No, of course not. It was the only way,' Maribel replied. 'I shall never forget that you saved my life, Anna.'

'I could not let him kill you.' Anna smiled, oddly shy and uncertain. 'We have something in common now, Maribel. We share a bond that can never be broken— it is a secret we must keep to the grave.'

'Yes, it is.' Maribel took her hand. 'We are friends, Anna, truly friends. What has happened here has changed us both for ever. I am no longer the lady you served. I am different and I can never go back to what I once was.'

'We both need to wash and change our gowns,' Anna said, looking at the dirt beneath her fingernails. 'You should speak to Captain Sylvester, ask when we are leaving.'

'Yes, I shall.'

Maribel pushed her hair back from her eyes. She was damp with sweat, her clothes sticking to her. There were blisters on her hands and her back ached. The hard labour had exhausted her, but she had a feeling of satisfaction, because she would never have believed herself capable of doing what she had just done.

A part of her felt ill at ease because a man's life had been lost, but Pike was evil. He had tried to have Justin killed and would have succeeded this time if Anna had not stopped him. Maribel knew that she would not have known how to shoot the pistol. Anna must have learned it from Higgins, just as she had learned to use a knife from Peg. So although she felt uneasy that a man's life had been taken, she believed it was inevitable. Pike had been their enemy from the beginning. It was always his life or theirs.

She went into the house, then knocked at Justin's door. He was sitting on the bed. He invited her to enter, looking at her face as she did so.

'Is it done?'

'Yes. We put branches over the grave. It is not deep enough and it will be found, but perhaps not just yet.'

'We shall leave in the morning with the tide. Higgins has instructions to see the ship provisioned immediately.'

'Anna had no choice but to shoot him. He would have murdered us all.'

'I should have seen to it before it got this far,' Justin said. 'You both did what you had to do, Maribel. Put all this from your mind.'

'I shall try.' She brushed the damp hair from her brow. 'Your shirt has blood on it. I think your wound has opened,' she scolded. 'You have done too much. I saw that you brushed away the marks we left when we dragged Pike into the woods.'

'I wish I could have done it all.' He reached up to trail his fingers over her cheek as she sat beside him. 'You have dirt on your face and your gown is muddy. You must wash and change it for another.' He took her hands and looked at them. 'Rub some ointment into your hands; they will be sore for some days.'

'Let me tend your shoulder first.'

'No!' He caught her hand as she attempted to push his shirt back. 'I can manage for myself. Wash and rest, Maribel. You should drink a little rum or some wine. You have had a shock.'

'We buried a man,' Maribel said. 'Anna is feeling guilty. It will take time to forget.'

'I know. It is something you learn to live with. I've never been able to accept it, which is why I didn't just kill Pike at the start—but it might have been better if I had.'

'Yes, perhaps.'

Maribel turned away. She needed to wash and change. The dress she was wearing would be discarded, because she could never wear it again without remembering.

She had told Anna to forget what had happened, because to dwell on Pike's death would cast a shadow over their lives. She shuddered, because she knew it was something she might never forget. They had done what was necessary and they must put it behind them and move on.

* * *

Maribel could not sleep. The night was hot and stuffy and in the morning they were to leave the island for ever. In a few short weeks they would be in England and she would be with her mother's family. She might never see Justin again.

Rising from her bed, she dressed in a thin gown, pushed her feet into light slippers and went through to the main room and then outside. Here it was a little cooler. Maribel knew that she was taking a risk to leave the house, but Pike was dead and she did not think anyone else was likely to come looking for her. Most of the men on the island respected Justin, even if they blamed her for what had happened here.

Was it her fault? She had done nothing wrong and yet it might be because of her that the island had been attacked. She tried to put all the terrible happenings of the past few days from her mind. Soon now she would leave this place and perhaps…

Maribel heard a twig snap behind her, but before she could turn something thick and heavy was thrown over her head. She screamed, but the sound was muffled and the blanket filled her mouth, making her gag on the coarse wool. Fighting and kicking, she felt herself being tossed over someone's shoulder. She was being carried away. As she realised that she had been kidnapped, panic swept over her.

Justin would think she had run away! He would think she did not care. He would never know that she loved him. She might never see him again; it would break her heart, but she was just another woman to him. He would find someone else and forget her.

It was unbearable beneath the blanket. She found it difficult to breathe and after a while she ceased to struggle because she no longer had the strength to fight. She could only wonder who had captured her and where she was being taken.

After a while, Maribel heard the sound of the sea. She knew that she was in a rowing boat and that she was being taken to a ship. Was it her father's ship? It was the only explanation that occurred to her, because surely no one else would have come to the island to kidnap her. Her father must have sent someone to steal her back. He had sent Captain Hendry to bring the information they needed so that he knew where to find her and now she was a prisoner.

What was going to happen to her now? Justin was angry with her. He would not rescue her a second time—why should he?

When Maribel opened her eyes again she found that she was lying on a bunk. Her mouth tasted dry and she knew that at some time after being brought to this cabin she had fainted. As yet she did not know whose ship she was on or who had captured her.

Hearing a key in the lock, she looked fearfully at the door, her heart pounding. It opened slowly and she saw a man standing in the opening looking at her. When she saw the man's face she shrank back, feeling frightened, but determined not to show it.

'Why have you brought me here?' she demanded. 'Are you taking me to my father?'

'Your father has no more use for you, Donna Sanchez. He has given you to me in return for a contract for his wines—and favours rendered.' An unpleasant smile touched his mouth.

'What do you mean he has given me to you? I was to marry your cousin.'

Samuel Hynes looked at her triumphantly. 'Sadly, news reached us that my cousin is dead. All that he once owned is mine—and that includes you. I knew that he might not live to see his wedding day. Why else do you imagine I agreed to fetch you? I wanted to make sure I had you fast before the news of his death reached your father.'

'I shall never marry you. Never! I would rather die.'

'You speak wildly, Madonna.' His mouth hardened. 'Have I said that I wished to wed you? I might simply use you for my pleasure.'

'I shall fight you. You may force me, but you will never truly have me.'

'I think you will learn to obey me in time,' Hynes said. 'You are too proud. I shall enjoy teaching you your manners, Maribel. However, it will suit me better to have you as a wife. Your father thinks to cheat us both of your fortune, but he has met his match in me. I shall have you and then I shall claim what belongs to me.'

Maribel stared at him, feeling sick and miserable. 'I wish that Pablo had never left me his fortune,' she said.

'It seems that no one cares what I want. No one cares for me. You all want my husband's estates.'

'Beautiful women are easy to find,' Hynes told her with a sneer. 'However, a beautiful rich woman is another matter. I shall leave you to rest and think carefully, Maribel. We could be married almost immediately on board ship and I should treat you fairly—but defy me and you will learn to regret it at your leisure.'

Maribel lay back against the pillows as he left her. Her head was aching and her heart felt as if it had been torn apart. Tears trickled down her cheeks. She had not known how fortunate she was when Justin took her captive. She had called him a pirate and accused him of being a rogue, but he was a true gentleman—and she loved him. The time spent at the island had taught her many lessons and she knew that she had been offered something true and special.

The tears fell faster as she realised that she would probably never see him again. She was now at the mercy of a ruthless devil; if she lived, her life would be unbearable.

'Do you know where Maribel is?' Justin demanded of Anna when he realised that she had gone that morning. 'Has she taken anything with her?'

'Only the gown she meant to wear today.' Anna looked at him tearfully. 'Surely she would not run away? She had nowhere to go.'

'She must be somewhere.'

Justin strode into Maribel's room, looking for

evidence that she had taken something with her. Her combs and perfume bottles were still there, as were her jewels. He whirled round as he heard a step behind him.

'Maribel…' Seeing Higgins, he frowned. 'What is it? Have you found her?'

'I have found signs of a struggle. What looks like the marks of several pairs of boots in the dust outside the house—and I have heard that a strange ship was seen at anchor outside the reef.'

'You think someone snatched her last night?'

'I've never trusted Hendry,' Higgins said sourly. 'Did you not wonder why Sabatini let him return? Or why he bothered to come back at all? He already had the ship. Why should he have come back to the island merely to bring you another message?'

'You believe Hendry brought Sabatini's ships here in return for his freedom? That the intention was to snatch Maribel all the time?' Justin frowned. 'There was a map that showed the way to some silver mines… I destroyed it because a man like that should not be allowed to have such power. He is evil.'

'You destroyed a map showing the location of silver mines?' Higgins looked at him intently. 'Those mines are worth a king's ransom.'

'I considered trying to find the mine, but decided it was cursed.'

'Sabatini must think you still have the map. Do you think that is why he has snatched her?'

'If it is, then I am at fault,' Justin said. 'I do not

know where they are taking her—but we must try to find them. I shall go to her father. He may hate me and he may take my life, but, it is the risk I must take.'

'Do you think that is wise?'

'I do not care whether or not it is wise,' Justin replied. 'I shall not ask anyone else to risk their life for me. You will drop me on shore and then go back to sea. I will meet you on the beach at midnight. If I am not there, come again the next night, but after that you must go and leave me to my fate.'

'Let me go in your stead?'

'No. You have been a good friend to me, but if I do not come the second night leave me and seek your own fortune.'

'Will you not take the air on deck, Madonna?' Samuel Hynes looked at her, his eyes narrowed. 'We are forced to put into port for repairs to the mainmast and it may be some weeks before we reach England.'

Maribel sighed. It was hot in the cabin and since the third night after leaving the island, when a storm had badly damaged their mainmast, they had been forced to drift aimlessly. Now that the ship had at last managed to limp to the nearest port, which was Gibraltar, the carpenters could make repairs while the stores were replenished. Under Moorish domination for many years, Gibraltar had briefly achieved independent status until the beginning of the century, when it was taken under Spanish rule. Although in no hurry to reach England, Maribel did not wish to spend more time than need be on board ship with this man. The looks he gave her made her skin creep and the thought of being his wife filled her with revulsion. Perhaps if she reached England she might find a way to escape him.

'You do not answer.' His face clouded with anger. 'Your father warned me of your pride and stubbornness, lady.' He moved closer, menacing, angry. 'He told me you are mine, and I would have you as my wife, but I have a mind not to wait. You are here and there is nothing to stop me taking my pleasure of you.'

'If you touch me, I shall kill myself.'

'Damn you!' He struck her once across the face and she fell backwards against a table, hurting her back, but she gave no sign of her pain. Lifting her head, she looked at him defiantly.

'If you force me, I shall never reach England alive.'

Samuel looked at her and hesitated. He wanted the girl, had wanted her since the first time he saw her. But he wanted the money as much or more. His cousin's estate was heavily encumbered, leaving him little but an empty house. He needed a fortune to restore it to the great house it had once been, and this girl was his means of achieving his aim. Her threat to take her own life had given him pause for thought. If he forced her to yield, she might find a way to kill herself and he would lose the rich prize that could be his for the taking.

He must be patient and wait a little longer. A shipboard marriage might be contested. It would be better to wait until they were in England and he could be certain of her. Once the repairs were made, the ship

would get under way once more and he could be sure
that that damned pirate was not lurking somewhere in
these waters!

Chapter Eight

Justin was in his cabin, lying on his bed, when Higgins knocked at the door and then entered. He rubbed at his shoulder, which was still sore, looking at his friend with raised brows; it was less than an hour since he had left the bridge to take a much-needed rest.

'Is something wrong?'

'Look-out has just spotted a ship not far ahead of us. It is the *Mistress Susanna*—Samuel Hynes's ship. Shall we go after it or let it be?'

'The *Mistress Susanna* was one of the ships that attacked the island. We cannot let this chance for retribution pass.' Justin frowned. 'My meeting with Sabatini will keep another day for if she is not there…'

His words died away unspoken, because he would not let himself think of what might happen to Maribel if she was not at her father's house. Samuel Hynes was no better than his cousin had been and would treat her badly.

He would find her even if he had to follow her to England!

'We shall take the ship. We need to replace the *Siren Eater* and the men must be itching for a fight. It might be better if Hynes resists.'

'After what happened on the island you will need to crack the whip, Cap'n, for the men's blood is up. And you cannot blame them.'

'We will have no brutality, no wanton killing. Tell the men to chase and attack Hynes's ship, but when we board her any man caught using unnecessary violence will answer to me.'

Maribel turned as her cabin door opened. They had left Gibraltar that morning and were once more under sail. She was expecting the cabin boy with food and water. He was a Spanish lad named Pedro. He had helped her after she was hurt by Captain Hynes and treated her with respect, but instead of the friendly boy, she saw the man she both feared and hated. Her heart sank; he had a purposeful gleam in his eyes and she knew why he had come.

'Stay away from me!' she warned, brandishing her dagger. 'Come near me and I shall slash my wrists. I would rather die than be your whore.'

'I thought I had taught you a lesson?' Samuel moved nearer, watching her warily. 'If you take your own life, you will burn in hell—is that not your belief?'

'I do not care!'

'Oh, but I think you do.' He took another step closer.

Maribel held out her left arm, placing the blade against her white skin. Samuel halted. 'Do it, then,' he challenged. 'Kill yourself.'

'Do not think I should hesitate…' She touched the knife to her breast as he moved towards her, then a booming sound from above made him halt. He looked round as the cabin door was flung back and the cabin boy entered.

'We are being attacked,' he said, looking frightened. 'I was sent to fetch you.'

'Curses! Out of my way, imbecile,' Samuel growled and pushed past the lad, who looked at Maribel with scared eyes.

'Is it pirates?' Maribel asked, her heart thumping. She had prayed that Justin would come after her, but had not believed it would happen 'Did you see the name of the ship?'

'I could not see, but the look-out said it was named the *Defiance*. I was told that we were forced to surrender to these pirates before. The men are nervous and talking of surrender; they fear what may happen if they resist after what was done at the island.'

Maribel's heart raced as the lad went away. She felt the shudder as the two ships came together and heard the shouting and noise on deck as the pirates boarded. However, she could not hear sounds of fighting and she realised that the crew must have surrendered immediately, hoping that they would be allowed to go free, as they had been once before. She did not know if there was a cargo on board—she had remained in her cabin while they were in port and had no idea what had been loaded in the holds.

She sat on the edge of her bed and waited, and after a little while Pedro came to her. He grinned at her and she realised that he was no longer frightened.

'Is all well?' she asked.

'I was asked if a lady was on board and told to fetch you. The pirates have given quarter to all who surrender and will sail with them; the captain and those who refuse are to be put into a boat with food and water for six days and set adrift. If they return to Gibraltar, they will make land soon enough.'

'So the ship is not to be returned to its master?'

'Not this time. It has been taken as a prize and all those who sail with Captain Sylvester will receive their share.'

Maribel nodded. The crew set adrift in a longboat should make shore within the day, for they were not many hours out of Gibraltar. She followed the cabin boy on deck and discovered that some trunks were being taken aboard the *Defiance,* though it seemed there was no cargo, which was perhaps why the ship was being kept as their prize. She could see no sign of Justin or Captain Hynes, but Higgins was directing the transfer of trunks and men. He smiled as he saw her and came towards her.

'We were on our way to look for you at Don Sabatini's house, lady. It was touch and go whether we attacked the ship. I think Providence must have been watching over us.'

'Yes, I believe you are right.' Maribel felt her eyes sting with tears. 'Thank you for rescuing me once more. I am truly grateful—and I am sorry if I have caused you more trouble.'

'The captain will be glad to get you back,' Higgins told her with a gentle smile. 'Just don't expect him to admit it. He thought you might have run away.'

'With Captain Hynes?' Maribel shuddered. 'I would rather die than live as that man's whore!'

'Go below to your own cabin, lady. Anna is waiting for you. She has been worried sick.'

'Welcome back, lady,' Anna said as Maribel went to her cabin. 'I was worried about you. Captain Sylvester was so angry. He thought that you had run away, until Higgins told him you had been kidnapped. I told him you would not run away, but he would not listen to me.'

'It was so hot in my room and I was restless. I could not sleep and I went outside to get some air. Someone— I think there was more than one—crept up behind me and threw a blanket over me. I struggled and tried to escape, but they were too strong for me.'

'Have you been harmed?' Anna looked at her oddly. 'You were taken captive some days ago…'

'If you are asking if I was raped, the answer is that Hynes had it in mind to force me, but I defended myself with the knife Peg gave me. I have a bruise on my back where he hit me and I fell.'

'Let me see. Take off that gown. You will need to wash and change into fresh clothes. I shall—' She broke off, giving a cry of distress as she saw the bruise on Maribel's back. 'Oh, my lady, that looks so sore. That brute deserves to hang for what he has done to you! If Captain Sylvester knew…'

'You will please not tell him,' Maribel said. 'I do not want Hynes's death on my conscience.' She saw Anna's face pale and reached out to her. 'I did not mean to remind you, my good friend. I shall never forget what you did for me on the island.'

'I shall fetch you some water,' Anna said. 'It may be best to use salt water for that will ease the sting from your bruises.'

Maribel sighed as Anna went away. She felt tired and anxious and her eyes were gritty with the tears she was trying not to shed.

After she had washed all over in the salty water, Maribel rubbed a little of the salve into her back. Her cheek felt tender where Hynes had struck her when she fell and Anna had told her she had a bruise there as well.

She was still in her shift when the cabin door opened abruptly. Giving a little cry, she grabbed her shawl and held it against her as the man came in.

'Oh…it is you…' She stared at Justin, feeling vulnerable and unsure of him. She had been told he was very angry with her. 'I was just about to dress.'

'Your pardon, Madonna.' Justin's eyes were on her bare arms. Her soft olive-toned flesh was firm and sweet, her hair loose on her shoulders. He felt a rush of desire and it took all his strength of will not to grab her and take her to the bed. 'I did not think…forgive me. I shall turn my back while you put on your gown.'

'Thank you.' Maribel reached for a loose wrapping gown, tying the sash about her waist. Her heart was racing wildly, her head raised proudly. 'I am decent now, sir.'

Justin turned and looked at her. 'I came to see if you had all you needed. We have a long voyage ahead of us. I believe all your things were brought across from the island, but you must tell me if something is missing—it may be in the hold.'

'I have not looked, but I believe I have all I need, thank you,' Maribel said. She frowned. 'You took the ship captive this time and set her captain adrift?'

'The ship is the price for the crew's freedom, lady. My men were angry because of what happened on the island. I persuaded them to let Hynes and his officers go, but it went against the grain with some of them. I have given Hynes a message for your father.'

'Yes, of course. I understand. What happened on the island was wicked and unpardonable. I regret that I was the cause of so much pain and suffering.'

'It was not your fault, Maribel. I told you of the treasure map?' She nodded, looking at him enquiringly. 'I have destroyed it. Hynes told me that your father threatened to hang Hendry unless he led your father's ships to the island. But the *Defiance* was not there and he thought I was with the ship, so he destroyed what he could in revenge for what I had stolen from him.'

'Then it was for the map. Do you think it was the only one in existence?'

'I thought at first that there must be other copies. However, when we were at Mallorca, your father sent word that he would trade for the map...' Justin frowned. 'Hendry did not know where I intended to go next. He thought I might head for Cyprus. When I told him to rendezvous at the island I gave away my plans...and that was what your father wanted all the time...the map and revenge.'

'Yes, he wanted revenge.' Maribel shuddered, her throat tight. 'I know now that he never cared what became of me. He told Captain Hynes he could have me and do as he would with me. I think he hoped for my death, but...Hynes wanted to marry me for my fortune. He...would have raped me, but I managed to stop him...' She caught back a sob.

'The brute. Had I known, I would have hanged him from the yard-arm!' He moved towards her, stopping as she flinched. 'What did he do to you? You did not leave with him willingly?'

'No! How could you even think it?' Maribel hesitated, then untied her wrap and drew it back, lifting her bodice to show him the purple bruise on her back. 'This is what he did to me when I refused him; there are other smaller bruises on my arms.'

'And on your cheek, I think...' Justin took her chin in his hand, turning her face to look at the swelling that had begun to turn dark red. 'Had I known of this, I should not have been so lenient with him. Next time we meet he will not fare so well!' His eyes dwelled on her, hungry and yet oddly tender.

'Cover yourself, Madonna. I am sorry you have been treated so ill.'

'It was not your fault. You warned me not to venture outside at night alone and I ignored your advice.' She caught back the sob that almost broke her. 'Forgive me. When we first met, I called you such terrible names and you never treated me ill.'

'You must not cry.' Justin smiled at her. 'You are safe now. I shall not let harm come to you again. Very soon now you will be in England with your mother's family. You will be a lady again, living as you ought—I believe your uncle is a good man.'

'No, I shall not cry,' Maribel said, blinking back her tears. 'I am being foolish. I am safe now and, as you say, I shall soon be with my mother's family.'

In a few short weeks she would be in England. Perhaps then all the nightmares of the past months would be forgotten. She could return to being the lady she had been before she left Spain for the first time. It was what she had wanted from the start—to be with her mother's family. So why did she feel that her heart was breaking?

'Captain Sylvester says we are sailing under a fair wind and you may come on deck whenever you wish,' Anna said as she entered the cabin the next morning. 'If the weather continues to be good, you will be in England within a week or two.'

'Yes, I expect so.' Maribel got to her feet. She draped a lace shawl about her shoulders and went on deck. Her gown was one of the lightweight ones that Justin had given her. The heavy, elaborate gowns her father had sent as her trousseau lay unused in the chests in which they had been packed. Maribel preferred the simpler style of gown she had become used to on the island. Her Spanish clothes seemed outdated and ugly and she did not enjoy wearing them, though she might have to when she reached England—she had been told it was much colder than Spain.

What would her mother's family be like? Would they welcome her to their home? Justin had given her letters from her uncle to her mother. He spoke in fond terms and asked if she were well many times. It seemed that he had received no answer to his letters, though he had continued to write until her mother's death.

She pushed the fears and doubts concerning her relatives to the back of her mind. In a few days she would part from Justin, never to see him again—and it was breaking her heart. She did not want to leave him, nor did she wish to become a fine lady again; all that had changed on the island and she knew she could never be as she had been before her capture. If her mother's family took her in, she would be forced to live as they directed, behaving as a high-born lady and never knowing the freedom she had tasted on the island. She would never see Justin again. How could she bear it?

Was there any way she could change her destiny? Maribel's thoughts had been going round and round in her mind ever since she had been rescued for the second time. She was no longer the proud and sometimes cold lady she had been when she first sailed for England. Her life had changed the day she was taken captive the first time, and her experiences on the island had moulded her into a different woman. The fear and revulsion she had experienced at Captain Hynes's hands had made her realise how fortunate she had been to be taken captive by a man like Justin. She had called him a pirate, but he was a truly generous and gentle man despite his harsh looks when he was angry. When she had thought she might never see him again she had realised just how much he had come to mean to her. She loved him with all her heart, her mind and body. How could she bear it when the time came to part for ever?

It was fresh and cooler on deck than it had been in her cabin. Maribel took a turn round the deck, then went to the prow, looking out to sea. The sky was blue and appeared endless. Far away in the distance it seemed to end where the sky met the sea on the horizon; it was this strange phenomenon that had made people believe that the earth was flat until brave explorers began to prove that it was not so. She knew that it was a Spanish King who had funded the expedition that found a way to the West Indies and the New World, proving that the world was round and that it was not possible to fall off the edge.

Maribel wrinkled her brow. Anna and Higgins had such exciting plans for the future and they were willing to take risks. Was there really a chance of a better life in the New World? She knew that men like her father had used it only for the silver and precious things to be found there, stealing its resources and ill treating its inhabitants—but were there truly other men who chose to live in this New World? What kind of men were they?

'Why so pensive, Maribel?'

Justin's voice made her swing round to gaze at him.

'You are safe now. Once we are in England you must forget all that happened on the island—and what that beast did to you.'

'Would you have me forget everything that happened on the island?' Her eyes sought his. 'I thought for a moment…that day, on the other side of the island near the falls, before Higgins fired the warning shot…' She stopped, cheeks burning.

'What did you think, Maribel?' Justin's gaze was deep blue like the ocean and it held her fast. 'Tell me.'

'I thought perhaps there might be some other way…' She shook her head and turned from him. His eyes promised so much, but he did not love her. He would have spoken before this if he truly cared what became of her. 'It does not matter.'

'Does it not?' His voice was deep, husky with passion. 'I believe you fought Pike because you were afraid for my life. Anna fetched the pistol because she knew he was too strong for you—but you stood your ground with just a knife. Why did you do that?'

'I could not let him kill you.'

'Why?'

She whirled round to face him. 'Will you have it all? Will you shame me? I could not bear that you should die because—'

Justin reached for her, pulling her close. His mouth stopped her from confessing it all, his kiss so demanding that she melted into his body, almost swooning with pleasure. Heat pooled inside her, making her moan with wanting. When he let her go at last, she looked at him, touching her fingers to her lips, eyes wide and searching.

'Why did you do that?'

'Because I want you more than you will ever know. I am not worthy of you, Maribel. I have no right to ask you to be mine. You are a lady and you will make a good marriage to a man whose hands are not stained with blood, a man who does not live under the shadow of crimes that are punishable by death.'

'Supposing I do not wish to marry this man whose hands are white and soft because he has never lifted one finger for himself?'

Justin laughed softly. 'Is this the proud Spanish lady I first captured? I think you have changed, Maribel.'

'Of course I have changed.' She held out her hands, showing him the ridges that had been caused by hard work. 'I have learned what it is to work if I want to eat—and I should not want to become the lady I was.'

'But you must.' His expression was serious. 'What else can you do?'

Maribel stared at him. Tears were brimming and she felt like screaming. Why could he not see? Why would he not love her as she loved him?

'You are impossible! An arrogant, stupid…pirate!'

She ran from him, not heeding his cry. He called her name, but she would not look back. Her heart was breaking, because she knew there was nothing she could do but return to England and hope that her family would take her in.

Rushing down the iron ladder that led below decks, she entered her cabin and flung herself down on the bed, covering her face with her hands as the tears broke. Her life was ruined and all because he had stolen her heart with his kisses and his bold looks. Why had he kissed her so if he did not love her?

'Maribel. You must not weep for me. I am not worthy of you.'

'Go away. I hate you!' she cried without looking round.

'It would be much better if you did hate me.'

'Do you imagine I love you?' She raised her tear stained face, blazing with anger. 'You are an arrogant, stupid—'

'Pirate,' he finished for her and laughed. 'You have told me so many times that you do not like pirates. How can you love a pirate, Maribel?'

The softness in his voice broke her. She rolled over and got to her feet, flying at him in a temper. Her fists beat against his chest until he caught them, his eyes gleaming with humour as he looked down at her. She wanted to weep and scream, but most of all she wanted to be kissed.

'I don't love you. I hate you.'

'Liar…' Justin bent his head, his lips caressing hers softly. 'You know you want me, my sweet, beautiful temptress. You know that you have driven me to the edge with your smiles and your beauty, but I swore that I would not take you unwillingly.' His fingers brushed against her breasts and her flesh tingled beneath the silken material. Her body swayed towards him, heat building deep inside her as she felt the need sweep through her.

'Justin…' Her lips parted on a sigh. 'I am not unwilling. You must know it. You took me captive, but for a long, long time I have been your willing captive. Surely you knew?'

'Perhaps…' His hand caressed her cheek, his voice husky, throbbing with desire. 'I want you so much, but I am not worthy of you, my love.'

'You are a wicked pirate,' she said, her breath catching on a sob or a laugh. 'But I want you…I love you. Make love to me, Justin, for I cannot bear it if you do not. Your kisses lit a fire in me, but you did nothing more.'

'Only because I gave my word. You must know that I burn for you? You have kept me restless in my bed many a night.'

'Justin…' she breathed, moving closer, offering herself. 'Make me yours. I am asking you. Please, make me your own…love me.'

Justin gave a little moan; reaching for her hand, he led her back to the bed and sat down, pulling her down beside him. For a moment he sat looking into her lovely face, then he reached out and drew a finger over her lips, tracing their fullness.

'You have such a sensuous mouth. It begs for kisses.'

He leaned towards her, bending his head so that their

mouths touched. His kiss was soft at first, setting little butterflies of sensation winging down her spine; then, he pulled her to him, holding her so that her sensitised breasts pressed against his chest, his kiss intensifying, becoming hungry and demanding.

'My love,' he murmured in a voice made deep by passion. 'Let me look at you without these clothes, pretty as they are.' His fingers pulled at the lacings at the back of her gown, loosening them. As the bodice came free he pushed it down over her shoulders. Maribel unfastened the hooks that held her skirts in place and let them slide down over her hips. Now she was clad only in a shift made of such fine material that the pale tones of her flesh showed through. He touched the bruises, which had begun to fade. 'Do these still hurt you?'

'A little, but I do not mind them. Do not fear to touch me. I have longed for this moment so many nights.'

Justin smiled down at her. 'So beautiful, but I want to see you.'

With a swift upward movement, he tugged the shift over her head, his eyes feasting on the glorious body revealed to his eyes. Maribel was slender but full breasted, her nipples pink and pert as he leaned towards her, stroking first one and then the other with his tongue. She sighed with pleasure as his hands cupped her breasts and he buried his face against them, breathing in her scent and using his tongue to give her pleasure. Her body was melting in the heat of his desire, no longer her own to control. She gave a cry of intense pleasure as he licked his way between her breasts, down her navel to the damp moist hair that covered her femininity.

'You smell gorgeous…' he murmured huskily, his hands on her buttocks, pulling her in closer so that he could inhale her. His tongue seemed to set off little explosions of sensation within her, making her weak with desire so that she moaned, her fingers tangling in his hair and working at the back of his neck.

'Let me see you,' she said urgently, and reached for his shirt, ripping at the ties so urgently that it tore and he laughed at her impatience. He took it in his hands and ripped it apart, shrugging it off. Maribel drew a shuddering breath. 'I thought you were beautiful when I saw you chopping the wood. I should have liked to do this…' Her hands smoothed over his back, making him shudder and cry out. She pressed her mouth to his shoulder, sucking at him and then nipping him with her sharp white teeth. 'I want to taste you…' she murmured.

'Little witch…' he muttered hoarse with desire.

He bent to tug off his long boots, then stood and released his breeches. Maribel reached out, pushing them down over his hips so that they fell to the floor and he kicked them away. Now they were both naked. Her eyes feasted on his slim hips and strong thighs, then moved to the male glory that was fully erect and ready for her. She reached out to touch him, her hand stroking that part of him with tentative fingers. His manhood seemed to move and pulsate beneath her touch and she laughed as she heard his indrawn breath of rapture.

'Does that please you?' she asked, her eyes holding an appeal she was not aware of. 'I want to please you, Justin, but I am not sure…'

'But you were married?' His eyebrows arched. 'What are you telling me…have you not been with a man this way?' She shook her head and he frowned.

'My husband was a boy. He did not love me in this way, but as his childhood friend.'

'You should have told me. I thought…but you are virgin…'

Maribel reached out, catching his wrist, as he would have moved away. 'No, do not leave me now, I beg you. I want to be yours, Justin. I want to know how to please you, but you must teach me.'

'You are certain?' His eyes glowed with blue fire, searing her, his gaze searching deep into her soul. 'You want this truly?'

'I love you,' she said and lay down on the bed, gazing up at him trustingly. 'Show me how to be the woman you need.'

Justin hesitated, then sat down on the bed. He bent his head to kiss her, his mouth trailing kisses down her smooth navel. His tongue flicked at the inside of her thighs as he parted her legs, then moved to the moist heat of her femininity. He flicked at her delicately so that she whimpered and arched her back towards him, her body begging for more of the exquisite pleasure he gave her.

His hand caressed her throat and then her breasts. He lay beside her, pressing his flesh to hers so that their mutual heat flared as they kissed, tongues touching, flicking, tasting each other's sweetness. Maribel was quivering, her back arching at each touch as she whimpered and moaned, crying his name as he moved to cover her with his body.

She felt the heat of his manhood pressing against her and instinctively opened wide to accommodate the thick, thrusting shaft that pushed up inside her with sudden urgency. The pain was sharp as he broke through her hymen, but her cry of pain was smothered by kisses so sweet that she almost swooned with love for him. When he withdrew she reached for him, wanting him back inside her, wanting to feel him thrust deeper and deeper into her moist centre. Her body moved with his, her nails unconsciously scoring the smooth flesh on his shoulders as she lost all control and screamed his name aloud over and over again.

She felt his fluids come inside her and then his face was buried against her neck. His body was slick with sweat, as was hers. She stroked the back of his neck, tears trickling down her cheeks as she held him. For a few moments he lay still, his face pressed against her, then he raised his head and looked at her.

'Why are you crying?'

'Because you made me feel so wonderful.'

'I didn't hurt you?' He looked contrite. 'Your bruises still pain you. I was too impatient.'

'No, no, I wanted you as much as you wanted me.'

'Yet I hurt you?'

'A little just at first. I suspect it is always that way.'

'I have never taken a virgin before,' Justin said and touched her face. He looked regretful. 'I did not think you virgin when I teased you so unmercifully, Maribel. Forgive me?'

'There is nothing to forgive. You were as gentle with me as you could be. Besides, it was what I wanted.'

Justin rolled on to his back. 'Your husband must have been very young.'

'My own age, sixteen when we wed, barely seventeen when he died. Why do you ask that?' She turned her head on the pillow to look at him.

'I cannot imagine why a man of any age would not want to lie with you, Maribel. Even Tom was in love with you—the poor lad.'

'Poor Tom.' Maribel raised herself on one arm to gaze down at him. 'I think Pablo was perhaps not as other men—not as you are, Justin. I loved him dearly but I see now that we were friends, or close like sister and brother perhaps.'

'Yes, perhaps.' Justin sat up and reached for his breeches, pulling them on and then his boots. His shirt was too torn to wear and he grinned as he tossed it to her. 'Perhaps you would mend this for me?'

'Of course…' She sat up, her long hair falling forward over her breasts. 'I am yours to command, Justin. Your woman, your—'

'No! Not whore, never that,' he said and frowned. 'When we reach England I shall take you to your mother's family, Maribel… Nay, do not look so. I mean not to abandon you, my love. I must discover how the land lies. I shall wed you, Maribel, but things have altered now.'

'You will wed me? But you said…you wished only for a mistress.'

'I said many foolish things in my pride. I can never let you go. You must be my wife, but I cannot expect you to live as we have lived these past months. You must have a home worthy of you.'

'Surely you know that I would live anywhere with you?'

'We can never return to the island, nor would I wish that kind of a life for you. You are a lady, gently born. You deserve the life you were born for. I shall strive to give you all that you should have by rights. It may take some time—I must clear my name if I can, though I fear it may not be possible.' His expression was serious. 'If I am not welcome at my home it may be that we shall have to live elsewhere. I have money despite the loss of two ships. There is money held by the goldsmiths in London that was left for me by my great-grandfather, who died just after I was born. We may have to live in France or Italy, but I promise I will make a home worthy of you, my darling.'

'I shall be content to be with you wherever we live.'

'Yet I know that I can never be worthy of you. I wish…' He shook his head and smiled oddly. 'The past is gone. We may both regret things that were, but we shall have no regrets. We shall look to the future and it will be good for us.'

'Yes…it will be good for us.'

Something in his eyes caused a shiver to run down her spine. He was so urgent, so grim. What wasn't he telling her?

Chapter Nine

Justin went straight to his cabin to find a fresh shirt. He did not wish what had just happened to be whispered of by the crew. They might suspect it, but there was no need to confirm their suspicions. His conscience had begun to bother him from the moment he learned of Maribel's virginity. He could scarcely believe that she had been married for almost a year and remained a virgin. What kind of a man had her husband been? Perhaps the kind that preferred to lie with his own sex.

Justin knew that something had changed in him once he learned the truth. Until that moment he had fought the little voice in his head that told him she was special to him. He had tried to convince himself that she was just a beautiful woman and that all he felt for her was desire. Having had her in his arms, known her absolute surrender, he felt humbled and guilty for having destroyed her innocence. She was a lovely, loving woman and she deserved so much more than he could give her.

He must and would find a better life for them both. When he became a pirate he had had no choice, but now he must take his fate into his own hands.

How could he ask her to share the kind of life that might well be his in the future? Justin knew that his life would be forfeit if Queen Mary still lived. She would not listen to anything he had to say excusing the mutiny—in the eyes of her council he was already guilty of treason.

Only if Elizabeth had succeeded her sister would Justin have a chance of returning to his home. He believed that his mother would forgive anything, but his father might not wish to receive him. His great-grandfather's legacy was lodged with the goldsmiths in London. Justin could collect the gold and take Maribel to France or Italy; there they could mix with people of her own class, but would it be enough for her? Neither of them would have family about them. Would she come to resent him for taking her away from her family?

It might have been better if he had resisted her invitation, but the appeal in her eyes had broken his will, an overwhelming desire to make love to her sweeping all else from his mind. He knew that he would never have enough of her. Just the thought of her, of her scent and the softness of her body as she yielded to him was enough to make him hard again.

He couldn't give her up! He might not be worthy of her, but she was imprinted into his mind and his body and to lose her now would tear him apart.

Justin decided that he would take Maribel to her relatives and then visit his father. If the situation were favourable, he would journey to court to plead for his freedom and forgiveness. He thought of the chest of Spanish silver in his cabin. Perhaps if he presented that to Elizabeth as a gift—pray God she was now Queen!— she would find it in her heart to forgive him.

Later that evening Maribel glanced at Justin as he stood on the bridge. He was at the wheel as the order to bring down the sails and anchor was given. They had chosen to anchor just off the white cliffs of Dover, the plan being to use the rowing boats to take her and Justin and some of the crew ashore the next morning. Most of the men had voted to stay on board, because they feared they might hang if they set foot in England. She knew that Justin had promised he would secure pardons for them all if he could.

'I shall take you to your mother's family, Maribel,' he had told her the previous night when he came to her cabin. 'Once I know you are safe with them I shall journey to my home and then, if Elizabeth is Queen, to London. I shall ask her to pardon us all for the mutiny.'

'Will she grant you a pardon?' Maribel's eyes widened in fear. 'Supposing she refuses?'

'I shall hang and my men will sail away without me.'

'What of me?'

'You will be safe with your family.'

Maribel felt sick with fear. 'Why must you risk your life after everything we have found together? Turn the ship about. Let us sail for Italy or France. I beg you not to do this, Justin.'

'I have to do it.' His mouth set into a hard line. 'I have money with the goldsmiths and I must claim it if we are to live as a gentleman and his wife should. I owe it to my family to explain what happened when I disappeared—and I owe it to myself to at least try to clear my name, Maribel. Please try to understand how I feel.'

She looked into his eyes, then shook her head. 'Our love is more important than all the rest. You have your ship. You could earn enough money for us to live on without this foolishness.'

Justin reached out, taking her chin in his hand, tipping it so that he forced her to look at him. 'Will you scold me, lady? Have I found myself a nagging wife?'

Maribel shook her head. 'You make fun of me! I do not find this amusing, sir. If they hang you it will break my heart. I shall have nothing to live for.' Tears hung on her lashes and then slipped down her cheeks. 'Please, I beg you, let us go now while we may.'

'But I cannot claim you as my wife unless I have made some effort to throw off the shadow that hangs over me. I am a pirate, Maribel, and as such I am not worthy. I must see my family and receive my father's blessing if he will give it—and hope for mercy from my Queen.'

Maribel was torn between anger and disappointment. How could he imagine that honour was more important than the way they felt about each other? She turned away from him, holding back the torrent of anger and despair that welled inside her. If he were willing to throw everything they had away on a whim, he could not feel as she did; he could not truly love her.

Never had she felt such unease. Her love for Pablo and the grief when he died were a pale shadow of her present emotions. She did not know how she would bear it if she lost Justin after what had happened between them. It had been hard enough when she had thought he did not love her; it would be unbearable after their lovemaking.

'Do not be angry, my love,' Justin put his arms about her, nestling his face into the softness of her hair and holding her back pressed against him. 'I do this for you so that you can hold your head high and be proud of the man you call husband.'

She turned in his arms, looking up at him, intense passion in her face. 'Swear to me that you will come for me? Swear that you will not just sail away and leave me with my family!'

'You must know I would not?' His fingers trailed her cheek and her throat. He bent his head to kiss the hollow at the base of her throat. 'If I live, I shall come back to claim you—you have my word.'

Maribel had accepted his promise—what else could she do?

Yet as she watched the boats being lowered, nerves started to jangle. Until this moment she had not truly thought of what it would be like to meet her family— or of what she would tell them.

If she told the whole truth, they would condemn

Justin as a pirate and forbid her to see him again. She must think of some way to explain how and why she had come to them on the ship of a man who was not related to her.

Her cheeks became hot as she thought about how it would seem to her mother's family if they knew she had been a pirate's willing captive. How could she explain that she had lived on his ship and in his house on the island? It was impossible!

She knew that she must speak to Justin, ask him what she ought to say before they arrived at her family's home.

Maribel turned in Justin's arms. Before they made love he had told her that they would be rowing for shore the next morning. The knowledge that they must part so soon had made her cling to him desperately, as his loving took her to new heights. She moaned with pleasure, enjoying the moment of surrender as she gave herself completely to him.

'What shall I say to my uncle?' she asked, her face pressed against his chest, tasting the salt of his sweat and inhaling his scent. 'He will want to know how we met—and what my father had to say.'

'You must leave this to me.' Justin's hand moved down the arch of her back, stroking the soft skin so that she moaned and pressed herself against him. 'I have thought of how it should be handled a great deal and all I ask is that you follow my lead and agree with what I say.'

Maribel raised up to look down at him, her eyes on

his face, trying to read his mind without success. He looked serious, but gave her no hint of what he intended. Instead, he reached up and drew her down to him, rolling her beneath him in the bed and kissing her with such passion that she forgot everything but the need to feel him inside her.

'I shall take care of you,' he promised huskily. 'You belong to me now and nothing shall ever part us. I promise you that everything will be well, my love.'

'Yes…' She smiled up at him, her thighs parting as he moved between them, her hips arching to meet the thrust of his passion. 'I love you. I shall always belong to you.'

They had been riding south along the coast road for some hours and with each mile they covered Maribel's feeling of apprehension had grown.

'What will you say to my aunt and uncle?' she asked when they stopped to rest the horses. 'I fear they will be angry if they know I was your captive.' He had told her to trust him and she did, yet she could not help feeling nervous as the time to meet her family drew closer.

'We shall rest at an inn I know of not far from here. One of my men will take a letter from me to your relatives, telling them that you are coming to visit them. They will be prepared for good news, Maribel—for you are visiting them with your betrothed husband: Justin Devere, son of Lady and Sir John Devere of Devereham House—and great-grandson of Lord Robert Melford, also grandson of the Earl of Rundle.'

'Your name is Devere?' Maribel's eyes widened. 'You are the grandson of an earl? Why have you never told me this?'

'On board the *Defiance* I was a pirate and a mutineer. Here in England I am a gentleman. I did what I thought best to protect my family from the shame of hearing from others what I had become.'

'But why did you…?' She searched his face for the truth. 'Why were you ever a part of that crew, Justin? You have told me that you were shanghaied and something of the mutiny, but not why you were about to board a ship in the first place?'

'I was leaving England under a cloud of suspicion. Queen Mary had sent to arrest me for treason, though I was not guilty. My father thought I should spend time with my cousin in France, but on the waterfront I was knocked on the head from behind as I fought other ruffians. When I regained my senses we were at sea and I was forced to serve behind the mast—but not until I had been given more than fifty lashes to bring me into line. Had it not been for Higgins I should probably have died after the beating. I survived and the crew came to respect me. When a young lad was beaten near to death the crew would not go on with Captain Smythe. I was asked to join the mutiny. Had I refused, they would probably have marooned the officers on a deserted island or simply hanged us. I decided that I would lead them and in that way I saved the lives of Captain Smythe and his officers.'

'So you never wished for a life at sea?' Maribel

arched her fine brows. 'I am glad you have told me this, Justin—but you make a bold pirate.'

'I did what I had to do.'

'If you had not, we should not have met. I should now be wed to Lord Roberts, or, worse, I could have been his cousin's whore.' Maribel shuddered. 'I should prefer to lie in my grave than submit to either man.' She reached out to touch his hand. 'I love you, Justin. Please remember that I would rather wed a pirate than live without you as a fine lady.'

Justin gazed down at her, his eyes seeming to search her face. 'You must not be anxious for my sake. When we landed in England I asked questions of men on the waterfront and I learned that Elizabeth is now England's queen. I shall speak to my father and then ride to London to beg an audience with her Majesty.'

'Will she grant it?'

'I have every hope that she will.' He reached out to touch her face. 'Do not fear for me, my love. I shall return to you and all will be well.'

'I shall pray that it is so.' Tears misted her eyes as he helped her to remount. He had reassured her on many counts, but her apprehension grew as they neared their journey's end.

The house of Sir Henry Fildene sat just above the cliffs some thirty-odd miles on the coast road from Dover. It was a large old house, built of stone in the last century with an undercroft, small-paned windows and a sloping thatched roof. The approach was across an expanse of grass and rock, for it faced square to the ocean and a sandy cove set at the foot of steep cliffs. The house looked slightly forbidding and Maribel guessed that it had once been a fortress or look-out station in case of attack from the sea. In the event of a force of ships sent to invade England, a beacon would be lit on these cliffs, where it could clearly be seen for miles around. Other beacons would then be lit so that the news could swiftly be passed to London.

A stout wall surrounded the house, but at the approach from the land side there was a large iron gate, a moat and a wooden drawbridge, which was down, as if the occupants were expecting visitors. The small party of Justin, Higgins, Anna and Maribel rode over the bridge, their horses' hooves clattering on the thick boards.

'I believe we are expected,' Justin said as he saw a group of men and women gathered in the courtyard. He smiled at her. 'Have courage, Madonna.'

Maribel felt as if her face were frozen though the day was mild enough. She attempted a smile as he dismounted and came to lift her down, but found that she was trembling with nerves.

'Remember you are a lady and my betrothed.'

Maribel's head went up at the reminder. A tall man with greying hair and a lined face moved towards them. He stared at her for a moment and then inclined his head.

'You are Marguerite's daughter. I can see her in you. Indeed, you are very like your mother, my child.'

'Thank you. Forgive me, I do not know you.'

'How should you?' He held out his hand to her. 'I am your Uncle Henry. My sister and I were close when we were young, but my father made a match for her with Don Miguel Sabatini and I lost contact with her. I wrote to her often, but she replied only a few times before she died—and your father wrote only twice to tell me of your birth and her death. I was grieved that she died so young. I would have come to visit, but duty kept me here. My father died and I was forced to repair our fortunes before thinking of my own wishes—but I thought of you often and I am so pleased that you have chosen to come to us until you marry.' His steady gaze went to Justin's face. 'Captain Devere. I believe I once met your father, sir. It was years ago, but he spoke then of his son as being a fine young man.'

'I thank you for your welcome, Sir Henry. Perhaps we may talk again later? I am hoping that you will take my lady into your home while I perform some necessary duties. I shall return for her as soon as I have visited the court.'

'You wish to pay your respects to the new Queen.' Sir Henry nodded. If he wondered why Justin did not wish to take his betrothed with him, he did not ask. 'Please leave your horses to my grooms, sir. My wife is most anxious to greet Maribel. We have sons, but no daughters, and she hath always wished for one.' His gaze returned to Maribel. 'Come and meet Lady Fildene—she is anxious to welcome you to her home.'

Maribel's nerves abated a little as she moved with

him to meet the rather small, plump lady waiting to greet her. Lady Fildene smiled and embraced her warmly, clasping her to her ample bosom.

'How beautiful you are, my dearest child. We are so glad to have you with us if only for a time. I know my husband wrote to your father asking that you might come to us for a while, but he received no answer to his letters.'

'My father was not always kind, ma'am,' Maribel said. 'I think his marriage to my mother was not as happy as it might have been—for either of them.'

'Henry told me that she did not wish to wed him,' the lady said, placing a hand on Maribel's arm and drawing her into the entrance hall of what was clearly a grand house. The ceilings were high; the walls were of stone, but covered with rich tapestries that gave the rooms a warmth and colour not always seen in older homes. 'Your maid will be shown to your apartments, my dear. Everything is being prepared, though we had little notice of your coming.'

'I think it was not possible to let you know sooner,' Maribel told her. She was very conscious of the fact that it had been some time since she had left her home in Spain, and she was most certainly not the same girl. Her skin was no longer the pale olive it had been when she protected it by staying out of the midday sun. On the island she had become careless, allowing her skin to be kissed by the sun to a pale gold, a little freckling appearing across her nose. She was wearing gloves, but she knew her hands had not yet become as soft and smooth as they had once been. 'I am sorry to be a trouble to you.'

'You could never be a trouble to us, dearest girl. We are delighted to have you with us, even if only for a short time.'

'I am happy to be here,' Maribel replied, her fears falling away as she saw the genuine welcome in the lady's eyes. 'I shall enjoy getting to know my mother's family.'

'My sons Beavis and William are married and living in London,' Lady Fildene said. 'However, my son Michael is expected home any day now. He has been to the north on business for his father. We import wines, you know. Mostly from France these days, though it was because of the Spanish wines we once imported that my father-in-law entrusted his daughter to your father. I am sorry to learn that the marriage was not a good one.'

'I think my mother may have been unhappy, but I do not remember her. My stepmother was kind to me and I was happy enough until she died soon after my husband.'

'You were married? We did not know that. How sad to lose a husband at your age.'

'I was sad—but then I met Justin,' Maribel replied, her mouth curving. 'I think I shall be very content as his wife.'

'His family are respected and wealthy,' her aunt said. 'Everyone knows of Lord Robert Melford and the important family he founded. I believe they are all well connected and popular at court, though we do not often visit London ourselves. My husband was never one to seek royal favour, though we have recently been honoured by a royal contract for our fine wines.'

Maribel was not sure whether her aunt sounded regretful or a little jealous of those who had the royal favour. She sensibly kept her silence. Since she had only just learned Justin's true name it would not do to pretend to knowledge about his family that she did not have.

Glancing back, she saw him talking with her uncle. He seemed at ease and gave no sign of being anything other than he claimed to be. Clearly he had put the memory of his time at sea behind him, and she must too. She would have to be careful when answering her aunt's questions—she did not wish to reveal that she had been a pirate's captive.

'I shall return for you as soon as I can,' Justin told Maribel as he took his leave two days later. 'At least I know that you are safe here with your family. Your uncle is truly pleased to have you here, as he has made plain to me—and I believe his wife to be a good woman.'

'Lady Fildene is both kind and generous,' Maribel admitted. 'I like her very well. She is a good chatelaine and she loves her family. Her son Michael is expected home soon and I think he must be her favourite. Even so, I would rather come with you if I could, Justin, but I know I may not for I should only hamper you.'

'I am sorry I must leave you, but I know you are safe here. I shall travel faster alone, my love—but I shall think of you often. As soon as I am free to do so, I shall return and take you to my home, where we shall be wed.'

'I pray that you will return to me safely. You know that I love you.'

'As I love you. Take care of yourself until I come to claim you.'

Maribel went to his arms, clinging to him until he disengaged, pushing her back. 'Be careful, my love. It is not seemly to show such passion. We may be observed and I would not have your aunt lose her good opinion of you.'

Tears crowded in her throat. It was on the tip of her tongue to beg him to take her with him, but she knew that he would refuse. He had decided that she must remain here in safety with her aunt and uncle and she could not make him change his mind. Parting from him would tear her in two, but she must bear it as best she could and pray for his safe return.

Reluctantly she drew away, 'I should not like to shock her. I am very careful how I answer her for she would be shocked if she knew where I had recently been.'

'Be patient for a while. We shall soon be together.'

Justin touched her face lightly and then turned away. Higgins was waiting nearby with his horse.

'Farewell, Justin.'

'Farewell, my dearest one. I shall return.'

Maribel watched as he rode out of the courtyard. A breeze had sprung up suddenly, bringing storm clouds from the sea. The dark sky looked ominous and she shivered as she turned and went into the house. The time would seem long while Justin was gone. She hardly knew how to occupy her time, because the pretty sewing she had once delighted in for hour after hour was not enough to fill her days. She disliked the damp coolness of the English weather, finding the grey skies depressing, and thought wistfully of the time she had spent at the island and the long voyage back to England. Did the sun ever shine in this land? How many days would pass before Justin came to claim her as his bride—and how would she live if for some reason he never came? She thrust the thought away for it was unbearable. She must believe that he would return or she had nothing.

Justin was aware of a shadow hovering at the back of his mind as he rode the last few leagues to his father's home. Higgins had wanted to accompany him, but he would not allow it.

'If I am to be hanged as a mutineer and a pirate I will not take you with me, my friend. Remain near my lady and guard her until my return. I shall bring your pardon if I am spared. If not, you must take the ships and sail away. They will both be yours then.'

'You risk your life for nothing, Justin. I have not found English justice fair in the past. I do not expect it now.'

'You may well be right, which is why I ask you to remain with Maribel until…' Justin shook his head. 'If I do not return, she is safe enough with her uncle.'

'Aye, she is safe enough.'

They clasped hands and then Justin mounted his horse and rode away. He had not looked back—it was costing him a great deal to leave Maribel. If his heart had ruled him, he would have turned back, swept her up on his horse and taken her far away. His head told him that he would never be at peace if he did not at least try to obtain his father's blessing and the Queen's pardon. He could not take her with him, but he had ridden off with a heavy heart.

Now that he was close to his family estate, Justin felt uneasy. What kind of a welcome awaited him in his father's house? John Devere was an honest man. He had taught his son to live with honour. Would he be able to accept Justin for what he was—a mutineer and a pirate?

As Justin dismounted in the courtyard of his home a groom came running towards him. He hesitated as he drew near, stared at Justin in stunned disbelief for a moment, and then grinned.

'God be praised! 'Tis Master Justin home at last.' The groom took the reins of Justin's horse. 'We thought you dead, sir. Your lady mother has been grieving for you these past months.'

'I was lost, Jedruth, but now I am found,' Justin said and clapped him on the shoulder, feeling overcome by the man's obvious delight. 'Tell me, are my parents within?'

'Your lady mother is at home, sir, but the master has gone this day to visit a neighbour. He should be back this evening.'

'Thank you. I shall see my mother immediately.'

Justin went into the house to be greeted by a shriek

from the keeper of the household as she saw him. 'Lord have mercy!' she cried and flung her arms up. 'If it isn't Master Justin—and the mistress crying her heart out for him day after day! Where have you been that you could not send a message to your mother? Wicked boy!'

'Forgive me, Lizzie.' Justin grabbed her in a bear hug. 'There were good reasons why I could not let my family know where I was. Tell me, where is my mother?'

'She is in her stillroom, of course. Where else would she be at this hour of the day?'

'Bless you!' Justin kissed her soundly on the mouth. She pushed him away and frowned at him, but smiled as he turned in the direction of his mother's stillroom and then crossed herself.

'The Lord be praised!'

Justin hurried to the room where Lady Devere prepared all the preserves that ensured they had jams and fruit in the winter, also creams and lotions that she used to cure the ills of the people who served her. He paused outside, almost fearing to enter, and knocked at the door.

'Come in,' her voice called and he opened the door. Lady Devere stood at a bench made of a scrubbed wood board and trestles. In front of her were bundles of leaves, dried herbs and berries, as well as stone jars and pots with squares of cloth, wax and string for sealing them. 'Yes, Lizzie, what is it?'

'It is not Lizzie…' Justin said and saw her shoulders stiffen. She turned slowly with a jar in her hand. When she saw him her eyes widened, she gave a little cry and swayed, dropping the jar she was holding so that it clattered onto the floor. 'Mother…forgive me…' He darted to support her, holding her close until she recovered. She straightened and pushed him away. Her eyes were filled with tears of love and forgiveness as she reached out to touch his face. 'I am so sorry, Mother…so very sorry for distressing you.'

'I thought you must be dead. Justin…my dearest son…' Lady Devere caught back a sob. 'Your father received a visit from a man called Captain Bolton. He told him that you had booked a passage with him to France, but failed to board, though your horse was lodged at the hostelry he told you of. It was months before he came to tell us, because he had been at sea. We were led to believe that you were somehow taken aboard another ship against your will.'

'Yes, that is what happened, Mother. I was shanghaied and forced to work for a cruel master who treated his crew ill. What happened after that is a long story. I had best wait until my father is here, for I would tell you both at the same time. I am not the man I was when I left my home—I have done things you may find impossible to forgive.'

'You could never do anything so wicked that I would not love and forgive you,' Lady Devere said. She put her arms about him, kissing him on the forehead. 'You look well, my son. I am glad to have you home. I care only that you are alive and well.'

'I thank you for your love, Mother. I regret that I did

not let you know I was alive sooner, but…' He shook his head. 'I shall wait until Father is here. He should hear my story at the same time, for I would not seek advantage and I know he may not forgive as easily as you.'

'Maribel, my dear. May I speak with you for a moment, please?'

'Yes, Aunt? Did you need me?'

Maribel had been walking in the walled garden at the back of the house. Behind the high walls that protected them from the full force of the sea was a sheer drop to the beach below. To reach the cove, you had to walk a little distance along the cliff until you came to a path cut into the rock by some ancient mariners. Maribel had been considering whether to walk down to the beach, but as yet the weather had been too cool to entice her. She turned at the sound of her hostess's voice and walked back to meet her.

'There will be a fair in the village tomorrow, Maribel,' Lady Fildene said as the girl came up to her. 'We may purchase silks and materials for new gowns— and many trinkets that may please us perhaps.'

'I have little money to spare—most of what I have is still with the ship. Captain S…Justin said that he would arrange for my trunks to be sent on, but I have only what was brought on the pack horses thus far.'

'Which is why I thought we should visit the fair to buy silks from the merchants. We can sew some gowns for you between us, Maribel. What you have is charming, but the Spanish style is heavier than the

English fashion. I believe you would feel more comfortable in something new.'

'I am sure I would. Justin—' Maribel broke off. It was difficult to remember that she must not mention her time on the island. 'I do have some simpler gowns in my trunks, but it would be pleasant to make a new gown.'

'Your uncle would be happy to make you a gift of the gowns,' her aunt told her. 'It has given us such pleasure to have you here, my dear. I hope you will visit us again when you are married to Captain Devere?'

'Yes, I am certain we shall,' Maribel told her. 'You and my uncle are both so kind to me.'

'We love you as your mother's child—and as the daughter we never had.'

Maribel's cheeks felt warm, for she felt uneasy at deceiving these good people. What would they think if they knew the truth? She would feel terrible if her aunt ever discovered that she had been so indiscreet as to become a pirate's mistress, for that was what she was until Justin married her.

Justin would return soon and marry her. Her aunt and uncle need never know the truth! She thrust the uneasy thoughts from her mind.

'Then I should love to visit the fair with you tomorrow, Aunt.'

'Justin!' John Devere came rushing into the parlour where his son and wife sat together. 'I could scarcely believe it when they told me you were here! I thought you lost to us for good.'

Justin stood up. He held out his hand, but his father smiled and embraced him.

'Welcome home, my son. This is a wonderful day!'

'Perhaps you should hear my story first, Father. You may not be so pleased once you know what happened—what I have done.'

John moved back, his gaze narrowed and questing. 'Should this be said before your mother?'

'I would wish Mother to hear it all. I have done things that may shame you, Father—but I ask for your understanding.'

'You mean the mutiny? I have heard that there was a possibility that you led a mutiny against a cruel master—namely Captain Smythe?'

'You knew that and yet you welcomed me home?'

'I heard from Captain Bolton that you might have been shanghaied aboard Smythe's ship. He visited us concerning a horse and told me what conditions aboard such a ship would be like and that he had heard the captain's life had been saved by one of the mutineers. Apparently, the leader forced the others to put the captain and his officers ashore at Venice rather than hanging them as others wanted. Was that what happened, Justin?'

'Yes, Father. I must explain what happened. When a young lad who had done little wrong was beaten half to death I could no longer hold out against the crew. They would have killed Smythe, his officers and me if I had not taken charge. I did not think I had a choice.'

'You did what you had to do,' Sir John agreed.

'Mutiny is a serious offence, but I must tell you that some of Smythe's officers reported him for gross misconduct, blaming him for losing the ship and putting their lives at risk. He has lost his master's ticket and will not sail as the captain of a ship again.'

'I am glad to hear it, sir. It is time that men like Smythe were shown for the bullies they are. However, that is not the end of my story. I fear there is worse to come. Something for which I may not be so easily acquitted.'

'You had best tell us then, Justin.'

'When we took the ship and set the captain ashore, I became its captain in his stead, but we sailed by the rules of the brethren, which make all men equal.'

'Brethren—you mean pirates?' John's eyes narrowed. 'You became a pirate? You preyed on the ships of others and stole what was theirs—you killed men for gain?'

'We took the cargoes we captured and sold them. We did not kill wantonly, Father. If the ship surrendered immediately there was no bloodshed, though a few may have been killed, those that refused the truce and tried to resist. Not by my hand, but by others. I have killed only when forced.'

'But the ships were taken by your order?'

Justin met his gaze. 'Yes, sir. I was the captain. I gave the orders, which my men obeyed. I sold the prizes we took and distributed the gains between them, and kept my share. I have ordered men flogged and I have killed men in fair fight—but I punished the crew only when I had no choice.'

'You are by your own admission a pirate?'

'Yes, Father.'

'Then you have shamed your family and yourself.'

His father stared at him a moment longer, then turned and walked away, leaving the room.

'Father…forgive me…'

'It will take time.' Lady Devere stood up. She placed a gentle hand on her son's arm. 'Do not be hurt or bitter, Justin. Your father is an honest man. This news has shocked and distressed him. He was always so proud of you and now…'

'I have brought shame on him and myself.'

'No, Justin.' Lady Devere's eyes were soft and moist with tears. 'You did what you had to do—what seemed right at the time. You were forced to lead the mutiny and then it must have seemed that you had no choice but to become a pirate. I understand, dearest. Your father will learn to think as I do and to forgive you.'

'You will persuade him, Mother.' Justin's face was fiercely proud. 'You may persuade him to make a show of forgiveness, but in his heart he will never forget what I have done. He will never truly forgive me; he will never be proud to call me son.'

'He is a proud man, Justin—proud of you and his honour. Give him time to think this through.'

'I had to tell him, to tell you both. You must feel that I have let you down, Mother. I did have a choice. I could have put the captain and his officers in chains and sailed back to England to take my chances.'

'Would the crew have accepted your decision?'

'I am not sure. I did not offer them the choice.'

Lady Devere touched his cheek. 'You know that they would not have listened if you had. You would have died with the captain and his officers. They owe their lives to you, my son. You have done the right thing now. Your father will understand in time.'

'I shall leave in the morning, Mother.'

'Why?' She looked at him in alarm. 'Where will you go?'

'To London to beg an audience with the Queen. If I am to live as I was born to live and hold my head high, I must seek a royal pardon. Only then can I build my house and bring honour to the woman I love.'

'The woman you love?' Lady Devere's eyes widened. 'You have said nothing of this, Justin. Please tell me about this lady—she is a lady?'

'A beautiful, innocent, perfect lady. Her father is a Spanish Don. He meant to sell her to a rogue so that he could steal her lands and fortune, but I stole her away from the rogue who would have harmed her. I love Maribel and she loves me.'

'Maribel, that is a beautiful name,' his mother said and smiled. 'You will bring this lady to see me, Justin. Give me your word that you will return once more and bring your bride with you.'

'Maribel is not yet my wife, for I wished to clear the shadow that hangs over me if possible. She is with her mother's family and I shall return to claim her as soon as I am able.'

'Supposing the Queen refuses to see you?'

'If I am at liberty I shall sail away and never return to England.'

'And if you are thrown into the Tower?'

'I must take my chances, Mother. I must pay my respects to Queen Elizabeth. I pray that she will remember me as a loyal supporter at a difficult time. I shall arrange for a gift to be sent to her; if it pleases her, she may grant me a pardon.'

Lady Devere leaned forwards to kiss his cheek. 'My prayers are with you, my son. I shall speak to your father. It may hurt him to know that you were for a short time a pirate, but I believe he will forgive you.'

'Thank you.' Justin smiled. 'At least I know I have your forgiveness and your love.'

'Nothing could ever change that,' she said. 'You are my son.'

Maribel looked about her excitedly. She had never been to a fair such as this, because her father would not have approved. A large field had been set aside to accommodate all the merchants and pedlars that had made their way here for the festival. All kinds of goods were set out, either on blankets set on the ground or on boards and trestles. There were men of several races displaying their wares; men with dark skins and eyes from the east with perfumes and trinkets made of ivory, silver and horn. Also merchants of France and Italy selling materials so fine and beautiful that Maribel could not resist touching them, letting the silk run through her fingers. Some of the merchants had leather belts and jerkins tooled with gold and vibrant colours, others had slippers and purses of leather or velvet, still more sold cures with strange-sounding names and relics from the saints. One man had a sliver of wood in a silver casket that he swore came from the Cross of Our Lord Himself.

'Do not buy any of the relics,' Lady Fildene advised. 'Rarely are they true relics and thus have no magical properties. Many of the baubles you see are merely glass and cheap metal—but the perfumes are usually good and the material is quality.'

'I love this green silk and the bronze velvet is beautiful. It would make a wonderful cloak to wear over a cream gown.'

'Are you thinking of your wedding, Maribel?'

'I am not certain whether I wish to make my wedding gown just yet. It might be better to wait until Justin returns—' Maribel broke off as she saw a man looking at her. He was standing some distance away, beyond the stalls, in a part of the field where contests and games of chance were being held. She turned away immediately, her heart thumping. It could not be! She must be mistaken. 'I think perhaps I should like to go home, Aunt. I have a sudden headache.'

'My poor child.' Lady Fildene looked at her with sympathy. 'You have not bought anything yet. But you must go back and rest. I shall purchase the silk and velvets you have chosen and have them sent to us. Go now, dearest. You look exceeding pale.'

Maribel thanked her in a low voice. She walked slowly from the field so as to avoid looking as if she were in a panic, climbing the steep hill towards her uncle's house. Her heart was pumping hard as she increased her pace, wanting to be safe, afraid that *he* had known her and would come after her. Reaching the drawbridge, she glanced back, shading her eyes against the sun that had come out from behind the clouds. She could see the figure of a man some distance away. He was just standing there, staring at her, but making no move to follow.

Perhaps she had been mistaken. Surely it could not have been Samuel Hynes? How could he have been here? Why would he have come to this quiet village? Had he known she was living with her uncle and aunt?

She was almost certain that he had seen her even before she had noticed him. Yet he had made no attempt to speak to her or to accost her. If he had come to abduct her, he would have surely taken his chance. No, he must have visited the fair for purposes of his own. What would he do now that he had seen her?

Maribel felt sick and frightened. Her uncle would protect her from Hynes if she told him that she was in danger, but to do that she must explain everything…tell him that she had hidden the truth from him. She had allowed him to believe that Justin was her betrothed and implied that she had her father's blessing. Sir Henry would have every right to be angry if he knew the whole.

No, she could not tell him! She must keep her secret and make certain that she stayed safe within her uncle's house. Samuel Hynes would not come looking for her there.

* * *

'Your fortune is safe with us, sir,' the goldsmith assured Justin. 'The funds lodged with us by your esteemed great-grandfather, Lord Robert Melford, have grown to almost twice that placed in our care when you were born. The money is available whenever you wish for it, Mr Devere.'

'Thank you. I may wish for a part of my fortune to be transferred to France or perhaps Italy. I have not yet made up my mind. Can you recommend a safe house for my business?'

'I have a cousin in Lombardy. He is well trusted by the most noble of the land, sir. I could write a letter of introduction. He would advance you anything you required against your funds held here and they need never leave England.'

'I shall let you know of my decision in good time, sir. Meanwhile, I have this chest of raw silver. I would like to barter it for a precious jewel—something that might please a noble lady. Something worthy of a queen.'

'Ah, yes, I think I may have the very thing.' The goldsmith smiled. 'Wait there, sir. I shall bring you something I think may please the most discerning lady.'

Justin nodded, glancing round the goldsmith's shop. It was sparsely furnished and nothing of great value was on display, for amongst the common folk there was some dislike of the trade and the goldsmiths, who were often of the Jewish faith. It was not unknown for their shops to be attacked by those who disliked repaying money loaned to them and felt they had been cheated. However, Master Baldini was well known for his honesty.

'This may be what you wish for, sir?'

The goldsmith laid a packet of black velvet on the counter and opened it, displaying a large ruby of such a deep blood red that Justin was struck by its beauty. It had not been mounted, but could easily take pride of place in a necklace or a crown.

'That is magnificent, Master Baldini. Will you accept the silver in return?'

The goldsmith looked at the silver, examined its quality and nodded. 'It is a fair exchange, sir. I shall be pleased to trade with you for the ruby.'

'Thank you. I may return to purchase another trinket—something as precious as the ruby, but simpler, more suitable for the lady I intend to wed.'

'I have many such trinkets, sir. Perhaps pearls might be what you would wish for?'

'Yes, pearls would do very well.' Justin offered his hand. 'My thanks, Master Baldini. I shall visit you again before I leave London.'

'May your business go well, sir.'

'I thank you for your good wishes. I pray it will— my future depends upon it.'

Justin left the shop, the ruby safe inside his inner jerkin. He had asked for an audience with Queen Elizabeth and been told that he might have to wait some weeks before it was granted. He was by no means the only man who desired an audience with England's new Queen. Ambassadors from France, Spain, the Netherlands and Italy were only some of those ahead of him in the queue, along with many English nobles.

It was possible that he would have to kick his heels for weeks before being granted an audience. The enforced separation from Maribel was hard to bear. His thoughts were always with her, for he knew she would be thinking of him, anxious for his return. However, he must attend the court every day and wait as patiently as he could.

At least she was safe in her uncle's house. He hoped that she would not think he had deserted her, but there was little he could do except wait for the moment.

'Michael has sent word that he will arrive by this afternoon at the latest,' Lady Fildene told Maribel that morning when she asked what was going on and why the servants were hurrying about their work with more urgency than usual. 'He says that he is bringing a guest with him—a gentleman who may put some business our way.'

'Oh, that sounds promising,' Maribel replied going to sit beside her on the oaken bench. It had a high carved back and would have been uncomfortable to sit on had her aunt not made thick cushions to make it easier. 'I know my uncle trades in wine, as do other English gentlemen. You said he mostly imports wine from Italy and France, I think?'

'Yes, that is true. We have not bought from Spain for a long time, but we may do so soon, because it is Spanish wine we have been offered—from Don Sabatini's winery, I understand.'

'My father's wine?' Maribel drew her breath in sharply. 'It is not he that your son brings here, Aunt?'

Lady Fildene looked at her. 'You have turned pale, Maribel. Does something bother you? The mention of your father? It is not he that visits with Michael, but a man who imports wine from him. We are to be offered an interest in bringing over a cargo of wine, but my husband may not accept. He would not if he thought it might harm you.' Her gaze narrowed. 'Did your father do something to hurt you, Maribel?'

'Yes…' She shook her head as her aunt's brows rose. 'I cannot speak of it. Forgive me. Will you excuse me, please? I must think.'

Maribel left the room hastily. Her heart was racing. She knew only too well that the man importing her father's wine must be Samuel Hynes.

It *was* he she had seen at the fair. Each day since then she had wondered if he would come to the house and demand to see her…if he would betray her to her uncle. She felt sick at heart and uneasy. Supposing Hynes claimed her for his bride as he'd threatened? Would she be forced to go with him? Would her uncle throw her from his house if he knew what had happened to her— that she had been Justin's captive and then his lover?

Could her father demand that she be returned to him or handed over to the man he had chosen as her husband?

Maribel paced the floor of her bedchamber. She was anxious, afraid of what might happen when the visitor arrived. It might be better to confess all to her aunt, who was kind hearted—but supposing she turned from her? Maribel knew that without Justin to protect her she would not be safe outside her uncle's house. Higgins was around somewhere, but she did not think there was much he could do to help her, especially if her uncle was of a mind to hand her over to her father's agent.

She did not know which way to turn for the best. Justin had left for London more than two weeks previously. How much longer would it be before he returned?

She wished that he was with her. He would tell her what she ought to do or take her away. She had been happy enough here despite missing him every day he stayed away, but now she was on thorns. What ought she to do?

'Maribel, my dear…' She heard the knock at the door and her aunt's voice. 'May I come in, please?'

'Yes, of course.' Maribel opened the door to admit her. 'I was about to come down, Aunt.'

'Something is troubling you, my love. Will you not tell me?'

Maribel hesitated. If she ignored this chance it might be too late. She took a deep breath and then inclined her head.

'I must begin at the very beginning. I beg you will forgive me—I have not been entirely honest with you. When I first came here I did not know you and was afraid that you might turn me away. It is true that I am promised to Captain Devere, but we were not betrothed in the proper manner. My father wished me to marry a man I had never seen—a man called Lord William Roberts of Helbourne.'

'Impossible! That wicked man...' Lady Fildene's face reflected her shock. 'I have heard of him and the very idea offends me. How could your father suggest such a thing?'

'He hated me, as I believe he once hated my mother. I begged to be allowed to wait and perhaps choose a husband for myself, but he would not listen. Lord Roberts sent his cousin to fetch me and I was forced to go with him, but then...I met Captain Devere. We fell in love and he asked me to wed him.'

'How did you meet Captain Devere?' Her aunt's eyes were on her face. 'I have felt there is some mystery, Maribel...something you did not wish to tell me? Will you not be honest with me so that I may protect you from those that would harm you or take advantage of your innocence?'

'Justin attacked the ship and forced Captain Hynes to give me up to him. At first I believe he had some thought of a ransom, but then—' She broke off as she saw her aunt's face. 'No, it is not like that, Aunt. He truly loves me and I him. Justin would never harm me.'

'Is Captain Devere a privateer?' Lady Fildene frowned, clearly doubtful. 'What is his business? I thought it strange that he should leave you here and go off on some secret mission.'

'It is not secret. He has gone to seek an audience with the Queen...' Maribel's eyes filled with tears. 'Please do not judge him or me, Aunt. I was treated ill by my father and by Captain Hynes. He tried to—to seduce me while I was on his ship. He said he had my father's permission to do as he would with me. If Justin had not attacked the ship, I might be dead, for I would have taken my life rather than live as his thing.'

'My poor, poor child,' her aunt said and held out her arms. 'I am not certain how your uncle will feel about a marriage between you and Captain Devere, for he would frown upon such a trade. Pirates and privateers are the scourge of the seas and cost many an honest merchant a great deal of money. However, you are not to be judged or chastised for you had no choice in all this, my love. Do not fear this man. You shall not be given up to him. My husband will listen to a business proposition if he makes it, but nothing will affect you. I give you my word. You shall not be forced to leave this house against your will.'

'And Justin?' Maribel looked at her uncertainly. She half-wished that she had not told her aunt anything. 'I love him so very much.'

'If that gentleman returns, he will explain himself to your uncle and me,' Lady Fildene said, looking grim. 'If we are satisfied the wedding will go ahead, but he must be prepared to tell us everything.'

Maribel was silent. Her aunt was asking for no more than was due, for she had taken her into her home and treated her kindly, but if she and her husband sought to deny the marriage, Maribel would defy them and run away with the man she loved. She had obeyed her father as a dutiful daughter ought, but never again would she go against the dictates of her heart. She belonged with Justin and she would sail with him to the ends of the earth. Let him only return to her and she would not ask for anything more. Riches and fine clothes meant nothing. Only in her bold pirate's arms could she find happiness.

Chapter Ten

'Her Majesty will see you now, sir. Please come with me.'

Justin inclined his head to the flunky who had summoned him and followed in his footsteps. He had waited every day for the past ten, containing his impatience as best he could, but he knew that he might have been kept waiting so much longer. Some of the gentlemen he had spoken to had already been kept in limbo for far longer. After traversing some steps and a long corridor, the footman paused outside a door, indicating that Justin might enter.

'Her Majesty will be with you shortly.'

Justin thanked him and opened the door. He entered a large room, which had been hung with rich tapestry and was furnished with a beautiful cabinet of carved oak, several footstools and side tables. These were adorned with heavy silver chargers, ewers and candlesticks, an important chair set upon a little dais at the far end. As far as Justin could tell he was alone. He moved slowly towards the dais, then hesitated as he heard a woman's laugh and then a muffled whisper, which sounded like a man's voice. A curtain moved to the right of the chair and a woman came out.

Her red hair was hanging down her back, held only by a little jewelled cap at the back of her head. She looked like the young girl he had met before but her gown was exquisitely sewn with jewels, rows of pearls hanging about her white neck. She stood with one hand behind her back, her gaze bright and inquiring.

Justin went down on one knee. 'Your Majesty,' he said. 'I thank you for graciously allowing me this audience.'

'Have you forgot me, sir?' Elizabeth demanded with a twinkle in her eyes. 'I am still the same Bess you visited and teased, as I recall, when I was but a child and you a friend of Robin's.'

'I was privileged to know you then—and I am honoured to bend the knee to my Queen now.'

'Stand and face me. I have received the gift you sent me. It is a fine jewel and I shall have it mounted in a crown, I think.' Her shrewd eyes narrowed. 'Why have you given me such a precious thing, sir? I believe you must want something of me.'

'I have come to ask for the royal pardon, your Majesty. I was shanghaied and taken aboard Captain Smythe's vessel and eventually driven to mutiny, as I believe you may have been told by others.'

'Captain Smythe has been dealt with and all those

who took part in the mutiny are pardoned by my decree. Mutiny is a serious crime, but the man was a monster and he dared to sail under a royal flag, bringing disgrace to our name. He will do so no more. So, what more have you to tell me, sir?'

'I have sailed as a pirate, Majesty. I attacked Spanish and Portuguese merchantmen—and one English ship.'

'Why did you attack an English ship, sir? I can turn a blind eye if you attack Spanish treasure ships, for that country grows too rich and powerful and in time will seek to rule us. The Portuguese are greedy and will not share their trading agreements, keeping all the riches of the east for themselves. If a privateer wishes to attack ships from these nations I may choose not to know what they do—but I shall not tolerate attacks on English ships by an Englishman.'

'Hynes was in league with an evil Spaniard who tortured and killed men who worked for him in the silver mines. Sabatini intended to sell his daughter to a monster. I rescued her and gave him back his ship, but then he and the Don attacked the island where my ships were anchored, killing and injuring innocent men and women. They stole Maribel against her will, but I rescued her and she has consented to be my wife. This time I did not give him back his ship—and if I had the chance I would see him hang for his crimes.'

'Indeed?' Elizabeth's eyes gleamed. 'You take much for granted, sir. Mayhap I shall make an example of you to teach others what I expect of my young captains.

Perhaps you will be the one to hang. Kneel, Master Devere. I wish to see you penitent for your wicked crimes.'

A nerve flicked in Justin's cheek, but he went down on one knee before her, bowing his head, his eyes fixed on the hem of her gown. 'I know I have behaved recklessly, but I crave your Majesty's pardon.'

She made a sound that he interpreted as a laugh and there was the sound of movement, as someone joined her. He could see a pair of booted feet standing beside her, but did not raise his head.

'Well, what shall I do with him, Robin?'

'It is your choice, but you may one day have need of such men as Devere, Bess.'

Justin did not look up, but he knew that only one man would dare to speak to the Queen in such a manner. Lord Robert Dudley had been one of her most loyal friends during the difficult times when she was at the mercy of her sister Mary's whims.

'Give me your sword, Robin. Raise your head, Master Devere.'

Justin looked up as she brought the sword tip down on one shoulder and then the other. Elizabeth's eyes were bright with mischief. She had become a queen and must be treated with respect and reverence, but as yet there still remained the girl who had loved to laugh and play with her friends. She had been a captive at the mercy of her sister, treated as a bastard and at times in fear of her life, but courage and her own good sense had brought her through. Justin believed that at last England had a worthy queen.

'Arise, Sir Justin Devere. You are hereby made a knight of my realm. If you wish for it, I shall give you papers to sail as a privateer under my order.'

'Your Majesty...' Justin was surprised and overwhelmed—he had not expected such an honour. A pardon was all he had dared to hope for. 'I do not know how to thank you.'

'You were Robin's friend and mine in the past. I am Queen now, but I have enemies as well as friends. There may be a service you can do for me one day.'

'Your Majesty may call on me whenever you wish.'

Justin stood. He offered his hand to Robert Dudley. 'I am glad to see you, sir.'

'And I you, Devere. You must join me for supper. I should like to hear more of your adventures. Especially concerning Spanish treasure ships.'

'Thank you, I shall be pleased to. This evening, if you will, for I leave London almost immediately. The lady I have promised to wed waits anxiously for news.'

'Your uncle wishes you to come down,' Lady Fildene told Maribel that evening. 'Captain Hynes is with him. He has asked if he may speak with you, but he has laid no claims. I have held my peace so far, but do not fear that I shall allow this man to distress you.'

'Must I see him?' Maribel asked. 'I do not like or trust him. He is sly and may try to turn my uncle's mind his way.'

'I shall be with you all the time. Fear not, dearest.

You are under my protection. I promise no harm shall come to you.'

'Thank you.' Maribel smiled at her gratefully. 'I shall come, but you must not leave me alone with him.'

Maribel glanced at herself in the tiny silver mirror that hung from the chatelaine at her waist. She no longer dressed her hair in the Spanish way in ringlets either side of her face, but instead wore it loose down her back, tucked beneath a velvet hood in the manner of an English country lady.

Her heart raced as she accompanied her aunt down the wide stone steps leading to the great hall below. She could see her uncle, a young man who looked very like him and was clearly his son Michael, and Samuel Hynes. A shiver went through her as he glanced up and saw her. His eyes narrowed, gleaming with sudden excitement. Maribel's nerves jangled, but she kept her head high, giving him a haughty stare.

As she and her aunt advanced towards the little group, Samuel Hynes inclined his head to her.

'Good evening, Donna Maribel. I am glad to see you looking so well and none the worse for your adventures. I did not dare to hope that you would be brought safely to your family after that pirate abducted you from my ship.'

Maribel resisted the temptation to look at her uncle. 'Captain Devere is a man of honour. I was his willing captive, sir—for I did not wish to marry your cousin.' She wanted to fling her accusations of attempted rape in his face, but retained her dignity.

'If a pirate can be honourable, I suppose he has acted

in your best interests by bringing you here. I have a letter from your father to deliver to your hand. Don Sabatini insisted that it must come only to you.'

Maribel looked at her aunt, who nodded, then went forwards to receive it. She took the sealed paper from his hand. 'Thank you, sir. If that is all, I shall leave you to your business.'

'I pray you stay a little, lady. Your father's instructions to you are in the letter.'

'My father may no longer command me, sir. I am under the protection of my uncle.' She turned her head, but saw that her uncle and his son were leaving the room. Her aunt had withdrawn to the far side and was staring out of the window. Maribel felt as if she had been deserted, but she resisted the impulse to summon her aunt to her. 'I must tell you that I shall not return to Spain—nor will I submit to unreasonable demands.'

'I believe that Don Sabatini wishes to make amends. If you read his letter, you will discover that he has suffered a seizure and may never truly be himself again. He asks that you will allow me to take you to him so that he may give you his blessing and promises that you will not be forced into marriage.'

'Do you imagine I would trust you after what you did to me on board your ship? You hit me and kicked me as I lay on the floor. You threatened me with all manner of violence—' Maribel broke off as she heard something behind her and saw her aunt leave the room with her son. She had been left alone after all her aunt's promises! Fear coursed through her. 'Do not touch me, sir. I shall scream.'

Hynes moved towards her. 'Your uncle is interested only in the rich contract I bring him. He will send you back to your father and then I shall have what belongs to me.'

'No!' Maribel gave a scream of fright as he pounced on her, grabbing her arm. He pressed his face close to hers, his sneer of triumph making her shiver and tremble. 'No, my uncle would not…he could not…'

'You are quite right, my dear, I would not,' her uncle said, entering by a door situated behind Samuel Hynes. 'When Lady Fildene told me what this evil man had done I could hardly credit it, but when he asked to see you alone I made my little plan to test him.' He advanced on Hynes, his face set coldly. 'I have heard enough from you, sir. You may believe that I am interested in your talk of riches, but I assure you I care nothing for Sabatini's money. He took my sister from me and broke her heart. One letter telling of her unhappiness was all she sent me, but it told me everything. If he imagines I would allow my niece to return to Spain on this false pretence, then he is sadly mistaken. He may be ill, but unless Maribel wishes it she will not leave this house.'

'Damn you!' Samuel Hynes's face turned dark red with anger. 'Her father gave her to me and I mean to have her—whether she wills it or no!'

'You will leave my house instantly or I shall have my men arrest you and send for the militia.'

'You will pay for this—you and that hellcat!' Hynes said and stormed from the room.

'Uncle…' Maribel was pale as her uncle came

towards her and took her trembling hands in his. 'I thought for a moment that you had deserted me.'

'Forgive me. It was the only way, Maribel. I believed your story for I knew my sister was unhappy in her marriage, but I had to be certain just what was happening. I hoped that if Hynes believed you were alone he would say something to betray himself—and he did.'

'I cannot thank you enough for believing in me. Even had I wanted to visit my father I would not have trusted Captain Hynes. Besides, I must wait here until Justin returns.'

Her uncle looked severe. 'And when he does I shall have a few questions to ask that young man, Maribel. He must prove himself worthy of you, for I will not have you wed a pirate. You are a lady and it is not fitting.'

'I am sure that Justin will be able to satisfy all your questions when he comes, Uncle.'

'We shall see, Niece.'

Maribel was thoughtful as she returned to her own chamber. She had been wrong to doubt her uncle and aunt; they were both truly kind and concerned for her. Her uncle had sent Samuel Hynes away, but would he give up his attempts to claim her?

'Oh, Justin…' Maribel sighed. 'Where are you my love? I need you so.'

Something told her that Captain Hynes would not give up just because her uncle had sent him packing.

Samuel Hynes stood looking up at the house high above him. It would be impossible for a small force to scale the cliffs from this position and take the inhabitants by surprise. He had imagined that by wooing the son he might gain the father's trust, but he had lost his gamble. His one advantage was that he had learned Justin Devere was not here. He knew that he might have only one attempt to snatch the girl, because once Devere returned he would guard her too well.

The uncle was a wily old bird and had fooled him into thinking he was interested only in the rich contract he had offered. It might be prudent to give up the contest, let the girl go her way and forget her. He had Sabatini's contract in his pocket, but he wanted much more. Maribel probably did not guess what a wealthy heiress she was or that if she contested her father's guardianship in the courts she could regain all that was hers by right.

Sabatini had let slip far more than he realised in his rage at her capture. Hynes wanted the girl. He intended to humiliate her, to break her spirit and teach her to serve him like a slave. Once he had her fortune in his possession he would probably discard her, but marriage was necessary if he were to gain the riches she could bring him.

Hynes had recently inherited his cousin's title and what was left of his estate, but it was heavily encumbered by debt and of no consequence beside what he might gain if he could force Maribel to become his wife. If Sabatini were to die after they were wed, his fortune would probably come to Maribel and him. It might be possible to arrange a little accident for the proud Spaniard, but it would avail him nothing unless the girl was his wife.

Lord Roberts had needed the fortune she could bring him, but it was Hynes that had suggested sending an early portrait to fool both her and her father. It had made the trick easier when he discovered that Sabatini hated his daughter and hoped to keep control of her fortune even after she was married.

If it had not been for that damned pirate, Maribel would already be his to do with as he wished—and it would give Samuel pleasure to tame the vixen. Once he had her she would soon learn to know her master!

He was determined to have her, and he craved revenge on the man who had stolen her from him twice. He had tried persuasion, but now he must resort to cunning and force. Maribel was safe while she remained inside her uncle's house. Samuel must find a way of enticing her to leave it. He knew that she did not walk out alone as she had sometimes at her home in Spain, but she must long to walk on the beach when the weather was fine. If she thought that she was coming to meet that damned pirate, she might disobey her uncle and slip out alone.

On his ship with his crew to protect him, Devere was impossible to beat, but if he had been in London, as Michael Fildene had obligingly revealed when they were talking before the girl made her appearance, it should be possible to set a trap for him. He was travelling alone and might not be on his guard in his eagerness to claim his bride.

* * *

Justin decided that he would stop at the inn he had stayed at before when making his way to London. He could not hope to reach Maribel before nightfall and it was best to avoid the roads at night; a man travelling alone was easy prey for the bands of beggars and rogues who haunted the roads.

After his audience with the Queen, he had stayed in London only long enough to buy gifts for Maribel, most of which he had had sent to his father's house, along with other things he needed. It was Justin's intention to take Maribel to visit his mother. If his father would receive him, he would visit with his parents until he could find an estate he thought worthy of his wife. If not…perhaps he would take her to court, where he was certain she would be welcomed.

He was still surprised to find himself being addressed as Sir Justin, but did not imagine that a knighthood would weigh with his father. John Devere would not change his mind simply because the Queen chose to find his son's adventures worthy of honour.

At least he could hold his head up high, Justin thought as he dismounted and gave his horse to a groom. In the morning he would speak to Maribel's uncle and ask for her hand.

He was crossing the yard to the inn when he heard something behind him and whirled round. Seeing the three rogues advancing on him, Justin drew his sword. By the look of their faces they were out for more than the gold he carried and he was immediately wary. Once before he had been caught in a trap, his attention on the rogues who were attacking him from the front while another attacked him from behind. It would not happen this time. He gave a low piercing whistle and suddenly men came running towards him from the shadows—several more than he had expected.

'Higgins?'

'You sent word to meet you here, Cap'n. I brought a few of the men with me just in case.'

Justin smiled in the gloom. 'I applaud your caution, my friend. We'll make short work of these rogues between us.' He brandished his sword in anticipation. One of the would-be assassins pointed a pistol at Justin, but before he could press the trigger a knife thudded into his chest and the shot went wide. Seeing they were outnumbered, the two men who had threatened Justin disappeared into the shadows and a third man watching at a distance scowled and melted away.

'What made you think an attack might take place here?' Higgins asked as a couple of shots were fired after the fleeing rogues.

'As soon as you sent me word that Hynes had been seen lingering in the vicinity I suspected that he would try something. He could not know when I left London, unless he had someone watching me, and I had not noticed anything unusual; therefore, it was likely he would try to surprise me when I stopped at the inn. He may have men watching for me at various inns, but if he made enquiries he could have learned that I stopped here before.' Justin's brow furrowed. 'Is my lady safe? He has not tried to harm her?'

'Hynes made some attempt to persuade her to let him take her to his father. Anna told me there was some tale of Sabatini being ill and wanting to make amends. When her uncle left her alone with him, he tried to force her and was caught out. Fildene is no fool, but…' Higgins looked awkward. 'Anna says that he means to question you about your plans before he will permit the wedding. He will not have his niece marry a pirate.'

'Nor would I expect his blessing if that were the case. I believe he will be satisfied. Her Majesty hath seen fit to bestow a knighthood on me and I intend to take my bride to my father's house until I can find an estate fitting for her.'

'I am glad that the Queen pardoned you.' Higgins gave him a hard look. 'What of the rest of us? Are we to receive the royal pardon too?'

'You are all pardoned for the mutiny and Captain Smythe has lost his master's ticket. Her Majesty is willing to grant me letters of marque so that we could sail as privateers if we wished. She told me in confidence that she fears Spain; if that country grows too powerful, its king may cast covetous eyes on England's throne, and, as is well known, the Portuguese merchants will not share the secrets of their trading with the exotic lands of the east.'

'Rich pickings for the taking…' Higgins nodded his understanding for the Portuguese were the envy of other nations who craved a share of their special trading agreements. 'But 'tis not your intention to sail under licence to the Crown, is it?

'No. I could not ask Maribel to share life on board a privateer. I must make a home for her. She is a lady and deserves to be treated as such.'

Higgins looked thoughtful. 'Me and Anna—we have thought of settling down. We had thought of a trading post on the island, but...' He rubbed the bridge of his nose. 'I have been talking to some folk who think of sailing to the New World.'

'The Spanish grow wealthy on silver and gold stolen from the Incas and other tribes, but you could not compete with them.'

'It is not of gold or silver taken from the earth that these men dream, but of freedom and the wealth of the soil. They say that there are great forests where the game is so plentiful that a man would never starve. They talk of a settlement where they can build new lives for themselves, unhampered by old prejudices and unfair laws—a land where all men are equal and all can work to earn their fortunes.'

'Do you believe such ideals are possible?' Justin asked doubtfully.

'I may be pardoned for the mutiny, but there are men in England with long memories. I could be hanged for stealing a loaf of bread. I might be arrested for speaking out of turn to an aristocrat. I am thinking of buying a cargo and sailing for the New World. I know that there are men who sailed under you who have thought of it too. If men are to settle there, they will need ships to supply them with the goods they cannot provide for themselves.'

'What would you do—set up a trading post?'

'Aye, I've thought of it, but I'll need a regular supply, someone I can rely on to replenish my stocks once they have gone. I don't know what you have in mind for the *Defiance.* There's the *Mistress Susanna,* too—though that was promised to the men.'

'I might pay its price myself, but I am not yet certain of my plans.' Justin was thoughtful as they went into the inn together. 'I had thought to become a merchant adventurer when I was no longer a pirate, but things have changed. Give me a few days to think this over and I will give you my answer.'

'It will take me a week or two to get a cargo together. I've been asking what kind of things will be needed. For a start it will be tools and seed that are most wanted, but the settlers will no doubt take those things with them. I was thinking of other stuff: lamps and crockery, material for women to make new gowns and shirts for their menfolk.'

'You will make a fine shopkeeper,' Justin said and chuckled, clapping him on the back. 'I thank you for coming to my rescue this evening. I shall give your ideas some thought, but for the moment there is still the problem of Samuel Hynes. His first attempt to have me killed has failed, but there will no doubt be others.'

'Why are you looking so upset, Aunt?' Maribel asked as she walked into the parlour and found Lady

Fildene sitting over her needlework, tears trickling down her cheeks. 'Has something happened to distress you?'

'Michael has been telling his father that he would like to join some men who are making plans to sail for the New World. Sir Henry says that we must not hold him if he wishes to go; it is an adventure and he is a young man—but I had hoped he would marry and live here with us. His father had thought he would take over much of the business.'

'I am sorry. You will miss him if he goes,' Maribel said. 'But you have other sons who—' She broke off as the door opened and a maid entered carrying a small tray on which lay a small piece of parchment. She offered it to Maribel, who took it and saw her name inscribed. It had been folded and sealed with wax, but there was no insignia to indicate who had sent it. 'Who gave you this, Jess?'

'A young lad brought it, mistress. He said it was for you and that his master would be waiting for your answer.'

Maribel broke the seal and gave a little cry of pleasure. 'It is from Justin. He says that he will be here later today. He asks that I will meet him on the beach because he wishes to talk to me alone.'

'Show me…' Lady Fildene held out her hand and Maribel gave it to her. 'Is this Captain Devere's hand? Are you sure it came from him?'

'I do not think I have seen Justin's writing before this,' Maribel said and looked at her aunt. 'Do you think it could be a trap?'

'Is this the kind of thing your betrothed would ask you to do? I think it most improper for you to meet any man alone on a beach.'

'I do not know…' Maribel wrinkled her brow in thought. She was remembering the walks they had taken together on a beach, and the way Justin had kissed her. He might long to hold her in his arms and feel that he needed to be sure of her love after whatever had happened to him. 'Justin might wish to be alone with me before he spoke to my uncle. Yet I am not sure. I think I must show this letter to Uncle Henry.'

'Yes, my dear. That would be the best—ask your uncle what you should do.'

'I shall go and find him now.' She hesitated, then, 'You should not cry, dearest Aunt. If Michael understood how you felt, I am sure he would not leave you.'

'But he must not know,' the loving mother said at once. 'You must not tell him, Maribel. If it is his wish, I shall not stand in his way.'

Maribel inclined her head. Her aunt was so generous and she was sorry that her son seemed likely to leave his home. An adventure such as Michael was about to undertake must be fraught with danger—but it would be exciting. To begin a new life in a land where all were equal, valued for their contribution to the community rather than their birth. It was an interesting thought, but she pushed it from her mind as she went in search of her uncle. However, she was told that Sir Henry had gone out on business and would not be back until later that afternoon.

Maribel returned to her own chamber. As the sun began to move round the sky and the time for the meeting with Justin drew nearer she felt restless, unable to settle to her needlework. It was a fine day and Justin might be waiting for her on the beach, wondering where she was and thinking that she no longer loved him. Yet it might be a trap…

Making up her mind, Maribel found a light cape to wear over her gown. She would go down to the beach, but she would not go unprepared. She took out the knife Peg had given her on the island. If the note had come from Samuel Hynes, she would not be as weak and defenceless as she had been once before.

'You had my letter?' Justin asked as he was shown into Sir Henry's counting room. A large table was spread with ledgers and small piles of coin and talents were set out in readiness. 'Forgive me. I was told you were here, but I see you are busy.'

'My steward has made a reckoning of the rents and monies owed for this past month, but we are almost finished now. My servants and labourers will be coming for their pay at any moment but the steward will manage without me. Walk with me, sir. I would talk to you alone. I believe you bring good news with you?'

'Yes, the news is better than I had hoped, sir. I wished to talk to you…to tell you of my plans. Now that her Majesty has seen fit to give me a knighthood I mean to retire from the sea, but I may carry on trading. I have a fine ship and I am looking for a captain to sail it to the New World for me.'

'Indeed, that is interesting,' Sir Henry said. 'You must meet my son Michael—you may have something in common. You have answered my most pressing question, for I did not think I could allow Maribel to marry a pirate—or even a privateer. She is my sister's only child and has become a daughter to us. I want to be sure that she will be happy.'

'It is my chief concern.' Justin inclined his head. 'I have fortune enough to provide a good home for Maribel, to give her the life she is entitled to expect. I have always known that I could not wed her and continue the life I led before.'

'Then we are in agreement.' Sir Henry smiled. 'I know she has been waiting anxiously for your return and I think we should not keep her waiting a moment longer…but there is something else I must tell you. I have received news of Maribel's father. If it is true, he was taken ill of a seizure after a quarrel with someone and has since died—' He broke off as he saw his wife coming towards them. 'Lady Fildene, my dear. Sir Justin hath come to claim Maribel and I have given him my blessing.'

'Then why have I just seen her leaving the house alone?' Lady Fildene looked alarmed. 'This morning she received a letter that was supposed to have come from Captain Devere. I warned her that it might be a trap and she said she would ask you what she ought to do, Henry—did she not come to you?'

'I have been out all morning on business. What did this note say?'

'It asked her to meet Captain Devere on the beach…'

'Samuel Hynes! He tried to have me killed. When the attempt failed he thought he would abduct Maribel instead!' Justin cursed and turned on his heel. 'I must go.'

'I shall come with you.' Sir Henry said. He looked at his wife as Justin set off at a run. 'Rouse the household, madam. We must put a stop to this rascal's mischief once and for all. I should have seen to it before, but I thought her safe in the house.'

'I tried to warn her…' Lady Fildene shook her head at the folly of love and picked up a large brass bell, shaking it hard. As it reverberated through the house, servants came hurrying to answer her call. 'To the beach…to the beach…' she cried. 'My niece is in danger…'

Maribel followed the sloping path to the beach. The sun was bright but there was still a cool breeze from the water. Stopping for a moment to gaze out to sea, she saw the sails of a ship she thought might be the *Defiance*. Had Justin decided to bring his ship here? She had thought it left behind at Dover, but if he had managed to obtain the pardon he hoped might be his, he could have decided to bring his ship here. She was not entirely sure what he intended once he had settled his affairs. Were they to live here in England or perhaps in Italy or France?

Although her visit with her aunt and uncle had been pleasant, Maribel did not think she would care to live as they did for the rest of her life. Their way of life was not so very different from that she had known before she left for England the first time—but sailing with Justin on his ship and her stay on the island had opened her eyes, making her see that there was more to life than sitting in a drawing room in a pretty gown embroidering cushions.

Was she foolish to long for something different? She knew that she might have been more sensible to sit in her room at home and wait for Justin to come to her— but perhaps he had been testing her?

She could not see anyone on the beach, but she caught sight of movement near a rocky point at the far end and thought that perhaps a boat had been beached just out of sight. Her heart quickened. The true reason she had come to meet Justin was that after leaving her aunt and failing to find her uncle, she had wondered if Justin's reason for asking her to meet him was that he had been unable to secure a pardon. Perhaps he was a fugitive in hiding from those who wished to capture and hang him?

Maribel's mouth ran dry with fear, her pulses racing. It was surely the only reason Justin would ask her to meet him in such a clandestine way. She must be prepared to leave with him immediately because his life might be in danger every moment he stayed here!

Reaching the beach, Maribel glanced up at the cliff top once and then began to walk towards the point. Justin must be waiting for her, keeping out of sight until he was certain she was alone.

'Justin…I am here, my love—'

Maribel stopped as several men suddenly burst out from behind rocks that jutted into the sea and had hidden them from her gaze until this moment. She hesitated, her heart catching as she saw their faces and realised that these men were not Justin's. Immediately, she knew that her aunt had been right and she had foolishly walked into a trap.

Turning, she began to run back the way she had come. Her heart was thumping madly because here on this beach she was vulnerable. The ship anchored in the bay must be Samuel Hynes's ship and these men had come to take her captive. How foolish she had been! She ought to have known that Justin would not ask her to meet him alone.

She was breathing hard as she reached the bottom of the path leading back to the top of the cliff. Glancing up, she saw that a man was scrambling down to her as swiftly as he could manage. She knew him at once and her heart gave a little skip. Gathering her courage, she turned as the first of Samuel Hynes's men caught up to her. She whipped out her knife, brandishing it in front of her, sweeping it back and forth as she moved away from the cliff face to the open sand.

'Stay away from me or it will be the worse for you,' she cried. 'I know how to use this and I shall…' Maribel gave a little cry as one of the men lunged at her with his sword. She backed away, because a knife was no match for such a weapon. 'Stay back…'

Four of the men had surrounded her. One tried to

grab her from the back, but she whirled about and slashed his hand, making him yell in pain and retreat. Another man threatened her with his sword, the tip of his blade hovering near her throat.

'Have a care, Davy,' his companion warned. 'He wants her alive and all in one piece. It will be you he flogs if she is harmed.' He glanced over his shoulder, and, following his gaze, Maribel saw that Captain Hynes was near the boat that had brought them ashore.

'Damn the wench!' The first man spat on the sand. 'He swore she would be easy to abduct once he got her here.'

A shout from Justin warned them that he was nearly at the foot of the cliffs. The men swung round to look and all of a sudden a crowd of faces appeared at the top of the cliffs, men and women, all carrying weapons of some kind, had followed and were about to pour down the steep path. Someone pointed an arquebus at the would-be abductors and fired. The shot went wide, for at this distance it could never have hit its mark, but the sound was enough to startle the men.

'Leave her! We shall all be killed…' one of them cried.

The one pointing his sword at Maribel's throat hesitated, then, seeing his friends fleeing, turned and followed as fast as he could in their wake.

Justin reached Maribel before the scoundrel could regain the safety of the jutting rocks. He fired after them and his ball struck home, winging one man in the arm. The man's screams echoed, as he yelled for his friends to help him and was ignored. He fell to his knees, struggled to his feet once more and set off towards the boat, which had already been pushed out into water deep enough to float it. His pleas for help were disregarded as the others began to row frantically for open water.

Sir Henry's household had reached the beach and several shots were fired as the wounded sailor ran into the water, floundering after the boat and eventually falling face down into the sea as another shot struck his back.

Maribel gazed up at Justin as he stood before her, his eyes intent on her face. 'I was so foolish,' she said, catching her breath. 'I should have known that you would never tell me to meet you here. I thought that you might be in danger of your life.'

'And so you risked yours…' He smiled and shook his head. 'If you insist on taking such foolish risks, I must teach you to use a sword or, better still a pistol, my love. Peg's knife served you well—without it they might have had you in the boat before I could reach you—but 'tis no match for a cutlass.' He shuddered. 'It would have served only to delay them, Maribel. Had your aunt not seen you leaving the house I might still have been talking with your uncle and it might have been too late.'

'Justin…' Tears welled in her eyes. 'Forgive me. I have missed you so much. When the letter came I suspected a trap, but I longed to see you and I was afraid if I did not meet you, you might go away and I should never see you again.'

'My sweet, lovely, foolish darling,' Justin said and trailed his fingers down her cheek, wiping away the tears. 'I would never have gone without giving you the chance to come with me. Had I been a fugitive and risked death to come to you I would still have done it— but I am a free man. The Queen has pardoned me and there is nothing to stop us marrying.'

'Justin…' She breathed and moved closer to him. She was longing for him to sweep her into his arms, but at that moment her uncle arrived, sword in hand. 'Uncle…I fear my foolish behaviour has caused you some trouble.'

'Foolish it was, child, for you should have consulted me,' Sir Henry said, but looked pleased with himself. 'I believe we showed those villains that we are not to be messed with, Sir Justin. If Hynes has the sense he was born with, he will sail away and not bother us again.'

Justin inclined his head, but when Maribel looked at him she saw there was a grim set to his mouth.

'Is it true?' she asked. 'Are you now Sir Justin?'

His gaze came back to her and he smiled, putting his arm about her waist. 'Shall you enjoy being Lady Devere?'

'I do not mind what I am called if I am with you,' she declared passionately. 'I will be your lady, your wife or your mistress…just as long as you never leave me again!'

Chapter Eleven

'You must know that I would not,' Justin said. He gazed down at her, his expression serious. 'If I seem distant or reserved it is because I have something on my mind, Maribel. I love you with all my heart. I wrote to your uncle and told him of my coming, but he was out when the letter arrived and I was with him when your aunt told us she had seen you heading towards the beach.' Justin caressed her cheek with his fingertips. 'You uncle has seen fit to allow the wedding. If you will have me, my darling, we shall be wed as soon as it can be arranged. Then I shall take you to meet my mother. After that…'

'You are anxious for my safety,' she said, looking into his eyes. 'Surely I must be safe once we are wed?'

'Yes, of course.' Justin promised. He took her hand and held it firmly. 'Yet still you must take care not to walk alone.'

'You fear that Hynes may try again? Surely he must

know that he has lost? I would kill myself rather than wed him—and it is my fortune he wants.'

'Perhaps.' Justin's brow furrowed. 'We have had news that your father may have died of a seizure.'

'My father may be dead?' Maribel was shocked by the news, but could not grieve for a man she had never truly known. 'God rest his soul. He did not love me, but I would not have wished him dead.'

'Of course you could not.' Justin took her hand. 'He did not deserve a daughter like you—indeed, I have wondered if he believed you were not his child.'

'He believed my mother had betrayed him?' Her eyes opened wide. 'Was that why he hated me?'

'It may have been or he may simply have been driven by greed. But his death has consequences. Even if he has left you nothing of what he owned, your husband's fortune will be at your disposal. I do not think you know the extent of the fortune your husband left you, but I imagine it may be considerable. Until we are wed, Hynes may not be the only man to covet what is yours.'

'Yes, I see. I knew Pablo was wealthy, but I do not care for riches. I was far happier when we lived simply on the island—at least I would have been had it not been for Captain Pike.'

Justin smiled wryly. 'You are too beautiful, my love. Men will always find you attractive, but once we are married no decent man would try to take advantage.'

'Let it be as soon as possible,' Maribel said and saw the gleam in his eyes. 'I want only to be your wife.

Nothing else matters. I do not care about the money. I never did.'

'I promise I shall keep you safe.' Justin bent his head, touching his mouth to hers in a soft kiss that held the promise of much more. 'I cannot wait for the moment you are truly mine.'

'I have been yours since the moment you took me captive.' Maribel smiled at him with love in her eyes. 'My uncle waits. We should go back to the house so that the arrangements for the wedding may be made.'

'You make a beautiful bride, my love,' Lady Fildene said as she gave Maribel a blue lace ribbon for her posy. Maribel was dressed in a gown of pale grey with trimmings of silver, a lace veil over her hair caught with jewelled combs in the Spanish way. 'I wish you every happiness, Maribel. Perhaps you will visit us sometimes?'

Maribel kissed her cheek. 'If I cannot visit I will certainly write to you, dearest Aunt. You have been kindness itself and I wish that I had known you years ago.'

'It has given us great happiness to have you here for this time.' Lady Fildene pressed a gift into her hands. 'This locket will remind you of your mother—it has her likeness inside. It was painted when she was very young and your uncle treasured it, but he says that it should be yours.'

Maribel opened it and saw a young girl who looked much as she did when a year or so younger. 'I shall treasure it always, Aunt—but are you sure my uncle can bear to part with it?'

'I believe he has other keepsakes. He wishes you to have this, Maribel.'

'I must thank him.' She fastened the locket about her neck with a ribbon. 'But he will be waiting downstairs, for it must be time to leave.'

'Yes, we must not keep the gentlemen waiting. Sir Justin will be anxious to see you, Maribel.'

'He loves me. I am so lucky, Aunt. There was a time when I believed my destiny would bring me little happiness, but now I know that I am the most fortunate of women.'

'Yes, my dear, I believe you are.' Lady Fildene smiled at her. 'Sir Justin will take good care of you, I have no doubt.'

'I am certain it is uppermost in his mind.' Maribel picked up her posy of pink roses. 'I am ready.'

Seeing her uncle waiting for her, she went up to him. He smiled and kissed her on the cheek, then took her hand.

'I believe you have found yourself a true man, Niece. He is the proper custodian for your person and your wealth.'

'I know that Justin has no desire to benefit from anything that was mine before I wed him. If my father is truly dead, he will sell my property in Spain and put it to good use elsewhere. I have friends I would like to help—and there are people who recently lost much of what they own. Justin will use some of my money to help them. We have talked of what I wish and he has agreed to do what I ask.'

'It is rare that a man is so uninterested in the marriage portion, but in this case you are right. Sir Justin is heir to a large fortune and has no need of anything you might have owned.'

'I am very fortunate in my husband-to-be.'

'Then I shall write to Spain and confirm what we have been told.' Her uncle smiled at her. 'The groom is waiting. Go to him with an easy heart, Maribel. You will no longer be the target for greedy men who want your fortune.'

'Thank you.' She smiled, kissed him again and went to meet her soon-to-be husband.

'As soon as the wedding is over, you will go aboard the ship at Dover and wait for my instructions,' Justin told Higgins as they stood outside the church for a few moments. 'You need not fear reprisals for yourself or the crew.'

'I have told you that we have a mind to sail for the New World, sir.'

'Aye. I am still thinking of your proposals and will send word once I have spoken with my mother.'

'You have not made up your mind about becoming a privateer? The letters of marque from the Queen would grant us safe passage.'

'I am not certain of my plans yet, but you shall know—as soon as I have spoken to my mother and my wife.' Justin heard the sound of approaching carriages. 'As soon as you can, take Anna and go to the ship. Tell the men that they are free to leave or stay, but I would ask one more service of them.'

Higgins looked at him in silence for a moment, then inclined his head. 'We all of us owe you that, Cap'n. My plans can wait for a while.'

'Thank you,' Justin said and smiled. 'And now if you will excuse me, I have an appointment to keep inside the church.'

Maribel saw Justin standing before the altar waiting for her. He turned his head to look at her and the expression in his eyes made her heart leap. She walked towards him proudly, feelings of joy and anticipation surging through her. She had been his willing captive, but now she would be his wife! They would live together for the rest of their lives!

Maribel glanced about her as they left the church. Bells were pealing and the villagers had gathered to throw rose petals, but she noticed several heavily armed men amongst the crowd.

'Who are those men?' she whispered to Justin.

'Just some men I have engaged to serve us, my love. Nothing for you to worry about.'

Maribel noticed a nerve flicking in his throat and the way his eyes scanned the faces of the villagers and a shiver went down her spine. She knew without being told that he and her uncle had been prepared in case another attempt should be made on her life outside the church. Yet surely Captain Hynes must know that he had lost, for he could not hope to benefit once she was married.

However, she was determined that she would not allow the worrying thought to spoil her wedding day.

She raised her head, smiling at her husband as he led her towards their carriage. Her uncle was giving a reception for them and they would stay under his roof for this one night. In the morning they would travel to the home of Justin's parents.

Maribel was eager to meet his family and yet she sensed that something was not right…that something more than the threat of another attack was playing on Justin's mind.

'I thought that we should never be alone.' Justin said, a rueful look on his face as he gazed down at her. 'Your uncle has too many friends, my love. I wished to be alone with you before this, because we have a long journey before us on the morrow.'

Maribel reached up to kiss him on the lips, her eyes questioning. 'Something troubles you, my love. Something more than Samuel Hynes, I think—will you not tell me what plays on your mind?'

'I said nothing to your uncle, Maribel.' Justin's expression was serious. 'My mother forgave me, as mothers will, without asking my story—but my father feels that I have shamed him. He walked from the room when I told him where I had been and I fear he will not wish to receive us.'

'Justin…' Maribel's heart caught because she knew how much the breach with his father must pain him. 'I am sorry. Surely he will find it in his heart to forgive what you did now that the Queen has given you a royal pardon?'

'My father is a proud man. I think perhaps too proud for his own good. It was he who told me I must leave England rather than shame the family when I was unjustly accused of being a traitor. I am not sure that he will forgive or acknowledge me.'

'I see that it hurts you,' Maribel touched his face with her fingertips. 'What will you do if he refuses to see us?'

'My mother may wish to say farewell to us. After that we shall leave.'

'Where shall we go? I thought you hoped to buy an estate close by your father's?'

'If I did that, my mother would visit us and that might cause an estrangement between them. I could not be responsible for that—so I think we shall leave England.' Justin's gaze was intent as it searched her face. 'Would you mind if we did not live in England?'

'I shall be happy wherever we live. I want only to be with you, Justin.' She held his hand to her cheek and then kissed the palm. 'For your sake I pray that your father can find it in his heart to receive you, but if he cannot we shall leave England and make our home elsewhere.'

'I thought Italy or France. It would be warmer for you as you have been used to the climate of Spain.'

'Perhaps,' Maribel said, 'but I have been thinking. There is somewhere else we might go.'

'Where? Tell me and—'

Maribel put her fingers to his lips. 'This is our wedding night, Justin. Make love to me. You have not loved me since that last time on the ship and I was but half-alive without you. I long for you to make me whole again. I missed you so when you were away.'

'My beloved…' Justin moaned softly as he buried his lips against her soft white throat. 'You are right. These things can wait. I burn for you. I love and want you so much.'

He bent down and swept her off her feet, carrying her to their bed. Removing the delicate lace nightgown, he gazed down at her body and then bent to kiss her. Maribel gasped as his tongue stroked and caressed the rosy peaks of her breasts, making her arch towards him, inviting him to take her to the heights of pleasure once more.

'I want you so much.'

'I adore you, my darling.'

'Oh, Justin.'

Maribel clung to him as she felt the burn of his flesh, opening to his thrusting manhood and giving a scream of pleasure as he entered her. She had longed for this, for the touch and taste of him, and it was all that she had remembered and more. Their bodies moved together in perfect harmony, reaching a swift and exquisite climax.

She lay gazing up at him, eyes soft and dark with desire. Justin stroked her side, her thigh, her cheek, as they looked into each other's eyes. She sighed and melted with love, her hands seeking the smooth hardness of his back. Her hands caressed him, smoothing over his shoulders and down his back. He bent his head, his tongue seeking out the secret places of her flesh, his touch making her arch and whimper with need until they came together in a slow, sensual loving that ended in a blaze of overwhelming sensation that left both satiated, at peace and soon to sleep.

In the night Maribel woke and turned to Justin. She was sure she had heard him cry out and she leaned over to see what ailed him. As she did so, he woke and looked at her.

'You are here,' he said and reached out to take her in his arms. 'I dreamed that I had lost you…but it was foolish, for you are not as she was, my darling.'

'What do you mean?' Maribel reached out to touch his cheek with her fingertips. 'Not as who was—do you mean the woman you once loved?'

'Yes. Loved, but learned to hate,' he told her. 'She was to have been my wife, but then she died—and before she died she told me that she loved another. He was poor and her family wanted her to marry for wealth and so she took me, but she loved him.'

'Oh, Justin…' Maribel's heart caught with love, understanding how he must have suffered. 'That is why you read that poem so often…' She bent over him to kiss him on the mouth. 'I shall never betray you. No other man could make my heart race as you do. I love you and you alone.'

'I know.' Justin smiled, pulling her closer and rolling her beneath him in the bed. 'Yet the dream was real and hurt me, for I could not bear to lose you, my only love.'

'You will not lose me until death us do part,' she promised and gave herself up to his kiss.

* * *

It was nearly dusk the next day when they reached Justin's home. He came to help her dismount, holding her in his arms and looking down into her lovely face for a moment while the men about them took the horses away to feed and stable them.

'I pray that your father will receive you,' she whispered. 'But if he does not, remember that together we are strong enough to face anything.'

'Yes, I know.'

Justin took her hand and they went into the front hall. A woman gave a cry of pleasure and came hurrying to meet them, her gentle face wreathed in smiles. Maribel looked at her. She guessed that this must be Lady Devere, but Justin's looks did not much favour her. He must get his size and colouring from the father…who was nowhere to be seen.

'Mother…may I present my wife, Maribel?' He held out his hand to her. 'My love—this is my mother, Lady Devere.'

'Ma'am, I am happy to meet you,' Maribel said and curtsied to her. 'I hope we find you well?'

'Indeed you do…and happy to meet you.' Justin's mother studied her face. 'I think my son has chosen his bride well. I believe you will make him happy.'

'She already has,' Justin said. 'My only concern is to be worthy of her—and to build her a home that is fit for her. I am grateful that Maribel has given me her trust and I ask for your blessing on our marriage.'

'It is willingly given.' Lady Devere hesitated. 'Your

father is not here, Justin. He left to visit your uncle's estate only this morning.'

Justin's brow creased. 'He had my letter?' She inclined her head, her eyes reflecting sorrow and disquiet. 'Yet he still went? Then I have my answer.'

'You must give him more time, dearest,' Lady Devere pleaded. 'I beg you not to be bitter or angry. Your father is a proud man. He did not try to forbid me to see you, for he knew that I should disobey him, but he cannot yet bring himself to see you.'

'I would not be the cause of dissent between you. With your permission we shall rest here the one night, for my lady is tired.'

'Your father will be gone for several days.'

'It would be an abuse of his forbearance if we stayed longer, Mother. We shall take our leave of you in the morning.'

'But where will you go?'

'That is up to my lady.' Justin turned to her, his brows arching in enquiry. 'Where would you live, my dearest one? I think Spain might not suit you, for you have sad memories there.'

'Will you truly let me choose?'

'Yes. I shall go anywhere you wish, Maribel.'

'Then…please may we go to the New World? I know that Anna and Higgins wish to set up a trading post in this new land. I hear that it is warmer than England, but much bigger than France or Italy. I believe that a man may take land for himself and make it fruitful if he is strong and he has the will.'

'The New World?' Justin stared at her. 'Have you also heard that it is primitive and wild? There are savages who may take exception to our commandeering land they believe is theirs? It would not be the life you have been used to, Maribel.'

'That is why I have chosen it.'

'I am not sure I understand.'

'I have no wish to sit sewing all day like a fine lady. I want to do the things I learned to do on the island. You could build us a fine house, Justin. Better and bigger than the one we had there—and we could have land that we farm, food that we grow ourselves. In time we may have children and then I may need help with the chores, but I want to be a good wife, to care for my home and family in a way that would be frowned on in gentle society. Think of it—a life where we may work together to build our fortunes. A country that is beginning anew without all the prejudice and unfairness of the Old World. You would help to build it with others of like minds, Justin.'

'To live and work with you would be heaven.' Justin trailed his fingers down her cheek. 'It will be even harder than it was on the island. It will not be a question of whether you wish to work harder than you have before. You may have to do far more in this new life than you did on the island, Maribel. Even though we have money, this new life you speak of will not be easily won.'

'I am not afraid of hard work. I think there are many good people who wish to leave the old countries and go to this new land. My cousin told me that people who feel trapped by laws and prejudice in England and other countries are thinking of becoming settlers. Why should we not be some of the first? We have money enough to buy whatever we need—and your ship can sail between the New and the Old World, bringing us more supplies. We can use some of the money Pablo left me to help others establish themselves, as well as helping the people whose homes were destroyed on the island. We could build a town for others to come and settle. Do you not think it would be a good life?'

Justin hesitated, studying her face and finding no sign of doubt. 'I must confess it has been in my mind to do some of the things you suggest. Higgins asked if I would let him commission my ship to supply the settlement, which he and others mean to start. I know that other ships are being prepared. Indeed, there is no reason why I should not commission others. The more ships we have to bring us the supplies we shall need in the early years, the better. But I would ask you to be certain, my love. It will be a long and arduous journey, much harder than that we took to the island. Things will become easier as the years pass, but at first it will be primitive.'

'I am prepared for long weeks, even months, at sea, and I know it will be difficult at first, but we are young and strong, Justin. I believe that we can make a good life for ourselves. My cousin tells me that the settlements are far from the silver mines that my countrymen exploit.'

'Yes, your uncle is certain there is nothing to stop you selling your estates, and he will see to the business for us. He is a good man and I trust him to treat fairly with you. I believe we shall be free and happy in this brave New World.' Fire leapt in him and he laughed as he gazed down at her. 'You are as courageous as you are beautiful, Maribel. It is little wonder that I lost my heart to you almost from the start.'

'Are you sure you wish to go to such a place?' Lady Devere looked at their faces and sighed as her hopes of seeing her son's children faded. 'Then you go with my blessing, my dearest ones. I have chests of things you may find useful in your new life, Maribel—materials of good cloth, wool and kersey and linens, which will serve you better than silk. Also items of pewter and cast iron that you will need for cooking—and I shall make you a gift of my recipes, which I have written in journals. Had I a daughter I would have passed them on to her, but they shall be for you.' Tears stood in her eyes. 'I shall miss you, Justin—and your lovely wife.'

'We shall send word of how we go on, Mother,' Justin promised and took her hand. 'If my ships trade successfully, I shall purchase others and perhaps one day we may return to England to spend time with you—and you may come to us if you wish. We shall send news of our lives when the ships return to England and you may write to us. Mayhap one day your grandson will visit in our stead.'

'I pray that you find happiness and whatever you both seek in this New World,' Lady Devere said. 'Now come upstairs with me, Maribel. I want you to choose some things to take with you. It is best that you go well prepared for when you land safely—God willing!—it may be months or even a year or more before fresh supplies can be brought. The sea is a fickle mistress and ships do not always arrive when they should.'

'Go with my mother,' Justin said. 'With your permission, Mother. I shall write a letter for my father before we dine together.'

'Yes, you should. Try to forgive him, Justin. I believe he may regret his decision when he learns what has happened here.'

Justin watched as the two ladies went upstairs together. They talked and laughed and he was torn with regret. He was excited by the adventure that lay before him, but he would have liked to make his peace with his father before he left England.

Justin had no doubts that the future would be a success. Years might pass before they accomplished all their dreams. It had taken some years before the pirates had established their houses and inns on the island and who knew what would happen in this new land? Yet the idea had fired Justin with enthusiasm. Maribel's trust in him to make a good life for them was a challenge in itself. He had wondered if he would miss the freedom he had experienced as a pirate, but now he was filled with a sense of adventure.

His mind worked swiftly. They must gather as many men and women of the same mind as they could, for the more settlers the better. He would hire a good carpenter to build a small house for the time being, and then, when he found the right land, he would build something bigger and better. He would also commission several more ships, because one thing the settlers must have was a supply of necessities from the Old World until they could produce all they required. Storms and crop failures could lead to the failure of their bright hopes, but with a fleet of ships to keep them supplied they could survive the first years.

Smiling, Justin sat down to write the letter to his father. He bore no ill will to any man—if he had not been shanghaied and forced to sail as a pirate, he would not have met his Maribel. Yet there was still a small shadow in his heart; he regretted that he had parted from his father with anger between them.

Maribel was standing outside the inn looking towards the sea. In the morning they would embark and then their great adventure would begin. Hearing the sound of heavy footsteps behind her, she turned. Her heart was beating fast; despite her uncle's assurances that she was now safe from any further attempt to kidnap her, she sometimes worried that Samuel Hynes might try to be revenged on them. When she turned and saw the man looking at her, her heart missed a beat for there was such an odd expression in his eyes.

'Did you wish to speak with me, sir?'

'You are the wife of Sir Justin Devere?'

'Yes, I am.' Maribel's gaze dwelled on his face a

moment longer and then she smiled. 'You are Justin's father, aren't you?'

'How did you know? I do not think we are much alike; I think he favours his mother.'

'I don't agree; he resembles you in more than just looks…a set of the mouth that can seem harsh to those who do not know Justin well. You have it too.'

'Do I?' John Devere smiled at her. 'How observant you are, lady.'

'Please, you must call me Maribel. I am so happy to meet you. I know Justin hoped that you would come to take your farewell of us before the ships sail, though he has not said anything of his hopes.'

'You are set on going? I thought that perhaps you were leaving because of my unkindness?' There was a look of unconscious appeal in Sir John's eyes. 'Is it too late to beg my son for forgiveness?'

'I do not think you need to beg for forgiveness,' Maribel said. 'Justin would be happier to part as friends, but he bears no malice in his heart.'

'I have realised that I am much to blame for what happened to him. I sent him away with anger in my heart, but I never ceased to love him.'

'My husband will be happy to hear your words, sir,' Maribel said. She smiled as she saw Justin walking towards him and knew that he had seen his father. 'I do not think he will change his mind about leaving, for all our plans are made, but he will be glad of your blessing, sir.'

'I shall be glad to give it.'

Maribel smiled. She went to meet her husband, kissed him and then left him to make his peace with his father while she talked to some of the other women who were preparing to make the difficult and dangerous journey to a land that they had never seen. Maribel had no doubts or fears concerning the future. She had been frightened of life before she was taken captive by pirates, but now she was bold enough to face anything, as long as she had the man she loved beside her.

'Take a last look at England, my darling,' Justin said, his arm about her waist as the *Defiance* sailed out of port. 'There is still time to change your mind?'

'And disappoint all our friends?' Maribel laughed up at him, her eyes alight with excitement. 'I am not speaking of just the crew. My cousin Michael came with one of my uncle's ships as soon as he heard what we planned and others have joined us. For many of them it is a chance of a much better life, Justin, for they find the bonds of their lives here restrictive. In the New World it will not matter where a man was born; if he is honest and of good heart he will succeed. With God's help and a fair wind we shall find this new land and prosper there.'

'I am sure we shall,' Justin said and bent to kiss her. 'As you know, Higgins and I have commissioned two more ships to sail with us and a cargo that may make the difference between success and failure, for some of our friends come ill prepared. However, it is a brave adventure and I am certain that we shall find a place where we can live happily together; whether it be in the New World itself or an island in the West Indies matters little.' He glanced towards the shore once more and for a moment his expression was thoughtful, almost sombre.

She looked up at him. 'You do not regret what we have done? You do not regret leaving your home? We could have stayed now that your father has forgiven you and mine can no longer threaten us. I shall be happy whatever you decide, Justin. I am excited about our adventure, but I would be content to live anywhere with you. You are not doing this just for me?'

Justin gazed down at her and smiled. 'My home is right here beside me and will ever be while I have you, my love. We shall not speak of these things again. A new life awaits us and we shall make the most of it.'

'Yes, Justin,' she whispered and lifted her face for his kiss. 'The future is ours to make of it what we will— and I know that whatever fate befalls us, we shall be together for as long as we live.'

* * * * *

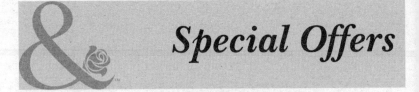

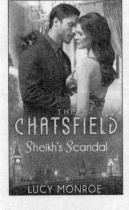

The Regency Ballroom Collection

A twelve-book collection led by Louise Allen
and written by the top authors and rising
stars of historical romance!

Classic tales of scandal and seduction in
the Regency ballroom

**Take your place on the ballroom floor now, at:
www.millsandboon.co.uk**

0214/MB458

The World of Mills & Boon®

There's a Mills & Boon® series that's perfect for you. We publish ten series and, with new titles every month, you never have to wait long for your favourite to come along.

By Request

Relive the romance with the best of the best
12 stories every month

Cherish™

Experience the ultimate rush of falling in love
12 new stories every month

Desire™

Passionate and dramatic love stories
6 new stories every month

nocturne™

An exhilarating underworld of dark desires
Up to 3 new stories every month

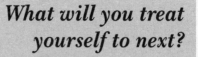

Discover more romance at

www.millsandboon.co.uk

- ❤ WIN great prizes in our exclusive competitions
- ❤ BUY new titles before they hit the shops
- ❤ BROWSE new books and REVIEW your favourites
- ❤ SAVE on new books with the Mills & Boon® Bookclub™
- ❤ DISCOVER new authors

PLUS, to chat about your favourite reads, get the latest news and find special offers:

- ❤ Find us on facebook.com/millsandboon
- ❤ Follow us on twitter.com/millsandboonuk
- ❤ Sign up to our newsletter at millsandboon.co.uk